Schorjun

To my loving wife, Linda and our children,
Errol Jr., Erolin, Erica and Emerson.

Schorjun

Book 1

Errol Rollins

Copyright © 2022 by Errol Rollins.

Library of Congress Control Number:		2022918088
ISBN:	Hardcover	978-1-6698-3830-2
	Softcover	978-1-6698-3829-6
	eBook	978-1-6698-3828-9

All rights reserved. No part of this book may be reproduced or transmitted in any form or by any means, electronic or mechanical, including photocopying, recording, or by any information storage and retrieval system, without permission in writing from the copyright owner.

Any people depicted in stock imagery provided by Getty Images are models, and such images are being used for illustrative purposes only.
Certain stock imagery © Getty Images.

Print information available on the last page.

Rev. date: 10/17/2022

To order additional copies of this book, contact:
Xlibris
844-714-8691
www.Xlibris.com
Orders@Xlibris.com
843943

Book 1

Chapter 1

Erwin sat in the comfortable brown suite in the living room as the chandelier glowed softly from the cream oak ceiling. He pressed the remote control and flipped the channel of the television as his narrow brown eyes roved the screen. The fleeting blue background instantly came alive with swirling, rippling water. The water swelled with its motion; a straight upright aerial-like object glided through it. Erwin thought he knew what it was; his eyes were fixed on it. Forcefully, the body of water broke, it spouted, then the object surged with a force in the air; its full length curved like a crescent; the mammoth creature gaped. Its large menacing fangs made Erwin shudder. The great white shark appeared suspended momentarily and then plummeted into the deep blue water of the ocean with a huge splash. Minutes after, the deadly creature rose to the swirling surface again, showing its sharp teeth. It seemed ready to pierce the flesh of any unsuspecting prey; it wriggled and swayed before submerging itself.

Erwin pondered the behavior and nature of the animal. He thought of the swiftness of movement and the destruction it unleashes on its prey. He flipped the channel, and flush on the screen was opera, a soprano rendering a song rich in melody. He flipped the channel again. A hot game of college basketball was being played. Before he could have recognized the teams, Margaret walked into the living room. "Erwin, aren't you going to bed? Mom said it's time for you to be in bed."

"I just started lookin' at the game. I wanna see some more of it," Erwin answered, looking at his sister somewhat dubiously.

"You heard what Mom said. And it's already ten thirty," Margaret said courtly, turning away heading for her room.

"Shhhh." Erwin sighed, pressed the remote control, and blacked out the television screen. He raised himself almost labored from the three-piece suite. He was quite tall for his age and had recently gained much weight as he developed a habit of gorging or devouring fast food with a passion. Perhaps it was a teenage fad or inclination. Unbuttoning his shirt, he walked toward the kitchen, his steps sounding and reflecting heaviness. He opened the refrigerator and took a bottle of apple juice from it. Reaching for a glass decorated with red and yellow flowers and green leaves, he poured the juice, which settled just below the rim. He raised his heavy arm and brought the glass to his slightly parted lips. He gulped the beverage in one act. Erwin then placed the colorful glass in the sink and walked toward his bedroom.

"Are you still sleeping, Erwin?" asked Mrs. Nichols, her eyes squinting as she stood in the room. "It's already six thirty."

Erwin was still snug asleep. He did not hear a word his mother said. She touched him and roused him from his deep slumber. "Erwin, Erwin, it's time to get up, hon. It's already six thirty."

"Uhhhh, mmmmm," moaned Erwin and turned on his side. He pulled his legs up, his head resting on his left palm; he took the posture of a developed fetus. He pulled the comforter up to the level of his shoulder. Returning to his room minutes after, his mom said, "Okay, it's time now."

Erwin pushed away the heavy, blue, red, and green criss-cross-patterned comforter that brought warmth and comfort to his body during the cold nights. With the drop in temperature, the radiator pushed heat into the room, into the home, with a hiss and buzz. The home was generally warm, warm from the love generated by Erwin's parents and the generator's flow of heat. Mrs. Nichols had emerged from the bathroom after a shower that was considered therapeutic in its effect, ridding her body and her head of any lingering drowsy feeling.

Feline-like she stepped lightly into her bedroom. She glanced at the little clock on the chest of drawers; it was yet early, but she was ever conscious of the time as the hand ticked. Mrs. Nichols reached for the brown comb lying among her accoutrements. She glided it through her luster of hair. She then sprayed her hair, grooming each strand, setting it at the back of her neck, allowing it to nestle on her shoulder. Looking into the mirror, she seemed satisfied with the style. Softly and meticulously, she applied a coat of foundation to her bland face and then a layer of makeup. She touched up her lashes with dark mascara. She moved swiftly but efficiently. Finally, decked in a gray skirt suit with a rich body fragrance flowing through the room, she stepped into the passageway separating the bedrooms.

She quietly called, "Erwin, are you in the bathroom as yet?"

"I'm going now, Mom," Erwin answered, still sleepy-eyed.

He edged his way to the bathroom. Pulling off his blue-and-white striped pajamas, he splashed water in his face from the faucet fixed over the white porcelain sink. He shook his head from the stabbing cold of the water, but it was reviving. Leaning over to the right, he turned the knob; the crystal-like sprays gushed from the overhanging tap and splattered in the tub, forming shiny beads along the sides. After fifteen minutes, Erwin was back in his bedroom.

His mother called, "Erwin, hurry and get dressed. I'm leaving. See you this evening." She was leaving an hour after Mr. Nichols had left for work.

"Okay, Mom, bye," he answered.

"Bye, hon," she replied.

Margaret was busy getting herself ready to leave. Mrs. Nichols knocked on her door and entered.

"Hi, honey. Good morning" said Mrs. Nichols with a broad smile.

"Hi, Mom. Good morning," responded Margaret while she groomed her hair. She was already dressed in a brown flowered blouse and blue denim jeans, smoothly pressed.

"I'll see you this evening. Have a wonderful day, and see to it that Erwin leaves on time," Mrs. Nichols said, placing a smooch on the round, smooth cheeks of her medium-build daughter, whose hair, long, lustered and flowing, settled on her round shoulder.

"Yes, Mom." Margaret's lips parted; they stretched, revealing immaculately white, even, close teeth in a full sweet smile. Mrs. Nichols looped her black, leather bag across her right shoulder and headed for the door. Turning the doorknob, she stepped out in the early morning trudge.

Erwin doused himself with a light cologne that emitted an apple and cherry fragrance. He donned full, baggy, blue jeans and a sky blue long-sleeve jersey, black sweater, and a bright red and blue jacket that reached him about the waist. The next five minutes he was walking down the sidewalk toward the bus stop about a block and a half away. Margaret left about two minutes after him. He walked along briskly; he arched his shoulder and pulled the straps of his haversack to position it more comfortably on his back.

Through the door of a brown, four-story brick building came Andju. The heavy metal door slowly glided back on its hinges and span and shut tightly. Andju walked along the narrow footpath that led to the sidewalk. He glanced over his right shoulder and stopped on the sidewalk. He turned and fleetingly looked up at the four-story building from which he came. Erwin quickened his steps and caught up with Andju, a slim figure of a boy with slanting brown eyes, compared to the bullish Erwin.

"Hey, son, what up?" said Erwin

"I'm good," answered Andju, looking up at Erwin.

"I ain't see you fuh like a whole week. Where was you at?" asked Erwin, giving Andju a fist bump. Gleefully Andju returned it.

"I played basketball in da park like after five o'clock," replied Andju, stepping off. "You wasn't there?"

"Ah, I went there like only three days. A got there after seven. The other days I was just flipping them channels at home as I watched TV."

"I spent like an hour and a half playin' with Dexter and Terence every afternoon. We left before seven. On Thursday and Friday, Dexter's mom wanted him to come in early 'cause she had to go out. So all of us left."

"I didn't go that early. And I didn't go on Thursday and Friday last week."

Andju pulled up a little the zipper on his green light jacket.

"You know Kalo?" Erwin asked, his voice sounding a bit deeper now.

"Who?" asked Andju, probably not having heard the name clearly.

"Kalo. That short, heavy kid. He got a full nose. He rides a bike sometimes."

"Yeh, yeh, I know him. We play ball together, too."

"You know he's always laughin' and jokin'. Taunting everybody when he's in da park."

"Mannn, you better believe it. He's so funny."

"I saw him yesterday comin' from da store. He looked so worried. His eyes looked red to me."

"What's wrong with him?"

"I asked him wha' happen. He said his mom had shortness of breath. She was like breathin' heavily while comin' from da supermarket. After she got in da house and sat down, she felt like her breath was cutting, he said. They had to take her to da hospital. She had to stay in."

"She must be suffering from asthma. That to me sounds like an asthma attack. Da sh—t could be somethin' else. My cousin suffers from that, and like he was just gaspin' fuh breath, yo. That's horrible to see. I thought he was goin' to pass out. They had to call da ambulance. He was admitted to da hospital. He spent two days there. When he came out, he had another attack two days later, and his mom had to rush him back to da hospital. He had an oxygen tank hook up to give him oxygen. Tubes was in his nose. That's da only way he coulda breathed properly. He felt a bit better afterwards, but he was weak. He looked sick."

"Ah, da sh—t is horrible. Those tubes in your nose. I can't take that."

"So what, she's still in hospital?"

"I donno. I'll ask him if I see him today."

"It's tough when your old lady is in hospital. You gotta run there every day; then you're worried. You wanna know wha happening. If she gonna improve and how quickly. It ain't a nice situation."

"You betta believe it, son."

Erwin and Andju continued north toward the bus stop.

The speedometer was reading sixty-five, and the gas was at the halfway mark as shown in the gauge. The traffic was really flowing.

Said Kathy, looking up, "We should get there at seven-fifteen."

"As long as the traffic flows like this it's fine," answered Mark.

Mr. Linsmun drove along the Belt Parkway in his gray sedan. Mrs. Linsmun sat in the front seat reading the newspapers. She pushed away strands of light-brown hair that fell in her face and turned the page. The traffic was flowing steady, and he was doing a reasonable seventy miles per hour now to keep up with the flow. It was cold outside, and the exhausts from the cars in front of him jetted misty vapor in the atmosphere. A gray, windy day it was. The trunks and branches of trees looked withered; they appeared ashen in tone. It seemed as if the bark peeled from their trunks and branches. The Belt appeared dreary, begging for the sun to burst out in a dazzling sparkle along its winding path.

The pace was maintained. Mr. Linsmun signaled, looked over his right shoulder, and entered the right lane. He accelerated and made a three-car gap with an SUV behind him. Soft music resonated from the radio on the FM band and added to the warmth of the cabin of the automobile. It was an instrumental, melodic and rich, but Mr. Linsmun could not remember the group that played it. He thought for a moment but soon gave up. Traffic slowed down. Mrs. Linsmun moved the newspapers and glanced at the clock on the dashboard. She thought, *We still have time*. Seconds after, traffic picked up again. They had another mile and a half to travel before they exit the Belt. The ride was now a little bumpy as the car gunned along the highway, the length of which was rather coarse.

Mrs. Linsmun lowered the papers. Said she without notice, "Mark, the weather is going to be horrible for the remainder of the week. We're going to have about six inches of snow."

"It's going to be a mess driving on some of the local roads," Mark answered.

"We'll have to leave earlier to avoid the backup in traffic after we get off the Belt," Mrs. Linsmun said, looking across at her husband, who kept his eyes on the road.

"There might even be a backup on the Belt. Kathy, we have to hope this one doesn't hit hard."

"And then there's the shoveling of snow. I can't stand that. It's so fatiguing, so tiresome. The last time there was that big snowstorm I almost dislocated my right shoulder shoveling snow when the storm caught you and Michael upstate."

"Oh, it was disgusting and scary. The snow was so heavy on the highway, we couldn't see beyond three or four feet. That's how bad it was. They later pulled us off the road and closed down the highway. I don't want to go through that again."

"It's horrible, Mark. I don't even want to talk about it."

"I understand, Kathy," remarked Mr. Linsmun. He pushed his auburn hair from his forehead.

The car continued along the highway. The sign above showed that they had a half mile to cover before the next exit. Soon after, Mr. Linsmun tipped the lever, and the right signal was activated. He hit the access road, and the car was now moving along the exit toward Pennsylvania Avenue. He stopped at the first intersection he came to as the traffic signals had just changed to red. The lights soon flipped to green, and the gray sedan drove along the busy avenue. Cars and jeeps or light trucks were cutting from one lane to the next as drivers seemed in a rush. At the overpass above which the Number 3 train ran, he noticed three men standing on the sidewalk, one of whom was leaning against a storefront, the hoods of their black coats pulled over their heads to ward off the stiff wind and cold. The tallest of the three sipped a cup of coffee, the steam swirling in the cold morning air from the opening in the cover of the styrofoam cup. Mr. Linsmun thought, *This is not a morning to be standing aimlessly in the cold.* The Linsmuns headed north and signaled for a left turn on Atlantic Avenue.

They proceeded at a steady pace almost catching every green light. The trains rumbled above as they sped both east and west toward their destination. The rumble penetrated the interior or cabin of the car even with the windows up. The car moved with the traffic and then pulled up behind others at Grand Avenue. Moments after, the vehicle was rolling again. The sedan then negotiated a right turn on Smith Street and finally reached Willoughby Street, where Mrs. Linsmun disembarked after giving her husband a smooch. She made her way to her office while he headed to work.

Meanwhile, on the N train, Ortis, of medium height and build, finally sat as a commuter and got up to leave at the next station. He held his black haversack. There was not much room for him to shift or move freely. His Spider-Man book was in his bag, but he resisted taking it out. His eyes were a little heavy, and he realized that his head jerked forward as the train rumbled into the Forty-Fifth Street Station. Hurriedly, passengers, cloaked in down and trench coats, made for the platform as the anxious eyes of those waiting to board stared into cars while others burrowed their way into the train. Within seconds, the door was shut after an announcement echoed through the cars.

Many commuters buried their eyes in some form of literature—a novel, a textbook, newspapers, or a magazine—hungry or desirous of gaining or assimilating a bit more information, a bit more knowledge. The Manhattan-bound train thundered out of the station. It pulled into two other stations to let out and take on passengers before it stopped at the Fourth Avenue Station. Many commuters rushed for the platform. Ortis made his way up the stairs for the street above.

It was crowded on the Number 65 bus. Julie Chin sat quietly. Her expression was pensive, and shallow lines settled along both cheeks. Passengers gripped the overhead hand bars to steady themselves as the bus gathered motion. Julie looked up at some of the commuters and then looked to the floor. She was a petite person, and her long, black hair, in a ponytail, settled on her back. "Excuse me, excuse me," said a hefty female passenger as she angled herself among the commuters to make her way to the back. Standees shifted or leaned over a little to make room. "Thank you, thank you," echoed the middle-aged woman as she moved along the crowded aisle. She finally got a seat at the back of the bus where she placed her bags on the floor. She moved her legs and feet in, locking the white and yellow plastic bags. Leaning forward slightly, she took out a magazine which she began scanning.

The bus hurried on, and each stop it came to, it let out two or three passengers but some eight to ten people jostled and rubbed shoulders to get on to the commuter conveyance. Julie just sat there observing the movement in the bus. She hoped the bus would speed on toward her destination, but the driver drove at his usual pace. The bus then pulled up at a stop sign, and Julie Chin got off. She settled the haversack on her back and walked briskly along the sidewalk. She then turned into Sixth Avenue.

Chapter 2

Mr. Linsmun drove his car into the parking lot in the compound south of the building. He backed in and parked. He gripped his briefcase, got out of the car, and walked across the lot to the building. In a few seconds he was making his way through the door and up the stairs. Erwin had just disembarked one of the buses he traveled on daily and stepped on to the sidewalk. He adjusted his haversack on his back and moved along. The cold air tickled, rather, irritated his nostrils. "Ha chu, ha chu," he sneezed. He made a few more steps and sneezed again. Reaching into the front pocket of his blue denim jeans, he pulled out a few sheets of tissue. Taking one from the set, he wiped his nose. He blew hard and wiped his nose again to clear his head, which appeared a little stuffy. It was windy, and the slim branches of the trees danced to the motion of the wind. Erwin felt the briskness of it on the back of his neck. He pulled the collar of his jacket causing it to reach him just beyond the hairline on his neck.

He crossed the road as the traffic signal indicated "Walk." Although it was cold outside, it did not really bother Erwin that much as he gingerly strode along the sidewalk to the next block. Before he could have crossed the next street, two of his friends met him. A number of his counterparts stood in front of the deli just at the corner.

"Erwin, what up?" shouted Daniel with a big grin on his face as his denim jeans sagged, almost falling off his waist.

"I cool, yo," replied Erwin, giving him a pound as their fists bumped.

"Hey, dog, what up," said Troy, performing the same ritual of greetings.

"Nothin' much, just cool, son," answered Erwin.

"You saw da match last night," asked Daniel, a tall, slim teen, decked in full, black jeans, blue sweater, and black coat that settled open about his waist. The hood covered his head.

"Which game?" asked Erwin.

"Basketball," said Daniel sharply, turning his head as if expecting an affirmative reply.

"Nah, I didn't look. I fell asleep early," replied Erwin.

"Yo, da game was pumped up. Everybody was shooting like crazy. Da was something else," remarked Daniel excitedly.

"I saw it. The Pinters was scoring a lot of jump shots. They had like four three-pointers back to back. Everybody was like wild," said Troy, who wore a blue coat, gray shiny jeans that was off his waist and black sneakers. "Da game was bad."

As they talked on the sidewalk, Julie Chin passed by. "Hi, Julie," said Troy, a grin spreading across his round face with dimpled cheeks.

"Hi," Julie answered slightly, looking across at the boys as they conversed.

Meanwhile, at A to Z Deli, youngsters were in and out of the premises.

"Carl, how much for this soda?" a young lady asked, fumbling in her haversack.

"It's a dollar. You don't know that by now. You buy it every day," the deli owner said as he moved behind the counter.

"I don't buy this one," she replied.

"It's a dollar," stressed Carl, a small man with a big moustache and full piercing eyes. The young lady paid and left.

"Carl, I been standing here long, and you're not looking at me. I want this pack of cookie," a male youngster said loudly.

"Look, look this, Carl, I got to go," was the resonating voice of yet another youth.

"You got to wait. It's I alone. I only got two hands," said Carl, who was kept extremely busy since he had no help that morning. His two assistants did not come to work.

"Look, I'm gonna put these things down and walk out this shop," said one young lady.

"He's moving as if he's sick this morning," the young lady's friend, another female, said.

"We gonna be late if we keep standing here," a heavy-faced lad, with deep brown eyes, said.

"Let's go. We shouldn't wait all this time in here," the next youngster, standing at his side, mentioned.

"But I want this stuff," the heavy-faced boy echoed.

"Hey, Carl, what's happening over here," another teen shouted.

Carl was trying the best he could to dispatch his young customers, who had grown impatient with the amount of time they had to wait to pay for the snacks and sodas they bought. Carl finally put their stuff in bags, accepted his payment, and gave them the items they bought. They then hurried off.

Next door at Chilco's Restaurant, a number of young customers gathered at the counter while some sat at tables and chairs that were available.

"Gimme a bacon and egg sandwich," a tall, husky youth of about eighteen uttered in a strong, raspy voice.

"Hey, leh me get da same stuff, man. I'm hungry," one of his colleagues in a red coat shrieked.

"Hold on, you'd get served in a minute," said Ramon from behind the counter.

A young lady who looked like nineteen or twenty, with a red woolen scarf wrapped around her head, said, "I want a nice, juicy cheeseburger . . ."

"We always sell nice, juicy cheeseburgers. If not you wouldn't be here. All our food is juicy and tasty," Hendy interrupted with a bright smile.

"I want a special one," the young lady replied.

"You gonna get a special one," Hendy answered. The young lady removed her bag, slung across her shoulder.

He turned and said to one of the three workers preparing the snacks and cooking the various menus, "Another cheeseburger. A special one with lettuce, tomatoes, and olives." A grin settled on his face as he turned around to face the young lady.

She looked at him straight up.

"You see I order a special one," he said, his smile broadening.

"Thank you," the girl replied, a faint smile spreading across her face.

"What you gonna drink with it?" Hendy asked, the smile fading from his face.

"A bottle of fruit punch," she answered.

"Two seventy-five," he said.

The young lady opened her purse, pulled out two crisp dollar bills and three quarters. Hendy punched the cash register, opened the drawer and collected the money which he deposited in the drawer.

"Next!" he yelled.

A few minutes later, the young lady received her juicy cheeseburger and bottle of fruit punch and swiftly exited the restaurant.

"Wha' happenin' here, bro? Other people gettin' through," the young man in the red coat blurted out.

"Take it easy, yuh stuff is comin' up," Ramon cautioned.

"I heard that before," the youngster rebutted.

Behind the wall, about six feet from the counter, kitchen staff was busy peeling and cutting vegetables, toasting rolls and slices of bread, frying and baking meat and potatoes. They prepared ham and cheeseburgers and sandwiches and an assorted menu. A number of young people sat at tables in the restaurant.

Richard, a heavyset youngster with a thick neck, a bulgy face, and a slight beard, bit his combo cheeseburger. He uttered throatily with a full mouth, "This taste good! This sh—t is good, son."

His friend, Peter, stocky, with freckles on his face, savored a big bite of his cheeseburger. "Ummm, I like this! It gonna do me good for da rest uh da morning."

"With these two biggies and a box of juice I'm ready to go."

"We're ready to go, son."

"Wha' you drinkin'?"

"A fruit punch, nice and cold."

"Good drink. I buy da sometimes, but I ain't want da so early. I wanted somethin' a little acid. About midday I'll take a punch. Pass me da mustard. This guy didn't put any mustard on muh burger. I feel like telling him, 'Next time put mustard on muh stuff, you hear me.' He knows it. We buy here steady, mannn."

Taking the yellow plastic bottle which Peter pushed diagonally across the table, Richard lathered his burger with mustard and took a big bite.

"Ummm. This is even better. I like this sh—t, yo."

"I ain't know you go fuh mustard da much."

"Yeh, it makes muh food taste better."

"I hardly use da stuff.'

"I like it and I use it. Some people don't go fuh such things. My mom always makes sure she buys a bottle or two when she buys groceries. Maybe, I'm like my paps. He likes it."

"Gimme muh ketchup, bro. I go fuh that anytime. I use a lot of that at home."

The din and aroma surged in the restaurant. Some youngsters were making their exit while others were entering to have their fill.

Chapter 3

A throng began entering the U-shaped building. Almost everyone was slowly moving along. Some were hurrying as if they were on a special mission but were soon impeded in movement by those ahead of them. Voices shrieked and bellowed. The sound was discordant. The yard was not yet cleared. Mr. Linsmun, along with other staff, was still out there ensuring that everyone entered the building. It was cold and the breeze was brisk. The bare branches of the weather-beaten trees in the opposite yards swayed incessantly. With everyone now in the building, Mr. Linsmun entered through the eastern door followed by Ms. Piggot and Mr. Delph. Other staff members made their way into the building from the biting cold. Mr. Eisenburg and Ms. Cort entered by one of the southern doors. Many people were running in the hallway; some stood around idle while others walked back and forth as if they had no place to go. It looked like chaos reigned in the halls. There were shouts, screams, laughter, and laments. The hallways were packed, and no one seemed inclined to budge. One had to angle his or her way through the crowd.

Mr. Linsmun removed his scarf and took off his black long coat as he climbed the stairs and reached the second floor.

He barked through his bullhorn, "Stop running, stop shouting and screaming. Keep moving." His order went on deaf ears.

Said he, again, "No running in the hallway. Let's move it. No standing around."

He was soundly ignored by many. A few began to drift.

"Come on, guys, you got to keep moving. You can't stand around here. Time is going," uttered Mr. Eisenburg sternly while he watched over the third floor with Mr. Delph. Movement was slow.

"Get into your rooms. No standing and running in the hallway," Ms. Cort's shrill voice echoed as she stood on the first floor.

Mr. Eisenburg, Ms. Cort, and Mr. Linsmun continued to bark into their megaphones in an effort to clear the halls, and yet the swift and hilarious movement persisted on the first floor more than the upper floors. "Get into your rooms," was the constant, repetitive call that filled the hall. Many youngsters were adamant; some reluctantly complied, and still others mused in the hallway. The screams, yells, and chatter were deafening.

The sergeant of security was on the first floor. Two other security officers were a distance behind him.

Bellowed Sergeant Grogan, hefty and tall and dressed in black regulation pants and black long-sleeve shirt and tie, "Clear the hallway, clear the hallway! Let's go! Keep moving!"

His words fell on deaf ears. No one really heeded his instructions initially. Most seemed not to care what he or Ms. Cort and her colleagues were saying. Hesitantly, many began leaving the halls on the first floor and climbed the stairwells when Sergeant Grogan whipped his radio from his side and called for backup. "Two more officers are needed on the first floor," he ordered firmly. Shortly, there were five security officers attempting to clear the hallway on the first floor. Efforts were also made to clear the second, third, and fourth floors by other security personnel and supervisory staff.

Stepping up to a group of four on the second floor, Security Officer Stanhope uttered, firmly, "Guys, clear the hall. You can't stand here."

"Who you talkin' to?" said a stout female. "We minding our own business."

"Minding your own business," retorted the officer. "It's time to be in your room."

She and her male colleagues looked at the officer cross-eyed and made their way into the room. Shouting into his bullhorn, Mr. Linsmun urged, "Everybody, clear the hall." It was an extremely difficult task. Security officers moved along all the floors, but the crowd was thick. The shouts, screams, and yells were intense.

"Clear the halls, let's go, let's go," shouted Officer Pandang, veins bulging in his forehead.

Mr. Eisenburg accosted three young men, "Where are you going? You ought to be going in the opposite direction right now."

"Why?" one of them asked.

"Because your room is not where you're going. Come on, get to your room," demanded Mr. Eisenburg.

"A few of you are still in the hallway. You have to move, guys" ordered Mr. Delph, as he approached Mr. Eisenburg while they supervised the flow of traffic on the third floor.

The young men and young women began to move casually as though they care little about going to where they belong.

Said Mr. Delph, with a grimace on his face, "It's so difficult to get these youngsters out of the hallway. It's early and it's so much of a task to clear the halls."

"It could be rather irritating," remarked Mr. Eisenburg.

Finally, after much effort, the halls were cleared.

Loud noise came from many of the rooms. In a few minutes, Mrs. Hutchenson had order and quiet in her room, room 2-802.

"You're not going to keep talking when there is work to be done!" she exclaimed vehemently to class 802.

She was stern. One look at her and one realizes she means business. Her voice was now raised.

"You will write in your journals your impressions about Chapter 7 and what you think was the author's purpose in writing that chapter," Mrs. Hutchenson instructed her students firmly.

"What book is it we're reading?" asked Michael, rummaging through his book bag.

"Michael, you couldn't be serious in asking that question. We started and finished that chapter two days ago," retorted Mrs. Hutchenson, her brown eyes fixed firmly on him.

"Oh, I got it. I had forgotten. We're reading *The Scarlet Patches*," blurted out Michael, peering in his bag and pulling the book from it.

Many students in Mrs. Hutchenson's class were browsing through Chapter 7 while some had begun writing. A few were still trying to get started.

Barked Mrs. Hutchenson, her full, jowly, double-chin face shaking, "The few of you who haven't started anything, you better get cracking. We don't have time to waste."

Some blank stares met her eyes and then lowered into the books. Some of them began scribbling rough drafts of what they wanted to say. The teacher then moved around the class checking to see how students were responding to the reading. It was quiet in the room, as everyone was focused or was getting into that mood. She stopped and leaned over to glimpse at what Erwin was writing.

Said she, "That's your impression, part of it?"

"Yeh," answered Erwin, looking up at her.

"Okay. Continue writing. You still have to write about the author's intent or purpose about the chapter, Erwin," she reminded him.

"I know," Erwin replied.

"How are you getting through, Julie?" she asked, walking to the middle of the class.

"I'm on to writing about the author's purpose," Julie responded, her eyes squinting as she looked up at the teacher.

"Are you finished writing about your impression?" Mrs. Hutchenson inquired.

"Yes, but I'm going to write some more when I finish this," said Julie.

"That's fine," the teacher answered.

Turning to Joseph, she said, "How far have you gone with your impression, Joseph?"

"I'm finished writing my first paragraph," Joseph answered, a glow resting on his face as he looked up at his teacher.

"Okay, that's fine. Continue," Mrs. Hutchenson encouraged.

She checked on a few more students in class 802 and made suggestions about what they should include in their writing. As the students continued to work, she went to a section of the bulletin board where the names of the students of the various classes she taught were written. She checked the names of those students whom she had given gold, silver, and bronze stars as incentives for the quality of work done.

On the third floor, Mr. James worked with his ninth grade math class, class 902. Almost everyone was absorbed in the new lesson on Pythagoras's theorem, apart from two or three who were squeaking and were not noticed by the teacher. The class of thirty-two students sat in groups of four. Mr. James read, "Why is the Pythagoras theorem an important mathematical concept?"

He paused and looked at the class as if expecting a response.

He then said to the class, "Copy your aim into your notebooks."

A number of students had already begun copying the aim before it was read by the teacher.

Mr. James read the objective, "How can we use this concept in solving mathematical problems?"

Some students had finished copying the aim and had started to copy the objective. A brief discussion on a topic of math followed as he motivated the students for the lesson.

"Delve into your background knowledge and give the class a definition or tell us what you know about this theorem," Mr. James said. The expression now on the faces of the students indicated that they were thinking hard.

Said Ingram, "It has to do with parallelograms."

"No," replied Mr. James kindly. "Anyone else can tell me something about this theorem?"

"It deals with triangles," said Nichola, a tall, slim young lady with thick eyebrows.

"What kind of triangles?" inquired the math teacher.

Nichola tightened her lips and opened her eyes wide as she seemed perplexed by the question.

She thought hard and then said, "Isosceles triangles."

"No, Nichola," answered the teacher. "Can anyone help her?"

Two students raised their hands.

"Yes, let me hear you, Renzel," uttered Mr. James, removing his silver frame spectacle from his eyes

Said Renzel, "The theorem deals with the hypotenuse."

"Very good! Tell us some more about the hypotenuse," the teacher urged.

"Mr. James, I already told you about the hypotenuse," protested Renzel.

"But you did not explain what it states," Mr. James pointed out.

"All right, it means a square equals . . ." Renzel paused and a cast or expression of bewilderment spread across his face. "Aright, it means a square equals…" Rondell paused and a cast or expression of bewilderment spread across his face.

"Come on, Renzel," said Mr. James with expectation.

"I can't remember the rest," lamented Renzel.

"Okay, okay," Mr. James repeated himself. "Any volunteers?"

No one volunteered. Eyes were fixed on Mr. James and the chalkboard. A slight chatter emanated among some of the students as they tried to figure out the exact definition of the theorem.

Said Mr. James thoughtfully, "Most if not all of you should be throwing that definition at me. Some of this work you did in the junior school, grades 6 to 8, when you were on the first and second floors. It surprises me that you have forgotten your theorems already . . ."

"It's not that we forgot the theorem but just that some people don't know how to put it over because we may not say it the exact way," Troy interrupted. "It's quite a while since we did it."

"That was in the seventh grade," joined in Alberto, scratching his chin.

"All right! In the interest of time let us move on. Open your textbooks and turn to page 227. Can someone read the theorem for us," said Mr. James as he scanned the class to see that everyone had a textbook opened and was looking at the page.

Troy began to read. "Pythagoras's theorem states that the square on the hypotenuse is equal to the sum of the squares on the other two sides in a right-angled triangle."

"Very good, Troy," complimented the teacher. "Kindly read that for yourselves now."

Students buried their eyes in their math textbooks while they read the theorem.

The teacher gave them a few seconds before he loudly reiterated, "The Pythagoras theorem states that the square on the hypotenuse is equal to the sum of the squares on the other sides."

The students looked up at him with eyes of expectancy. Most of the students in class 903 were willing to learn apart from a small number who was not motivated or clearly indifferent to learning. That number was mainly made up of four or five students. Students knew that Mr. James was a stern and no-nonsense teacher. They realized that he could be harsh but was a kind and compassionate teacher whom they could rely on to help them overcome their fears and struggles with math. Arriving in class 3-903 on the third floor meant it was time for work, and work they were doing.

With his medium-build frame and wiry muscular body, he turned and faced the board with a sharpness of movement. He removed the magnet, and the bottom of the chart paper fell, revealing the full length of the ruled chart paper on which was a colorful diagram of a right-angle triangle labeled ABC. On the hypotenuse labeled AB was drawn a brightly colored red square. On the base BC was drawn another brightly colored square in the color of yellow, and yet another square was drawn on line CA. It was colored a bright green. A vividly graphic illustration was presented on the chart attached to the chalkboard.

"This diagram on the board with the three squares in bright colors present stark imagery to create more visual and mental stimulation. You should immediately get the picture of what is meant by the squares and their location," Mr. James emphasized, turning at an angle to face the class as he modeled what he expected the class to learn and to do.

Some students nodded their heads and a brightness radiated in their faces as they began to cognize the concept that was portrayed.

In his deep raspy voice, Mr. James echoed, "In the triangle, side AB equals BC plus CA. Another way to look at it or understand it is to state that side AB is X square, side BC is Y square, and side CA is Z square. Therefore, X square equals the sum of Y square and Z square. Do you follow?"

In unison, about more than half of the class said, "Yes!"

Mr. James repeated what he said and continued to model the lesson. He looked at the students and then looked at the board pointing to the colored squares on the right-angle triangle.

Said he, "In other words, the red square or box is equal to both the yellow square and green square together.

"So, Mr. James, what you're saying is when you put the yellow and green squares or boxes together they equal the red square?" inquired Daniel.

"Absolutely," said Mr. James, with a nod.

"Then, X square equals Y square and Z square put together?" asked Ingram.

"Correct," replied the math teacher. "We'll now have to find the square root to get the answer."

Further questions were asked by students, and brief discussions were held in the usual small groups. The teacher allowed the groups to talk for about five or more minutes, sharing what they learned about the lesson. The discussions with the teacher's guidance focused on the importance of the theorem in solving mathematical and technical problems related to building and construction.

"Class, we'll now prove the theorem. We'll check the sides of the right-angle triangle. So what we're going to do is, instead of using x, y and z, we will use numbers, in the unit of inches, for sides BC and CA. Each of the two sides will now have a number. We'll have to find the number for AB. Okay," said Mr. James, turning to face the chalkboard. He then wrote numbers, in inches, on the two sides of the triangle and using that figure as an example, he began calculating the square root. Students looked intently at what the math teacher was doing. A few of them asked questions to get a clearer picture of how they had to work.

"Now, students, I want you to work on problems 1 to 10 in exercise 14," the seasoned, veteran math teacher ordered. Students became busy working on the problems as Mr. James walked around the class to give assistance to many of them. With the conclusion of the lesson students were given points as a form of incentives which were cumulative. At the end of the month, Mr. James gave students awards for participation and outstanding work as most teachers did. Certificates of credit were awarded to the hardworking students.

In the rooms on the first floor, as in all the classes in the building, there were students who were avidly seeking knowledge while there were those who did not seem to care. Ms. Vine was making every effort to get her lesson done. She was teaching language arts in the seventh grade, class 704, located on the first floor in room 1-704. Her class was on the east wing of the school. A pale gray was the hue or color of the classroom in front of which she stood. On the chalkboard was written the aim of the lesson, which dealt with identifying and explaining the importance of the main idea and supporting details of the story, which was "The Challenges of Conquering Mount Everest." Two paragraphs were read. There was shared reading.

"What is the main idea in the two paragraphs we've just read? Any volunteers?" Ms. Vine asked, looking around the class.

No one appeared eager to answer. Jaime had his head on the desk. Kevin also had his head on the desk. He then pulled the hood of his black sweater over his head. Jasmine was busy with a crossword puzzle while others in some of the groups were engaged in their bit of conversation.

"What is the main idea in the passages read?" Ms. Vine questioned, looking steadfast at him.

Nakon curled his lips, rubbed his chin, indicating that he was uneasy, then said, "Preparation to climb."

"Good!" she said. She then turned and wrote the response in the upper section of the diagram drawn on the chalkboard.

Facing the class again, she said, "Lakendra, give me one supporting detail."

Looking at the teacher, Lakendra bit her top lip and tapped the desk with her right index finger before she answered, "They bought tools and backpacks."

Suggested Rachel eagerly, "They had to collect supplies of food and items for first aid."

"Very good responses, Lakendra and Rachel," stated the language arts teacher before turning to write the two supporting details on the board, in the lower section of the diagram. "We'll continue reading. 'It was a blistery cold and windy day and it was becoming dark very early. The climbers had to light a fire at the mountain foot . . .'"

Ms. Vine read an entire page and a half so that students could follow the flow of the story and understand the relevance, the essence, of it. She then paused. She walked to the center of the room and looked around.

"I read a page and a half so you could follow how the story unfolded," Ms. Vine mentioned. Some of the students watched her as she walked around. Nakon Said she, "What are some of the challenges or maybe one of the challenges of climbing such a high mountain as Mount Everest? Let's hear you, Jack?"

"Me, I ain't challenging anything. I ain't no wrestler," answered Jack, with a scowl on his face.

"That's not what I asked you, and that's not the response needed," remarked Ms. Vine, somewhat surprised at the answer Jack gave.

"I don't care," Jack retorted.

"Jack, she dissed you, ha, ha, ha." Mike laughed. *Bang! Bang! Bang!* Mike banged the desk with his fist as he amused himself.

"She could f . . . outta here," Jack spouted, his round baby face becoming red.

"Ooooh, ha, ha, ha-ah, ha, ha, ha," the class burst out in laughter.

"You're cursing me, Jack?" Ms. Vine fumed.

"I ain't talkin' to you," grunted Jack.

"I'm going to write you a referral and call your parents,"

"I ain't do you anythin'. You dissed me. I answered your question."

"But it wasn't an appropriate answer,"

"I ain't say anything to you,"

"Ha, ha, ha." The laughter continued.

Bang! Bang! Bang! Bang! Bang! Bang! "Yeah, yeah, yeah . . ." the banging and shouting rose as many became wild with excitement.

"Be quiet! Stop shouting and banging!" Ms. Vine yelled.

The noise continued. Students were still beating on the desk and talking and laughing loudly. The teacher tried desperately to control the class and continue the lesson, but students or most of them were not paying any attention.

"Let me have your attention, class! Be quiet! Stop talking!" the subject teacher shrieked. Her voice became subdued by the ruckus created in the class.

"I'm going downtown with my sister as soon as I get home," said Fatima with her notebook and textbook closed in front of her on the desk.

"Where you goin'?" asked Jasmine with interest, looking up from the crossword puzzle she was busy working on while the story was read.

"We goin' to a new store opened last week. I don't remember the name, but it got some real good stuff my sister told me," Fatima stated, her lips parting into a broad smile as her head bobbed while she pulled a candy from her bag, removed the wrapper, threw it on the floor, and put the candy in her mouth.

"Ych?" Jasmine seemed to question.

"Yeh! Sneakers, jackets, some hot jeans. And the price is good. Man, I can't wait to get there." Fatima's eyes becoming bright with excitement. She gave Jasmine a candy. She, too, threw the wrapper on the floor.

"How you getting there?" Jasmine asked as she appeared quite interested in some of the bargains.

"By train. Soon as I get home and get a bite we're outta there. We gonna just hop on da D train and bang, we're there."

"You gonna show me what you get."

"Hell, no."

Jasmine's face dropped.

"Cool, cool it. I just playin'. I'm just playing you. What, you could come at my house tomorrow and I'll show you what I got."

"Aright. After school."

"Yeah"

"Would you two stop talking? We're about to continue reading the story," the teacher said exasperatedly.

Jasmine turned and looked at her teacher like a raging bull. Her eyes were wide, her lips pursed, and the muscles in her face tight. She felt a hotness in her face.

"Why you in my face?" Jasmine yelled.

Ms. Vine knitted her brow, the clefts showing vertically deep on her forehead, "You are so rude. The two of you are sitting talking and you're asking me why I'm in your face. Cut it! Both of you open your books now as we continue reading."

"But they're talking over there and you only coming over here. Tell them to stop talking, too, shu," Jasmine argued, now turning her head away from the teacher.

"You continue talking and you'll get a call home," remonstrated Ms. Vine, backing away and pushing back with her right hand, with bright-red manicured fingers, strands of hair that fell in her face.

Jasmine pouted her lips. She instantly became quiet. Her friend Fatima did not say anything as she normally does.

"Gimme my stuff, gimme my stuff," was the loud noise that came from the side of the room next to one of the windows.

"What's going on there? What's going on?" demanded the teacher.

"He got my Star Game. He took it from my desk," Ortis said frantically.

"Jason, give me the Star Game. No playing in this class," said the teacher as she walked over to them.

"I ain't got anythin' fuh him. Look, your stuff on da floor," shouted Jason.

"You put it there," cried Ortis, pushing back his chair and bending to pick up his gadget.

"Stop punching me, Derrick," bawled Jundon, storming out of his seat.

"I just playin'." Derrick laughed, pulling his hood over his head.

"I ain't playin' with you," Jundon complained. "You hurtin' my arm."

Ms. Vine looked across at the two students while she leaned toward Jason and Ortis, who sat next to each other, "I'm coming there in a second." The noise continued.

"Give it to me, Ortis," ordered Ms. Vine.

"I'm putting it away," shrieked Ortis, with the game in his hand and fumbling with his bag.

"Give me the Star Game."

"I can't. I'm putting it in my bag"

"Don't let me see it again or you'll be in big trouble. And leave his thing alone, Jason," Ms. Vine warned.

Ortis put his Star Game in his backpack and zipped it while the teacher walked over to Derrick and Jundon. Jason rested his head on the desk and looked away from Ortis who opened his book and began reading.

"What's the matter with the two of you? Can't you settle down and stop behaving like, ah, as if something is wrong with you. If I got to come back to you I'm writing referrals, you get it? Plus I'm calling your home, Derrick."

"What?" answered Derrick.

"What?" echoed Ms. Vine.

It was difficult to bring the class under control, but with much effort, there was some semblance of order in the room. Ms. Vine stood in the corner of it and continued reading. There were some students who were not paying attention but whispered to each other so that the class was not disturbed again.

Ms. Vine read, "About five hundred feet up the mountain the wind began blowing very strong. The four climbers could not move much on the steep snow-covered mountain. With the heavy haversacks on their backs and the violent wind lashing against their bodies, they had come to a standstill. The white powdery snow now swirled in their faces from the mountaintop. It was cold. Moments after they began to edge forward . . ."

Ms. Vine paused and then continued reading. She abruptly stopped. Said she, "Students are talking at the back."

The talking stopped, and she proceeded and was able to read two more paragraphs. She asked students to state the main idea of the latter paragraphs read and to provide supporting details. Some reasonable answers were provided though some were off target.

Incidentally, Ms. Vine decided that because of some of the statements in the passages she read, to divert momentarily from the aim of the lesson to ask a question about figurative language since the reading was rich in that element.

Said Ms. Vine, "Kathy, is there any figure of speech in this last paragraph?"

"What she talkin' 'bout? How you gonna talk 'bout math when this is language arts, duh?" blurted out Kathy defiantly and disrespectfully.

"She's talking about figurative language, Kathy," cautioned Anne.

"What?" asked Kathy. Her brow knitted and her jaw dropped.

"She is talking about figurative language or figure of speech," Anne emphasized, shaking her head, the long black locks dangling just below her shoulder. "We did that about two months ago."

"Thank you, Anne. I'm talking about figure of speech or figurative language, Kathy. Let me explain that to you briefly . . ." said the teacher.

"Well," Kathy interrupted. Ms. Vine briefly explained figurative language to the class and then continued with the lesson.

Cling, cling, cling-cling, cling, cling! The bell sounded, ending the period shortly after.

"Yeah, yeah, yeah . . . bang, bang, bang . . ." was the loud outburst as students grabbed their bags and pushed and tumbled chairs and desks on the floor as they rushed out the classroom in a craze and into the hallway. Ms. Vine shook her head and placed her right hand on her forehead. She walked back to her desk and sat in the chair for a few seconds.

She said under her breath, "I can't believe this."

Ms. Vine got up and struggled as she picked up four desks and five chairs from the littered floor.

"It is important for us to grasp cause–effect from the story we read," said Mrs. Hutchenson as she pointed to the KWL chart on the chalkboard in class 802 in room 2-802. She was now pointing to the L column indicating what students had learned about cause and effect during the block period of ninety minutes. Students had their handouts in front of them with four cause-and-effect graphic organizers which they were working on from the articles they were reading in the text. Erwin rested his head on the palm of his left hand as he thoughtfully read the last article and worked on the last chart.

"We must complete the last graphic organizer before the end of this period today," ordered Mrs. Hutchenson as she walked around the class and directed students how to look for clues and the relevant information.

"Is this the last period?" whispered Blinny, looking across at Erwin.

"Yes," Erwin said, in a whisper, hoping he was not heard to stir the anger of Mrs. Hutchenson.

"Yeah!" Blinny exclaimed in a hush, making his fists and raising them in a victory sign.

Erwin gave him a stern look and continued reading the article. He could hear someone talking in the group behind him and hoped that the teacher did not hear him, but Mrs. Hutchenson was a keen observer in her class. Suddenly her voice rang out.

"Who is talking? Is it you, Arlon?" she queried.

Arlon did not answer.

"Come up here, get right up here," she bellowed, looking over her black square-framed glasses.

Arlon got out of his seat and timidly walked to Mrs. Hutchenson, at the front of the class, where she was assisting a student.

"You talking in my class? Didn't I give you work to do?" the teacher asked sternly.

"Yes," Arlon mumbled, standing stiff and straight in his baggy jeans, blue sweater, and black jacket.

"I didn't hear you!" she shrieked.

"Yes, Mrs. Hutchenson," Arlon replied, his voice a little firmer now.

"You better sit yourself down and get on with your work and don't let me hear a word," Mrs. Hutchenson's voice rose to the ceiling and reverberated in the entire room.

Arlon made an about-face and mockingly made a sad face as he walked back to his seat. Some students looked up briefly and then focused on the paper before them in an effort to complete the task. Immediately, Arlon got down to his work. Erwin compressed his lips while he wrote in the cause section, information he obtained from the article. He continued reading so that he could complete the effect section of the assignment. Students worked assiduously in Mrs. Hutchenson's class. They knew when they were with her it was time for serious work and no fooling around.

"We have five minutes before the end of this period, and I hope everyone is about finish," her voice boomed as she glanced at the class.

Students were busy trying to finish the assignment before the end of the period. Erwin breathed, "Huh," as he completed his task and put his pen on his desk. Other students had just finished and were reading over their work. Erwin had already done that.

Looking up from one of the student's work she was observing, Mrs. Hutchenson said, "Raise your hands if you are finished."

A number of students raised their hands. She then walked to her desk and sat.

"In a straight line, bring up your work and no talking. Humm, some of you are not yet finished. You can't finish because you were talking. Blinny, Arlon, Barbara, Salome, and others can't finish yet. You're going to do some extra work at home," roared Mrs. Hutchenson.

"I wasn't talking," Barbara objected, with a seriousness of expression on her face.

"I wasn't talking either," Blinny said, somewhat subdued.

"Those who are not finished, you're gonna sit here and finish it before you leave, and you're going to answer the questions on page 142 using the same graphic organizers. And let me get it in the morning."

"But we were doing our work," complained Blinny.

"I don't want to hear it. You were sitting there talking with Barbara, and now you're telling me you were doing your work and cannot finish as yet. You deserve a call home. Those who're still working, what number and section you're at?" questioned Mrs. Hutchenson, taking a deep breath as her wide, full chest heaved.

"I'm at number 10 and I'm doing the effect part," said Blinny.

"I'm at number 9 and I'm doing the effect section," answered Salome.

"I'm working on number 7. I'm still on the cause section," stated Arlon.

"All of you are going to sit there and finish it and then you'll do page 142 at home, in addition to your homework. I keep telling you we're not here to play. We come here to work, and some of you have not gotten it as yet. I hope you get it soon," Mrs. Hutchenson growled.

A hush descended on the class as students formed a line in handing in their work to the teacher. They returned to their seats to await dismissal. Seconds after, the bell rang signaling the end of the period and the beginning of homeroom.

Mrs. Hutchenson issued the class with a handout from the main office. "Take this notice home to your parents. They are invited to a meeting next week Monday afternoon at 6:00 p.m."

Some students folded the form and stuffed it in their desk while others dropped it on the floor at the back of the class unnoticed by Mrs. Hutchenson as she turned to put the rest of the forms on her desk and to put some other material in her desk drawer. "Put the chairs up," her voice shrieked.

Students rose from their seats and began placing chairs on their desk. *Bang!* a chair sounded on a desk.

"I didn't say slam the chairs on the desks. Put them up quietly. That's what I mean and you know it," Mrs. Hutchenson said firmly.

Instantly, the chairs were put up on the desks in a quiet manner with hardly a sound.

"Stand behind your desk. You know the routine before we leave here," she uttered.

There was silence in the class, and the majority who were to leave stood behind their desks to await the next instruction from the teacher. Those who were to remain continued with their work.

"Form two lines now," Mrs. Hutchenson ordered, standing in front of her desk.

Students moved away from behind their desks and formed two arrow-straight lines in front of the class. The bell rang again.

Said the no-nonsense teacher, "Good afternoon, class."

"Good afternoon, Mrs. Hutchenson," the class said, and 802 walked through the door and into the hallway. The buzz was great in the halls as other classes surged from their rooms. It meant angling and jostling each other to get to the stairwell and to the main exits. There was a constant tramp as students descended the stairwell.

Chapter 4

Erwin made his way down the stairwell to the exit. Moving within the crowd, he headed to the bus stop. Fatima was already down Sixth Avenue to get home. From there, she and her sister would be bound for the department store, Price Jam, to get their goodies. She let out a deep breath when she got to the door. "Huh." She put the key in the door, pushed it, and entered the warm living room of the brown, one-family brick home. She instantly pulled off her black down jacket and threw it on the arm of the brown three-piece suite as she felt the warmth closing in on her.

"Angela, you home," Fatima called out since the home was exceptionally quiet. There was no immediate response, so she stood at the foot of the inner stairway, covered with a strip of burgundy floral rug that led to the bedrooms on the second floor.

Holding the rail, she called, "Angela."

A voice from above sounded, "Yes."

"I'm home," Fatima answered with a tinge of excitement in her voice.

"You're home pretty early!" exclaimed Angela from her bedroom.

"I din stick around. I just hurried down da road and got da bus," Fatima answered while she moved to the kitchen.

Minutes after, her mouth was full sitting at the kitchen table while she ate voraciously. She was eager to go; she didn't even take her food to the mahogany dinner table in the dining room to eat. Angela had pulled on a close-fitting JXNY blue jeans and a hugging sky-blue, deep-neck jersey. She revealed much of her curvatures, her statistics. She applied a film of foundation to her supple brown face. Her shiny black hair fell back lushly in waves on her round shoulders. A coat of yellow bronze lipstick blended in smoothly with her complexion. She doused herself with her Bloomy Girl spray, the vapor of which engulfed her room with that passionate, irresistible air. Her gold circular earrings hung tauntingly from the lobes of her ears. Angela upped her large-size handbag, stepped forward, pulled the door open, and descended the stairs lightly. Her face looked much younger for her twenty-five years.

"Wow! Like you goin' to meet a, ah, goin' to meet Kenrick."

"Little girl, are you talking to me?"

"Ha, ha, ha, ha, ha. I hope you buy somethin' nice fuh me."

"I hope you have your money."

"I thought you woulda get somethin' fuh me."

"You think I took my day off to go downtown to buy things for you?"

"You promised to buy me a jacket."

"Your mom or dad is going to buy that."

"Man!"

"Don't man me."

"I say I was goin' to get that from you. You know, I got some money put away."

"Wow! That's nice. At least you didn't spend all your pocket money."

Fatima wiped her mouth with a flowered red-and-green paper towel, pushed in her chair, a black metal chair, emptied the plate, put it in the sink, and climbed the stairs in her red-and-black striped socks. She reached for her money in the bedroom that she and her sister shared. She counted it and hurried down the stairs.

"I'm ready to go, Fatima." Angela was already putting on her black below-the-waist leather jacket.

She had already donned long-pointed-tip, narrow-heeled, black leather boots.

"I'm comin'. Leh me put on my sneakers and jacket."

Fatima hurried to get herself together. In a minute, she and her older sister were making their way down the sidewalk. They hopped on the D train, and in ten minutes or a little more, Fatima and Angela were waltzing around Price Jam. It was a dazzling venue with all the glitter imaginable. Housed on two floors and a basement, it was teeming, buzzing with item getters. Fatima looked into one of the many quartz mirrors and flashed a smile.

"I don't know where to start," said the twelve-year-old Fatima, who was as tall as her sister.

She drifted away from her sister, and then they got back together. She drifted again, and they rejoined each other moments after. Fatima looked with excitement at many jeans and sneakers and jackets with fur collars. A sea of colors and their mixtures reigned, making it difficult for Fatima to make up her mind concerning what to choose. Angela graciously stepped around, carefully selecting what she wanted.

"I have a hundred and fifty dollars," said Fatima, pushing her hand into her right jeans pocket.

"How you get all that money? I thought you said you only had fifty."

"I save my money that Mom and Dad give me. I spend the ones you give me."

"That's fine. But to spend it all on clothes? You have a lot at home."

"You told me 'bout this store. You said you gonna get me a coat or somethin'."

"I'll get you two or three items as I promised you, maybe a coat and sneakers and something else. Now put away that money."

"Wow! Wow! I keep my dough. You gonna get me brand name, right?"

Big sister looked across at little sister and made a face.

Lil' sista tried on a red down coat, then she tried on a blue, looked herself in the mirror, and said, "How this look, Angela?"

Angela sized her up. "It looks cute."

Fatima took the coat off and checked some more. Big sista tried on a hip-length leather coat. Said she, "I don't need a third leather coat."

"But it looks nice," Fatima said, her off-white teeth gleaming in a half smile in the warm glow of the beaded chandelier.

Angela's eyes caught a brown coat made of heavy fabric and designed with cream fur on the collar. It was attractive. She put it on and twisted and turned as she looked in the mirror.

"I'm taking this. Doesn't it look nice, Fatima?"

"Ooooh, that looks cool, real cool. I like it."

Fatima stepped off a little and checked some other coats. She tried on a few. She then saw a royal blue with some stitched-on designs and fur collar. She tried it on, admired herself in the mirror, and blurted, "Yeah, yeah. I'm taking this." It reached her just below the waist. She pulled the little belt with the head and stepped off in style. Fatima took it off as her sister did, also, and headed for the footwear section. Fatima tried on some of the latest name-brand sneakers in an assortment of colors and design. An hour later, Angela and Fatima were in the long line heading to the cashier. Fatima hugged her blue jacket and blue jeans and her black-and-blue sneakers while Angela held her brown jacket, brown leather shoulder bag with thin straps and brown knee-length leather boots. Having cashed their items, they left Price Jam with four huge white plastic bags with red writing.

Erwin sat in the brown sofa flipping channels. He had already eaten dinner, and his sister, Margaret, was in her room writing a paper to hand in the next day. A key was inserted in the door lock and the knob turned. Mrs. Nichols pushed the door and entered her home. She kicked off her shoes and walked to the kitchen where she placed two plastic bags on the counter. She had stopped at the supermarket before coming in to purchase tomatoes, cucumbers, onions, oranges, bananas, and pears and a half-gallon bottle of apple juice. She took the items from the bags and put them in the refrigerator except the bananas. Mrs. Nichols wended her way to the living room.

"Hi, hon, good night," she said to Erwin, walking up to him and bending over and giving him a hug.

"Hi, Mom, good night," Erwin replied to his mother, raising his arms and holding her around her shoulders.

Mrs. Nichols then edged to her bedroom and dashed to the shower to revive and reinvigorate herself. The foamy and tingling sprays were therapeutic. She then stopped by Margaret's room.

"How was it today, girl." Mrs. Nichols giggled, lowering herself and throwing her arms around her daughter, who reciprocated in a firm grip.

"Oh, Mom, it was such a tough day with so much reading and all these papers. I didn't have time for myself. I couldn't scratch my head," said Margaret, a weak smile taking over her tired face.

"I understand, honey. I known it could be tough at times, but just hang in there." Mrs. Nichols smiled with her daughter.

They talked for a while before Mrs. Nichols helped herself to a cup of mint tea and a chicken sandwich which she prepared and slightly heated in the microwave.

"Hi, honey, how was your day?" Mrs. Nichols said as she reappeared in the living room and sat next to Erwin, who was watching college basketball. "How was school today?"

"Good. And how was work today?" inquired Erwin.

"It was a hectic day. There was so much to do like it wasn't going to end. Things only slowed down about twenty minutes before I left. I'm so tired. I'm going to take my bed in just a while after I briefly look at the news. Did you do your homework?"

"Yes, Mom."

"Did you finish it?"

"Yeah," Erwin replied with a little irritation in his voice.

"What did you have for homework today?"

"I had homework in four subjects."

"What subjects?"

"Ah, language arts, math, um, um, computer, and science."

"Let me see your books."

"What! I did my work," Erwin shrieked.

"You're not speaking to me in that voice."

"But I did my work."

"Let me see it."

"My bag is in my room."

"Go get it."

Erwin raised himself in a labored way and dragged his feet on the brown, soft-textured carpet of the living room of the sizeable one-flat detached-bungalow-type home in going to his room. He picked up his black backpack and went back to the living room. He unzipped it and rummaged through while his mother watched intently. Erwin took out two black hardcover notebooks and a folder.

"Erwin, please hurry. I want an early rest."

"What time Dad is coming home tonight?"

"Late. About eleven o'clock. He's been doing some late nights for the past week."

Erwin turned the pages in his folder with its hard cover, covered with a green-and-black heavy canvas material.

"Erwin!"

"Okay."

Erwin picked up one of the notebooks, flipped the pages to those where his math homework was written. He gave his mom the book. Mrs. Nichols began to go through the work. She sort of squinted her eyes. The countenance of her face changed somewhat. It looked tight and more serious. She turned the page, looked intently for a while as if she did some calculation. She glanced at Erwin, who kept his head straight in front of him and then looked back at the page in the notebook.

"You didn't finish your homework, and some of the work is wrong. You're doing integers and problems related to measurements."

"I didn't understand."

"Why didn't you tell your teacher?"

"He doesn't listen."

"How do you mean your teacher doesn't listen? He is there to teach you, and if you don't understand something that he's teaching, raise your hand and ask him to explain it again. Or ask a question if a point is not clear, Erwin. I hope you are paying attention and not fooling around when the lesson is taught."

"I pay attention. I don't fool around."

"Your dad and I have to find three thousand dollars every quarter to pay those fees, and I hope you're attentive so you could get your education."

Mrs. Nichols continued to go through his books and to ask questions.

"Turn off that television. It is distracting me."

Erwin pressed the button on the remote control, and the television screen went black.

His mother continued to check his book. Said she, "How come you did this problem wrong, Erwin?"

He asked, "Which problem, Mom? I did all of them."

"Number six. The calculation is not correct. You didn't use the correct formula. Number eight is wrong, too. What's going on? Take out that textbook and let me see the page you're working on. Focus is the key in doing well in your subjects."

Erwin dived into his bag and pulled out his textbook. "Look, Mom," he said, stretching his hand with the heavy math book.

"Find the page, please," his mother told him.

He turned to page 176 and gave his mom the book. She began reading the instructions and then she looked at some of the examples and problems.

"To find the circumference of a circle, you have to use 2 pie r as the formula. You did not do that."

"I did do that."

"Look here, it is not written. It is omitted." His mom showed him in his notebook.

"My bad," responded Erwin.

"What is that?" his mom questioned.

"Oh, my fault," he said, baring even off-white teeth.

"I keep telling you about all those slangs you're picking up. I didn't send you to school for you to be using all those meaningless words," Mrs. Nichols said. Her face tightened, and she shook her head. "Using this formula, let me see you work them now. You have to be more careful in the way you work, and to double-check your work."

"Okay, Mom," Erwin answered as he began working on the exercises.

His mother watched closely. She checked numbers six and eight and the steps he used to arrive at the answers when he was finished.

"Okay, these two are correct. Good."

She checked the other seven problems and integers and found they were correct.

"I know you're a good math student. You improved much since you went to Mr. Harper's tutoring on Monday and Wednesday evenings. You have to pay attention when you work and when you're in class. Let me see your English notebook."

Erwin gave his mother the notebook. She began reading some of the work he did that day and the day before.

The key turned in the door and the brown, solid cedarwood door, with carvings, designs, and a glass lookout about a quarter of the length from the top, glided open smoothly on its oiled hinges, and Mr. Andrew Nichols stepped beyond the threshold. His brown leather briefcase hit the carpeted floor with a slight thud, as he bent to loosen the laces of his black, wedged-toe shoes. He stepped out of his shoes on to the floor in his thick black socks, placed the footwear on racks in an area much away from the door, also his wife's footwear, upped his briefcase, and headed into the living room with a plastic bag in his right hand.

"Good night, Lorraine. Good night, Erwin," beamed Mr. Nichols, walking toward them.

"Good night, Dad," his son said.

"Good night, hon," his wife said, looking up from the book she held.

Mr. Nichols leaned his torso forward and planted a smooch on the oval face of his spouse. Erwin dropped the bag and notebook and got to his feet; with opened arms, he and his father bear-hugged. They both stood massive at six feet and above.

Releasing each other, Mr. Nichols said, "How you doing, son."

"I'm doing good, Dad," answered Erwin, his eyes glinting, his mouth agape, with even teeth sparkling in the soft glow of the chandelier, since he wanted to see his father who, over a week or more, left by five in the morning and returned by eleven, having had to work a double shift to clear up some backup assignments.

"You getting through with your homework?"

"Yeh, Mom helping me with some I didn't do right."

"All right, just pay attention."

"Yeh, Dad."

Queried Mrs. Nichols, "How come you're home so early?"

"We had a meeting with the executive board, so we were allowed to leave after the meeting instead of continuing to work overtime," replied Mr. Nichols, with the bag in his hand.

"That's nice that you're home early tonight."

"I was so happy when my supervisor said we could leave."

"Hi, Daddy. Good night! You're home early tonight," Margaret said, rushing from her bedroom and hugging her father, who reciprocated.

"Hi, baby. Good night. Yes, Daddy is home early tonight. The staff was allowed to leave early after a meeting. How you doing?" Mr. Nichols asked. His face brightened.

"I'm fine, Dad. It was a tough day with a lot of reading, but I'm just working quietly on a paper I have to hand in tomorrow," Margaret said gleefully.

Releasing his daughter, Mr. Nichols said, "How you're getting on with it?"

"Good!" remarked Margaret.

"Okay," Mr. Nichols agreed.

"What you have in that bag?" questioned Mrs. Nichols.

"I bought some food," Mr. Nichols answered.

"What you have?"

"I have a chicken fried rice, barbecue chicken, and vegetables."

"Well, I could take my full sleep, not having to get up after a nap to make your dinner. I don't know if I would have been getting up tonight. I'm so tired. Just as I'm finished checking Erwin's work I'm in my bed."

"Have your rest, honey. I'm gonna take care of this food in a minute. Let me just get out of these clothes and have a hot bath, which I need to feel revived."

"Okay, hon."

Mr. Nichols began slipping away.

Margaret headed for her bedroom, saying as she went, "See you in the morning, Dad. Good night."

"Good night now." His throaty voice bounced off the pastel walls of the living room.

Looking at the notebook in her hand, Mrs. Nichols said gently, "Erwin, you have to be more careful in working your math problems. Your language arts are pretty good. Just a slight mistake in one of your essays, and the questions you answered using the diagrams are correct."

"Mom, I take care," Erwin announced, turning to look at his mother with an expression of satisfaction.

Seeing that his work was correct, his mom said, "Let me see your science notebook, son."

Erwin shuffled three hardcover black notebooks and gave his mother the science notebook.

"What did you do in science today?"

"We did the circulatory system of the frog."

"That seems quite interesting." Mrs. Nichols looked at the notes and diagram in the notebook. Ten minutes after, she was making her way to her bedroom. As she went, she said, "No more television."

"Mom!" Erwin groaned.

"I said no more television. It's past nine o'clock. You should be going into your bed now. Come on, up you go."

Erwin got up from his seat.

"Did you read your storybook?" his mom asked, looking over her shoulder.

"Yes, I read about three chapters when I came home," Erwin answered as he walked to his room to have an early night.

The phone rang at 8:22 p.m. and Mr. Ocabin leaned over to his left and reached for the receiver while he sat in a brown chair in the living room. Said he, "Hello!"

"Good night! Is this Mr. Ocabin?"

"Yes, it is."

"I'm Ms. Vine, Jack's language arts teacher. I'm calling to inform you that Jack was very disrespectful in class today—"

"Oh, really," interrupted Mr. Ocabin, his blue eyes dilating somewhat.

"Yes, I asked him a question about the story the class was reading in the lesson, concerning mountain climbing, and his reply was that he is no wrestler. I figure he did not properly hear or understand the question. I told him that he did not give a suitable answer, and he said that he did not care. He then used the four-letter word saying I could get out the room. I found it to be very disrespectful and unacceptable."

"Jack, come here."

"Yes, Dad?"

"Your teacher said you were disrespectful in class. That you used the four-letter word to her after she asked you a question and told you that your answer was not right."

"No, Dad, I didn't do that," denied Jack, his jaw hung, his mouth open, a surprised and worried look on his face.

"She's on the phone right now saying you did it." Mr. Ocabin's face was flush with embarrassment.

"Nnnoo," Jack appealed, turning away.

"I would like you to talk to him seriously about his behavior so that there is improvement in the way he conducts himself. It's not the first time he has acted up," the teacher continued.

"Okay, Ms. Vine, I'll talk to him. I'll deal with this matter, and I'll see to it that it doesn't happen again."

Jack's mother, who was sitting nearby in the living room, gave an ear to what Mr. Ocabin was saying.

"Thank you, Mr. Ocabin," Ms. Vine said.

"You're welcome."

Mr. Ocabin reached over again and cradled the phone. He got to his feet. He seemed irritated by what Ms. Vine said.

Turning to face Jack and walking off he yelled, "Your butt is mine."

"Oh, no, Joseph, you can't say, you can't do that," Mrs. Ocabin complained, rising from her seat in the burgundy sofa where she sat watching television.

"I'm sorry. I didn't mean to say it and say it in that way. I'm just upset by what Jack did in school."

"I know, Joseph, but we have to speak to him. There're other things we need to do so that Jack wouldn't behave that way again."

"I feel bad that I said it and out of anger, but Jack has to know I'm working hard to pay that fee so that he could have his education."

"I know, Joseph, I know."

"I drive that forty-foot trailer from Boston to Los Angeles, so he could have an education at a private school. I don't know what to say to this that he is misbehaving, being disrespectful to his teacher. I never cursed at my teacher."

"Jack, you're going to be grounded," Mrs. Ocabin said as she scratched her head.

"But I didn't do anythin'."

"Let me see your books to see what you did today," his mother said visibly upset.

"She didn't teach anythin'. Everybody was acting up," Jack said with an expression of concern, as he pushed a few strands of blond hair from his face which showed a bit of red in his cheeks.

"What about the other subjects?" asked his father.

"Nobody teach anythin'."

"You're telling me none of the teachers taught anything."

"They don't teach anythin'."

"Then I would have to go to your school to find out what's happening," Jack's mother said.

"No, no, don't go, I don't want you there. We do do some work but not everybody works."

"What you mean that not everybody works?" Mrs. Ocabin questioned.

"Not every teacher do work with us," said Jack, looking away from his parents.

"I got the impression that you're not attentive in class, Jack," uttered Mrs. Ocabin, shifting in her seat.

"I pay attention, Mom," muttered Jack, walking off a little, as if he felt annoyed.

"Jack, sit down. I wanna talk to you," Mr. Ocabin said, still feeling a bit irritable.

Jack sat on the sofa next to his father. His father angled himself in the chair so that he could look at Jack in his eyes while he spoke to him.

"I'm very upset and disappointed about what the teacher said about your behavior. You don't curse your teacher and give all sorts of funny answers when she asks a question. You're the class clown? Your pocket money and video are doomed this week." Mr. Ocabin frowned.

"I'm going to talk to him too, and I'm going to take away some things from him," chimed in Mrs. Ocabin. Both parents continued to rebuke Jack about his unbecoming behavior.

"Take out your notebooks, and let me see what you did in school today," Mrs. Ocabin said. Jack got up and collected his backpack, which he placed in the closet near the door. He edged back and sat on the sofa next to his mother and father.

"Did you do your homework as yet?" asked Mr. Ocabin, his head bobbing a little.

"No, Dad," answered Jack, passing his hand over his lips.

"Okay, go to the desk and start your homework while your mom checks your classwork," Mr. Ocabin ordered, still feeling a little perturbed about the incident with Jack and his teacher. Jack rose from the sofa, took his books, and sat at the desk where he began his homework.

Mrs. Ocabin checked through his classwork notebooks and noted the work he did for the last two days. She then left the sofa, pulled a chair near the writing desk, and continued to check Jack's classwork.

With his biological science book in her hands, she noted that he did not complete the drawing and labeling the diagram of the respiratory system. What the teacher was trying to do is correlate, infuse, art and language into science.

Said Mrs. Ocabin, as Mr. Ocabin looked on attentively, "Jack, you did not complete your class work. This diagram is not completed. The drawing is not finished, and you have not completely labeled the diagram. What were you doing?"

"The teacher didn't give us enough time to do our work," answered Jack, looking up from the English homework he was working on.

"Jack, if you were paying attention you would have finished that task. Also, you didn't completely answer the question on how air travels to the lungs and what the lungs do. What is happening here, Jack? Let me have that science textbook to see what it says about the lungs and its function, so that you could complete this work," said Mrs. Ocabin, studying the work in his notebook.

Jack delved into his backpack, retrieved his science textbook, and gave it to his mother.

"Turn to the chapter the class is working on, and let me get it to see what is done. I want you to be attentive in class," cautioned Jack's mother.

"Jack, you have to stop playing and concentrate on your schoolwork. Your purpose at school is to learn and improve your work, your performance," Mr. Ocabin said, his voice rising somewhat.

Jack turned the pages of his textbook to chapter 10 and said, "Here, Mom." He gave his mother the book.

She began reading it, focusing on the diagrams and the information that went along with it that explained the functions of the lungs and the importance of the entire respiratory system. Jack, meanwhile, worked on his English assignment. He had to read a story and answer several questions related to the story. He then had to identify certain parts of speech in the story. He finally completed his English homework, then decided to start his math home assignment.

As he checked for his math textbook, his mom said, "Jack, we're going to complete this classwork, and we're going to do this science homework together."

"Okay, Mom," answered Jack. He was happy that his mother was helping him with his science.

Together, Jack and his mother worked on his science homework after they completed the incomplete classwork. With the science behind them, Jack was allowed to start his math homework as his mother observed what he did and the steps he used in arriving at answers to his assignment. Mrs. Ocabin then decided to check his work on a more regular basis, at least three times per week.

Alfreda sat at the writing desk with her notebooks and textbooks opened in front of her. She worked on a math problem that involved problem-solving. While she worked, her mother sat in an armchair next to her. Mrs. Ortega checked her daughter's math notebook to see what was done in class. Leaning over to her husband, she showed him what their daughter had done in class today. Both of them held the book and scanned it. They turned the page to the previous day to see what she had done. The class was working on equations. Mr. Ortega checked a number of the equations his daughter did. She did miss a step in two of the ten equations.

Said Mr. Ortega, after showing his wife that their daughter had made a mistake, "Alfreda, you made a mistake in doing two of the equations for class work."

Alfreda turned and looked at her father, then her mother, then back to her father in a dubious way, and said, "I didn't make any mistake. I did it right."

"No, look, I'm going through your work and two of the equations are not right. Let's work them together," Mr. Ortega said, rising from his seat and edging to the desk where his daughter sat. Leaning over the desk with her notebook which he placed on it, he began working the various steps, following examples from the math textbook, which he also placed on the desk.

"Ohhh, I messed up here. I missed this step," declared Alfreda, rolling her eyes.

"Okay, let me see how you would work it using the example and following the steps used," said Alfreda's father. Alfreda worked the math equations with her father watching closely what she did. Her mother continued to check the classwork she did in English, science, social studies, and Spanish as well as previous homework done in those subjects. They sat there with her for over two hours to ensure that her work was correctly done.

Chapter 5

The hallway was teeming with traffic as students made their way there on a bleak, cold wintry morning with a heavy overcast. It was gray, and the mood of many seemed somber. Heavy jackets and hoods, and layers of warm clothing, under jeans and pants brought some relief and warmth to all on a bitter, cold morning. The freezing weather with its temperature in single digits that resulted from a drop in the overnight temperature forced school officials of Jones High School to send students into the auditorium and gymnasium, instead of allowing them in the yard, before the beginning of school at 8:30 a.m. The shouts, screams, and laughter were tumultuous.

A small number of students had arrived since 8:00 a.m., as usual, and the flow began about fifteen minutes after on a normal day. Even after 8:30 a.m. there was a steady stream of students who appeared not to be bothered that they were late. They were chronic latecomers. Hundreds of students stood in or walked the hallways and displayed an unwillingness to go to the two accommodating areas. Ms. Cort, Mr. Eisenburg, Mr. Linsmun, and Mr. Delph were four of the seven deans who were in the hallways, while the others did duty in the auditorium and gym.

"This is not a nice morning with this awry weather," said Ms. Cort, holding her blue-and-white bullhorn in her right hand.

"We really couldn't keep these kids out there," concurred Mr. Linsmun, standing in his heavy, black long coat with both hands behind his back with his megaphone.

"It was so tough driving in here," said Mr. Eisenburg, clutching his radio with both hands.

"The weather is going to get worse over the next few days, which means we'll have to get the students in these two areas during those days, Rick," said Mr. Linsmun.

"Oh, it's not going to be a pleasant scene with all these kids in the hallway, and some of them are so reluctant to move," remarked Ms. Cort.

"Tell me about it," uttered Mr. Eisenburg.

Cling, cling, cling-cling, cling, cling-cling, cling, cling! The bell rang for the beginning of homeroom. There was a mad dash out of the auditorium and with more fury out of the gymnasium where the lower or junior school was assembled. "Yeah, yeah, yeah," "Hold on," "Wait fuh me," "Yo," "Son, chill," "Hey dog, what up," "My man, where you goin'?" and some expletives were some of the phrases, discordant in their tone, that spilled from the mouths of the many students.

In their sober and light-colored jackets, they jostled their way to get to the stairwells, leading to the main hall and the east wing on the first floor, dragging their bags on the floor or carrying them on their backs or slung across their shoulders. In haste, the younger ones descended the stairways to get to the first floor while those from the upper or senior school sluggishly took their time in climbing to the third and fourth floors. The rooms on each floor suddenly buzzed with activity. It was as though a storm had erupted in each room. Loud talking, chanting some out-of-place lyrics, and heavy beating on desks seemed to be the order of things during the initial part of homeroom. Teachers yelled in desperately attempting to bring their homerooms to order or some semblance of it. They found it difficult to do attendance or listen to the morning's announcements.

Back on the second floor, Mr. Linsmun tried to clear the hallway to get the eighth graders in their classrooms. Officers Pandang and

Stanhope and Sergeant Grogan moved along the east wing and the main hall ordering students out the hallway and into their rooms. Some were adamant. They stood their ground or moved reluctantly.

"Let's go, students. Move your bodies," the burly sergeant and ex-marine senior NCO roared, stopping in the middle of the main hallway. Some students budged; others did not.

"I said to clear the hallway now or I'm going to make a sweep," the sergeant roared again.

They began moving a little faster; the hallway began to clear apart from a few who showed stubbornness.

At the eastern end of the main hall, Officer Pandang said, "I'm not goin' to tell you guys to clear this area. You must go to your homeroom now."

"You got a problem," Millicent squeaked under her breath.

"I want you out the hallway. This's my last warning. You must be in your homeroom now," Officer Pandang ordered in a loud, stiff voice.

"He thinks he owns this school. Sh—t, we don't wanna go to no homeroom," Angelina said with a frown, her jet-black hair settled in a bun and her drooping costume earrings made her look as if she were on staff.

They edged their way along the hall and to the entrance to the stairwell and climbed their way to the fourth floor.

Ms. Cort and other security officers were busy on the first floor trying to clear it while Mr. Eisenburg and Mr. Delph and security personnel worked on the third floor. Other admin and security staff managed the fourth floor. On each of the floors were clusters of students who were reluctant to move.

"C'mon guys, no time to be idling on the floor," said Mr. Linsmun, as he approached them.

After considerable effort, the hallway on each floor was finally cleared almost at the end of the homeroom period. Moments after, fifteen minutes had gone. *Cling, cling, cling! Cling, cling, cling!* and the hallways were bustling with traffic again and hilarity. The din was so intense; one could not hear if he or she was called beyond two feet. It took the deans and security officers twenty minutes to get students into their classrooms for the beginning of the first period for the day.

Students from class 806 barged into Mrs. Hutchenson's room from the crowded and noisy hallway.

"Stop! Check yourselves! You are not coming in here with all that yelling," Mrs. Hutchenson confronted the class.

"Everybody making noise. Look what's happening out there," retorted Hector in a heavy voice as he walked with a swagger.

"I don't care what's happening out there. You're going to come in here quietly. This ain't no ballpark or music concert," Mrs. Hutchenson said firmly.

"You gonna stop us from talkin'? We got free speech, man," rebuffed Kenneth, swinging his bag and throwing it on the desk.

"But you're not going to come in here every time with that noise," the teacher emphasized, moving closer to the door.

"Yeah, yeah, we gonna party today," shouted three female students, with their arms around each other's shoulders, tramping into the room.

"Stop that now!" Mrs. Hutchenson ordered.

"Stop what? We gonna party," Makalia said, the tall, medium-build girl in the middle of the three girls.

"You're not going to party in here," the teacher told them.

The girls stopped in their tracks, still holding each other around the shoulder, and looked at the teacher with smirks on their faces. The teacher stood two feet away from them as they faced each other.

Merleen looked at Makalia in her eyes and said cynically, "She's getting on our case early."

Mrs. Hutchenson stood there fuming, irritated that her morning began awry with a class that was bent on challenging her authority and which taxes her in trying to bring it under control. A male student came through the door. "Blam!" He slammed the door shut. The noise shook the room and hurt the eardrums of many.

"What da f… wrong with you? You hurt my ear," yelled Hector, who sat near the door.

The latecomer ignored him and went to his seat. The girls stepped off and Makalia said, "She got a problem. Leave us alone. We're not bothering you."

They dragged the chairs from their desks and slumped in their seats. They threw their backpacks on the desks. Immediately, Merleen, with a broad grin that appeared to broaden her full, oval face, beat her right fist on the desk. *Bang, bang-bang, bang-bang, bang-bang, bang, bang!* William, who sat nearby in the next group of four, started chanting, "Yo, I need some dough, 'cause a gotta go to see ma homegirl Zo . . ."

"Yeah, yeah, c'mon, c'mon," some others encouraged.

"Cut that banging and singing in here," shouted Mrs. Hutchenson, her eyes wide, with furrows gouged in her forehead.

"C'mon, I need some dough, c'mon, I need some dough, yo . . ." Merleen, Makalia and Kenneth joined in and backed up William.

Mrs. Hutchenson stepped up to Merleen and her colleagues and barked, "I'll get your mothers up here right now. William, you chant again, and your father will be here. I'm not sticking this. Get it together. Stop the crap."

The banging and chanting ceased.

Said Merleen, with bright eyes, "We're just having some fun."

"Have fun in the yard or have fun at home," Mrs. Hutchenson belched.

"She's getting whack." William laughed.

"It's ten minutes into the period and you haven't settled down. We have work to do and much of it," remonstrated the teacher as she moved to the center of the room.

"I don't feel like workin' today," screamed Teddy, his face appearing wider under a thick layer of blond hair.

Then "Blop!" Pedro threw his green-and-black backpack on the floor just as he pushed the door and entered the classroom.

"What's your problem, Pedro?" shrieked Mrs. Hutchenson, turning to look in his direction.

"She got scared, she got scared, yo, ha, ha, ha." Pedro laughed. "Could you get me my bag, Mrs. Hutchenson?"

Mrs. Hutchenson squinted in looking at Pedro in dismay.

Said she, "You better get your bag off the floor and stop fooling around. It's too early for that. We have a lot of work to do, and this class is wasting time. Take out the book we're reading and your notebook."

Mrs. Hutchenson already had charts on the chalkboard, a list of vocabulary words, and a 'Do Now.' The aim and objectives of the lesson were clearly written. The students now had their reading texts on the desks, in addition to their notebooks. The talking and laughter had subsided, and those who were just sitting around began getting into their bags and taking out their books. Finally, the class had settled down, and Mrs. Hutchenson began her language arts lesson.

She struggled with the students who were disruptive, to bring order to the class, so some amount of work was done.

In a number of classes on the second floor, students seemed to be going out of their minds. There were shouts and screams and laughter as they engaged in mock fights or bantered among themselves. Ms. Bishop tried desperately to bring her class, 803, under control. She was getting there, and some students had already begun to do some work; a few of them half-heartedly as they carried on their own bit of conversation, much to the chagrin of Mrs. Bishop, who was explaining what she had wanted them to do.

Said she, "The questions you are working on are to prepare you for the test I'll give you next week."

"You givin' us a test next week?" asked Adrian, with much concern on his face.

"Yes. I told you that since the beginning of the week," replied Ms. Bishop.

"But you ain't teach anythin'," Adrian complained with wide-open eyes as he craned his neck toward the teacher.

"If you were paying attention and had stopped talking constantly then you would have known what was taught," rebutted Mrs. Bishop firmly without a blink.

Adrian sucked his teeth, becoming upset that a test was scheduled for the following week and that he was hardly knowledgeable of what was taught. Several students appeared focused and were seriously working on the questions as a form of practice. Notwithstanding, there were those who chose to malinger, though, in subdued tones. Mrs. Bishop subsequently stopped the class from writing and began questioning students about what they had done, soliciting responses from many of them and then explaining aspects of the questions which she felt students were not clear about. She then allowed them to continue answering the questions.

A sudden outburst broke the momentum of instruction and learning that was underway. Melissa yelled, "Ahhhhhh!" then *bang* as a desk hit the floor. She tumbled the desk on the floor as she jumped from her seat and dashed out the classroom because someone pelted her with a broken pencil that caught her in her face, her cheek. She skipped down the stairwell and stormed into the main office where visitors and parents were sitting and yelled, "I wanna call my f— house. I wanna talk to my mother."

"Oh, oh! Where you think you are, girl?" the school secretary demanded, her eyes distended with disdain.

Eyes of the adults turned up. Visitors were in disbelief at the way the young lady's arms were flailing, the smirk on her face, and the foulness of her mouth.

"You have no regard for your school and yourself," said an elderly man dressed in a dark suit, white shirt and blue-and-red tie, and tan trench coat, who sat in one of the chairs in the office waiting to see the principal, Mr. Richard Cottle.

Almost at the same time, a tall, thin, sixty-plus-year-old woman in a flowered sky blue dress and black coat rebuked, "These young girls these days seem not to have any respect at all."

Two younger women, parents, shook their heads and frowned in disappointment but said nothing.

"He had no right to f— throw that sh—t in my face," she blurted out with fury, bobbing her head, her dark, shiny hair swaying along her shoulder as her long, hanging, circular costume imitation gold earrings dangled from her stretched ear lobes.

"Mind how you talk to me, miss. I have grandchildren who're older than you," the elderly female visitor said, pursing her lips.

"I ain't care and I wasn't talkin' to you," Melissa rebutted, leaning against the counter and looking over her shoulder at the visitors and parents. "I wanna call my f— mother so she could come up here and smack da bitch in his face. Let him feel just how I feel."

"You can't carry on like that in here, Melissa. You have to calm down and respect this office and yourself," said the other secretary, Mrs. Caldwell.

The principal heard the commotion and pushed the door and came out. Said he, "What's the matter with you, young lady? Why are you cursing and carrying on in this office? Sit down. I'm going to suspend you for your behavior."

"You suspendin' me and he throw sh—t in my face. Look at my face." The young woman was full of venom and anger and showed no regard for authority.

"You cannot remain in this office and disrespect the staff and visitors, also myself. Call security for me, Mrs. Caldwell. You'll be taken to the dean's office and he'll find out what happened but you're not going to behave as if you're losing your mind in this office," the principal said in a firm deep voice.

"He started it. He threw that pencil which hit me in my face," Melissa said, still furious, as she slumped herself in a nearby chair in the office, a chair away from the adults.

Mrs. Caldwell got on the radio, "Come in, security, this is the main office."

"This is security, main desk," answered an officer, at the main entrance.

"Officer needed in main office."

"Roger."

Meanwhile, the principal said to Melissa, "You're going to be taken to the nurse, and I'll get the young man in here who hit you."

As the principal talked, Melissa turned her head away and sulked. Within a minute, a security officer was in the main office. "Is there a problem?" Officer Morgan asked.

"Take this student to the nurse. She has a slight bruise on her face. A male student threw a broken pencil that caught her in the face. Go to Ms. Bishop's class and find out who the student is and take him to Mr. Linsmun and ask him to deal with the matter. When she is finished with the nurse, take her to him, too. She has to be suspended for her disrespectful behavior in this office. I'll call him."

"Come on, let's go, young lady," Officer Morgan ordered.

Melissa sucked her teeth as she got up from the chair. She flounced out of the office at the side of the officer without a sign of embarrassment.

"She is a very disrespectful student," said the gentleman in the dark suit and trench coat that came to see the principal.

"I wonder what her mother would say about her behavior," voiced the elderly woman.

One of the two younger parents said, "I wouldn't like to have a daughter who behaves like that. I'll be very embarrassed."

"And she doesn't care," the other young parent agreed.

Said the principal, "These are some of the disrespectful students whom we have to deal with every day."

Melissa was taken to the nurse's office.

Back in class 803 in room 2-803, Nigel was removed from the classroom and escorted to the office of the dean by Officer Morgan after students who sat nearby mentioned that he threw the pencil which hit Melissa in her face. As Ms. Bishop grappled to get her lesson moving after the disruption, Lawrence turned to Alexander and said, "You got a pen? Mine not writin'."

"I ain't got an extra pen," uttered Alexander while he flipped through the pages in his notebook.

Lawrence reached over and picked up Alexander's pen as they sat next to each other at separate desks.

"Gimme my pen," Alexander said and pulled it from Lawrence's hand.

Lawrence turned and punched Alexander in his shoulder.

"Ahhhh," Alexander shouted. "Why you punch me?"

"You pulled da pen from me," Lawrence growled, making a face at Alexander.

"But this is my pen, man," protested Alexander.

Alexander pushed his desk and dragged his chair away from Lawrence and continued answering the questions as Ms. Bishop then instructed them to proceed with the written work in preparation for the forthcoming test.

During the afternoon session in Mr. James's math class, Lawrence scrapped or cancelled a loose-leaf paper he did work on that was incorrect. He crumpled the paper into a ball and threw it at Alexander.

"What's wrong with you? Don't throw no paper ball at me," Alexander complained.

"I ain't throw nothin' at you," said Lawrence, grinning broadly.

As Alexander worked on a math problem, Lawrence saw a piece of crayon on the floor. He bent over and picked it up. He looked at Alexander and pelted him with it.

"Ouch!" Alexander shrieked and looked around. The crayon hit him in his head.

Lawrence pretended as if he was working a problem and then looked up cunningly. He and Alexander's eyes met. A sly smile broke out on Lawrence's face.

"You throw that crayon at me?" Alexander yelled.

"Yes, Lawrence, you throw it at him. I saw you," said Michelle, a full-faced, bright-eyed young lady with thin eyebrows, decked in a pink-and-white sweater, blue wide-leg pants, and black boots. She wore a pair of hanging gold earrings and silver glossy lipstick. She sat at a nearby desk answering math questions.

"There is too much talking going on in the middle there," cautioned Mr. James as he checked how students were working the math problems.

"You saw me throw sh—t at him? Mind your own business," Lawrence burst out.

"Yes. I saw you throw that broken piece of crayon at him. You picked it up from the floor," Michelle maintained with a straight face and bright penetrating eyes.

"Don't throw nothin' at me," Alexander muttered. Anger was on his full round face.

"You's a snitch, Michelle," Lawrence fumed, resting his head on the desk and pulling the hood of his jacket over his head.

"But you hit him with the crayon. Why you're lying?" Michelle said.

"You's a snitch, man. You too nosy. Always checkin' to see wha' a brother doin'," Lawrence lamented.

At three o'clock after dismissal, Alexander had several game cards in his hands showing his friend, Adrian. Lawrence came from behind him and snatched the cards. Two fell on the floor. Lawrence ran along the hallway with six of the ten cards.

"Gimme my cards," shouted Alexander, holding the two remaining cards in his hands. "He gone with six of my cards."

"Why he snatched your cards," inquired Adrian.

"He's always taking my things and hitting me," said Alexander, bending over and picking up the two cards which fell on the floor.

"Why not tell your parents what he's doing to you. If it was me I'd tell my mother and she'd be up here on him. Nobody ain't gonna be hitting at me and taking my things. Hell, no. They didn't buy them for me. My parents got to work hard to give me what I want, and I'm not goin' to allow anyone to take my stuff or hit me and get away with it," said Adrian.

"I gonna tell my mother again," agreed Alexander.

As Alexander and Adrian reached the intersection near the school they parted, each going in the opposite direction. It was a frequent occurrence whereby Lawrence hit out at Alexander, pulled things from him, and demanded writing material. On the sidewalk, a block away from the school, Alexander saw Lawerence.

"Gimme my cards, Lawrence," said Alexander, hurrying up to catch him.

"I ain't got no cards fuh you." Lawrence grinned, stepping up his pace.

Alexander hurried after him.

"Wha' you followin' me for?" shrieked Lawrence.

"You snatched my game cards from me. You got about six of them," replied Alexander, looking upset.

"I ain't got your cards," Lawrence stressed, looking over his shoulder.

"Yes, you got my cards," emphasized Alexander.

"I got your cards?" Lawrence stopped and turned around to face Alexander.

"Yes," shouted Alexander.

Whack! Lawrence punched him in his face and ran.

"Ahhhhh, ahhhhhh," cried Alexander, bending over and holding the right side of his face.

Arriving home, Alexander complained to his mother about the things Lawrence did to him. His mother became equally upset. She vowed that she was going to take the necessary actions to put an end to the situation.

Chapter 6

Mr. James left the staff lounge; he made his way up the stairwell to the third floor to begin his third-period math class with the tenth graders, class 1003. He entered room 3-1003 and placed his charts on the board. He had already placed other teaching materials on the desk. Soon after, students began entering the room. Their shouts and laughter were deafening. Mr. James's eyes glared at the way they were entering his classroom. "Quiet down, students," he shouted from the front of the class. Most of the students were not yet seated. They stood around in small groups bantering. Some stood with their hoods on their heads and backpacks on their backs.

"It's time to get to your seats, guys. Time is going," the teacher said, stepping off from the front of the classroom to the center of it.

"What's his case?" said a student who sat on a desk.

"I'm tired of his sh—t," said another, leaning against the wall.

Mr. James, standing in front of them, said, "Terence, kindly get off the desk. It's not something you sit on. Sit in the chair. And you, Avery, find a seat, please."

"Who you talkin' to?" answered Terence, still sitting on the desk, clad in black jacket, black jeans sagging below his waist, and black-and-gray sneakers, with a thick crop of hair and a black Afro comb stuck in it.

"I'm talking to you, Terence," stressed Mr. James, who stood upright in his light blue, long-sleeve shirt; yellow-and-blue striped tie; tan pants; and shiny, black leather-sole shoes.

"Get outta my face," murmured Terence as he slid from the desk into his chair.

The teacher did not answer him.

Turning to Avery, the math teacher said, "You're not going to stand there."

"I don't have a seat," yelled Avery, shaking his head, the pom-pom of his green-and-black topee swaying from left to right.

"What is that?" Mr. James asked, pointing to a vacant chair nearby.

Avery sucked his teeth, moved off, and sat in his seat. Mr. James bit his lower lip, the inner part of which had become pink from the cold, and shook his head while walking away to accost two other groups of students who were still standing and talking.

"I've already said it." He faced the group closer to him. "You have to take your seats immediately as you enter this room."

"We're discussing something," said a female student who also sat on a desk with her feet in the chair.

"Do you sit on the table at home with your feet in the chair?" the teacher asked, in disgust.

"Yes, I sit on the table. My momma allow me. She don't say nothin'," said Tamara.

"You playin' yourself, Tamara. Don't lie." Donette laughed.

"Fuh real, my momma don't care where I sit and where I put my feet," reiterated Tamara.

"Kindly come off the desk, Tamara, and have a seat in a chair," Mr. James said firmly.

"Wait!" Tamara howled.

Mr. James knitted his brow, incensed by the disrespect and disregard for authority. Tamara took her sweet time and lowered herself in her chair.

"You happy now," she said with disdain for the teacher.

The math teacher did not answer her but said, "The rest of you, be seated."

They slowly edged to their respective seats where they sat as if they were in for a splash of entertainment instead of preparedness for serious learning of a vitally important subject.

Mr. James headed back to the front of the class and said, perhaps for the second time, "Good morning, students."

Nobody answered except for a female student who sat in the group in the middle of the room.

The teacher looked and realized that most of the students were settled.

He began, "We will continue working on factorization. After you complete your 'Do Now,' we will review the method that is used in factorization."

Some students had taken out their notebooks and had begun answering the "Do Now." Others had still not begun but sat and talked in a low-key manner. The teacher moved around the class and observed how students worked on the five problems written on chart paper which hung on the chalkboard. He stopped at a number of desks, leaned over, and checked the methods and steps students used in doing the problems. He put a check mark on the notebooks of students who were engaged and did the problems correctly. Moments later, he stood before the chalkboard and pointed to an example on the chart paper as he began explaining how it ought to be done.

He abruptly said, "Let me have your full attention, students. Some of you are not paying attention to what is explained on the board, and then you'll say you don't understand."

Some students pulled themselves together and looked straight ahead on the board and intently.

Mr. James continued explaining the work on the board. A fair number of students tried to figure out what he was saying. Their eyes appeared bright and absorbing. There were times when Mr. James taught with the classroom door wide open or ajar, and at other times he would step toward the door and close it. The door was ajar that morning while he taught. He modeled to students what he wanted them to do. Suddenly, a noise burst out in the hallway and echoed in his room, "Yeah, yeah, yeah . . .," followed by expletives which filled the air.

A student in the hallway yelled, "Fight, fight . . ."

Avery shouted with wide eyes, "Fight, fight, somebody getting his ass whop."

Instantly, desks were pushed forward and chairs backward. Students leaped from their seats and bolted out the classroom to the consternation of Mr. James, whose jaw dropped with his mouth agape. Other students dashed from their classrooms and bawled.

The commotion started in room 3-1006, four rooms down the hall from Mr. James's room. Students stumbled out Mr. Howard's accounting classroom. "Yeah, yeah, yeah . . .," and all the other discordant sounds were leaping into the hallway. "Break it up, break it up," Mr. Howard shouted as he moved in, among other students, to separate the two females who punched away at each other and grabbed at each other's hair.

"Whop her ass," a student in the crowd shouted.

"Who fightin', who getting' their ass whack?" another asked, excited about what was going on.

Before Mr. Howard, in angling his way, could get to the two fighters, the taller of the girls pushed the shorter one against the desk; she drifted as her opponent fired a punch at her. The short, heavy one lunged and dealt the other a blow to her chest. And the scramble and punching raged as the cussing heightened. Desks and chairs were pushed and tumbled as a few students tried to part them before Mr. Howard reached them, while others belched, "Ha, ha, ha-ha, ha, ha . . .," raising their hands in the air, flailing fake punches themselves. Mr. Howard grabbed one of the students by her left arm and pulled her away, placing himself between her and the other fighter. With his left arm, he kept the other student at bay. "Back off," he shouted.

"I gon f— you up," howled Kendra, the taller student, with short wavy hair, decked in a green, heavy jacket.

"Yeh, I gonna whop your ass." Nickita, the shorter one, coughed, panting for breath.

"Back off," Mr. Howard shouted again, angling his body and putting his arm as a shield, as the shorter girl tried to wriggle free from his grasp of her. Again, the taller one yelled, throwing a punch which did not land, "I gon f— you up, bitch. Yuh momma is a ho."

"Like yours, you stink ass," the shorter one bawled.

"Stop it," Mr. Howard barked as he led her toward the door.

Two other female students and a male tried to restrain Kendra. Two male teachers and a female dashed into the classroom. Mr. Mendez rushed toward Kendra, the taller student.

"Give me her. Loose her," he said quickly, taking hold of her from the students.

The other male teacher, Mr. Blair, moved in to assist Mr. Howard while Ms. Langevine headed to help Mr. Mendez in holding Kendra.

"This is awful, what these students are going on with," Ms. Langevine lamented, gripping the left arm of the student.

Students from the hallway were rushing into the room while others were bailing out. It was pandemonium.

"Nicky, bus her ass. Nicky could fight, yo." One student laughed, referring to the shorter student.

"Nah, she being whack. Kendra grabbed her head and punched it like mad," another student said.

"Ha, ha, ha, ah, ha, ha, ha," other students were cracking up with laughter.

The dean, Mr. Eisenburg, hurried down the hallway; soon after, Officer Stanhope ran down the hallway, too. The clatter of his shoes was muffled by the loud noise. Closely on his heels was Officer Stuart, making his way among the scores of students who clogged the halls.

Running from the west wing, the gym, a student blurted out, "What da f— goin' on."

"It's hot down there," a colleague shot back as he moved away from the area.

"Two sistas slugging it out," a heavyset youngster said while standing against the wall.

"It's action in reaction, ha, ha, ha." His friend, who also leaned against the wall, laughed.

"These homies getting at each other's throats," uttered the student who ran from the west wing.

Officer Pandang sprinted along the hallway on the second floor and leaped up stairwell number 6, closely followed by Officer Morgan and Sergeant Grogan. The security officers in black regulation uniform began running hard on the third floor, jostling students and angling their way among them to get to the scene of the commotion.

"Let's go, get off the floor. Go to your class," the sergeant howled as he moved among them.

"Clear the hallway!" Officer Pandang shrieked.

"Keep moving! Clear the hallway!" Officer Morgan echoed.

Students did not budge. The big crowd was at the entrance of and near to Mr. Howard's classroom. Mr. Howard and Mr. Blair escorted Nickita, the shorter student, from the room while Mr. Mendez and Ms. Langevine followed holding the forearm of Kendra, the taller of the two, restraining her from punching, while she said, "I gonna get you later."

"I'm ready, f—r," spouted Nickita.

"Allow us to pass," Mr. Howard said as the crowd gathered around.

"You got your ass whoped," said a young man from the crowd as Mr. Howard came forward with Nickita.

"She's always fighting somebody," remarked a female student who looked on.

"She's got to calm down. She's out of control," agreed another female student.

Reaching the entrance to room 3-1006, Sergeant Grogan said, "I'll take care of her."

He reached out and held Nickita's right arm as Mr. Howard released his grip on her arm. Mr. Blair also released her. Officer Stanhope moved forward and held her left arm. Arriving on the scene, Officer Morgan shouted, "Back off, clear the hall." He lunged forward and held Kendra, relieving Ms. Langevine while he and Mr. Mendez led her out of the room. Officer Stuart took over from Mr. Mendez at the door.

Mr. Eisenburg was at the door. Said he, "Take them to my office. I'm tired with this kind of behavior."

The security officers took the fighting girls to the dean's office.

"What you gonna do to them, Mr. Eisenburg?" queried a student wearing a red-and-black jacket.

"I want you in your class," said the dean, looking much perturbed.

"C'mon, clear the hallway," Mr. Blair ordered.

"Let's go, guys, let's go," shouted Mr. Mendez.

Students slowly began drifting to their respective classes.

"Let's move it, students," Mr. James said, standing in the hall as his class became empty as students dashed through the door to witness the sudden brawl.

"Return to your class, now," Mr. Russo said, standing at the door of his empty classroom, assisting in getting the hundreds of students back in their classes.

"Some of these students just don't care. They prefer to stand out here rather than being in their class learning," said Ms. Vivehouse with her hands resting on her full hips.

Some of the young men and women eyed her as they passed with scowls and disdain on their faces.

"I can't believe this. So early, just the beginning of the third period, and the fighting started," said Mr. Russo, stepping further into the hallway within earshot of Ms. Vivehouse.

"What a mess this is every day," lamented Ms. Vivehouse. "Come, guys, let's get to our rooms."

"Get to your classes," Mr. Einsenburg growled, pushing his gray hair from his face. Beads of perspiration spread on his forehead and nose, which looked pink.

Additional security personnel, Officers Pamela Kurt and Shirley Cook, were deployed on the floor to assist the teachers and dean in clearing the floor. It took more than twenty minutes for students to get into their classrooms. Back in his office, Mr. Eisenburg pulled the arm of his black, high-back leather chair and sat. He pulled the chair, with wheels, closer to his desk.

Turning to the two female students, he said, pointing to Nickita, "What is the reason for fighting in that class so early in the morning?"

"I had my CD player on the desk, and she picked it up to listen to a song. I tell her I wanna listen to something—" said Nickita with fierceness in her eyes while breathing hard.

"You're listening to CD players in class when you ought to be working, uh? I said no CD players or music and game equipment in the class," Mr. Eisenburg interrupted sternly, his eyes blinking frequently as his voice rose and fell.

"But she picked it up. I wasn't listening to it before," said the short, stocky girl.

"She lent me," interjected Kendra, rolling her slanted eyes.

"Shu, I don't want to hear it," the dean said. Both students got quiet.

"Continue," ordered Mr. Eisenburg, placing both arms on his desk.

"She wouldn't give it to me, and I pulled it and the cord came off and fell on the floor. I told her to fix it and she didn't," described Nickita.

"No, no," Kendra jumped in, shaking her head and gesturing with her body.

"Be quiet," ordered Mr. Eisenburg.

Continued Nickita, "I pulled the CD player from her and the cord fell on the floor. I bumped into her when I bent over to pick it up and she pushed me. I pushed her back and the fight started."

"What happened, Kendra?" the dean asked.

"She lend me the CD player 'cause I told her I wanna listen to something. She gave it to me and then she pulled it away, and the cord fell on the floor. She then bumped me hard when she bent over to pick up the cord. She bounced into me deliberately and I pushed her. She had no right to bump me," related Kendra.

"Is she going to lend you something and then pulled it away?" questioned the dean.

"That's what she did," emphasized Kendra.

"No, I didn't lend her it. She picked it up," chimed in Nickita in anger.

"Okay, I've heard both of you. Your parents will have to come up here," said Mr. Eisenburg as he pulled a few forms closer to him and began writing on them.

Both Kendra and Nickita eyed each other with cunning as they sat waiting on further instructions from the dean.

"Now, to both of you. You are each suspended for three days for fighting in class and bringing and playing a musical instrument there. Take these letters to your parents. Both of them have to be here in the morning. Also take this note to the in-house coordinator. You'll remain there for the rest of the day. Nickita, you go first," Mr. Eisenburg ordered.

Nickita got up with her backpack and left. Kendra remained seated there with other students. Ten minutes after she was told to go to in-house.

Chapter 7

Mr. Linsmun left his office because of the noise that poured in while he worked. He assisted in clearing the second floor after many students were out of their classes without passes during the third period. He walked back to his office in his crisp white shirt and red-and-blue striped tie with the bullhorn in his right hand. Inserting the key and turning the lock and the doorknob, he entered his office on the second floor in the main hallway and placed his loudspeaker on his desk. Pulling his black high-back leather swivel chair from the sizeable mahogany desk, he sat and opened a file on his desk. He glanced at the first document, flipped the others, and closed the manila file. He stretched his hand to the in-tray on his desk and removed three files. Opening the one on top, he began writing on the first page. *Cring, cring-cring, cring.* The phone on his desk rang. "Hello," he answered, placing the receiver to his ears.

"Mr. Linsmun, a parent is here to see you concerning her son," said Ms. Ellis, one of the four school secretaries.

"Send her up," Mr. Linsmun said.

Cradling the phone, Mr. Linsmun thought, *What is it now? So many problems in the classroom every day.*

There was a knock on the opened door of the dean's office shortly after. *Pap, pap, pap.*

"Come in," said Mr. Linsmun, raising his head and looking over his shoulder.

A heavyset, dark-skinned woman wearing a brown down coat and light-gray track pants and white sneakers entered the office. Her head was covered with a brown, woolen, bonnet-like headwear with a short peak. A concerned expression settled on her smoothed face with single lines running away from both lobes of her high-bridged nose. Her lips were covered with a thin layer of gel to ward off the icy cold atmosphere outside.

"Good morning. Are you Mr. Linsmun?" she said, her countenance remaining stoic.

"Good morning. Yes, I am. What can I do for you?" uttered Mr. Linsmun, reaching to shake the hand of the visitor. "You may have a seat."

"Thank you," the visitor said, a faint smile breaking on her full oval face.

"You're welcome," Mr. Linsmun replied.

"Mr. Linsmun, I'm Mrs. Parke, and I came to see you because my son, Alexander, told me that a student punched him in his face when he was going home, walking on the sidewalk a block away from school. The student did so because my son asked him for his game cards, which he snatched from him in the hallway, after dismissal at three o'clock. Earlier in the day, he pelted him with a crayon in his head and punched him in his shoulder because he didn't lend him his pen. When my son came home, his face was swollen just on the right cheek. It is still swollen, and it is paining him. It is not the first time this student has been bothering my son—"

"Which class is your son in, and who is the student that punched him?" interrupted Mr. Linsmun, a grim expression settling on his face.

"His name is Lawrence Mingo, and they're in class 803," said Mrs. Parke, folding her arms across her stomach.

"Okay," Mr. Linsmun said.

He stretched his hand across his desk and picked up a green folder. He opened it, checked the schedule of class 803, saw what subject the class had during the third period, where it was, and who was the teacher teaching the class. With that information, he picked up the intercom and dialed 2815, as the class was in the math lab.

"Mr. Zachary, this is Mr. Linsmun. Kindly send Lawrence Mingo and Alexander Parke to my office," said the dean.

"Sure, Mr. Linsmun," answered Mr. Zachary, teacher and supervisor of the math lab.

In a few minutes, the two students were making their way along the hallway, Alexander trailing Lawrence, to the dean's office. Both students walked into the office. Lawrence was surprised to see someone in the office, a parent. He glanced at the parent and then looked at Mr. Linsmun.

Said Mr. Linsmun, "I called both of you here because there is a complaint about you, Lawrence."

"Complain about me?" questioned Lawrence, anger showing in his face.

"Yes. Alexander, tell us what happened," said the dean.

Alexander explained what his mother had earlier said.

"I ain't do him nothin'. What da f— you sayin'. I ain't touch da nigga," Lawrence blurted.

"My son is no nigger. He has a name," protested Mrs. Parke, turning in her chair and staring at Lawrence, who did not make eye contact with her.

"I don't care," Lawrence answered, stepping back.

"I'm going to suspend you," said Mr. Linsmun.

"I don't care, sh—t. This is a p—sy ass place," Lawrence said and began walking out the room. "I gonna f— you up." He referred to Alexander.

"Let me get security," said Mr. Linsmun, who whipped his radio from his side and spoke. "Come in security."

"This is security," answered one of the officers.

"Security needed. Dean's office, second floor"

"Roger!"

Two security officers began making their way to the dean's office, but Lawrence had already slipped out of the office, darted down the hall, and rushed through the exit. He slid down the stairwell to the first floor.

"I'm going to move my son from this school, Mr. Linsmun. It's getting too dangerous here with these students out of control and having no respect for anyone," said Mrs. Parke, looking at the dean steadfast.

"It's tough here, Mrs. Parke, but if you want to move your son, I wouldn't stand in your way. It's your right," advised Mr. Linsmun.

In a jiffy, security officers Morgan and Stanhope were in the room with Mr. Linsmun, the parent, and Alexander.

"Lawrence Mingo, we have to get him. This parent is making a complaint. He cursed out and fled the office," Mr. Linsmun stated, quite embarrassed.

"Okay," said Officer Morgan. The two security officers dashed from the office to the hallway and down the stairwell in hot pursuit of Lawrence. They checked the hallway of the first floor, then the bathrooms. Lawrence was not there. Fifteen minutes after Officer Morgan communicated over his radio with Mr. Linsmun indicating that Lawrence was not located.

"Mrs. Parke, I'm sorry for this behavior, but this young man will get five days' suspension. He has to return with his parents, and we'll further investigate this matter," Mr. Linsmun explained, placing his hand on his forehead.

"I'm tired that Alexander comes home to tell me he is harassed by this boy. I don't like to call people's children names, but he is always bullying my son. I didn't come before because I felt something would be done by the school as I told Alexander to complain to his teacher whom I thought would take it up to somebody higher," Mrs. Parke complained.

"We're trying our best, but some students are giving us a tough time. They're many like Lawrence," explained Mr. Linsmun.

The security did not find Lawrence. They did not know if he had left the building or secreted himself somewhere in it. Others were called in to search. They searched all the floors, but Lawrence was not found.

Mr. Linsmun picked up his phone and called the home of Lawrence. The response he got was that the number was disconnected. Looking at the emergency contact card, he dialed another number but got no response. He then called the workplace of Mrs. Mingo. Someone answered the phone, and he asked to speak to Mrs. Mingo. A minute or two elapsed. Then a voice answered.

"Hello, this is Mrs. Mingo."

"Good morning. I'm Mr. Linsmun, the eighth grade dean of Jones High School, and I'm calling in connection with a matter involving your son, Lawrence. It is a very serious matter, and he would be suspended for five days. I would like you to come up to the school to assist in having this issue resolved in the interest of both parents," stated Mr. Linsmun candidly.

"What he did, sir?" inquired Mrs. Mingo, her face flush with concern.

"It was reported by a parent that Lawrence is always taking things from her son, punching him, and preventing him from doing his work and that he punched him in his face last Friday. When I called him in my office to find out what happened he used the N-word and threatened to attack the student in the presence of his parent. His behavior is unacceptable."

"Oh my goodness! I can't believe Lawrence did that."

"The parent came up to the school and made the complaint."

"I told Lawrence about getting involved in any problems."

"Anyway, Mrs. Mingo, you are required to come to the school tomorrow or before the week is out."

"Okay, Mr. Linsmun, I'll be there tomorrow morning."

"I look forward to seeing you. Thanks."

"You're welcome," Mrs. Mingo replied.

Mr. Linsmun cradled the phone.

Said he, turning to Mrs. Parke, "Lawrence's mother would be here tomorrow morning. I would like you to be here so we could deal with this matter and put an end to it."

"Yes, I would be here in the morning," answered Mrs. Parke, rising from her seat.

Alexander looked at his mother; she looked at him with worry on her face.

Said Mr. Linsmun, "Alexander, you may go back to your class. And thank you for coming, Mrs. Parke."

"You're welcome, Mr. Linsmun, and thanks for your assistance."

Alexander bit his top lip and made his way out of the dean's office followed by his mother. In the hallway, his mother moved forward and hugged him.

"Stay out of their way so they don't hit you. Don't say anything to them. I'm going to try to get you out of here," his mom said.

"Bye, Mom," said Alexander.

"Bye, Son," Mrs. Parke responded as she walked toward the exit. She turned and looked at her son once more as he made his way to his classroom.

Mr. Linsmun rubbed his chin and stared down at the file on his desk. He breathed, and a gush of air rushed from his stomach. He began writing in his log when loud talking distracted him. Officer Stanhope brought a student who cursed and prevented the teacher from conducting his lesson. He was told to sit in one of the several chairs in the dean's office. A few minutes passed, and two more students were brought in by Officer Pandang for cutting class and refusing to go to their classroom. By lunchtime, Mr. Linsmun had ten students in his office for various infractions. Some for cutting class, throwing objects at others, and fighting. A number of other students were in the offices of the other deans for various problems.

The afternoon session for Mr. Linsmun was not as hectic as the deans on the other floors. When the bell rang at three o'clock dismissing school for the day, he had already called and spoken to some of the parents, and those whom he did not reach, he gave letters to the students to take home to their parents requesting to see them. He made his way out of his office, pulled the door behind him, locking it shut, and tried to usher the students out of the building in order not to have a buildup of students in the hallway that lead to fights. With the eighth graders on the second floor out of the building, Mr. Linsmun returned to his office fifteen minutes later to begin writing up his log for the day and to do some paperwork.

Before the bell rang at 8:30 a.m. for the beginning of classes, Mrs. Parke was sitting in the main office waiting to see Mr. Linsmun in his office with Lawrence and his mother. She had checked in with security and was given her visitor's pass which she wore on her chest with her name clearly visible. At 9:00 a.m., when Mrs. Caldwell thought the students were in their classes and the hallway was cleared, she said, "Mrs. Parke, you can go up to see Mr. Linsmun. I just called and he's in his office."

"Thank you, miss," Mrs. Parke said, rising from her seat. She limped as if a pain gripped her knee and then steadied herself as she moved off in leaving the main office. She climbed the stairway and reached the dean's office. Knocking and entering, she said, "Good morning, Mr. Linsmun. I'm here again."

"Good morning, Mrs. Parke. I hope we can settle this matter this morning," Mr. Linsmun uttered, stoically.

"I hope so too," Mrs. Parke replied with a brief smile.

"I'm waiting on Mrs. Mingo," Mr. Linsmun said, stretching forth his hand and taking a file from the in-tray which he opened. Just as he opened the file, Mrs. Mingo and her son Lawrence made their way through the main door of the school. Mrs. Mingo checked in with security and then the main office and was directed to the dean's office on the second floor.

In entering the dean's office with Lawrence following, Mrs. Mingo said, "Good morning, Mr. Linsmun. I'm Mrs. Mingo, Lawrence's mother."

Looking up, Mr. Linsmun said, "Good morning, Mrs. Mingo."

Turning and glancing at the adult female sitting in a chair, Mrs. Mingo said, "Good morning."

Mrs. Parke answered, with a grim expression on her face, "Good morning."

Said Mr. Linsmun, "You may sit, Mrs. Mingo. And that's Mrs. Parke, the student's mother."

"Okay," Mrs. Mingo answered, looking over again at the other parent and nodding her head.

He then glanced at Lawrence, who edged into the office. The dean then called the classroom and summoned Alexander to his office. In a moment, Alexander was standing in front of the dean and opposite Lawrence.

Said Mr. Linsmun, sitting behind his large brown desk and decked in a light-blue long-sleeve shirt and burgundy tie, with his hands interlocked on his desk, "Mrs. Mingo, you were called to the school this morning as I indicated yesterday during my phone call, because a parent made a complaint that your son is harassing her son and has recently punched him in his face causing him to suffer bruises and pain in his cheek. When I called Lawrence and explained to him what Alexander's mother, Mrs. Parke, said about his attack on her son, Lawrence cursed out, calling Alexander the N-word and threatened to hurt him. He also left my office without permission and perhaps the building because security could not find him when they were called in. This behavior by Lawrence is reprehensible and unacceptable."

"Lawrence, this is what I send you to school for, to be fighting and calling people 'nigger.' Lawrence, this is what you did? Answer me," demanded Mrs. Mingo, anger and disappointment showing in her face with her voice rising slightly.

Lawrence remained mute. He looked timid and innocent.

"I can't believe this," Mrs. Mingo lamented. "I got to work so hard to send you to school, and this is what you're doing. Think about how much it costs for me to send you here."

Said Mr. Linsmun with a stern expression, "Mrs. Parke, tell us what your son mentioned to you."

Angling herself in the chair and looking at Mr. Linsmun she said, "My son Alexander came home on Friday and said that Lawrence punched him in his face while he was walking on the sidewalk a block away from school because he told him to return the game cards which he, Lawrence, snatched from him in the hallway after dismissal."

Mrs. Parke turned to face Mrs. Mingo.

She continued, "His face was swollen and bruised. I was very upset. He said your son would hit him. He would borrow Alexander's pen, and if my son didn't lend him or didn't have an extra pen to give him, he would punch and bully him to get what he wants. He prevents my son from learning. My son shouldn't have to go through this. And I'm very annoyed. Then when I came here yesterday to complain he's going to deny that he does anything to my son and then called him a nigger. Which parent must put up with this—"

Interrupted Mrs. Mingo, her face twitching, "Miss, I'm not going to condone my son's behavior. I understand how angry and upset you are. I give Lawrence pens and pencils. I give him whatever supplies he needs. He has no reason to be borrowing anything from other students—"

"I ain't borrow anythin' from him—" Lawrence chimed in, edging forward a bit.

"Be quiet! No one asked you anything. And I'm speaking," Mrs. Mingo rebuked. Lawrence became quiet and stood still.

Said Mrs. Mingo, "I told Lawrence not to get into trouble with anyone. I said I don't want to hear him getting into fights with anybody or taking anything away from them. I keep talking to him because recently I see him behaving in a way I don't like. Miss, ah, ah Mrs. Parke, I'm very sorry for what happened. Lawrence had no right to punch your son. I apologize. I gonna deal seriously with Lawrence. He's not going to continue like this."

She took a piece of tissue from her bag and wiped the corners of her eyes. She had become very emotional. She was very troubled by the manner in which her son had behaved.

"I accept your apology, Mrs. Mingo," said Mrs. Parke.

"Tell us what happened, Alexander," said the dean, leaning back in his chair.

"Lawrence always takes things from me, my pencils and paper. He hits me and snatches my things from me. In class on Friday, he punched me in my shoulder because I didn't give him a pen. He also pelted me with a crayon in my head, and when school dismissed and I was walking in the hallway, he came from behind and snatched my game cards and ran. He punched me in my face when I was going home after school when I asked him for my game cards which he snatched from me," Alexander explained to the dean.

"Mrs. Mingo, you heard it," said the dean

"Yes," answered Mrs. Mingo, looking very perturbed.

"Lawrence, what do you have to say? You heard what Alexander said you did to him," Mr. Linsmun uttered, casting his eyes on Lawrence.

"I ain't do nothin'. I ain't hit him," muttered Lawrence, lowering his head.

Joined in Mrs. Parke, "Miss, you cannot allow your child to be hitting and demanding things from another person's child. You have to do something about it."

"I talked to Lawrence seriously. His father also spoke to him because we see him behaving out of character by shouting and talking back to us," reported Mrs. Mingo.

"You have to do something about your child being confrontational with my son," Mrs. Parke said. "He even cursed and called my son a nigger."

"I was told he said that, and I'm angry about it," Mrs. Mingo uttered, shaking her head in dismay.

"Something you are not doing right that is causing your child to behave like that."

"His father and I will cut all the privileges he is having. No allowances, no games, no TV. He gonna be grounded. I'm disappointed and embarrassed."

"If that doesn't work, get some professional help before he gets further out of control."

"I'm going to talk to the counselor to see what help we could provide," suggested the dean.

"I would very much appreciate it, sir. And, Mrs. Parke, I'm truly sorry, again, for this behavior by Lawrence. I'm going to do everything so that he doesn't bother your son again," Mrs. Mingo told Mrs. Parke.

"I welcome that," replied Mrs. Parke.

Turning to Lawrence, Mrs. Mingo said, "I'm going to deal with you. Your father and I are going to see that you conduct yourself in a way that is respectful and acceptable. Apologize for what you did."

"But I ain't do nothin'," Lawrence declared, making a sad face.

"I don't want to hear you didn't do anything," Mrs. Mingo stated. "You never do anything."

"He takes my things, too," Lawrence snarled, putting his hand to his face and rubbing his nose.

"My son would never take anything from you," said Mrs. Parke, her eyes bulging a bit.

"And I give Lawrence all his supplies. I'm so upset," said Mrs. Mingo.

"Okay, ladies, I must thank you for coming here to have this matter resolved. Lawrence would be suspended, ah, Mrs. Mingo. He would remain at home for five days. His teachers would provide him with work which he is required to do during those days he's at home. He will submit them when he returns to school," said Mr. Linsmun.

"If he has to get that punishment he deserves it," Lawrence's mother said without reservation.

"Lawrence, let me warn you sternly that we're not going to tolerate your behavior. It is unacceptable, and any more complaints from any students or their parents would result in serious disciplinary action against you. It's time you settle down and focus on your schoolwork. I say this in the presence of your parent. Mrs. Mingo, you would have to take the necessary actions to curb your son's behavior. As I said before, we would provide some professional help. And, Lawrence, you cannot be bullying another student, demanding things from him, and when he doesn't give you, you attack him by punching and throwing things at him. This school is not going to tolerate this type of behavior—" rebuked Mr. Linsmun, rising from his swivel chair.

"But he takes my things, too," interrupted Lawrence.

"Be quiet! You already spoke," the dean ordered. "Sit there until I'm finished writing up your suspension letter."

Lawrence backed up and slumped in a chair with his backpack in his lap.

"Alexander, you may go to your class," instructed the dean.

Alexander turned and walked through the door of the dean's office.

"Again, thank you, Mrs. Parke and Mrs. Mingo, for coming here to put an end to this matter."

Said Mrs. Parke, "Thank you, Mr. Linsmun, for settling this matter."

"You're welcome," answered Mr. Linsmun, reaching out and shaking her hand.

Rising from her seat Mrs. Mingo acknowledged, "Thanks for bringing an end to this problem, Mr. Linsmun." She then stretched her arm and shook hands with Mr. Linsmun.

"I hope to see improvement in your son's behavior," the dean said.

"There will be, Mr. Linsmun. I'll see to it," Mrs. Mingo uttered.

"Very good," he said.

Mrs. Mingo turned to Mrs. Parke with an expression of worry on her usual placid face. Mrs. Parke looked at her without any animosity or anger and with a willingness to help. Mrs. Mingo reached out her hand after which Mrs. Parke reciprocated. Their gentle hands met and locked, and a level of warmth emanated from their physical connection to each other for a fleeting moment.

Said Mrs. Mingo, "Mrs. Parke, I'm very sorry for what Lawrence did."

"I understand, and I hope his behavior improves," Mrs. Parke expressed.

"Thank you," Mrs. Mingo said.

Both parents left the dean's office with Mrs. Mingo hurrying ahead to get to the subway.

Chapter 8

Officer Stanhope patrolled the second floor during the sixth period after lunch. He walked toward the east wing. His shiny black shoes made light thuds on the brown geometric tiled floor. His security accoutrement stacked around his waist on the broad black leather belt. Prim in his black, cotton, long-sleeve shirt with black tie and black gabardine pants, he bit the bottom of his lips as he stopped at the junction where the main hall met the hall of the east wing. With a thick palm and fingers, he rubbed the back of his head. He stood contemplatively for a while and then turned and headed in the direction from which he came.

On his way to the west wing, he made slow steps. He stopped and peered through the glass slot in the backdoor of one of the rooms. He shook his head disdainfully. The teacher was busy teaching a lesson. Some five or six students read comics and cartoons. Comic books and cartoons were opened bare on the desks for all to see. They carried on their own bit of conversation at the back of the class.

The young female teacher made a desperate effort to engage everyone, but many ignored her. About three or four of them drew cartoons in their notebooks and compared their drawings to see or determine whose was the best. They shaded the hair, eyes, and bodies of their objects. With determination and skill, they brought out the heavy muscle tones and actions of their comic heroes. Officer Stanhope stood long enough to make eye contact with one of the students. He whispered, hoping the student would read his lips, as he squeaked, "Do your work." The student brushed him off with a backhand stroke of his right hand. The student alerted the others to the officer's presence at the backdoor. One put a scowl on his face.

Another was very rude, showing the officer the middle finger, and yet another gave him the backhand. The security officer glared at the students and walked away. He thought, *These students don't care about their education. They don't want to learn. They'll find it out later.*

He walked along the hallway, which was surprisingly pretty clear, and looked in a few more classrooms. Some students were working; others were inattentive and hyperactive, being out of their seats and out of control. Reaching the west wing, the entrance to the boys' gym, he said, "What you're doing in the hallway?"

"We're going to the bathroom," two female students said in unison.

"Where's your pass?" Officer Stanhope questioned.

"What pass?" shouted the tall, frail, short-haired female student, gripping the plump arm of her short, stocky friend in close-fitting black jeans and black jersey and sweater.

Repeated the officer, "Your bathroom pass."

"We ain't got no pass," said the student, in faded blue jeans and red jersey, still holding on to the arm of the other student as though she was seeking support.

"You got to go back to your classroom and get a pass from your teacher," said the security officer.

"We ain't going back to that classroom. That mean, skinny teacher won't gave us a pass," blurted out the taller student, shaking her head.

"You got to get a pass to go to the bathroom. If you don't have a pass, it means you were not given permission to leave the class. You just walked out of the classroom," the officer stated, folding his arms across his chest.

"We told her we going to the bathroom," the shorter student said.

"We gon pee on ourself," the taller student lamented.

"You gonna wash our clothes or bring us fresh clothes when we pee on ourself?" the short, heavy student in a black top and jeans questioned.

"You got to get the pass," the officer reiterated firmly.

"We gonna pee right here, we ain't going back to no sh—ty classroom!" the student in the red top declared.

The officer exhaled and looked at them grimly, "Hurry up and get to the bathroom. The next time get a pass."

"She don't give anybody no pass," squealed the student in the black attire.

Together, the two female students made faces and walked away gingerly to the bathroom.

"You got to hurry, young ladies. No malingering in the hallway," the officer shouted.

The two students quickened their steps and disappeared into the bathroom. Officer Stanhope turned and walked back in the direction from which he came.

On all four floors the morning continued smoothly as well as part of the afternoon with the officers patrolling the hallways. It was difficult as usual for the security personnel and deans to get the students into their classrooms after the end of each period. Large numbers of students still milled around the hallways for some ten to fifteen minutes before they were barked upon or threatened with in-house suspension before they entered their classrooms. The male and female officers were having a little reprieve while classes were in session, but many students on each floor slipped into the hallway.

It was the seventh period, and a loud noise erupted in a classroom on the second floor. A girl jumped over a desk and lunged at a male student. She dealt him several blows in the head and face. "Yeah, yeah, yeah . . . ha, ha, ha . . ." was the outburst. "He being whack," someone in the class shouted. The student partly shielded his face and head with his arms, but the heavy female student pummeled him with solid punches.

"Stop it! End that nonsense now!" the young female teacher of class 807 shouted from the front of the class.

"You's a wimp. Havin' that sissy beatin' da sh—t outta yuh." A broad-shouldered, full-faced, double-chin student with a hood pulled over his head giggled.

"You taking that. She punching you all over your head," shrieked another.

"I ain't makin' joke with you," the female eighth grader shouted, her lips spreading while she punched and slapped him. "Don't throw anythin' at me."

"I ain't throw anythin' at you," the male student denied.

The female student, having satisfied herself, turned and walked back to her seat.

"You bust his ass," said one of her female colleagues.

"Yes, he mustn't throw anythin' at me. If it had hit me in my face what he would have said? I don't bother them. I come here, and I do my work," the young lady quarreled.

"You always allowing these girls to whack you. You got to do somethin' fuh yourself if not we gonna call you a sissy," another male student said.

"Carleen, you're not supposed to be punching at another student like that," the teacher rebuked, standing in front of her as she sat breathing heavily.

"Talk to him. He had no right to throw things at me, and you ain't do nothin' 'bout it," Carleen complained.

"I didn't see him throw anything at you—"

"You ain't see him throw those colored blocks at me?" Carleen interrupted. "Those lil building blocks!"

"Had I seen him I would've called the dean," said Mrs. Gringburg.

"You never do see anythin'," Carleen fumed.

"Those guys be throwing things all the time, and you don't say a thing," Carleen's friend told the teacher to her face.

"That's definitely not so," the business teacher said. She stepped over to the male student.

"What?" he said, looking up at Mrs. Gringburg.

"You ought not to be throwing things at other students. You could hurt them. Then you would be in a lot of trouble. The next time someone said you throw something at him or her I'm going to send you to the dean's office and ask that your parents come up here. This is nonsense. You ought to be working rather than fooling around throwing things at other students," the teacher rebuked.

"You see me throw anythin' at her? No. But you see her hittin' da sh—t outta me and you did nothin'. If I'd punch her in her face you woulda been calling security on me. Get outta here," Kendell shouted.

"No, no, I'm not going to take this from you," Mrs. Gringburg said, shaking her head.

"Talk to her. She smack me and you stand there doing nothin'," Kendell grumbled.

The security officer on the floor heard the skirmish and rushed to the door of the classroom.

"What's happening in here?" he questioned. "Why all this noise?"

"Carleen jumped on the desk to get at Kendell, and she started beating him in the head," said a small-sized eighth grader, baring even white teeth as his mouth opened widely.

"Look this is no joke. Mrs. Gringburg, what happened? There was a lot of noise coming from here," said Officer Stanhope.

"Carleen said—"

"Who's Carleen?" Officer Stanhope interjected, looking around the room.

"The girl over there with the yellow-and-red sweater," Mrs. Gringburg pointed to the student. "She said Kendell threw some building blocks at here, so she jumped on the desk to get at him, and she started punching him. It's ridiculous the way these students behave."

"Write it up, miss, and I'll take them," he advised.

"Okay, I'll write it up," answered the teacher.

"Let's go, the two of you," said the officer.

"Go where?" asked Kendell, frowning.

"Get up," ordered Officer Stanhope. Kendell did not budge.

"Young lady, let's go, too," the security officer beckoned at Carleen. Carleen looked away.

"Young man, let's go," the officer repeated.

"I ain't goin' nowhere. I ain't do nothin'," remonstrated Kendell.

"Bro, listen to wha' da dude is saying. Get up and go. Don't create more problems fuh yourself," suggested another student.

Kendell heeded the advice of his homeboy and rose from his seat. Carleen grabbed her bag from the desk and blazed out the room, into the hallway where she waited near the door for the officer. She was visibly upset since she did not initially create the problem as she sat reading a section in the business studies book as the teacher had instructed. Kendell picked up his bag, slung it over his right shoulder with the strap, and walked toward the door with the officer.

Said Officer Stanhope, as he walked with them to the dean's office, "I don't know what's wrong with you students. When you're going to get serious? Your parents send you here to learn. They're paying so much money for your education, and you're fooling around when the teacher is teaching. How you're going to learn that way?"

The two students did not answer but walked along with him to Mr. Linsmun's office.

"Mr. Linsmun, I have these students for you," said Officer Pandang.

Mr. Linsmun looked up from what he was writing. The security officer related to him what occurred in the classroom of Mrs. Gringburg.

"Sit there. I'll deal with you in a minute," Mr. Linsmun said, glancing at them with disgust.

The officer turned and left the room. The dean continued writing in a file while two other students sat waiting to hear from him.

Chapter 9

The next morning began as usual with loud talking and screaming among students. The deans and assistant principals had made their rounds on each of the floors before returning to their offices to begin their administrative duties. At the end of the first period, Kendra and her mother arrived and sat in the main office before they were sent upstairs to the tenth grade dean's office. Mrs. Simpson knocked on the door. *Pap, pap, pap.*

"Come in," a deep, husky voice said.

Mrs. Simpson and Kendra stepped into the office.

"Good morning, sir," said Mrs. Simpson, clad in a tan long coat. She was a medium-build woman.

"Good morning," answered Mr. Eisenburg, looking up from the file he was writing in that lay on his desk. "And you are?"

He did not see Kendra, who stood behind her mother.

"Oh, I'm Mrs. Simpson. Kendra's mother," replied the parent.

"I'm Mr. Eisenburg, dean of the tenth grade. Nice to meet you," said Mr. Eisenburg very diplomatically.

"Nice to meet you, too," the parent of Kendra responded politely.

"You may have a seat, and we'll wait until the other parent arrives," said the dean.

Kendra took a seat without even being told to do so. Before the middle of the second period, Nickita and her mother arrived at the school, did the normal protocol, and were directed to the main office and subsequently to the dean's office. Both mother and daughter waltzed into the room without knocking. "Good morning. I was given a letter by my daughter to come because of an altercation in the classroom," she rattled off looking at Mr. Eisenburg.

Said Mr. Eisenburg, "Good morning."

Turning, Nickita's mother said, "Good morning."

Mrs. Simpson answered, "Good morning."

"You may have a seat," the dean said.

Both mother and daughter sat in the brown cushioned chairs in the dean's office.

Said Mr. Eisenburg, his eyes shifting from one parent to the next, "Your daughters, Kendra and Nickita, were involved in a fight because, as it was explained to me, Kendra borrowed Nickita's CD player, and when Nickita said she wanted to listen to something, Kendra refused to give it up. And first of all, CD players and other gadgets of that type are not allowed to be played in school, moreover, during a lesson. Both of them broke the school's rules and would be punished accordingly. For the benefit of both parents, I'm going to ask each student to explain what started the fight. Nickita, tell us what happened."

"Kendra picked up my CD player, which I had on the desk, and started listening to it. I told her I wanted to listen to something. I held it and she pulled it away and the earphone cord disconnected and fell on the floor. I told her to fix it. She didn't. I bent over to pick it up from the floor and she pushed me. I straightened up and pushed her back, and that's how the fight started," explained Nickita, rubbing her palms together.

Both parents listened keenly to what Nickita said.

"Okay. Thanks, Nickita. Kendra, tell us what happened," the dean ordered.

"I ask Nickita to lend me the CD player. She lend me and when I was listening to it she pulled it away. The cord fell and she bumped me willfully when she bent over to pick it up. I pushed her 'cause she bumped me real hard. She pushed me back and the fight started," Kendra pointed out with a straight face.

"This is what appears to have happened from their accounts, as each is saying something slightly different. Firstly, fighting should not take place in school. There should be no fighting whatsoever. Secondly, musical gadgets or objects are not allowed in class and the building. We warn students about this. They break the rules and they are punished—" the dean said.

Interrupted Mrs. Mofatt, "Kendra had no right to pick up Nickita's CD player. I agree that Nickita should not come to school with it. I told her that before. It should be in her bag and not on the desk. Kendra should not have pushed her when she bent over to pick up the cord."

"But Nickita lend her, and she should not pull it away from Kendra like that. She lend her," Mrs. Simpson protested, her neck becoming stiff and straight.

"Your daughter should not have picked up her thing," Mrs. Mofatt emphasized.

"Kendra said Nickita allowed her to listen to the CD player and then she pulled it away," Kendra's mother, Mrs. Simpson, rebutted.

"No. She said Kendra picked it up from the desk. My daughter was not listening to it. She was getting her book from her bag," Nickita's mother opposed, her voice rising.

"But she borrows stuff from Kendra too. Kendra said she lends her stuff when she brings it to school, so your daughter shouldn't have to behave like that," Kendra's mother declared.

"I'm not going to prolong this. All I'm saying is that your child had no right to touch my child's thing, causing a fight to occur," Nickita's mom uttered.

"But she lend her. They were friends, and I don't see why they should fight over that, and you shouldn't have an attitude about Kendra touching Nickita's things because Kendra shows her things to Nickita too," Kendra's mother growled.

"I don't have to get an attitude about Nickita showing Kendra her things," Mrs. Mofatt said heatedly, turning to face Mrs. Simpson.

"Yes, you're getting an attitude, which is not necessary. These are children and we have to talk to them. We don't have to get puffed up and arrogant," declared Mrs. Simpson.

"Who is getting puffed up and arrogant? You're more getting puffed up and arrogant," retorted Mrs. Mofatt, turning away her face. "All I said is that she shouldn't touch my daughter's stuff if my daughter doesn't want her to do so."

"But my daughter allows her to touch and use her stuff," said Mrs. Simpson matter-of-factly.

Mr. Eisenburg stepped in and said, "Parents, there is no need for this verbal exchange. You have to show some example. These children behave like this all the time. They lend each other stuff, and then they quarrel and get fistic over their things."

"I understand that," said Mrs. Simpson in an apologetic tone.

"The point is that during a teaching session, they should not have those things out. They are not allowed to have them out or even bring them to school, and fighting is definitely not tolerated," Mr. Eisenburg explained to both parents as Kendra and Nicky listened somewhat half-heartedly.

"I told Nicky not to bring such things to school," joined in Nickita's mother.

"Because they broke the rules and fought in school, they are suspended for three days," said the dean. "Both of them will remain home until the suspension is over."

"I'm sorry this had to happen," remarked Kendra's mother, fumbling in her coat pocket and pulling a sheet of tissue with which she wiped her face. "Kendra is not going to borrow anybody's things, and she is not going to bring any music-playing gadget to school.

"Nickita would not walk with any CD player to school again," Mrs. Mofatt uttered in a subdued voice.

"Ladies, I thank you for coming here for us to take care of this matter and to let you know the punishment your children would receive for breaking the rules and fighting in class. They ought to be learning while in class. The teacher is conducting a lesson, and they are inattentive, fidgeting, and listening to something other than what the teacher is saying or what he requires them to do as an activity. That is unacceptable, and owing to their lack of attention and ill behavior, which caused the fight, the entire class was disrupted, which prevented other students from learning. That's a serious infraction of the rules and policy of the school. Any further misconduct by Nickita and Kendra would result in more serious punishment against them. This matter is settled and the punishment imposed. They would be provided with work by their subject teachers for the period they would be at home. You may wait in the main office where teachers would bring the assigned work for the three days. Again, thank you for coming," the dean finally said.

"Thank you, sir," Mrs. Simpson's voice squeaked as she and Kendra rose from their seats.

Mrs. Simpson stretched out her hand and reached that of Mr. Eisenburg as she made her way out of the office with her daughter after receiving her daughter's letter of suspension. Mrs. Mofatt rose from her seat and pulled her black coat around her, which was opened to the bottom.

Looking at Nickita, who had also risen, Mrs. Mofatt edged to Mr. Eisenburg's desk and said, "Mr. Eisenburg, I'm sorry this happened. Coming up here to waste your time and waste mine too. Nickita is not going to bring any of her stuff to school to disturb the lesson."

"I appreciate that," answered Mr. Eisenburg, nodding his head in approval.

Turning to Nickita, Mrs. Mofatt snarled, "You're not bringing any of those things in here again. I'm gonna check your bag before you leave."

Nicky looked to the ceiling. The white at the bottom of her eyes seemed more vivid while she pursed her lips and appeared meek.

"Thank you," Mrs. Mofatt said, looking over her burgundy metal-framed glasses.

"Thank you for coming," Mr. Eisenburg said, rising and shaking the hand of Mrs. Mofatt.

"You're welcome, sir," said Mrs. Mofatt, stepping gingerly toward the door with Nicky striding behind her.

Mr. Eisenburg sighed and shook his head. He thought, *If these parents could talk to their kids more, and advise them it would be better in here.* The dean then got down to some serious paperwork that he had to finish for the principal.

Things could be quiet for a moment, and then suddenly a situation would erupt that would send students bailing out the classroom into the hall. Some students sat somewhat dejected and immersed in their own thoughts without participating in the classwork. Mr. Wren, a young, athletic-build math teacher, grappled to get his sixth graders, class 605, under control during the fourth period and to see to it that they did some work. Students ran and jumped and engaged in some indecent talk.

Someone threw a paper ball that hit Philipi. Said Philipi, "What yuh doin' yo. Don't leh me come and smack you in yuh face."

Mia shot back, "You can't smack me, you dum d—ck. You a bum."

"Throw another one at me and see wha' I gonna do and who you callin' d—ck head," threatened Philipi.

Mia headed the threat and did not hurl any more paper balls at Philipi, nor did she describe him with any more slurs.

The obscenity was unbearable. In another row of seats, Ashlina pushed Cina, and she stumbled forward. "What da f— yuh doin'?" Cina blurted out, turning to face Ashlina.

"Where's my game?" asked Ashlina.

"I ain't got anythin' fuh you," Cina snarled, walking away.

Ashlina pushed Cina's head.

"Stop!" Cina shouted as Ashlina ran out the class into the hallway bound for the stairway. Cina went through the door after her; she did not run.

Facing Ashlina, Cina yelled, "You fat piece a sh—t! You wish you was like me."

A school aide who was coming down the stairwell from the second floor turned and said to Cina, "What you said to her wasn't nice. You shouldn't say that."

"I don't care. She started with me," Cina answered.

"I gonna catch yuh, Cina," shouted Ashlina, turning back and heading to her classroom.

"She is so rude," said the school aide.

Back in the class in the front row, as some of the classes were arranged in rows rather than groups of four or five, Kassima sat next to Rupert. Looking down at her sneakers, she said, "Rupert, tie my sneaker lace mad fast."

"What?" Rupert asked, squinting his eyes at her.

"Do it mad fast," she yelled, banging on the desk with her right fist.

"Why can't you do it yourself? It's on your foot," Rupert answered back.

"Bop," Kassima slugged him in his back.

"Why you hitting me? I ain't do you nothin'," complained Rupert, heaving his chest.

"'Cause you didn't tie my lace." Kassima chuckled.

Rupert shook his head in surprise and continued to follow what the teacher was saying.

Mr. Wren stopped what he was discussing and said, "It's time that you settle down and stop talking."

"We settled down," replied Kassima, with a big grin on her face.

Turning to Jerome, who sat next to Rupert, Mr. Wren said, "Give me the answer to the first problem."

Uttered Jerome, "How you treatin' me like I'm smart when I feel like I'm dumb."

Mr. Wren looked at him with surprise in his eyes and said, "Jerome, you could say something better than that. And you know you could do what I ask you to do. If not, you could make a good effort."

"I'm playin', I'm playin' with you." Jerome giggled and pawed at Mr. Wren's hand.

"Jerome, this is not time to play. We have much work to do," cautioned Mr. Wren, who walked off, turned, and faced the class.

From the back of the class, a noise ripped through the room. "Mr. Wren, this place is hot. We need a fan or air condition unit. We could die. We could drown in our own sweat. Come on, Mr. Wren, tell them to do somethin'. It's serious." Mia grinned.

It was a cold day, and the heat was coming up with a hissing sound to give warmth to the classrooms.

"It would be good if you take off that heavy coat then you would not feel hot. Put the coat in the closet," said Mr. Wren to Mia, who now giggled.

Less than half the class was attentive. As the teacher spoke a student belched loudly in the middle of the class while another student worked a math problem on the chalkboard during which Mr. Wren closely monitored the steps used to arrive at the answer. Turning, he said, "At least you could have said, 'Excuse me,' Arrond."

Arrond replied, "That's not my religion."

"Ha, ha, ha, ha, ahhh, ha, ha, ha." The class laughed at his funny reply.

Uttered Mr. Wren, "It means having manners. It has nothing to do with religion."

"So," mumbled Arrond, slouching in his chair and rubbing his chest and puffing his cheeks in attempting to burp again.

Mr. Wren did not prolong the exchange but observed how the student worked the math problem and then commended her for doing it correctly while showing all the steps.

Instructed Mr. Wren, "Do exercise 4, numbers 1 to 5 after which we're going to work on our class project."

Students spent the next fifteen minutes doing the exercise. At the end of it, Mr. Wren collected their notebooks, which he put on his desk.

Facing the class, Mr. Wren ordered, "Students, take out your class project. We will continue to work in groups of four."

Students began taking out their poster boards, construction paper, markers, books, glue, and other materials. There was much excitement and involvement in the task they pursued though a few students were not fully engaged.

Around the corner, meters away from Mr. Wren's classroom in the east wing, and adjacent to the west wing, which housed the auditorium, students in Mr. Carrington's sixth grade math class, 602, worked on a past practice test, which involved problem-solving, measurement, and decimals in preparation for a test scheduled for the middle of the next week. Mr. Carrington worked with his sixth graders, and many of them were the essence of concentration throughout the fourth period. Some worked together in groups while others worked independently. He walked around, helping students as they worked, checking to see how far they had gone and the methods and skills they applied to the problems.

"How many questions have you done so far, Louisa?" Mr. Carrington asked, leaning over and glancing at her math booklet and paper.

"I finished ten. I have five more to do," she answered. Her eyes sparkled as she was working assiduously.

"Fine! Continue working," the teacher encouraged.

Looking over at Jessica, whose blond hair shimmered in the light as she leaned her head on one side, cradling it with her left palm and red manicured fingers, the teacher asked, "How many have you finished?"

She looked up at him, squinted and said, "Ten, Mr. Carrington. We're working together."

"Good," Mr. Carrington said, and moved to another desk where he pressed the top of his red ink ballpen. "How are you getting on, Roderick?"

"Ah, ah, I'm on number seven," Roderick answered. The teacher saw the strain on Roderick's face and began to work with him, writing in his notebook, asking him questions, and showing him the method in solving the problem he worked on. Roderick's face brightened as he grasped the method and continued working. Mr. Carrington then stepped over to Amanda.

Said he, "Amanda, how many questions have you done?"

"I finished nine. I'm on number ten," Amanda answered with a glance at the teacher and then looked back in her workbook.

"Okay. Continue working," Mr. Carrington encouraged.

Amanda buried her head in her book and continued working feverishly. The teacher checked a number of students' work before inviting them to a discussion on what they did. Later on, Mr. Carrington stood next to the class list on heavy construction paper, tacked against the wall. He placed gold, silver, and bronze stars against the names of students who worked seriously and got ten or more of the fifteen problems right. He usually, like other teachers, gave various types of incentives to encourage students to perform well in their class and homework activities.

In most of the sixth and seventh grade classes on the first floor, students, both boys and girls, ran wild. They hit and kicked at each other in an aggressive form of play as they stumbled into garbage bins in the classrooms, spilling litter on the floor. Some students grabbed garbage bins and hurled them through the air at other students. The bins crashed on the floor spewing garbage all over the rooms and sending students scampering for cover to avoid being hit and to protect themselves from getting their clothes soiled or dirty. It was unbelievable to see the way some of the out-of-control students behave.

Idin, a short, thin student in class 603, stood up in his chair and, seconds after, jumped on his desk. He then jumped from his desk to another desk. Ezren joined him. The teacher shouted at them, reprimanding them for their callous and disrespectful behavior. Idin shouted back at the teacher and continued jumping from one desk to another. Xavil, Cleo, and Wanda folded loose-leaf paper into balls and began pelting them at each other. Girls threw or pelted at boys and boys pelted back at girls. There was a foray amidst the shouts and yells. Idin, Xavil, Ezren, and Octar, male students, then somersaulted, jumping and flipping their bodies, bringing their feet over their heads and landing flat on their feet, at the back of the classroom. They pushed some chairs and tables aside, tumbling some on the floor in order to make more room for their disruptive activities. Two girls, Cleo and Wanda, joined them in the somersault or cartwheel.

The teacher hurried across to them and ordered, "Stop this gimmick. Get to your seats. Stop the foolishness. You're looking to hurt yourselves."

They blatantly ignored him. Cleo and Wanda cartwheeled, and the onlookers came alive with delight. "Yeah, yeah" was the loud response. They laughed and jumped around.

One young man shouted, "Do it again, Cleo, do it again."

A young lady shrieked, "Do that flip one more time."

And Cleo somersaulted again to the roar and applause of the group.

Waving a sheet of paper in his right hand, the twenty-two-year-old teacher warned, "A number of homes gonna be called this evening."

Said one female onlooker, "You're not calling my home fuh sure 'cause I ain't do nothin'."

"Whether you're cartwheeling or looking on, your home is going to be called, I promise you. You're not going to continue with this crazy behavior in this class. If I got to get your parents up here I'll do it, trust me," the teacher rebuked, a grim countenance settling on his narrow clean-shaven face with strong jaws.

Two or three students ambled their way back to their seats but continued to delight in the cartwheel performed by the nimble young men and women.

Vilmena, clad in a black sweater, stepped up to the teacher and said, looking him straight in the face without a blink, "Why you callin' our house? We just havin' some fun. Chill, mannn, you use to do this too. Tell me I lie."

"I want you to go to your seat and get busy with your work," the young male teacher said.

"Tell yuh, I know you use to do this, too," the female student said, stabbing her fist in the air.

Ursila, who wore a green-and-yellow sweater, walked up to the teacher and said to him, "You cool, yo. You ain't callin' nobody's house."

"He ain't bluffing. He say he gonna call," said Yvonne, who stood in a red long coat.

Grinning broadly and showing even white teeth, Ursila said to the teacher, "You know you ain't callin' nobody house."

"I'm going to," said the teacher.

"You ain't calling anybody's home. You's my nigga. You's my homie." Cleo giggled as she stepped up in front of Mr. Carrington.

"What? What you just said? Calling me the N-word," Mr. Carrington fumed.

"Wha' you fussing 'bout 'cause I say nigga? You heard that before, Mr. Carry." Cleo laughed, backing away from the teacher and giving him the V sign with her middle and index fingers.

"I definitely got to call your home, and I'll let the dean know about this," Mr. Carrinngton said. He was definitely upset with the behavior of Cleo and some of the students.

"The rest of you, find your seats," the teacher ordered, but it was difficult for him to gain the attention of most of them as the noise soared.

As frustration gripped him, he headed to the door and opened it. The din rippled into the hallway. Several students were cutting class, and they walked the hallway in the east wing. Others idled and looked through the windows, as no security officer was present patrolling the area.

Mr. Carrington looked up and down the hallway in seeking the assistance of a supervisor or security officer, but none of them was present. He stepped back into the classroom and watched with disdain as some of the students ran amok in his class. Like some of the other rooms, his did not have a working intercom, which would enable him to contact security or the dean. Looking at his watch, he saw that he had fifteen more minutes to go through the ordeal with the students not listening or doing anything that involved learning during the sixth period. He tried working individually with the students who worked, who did the various math problems, though in a somewhat half-hearted manner, as the ruckus distracted them. Mr. Carrington made a note of Cleo's behavior and the others who cartwheeled in his notebook and later on in the day called their homes. He also informed the dean. Their parents came up to the school to see the teacher and the dean. Cleo was suspended for three days, and other students were placed in in-house suspensions for two days.

Chapter 10

Mr. James switched off the lights in his classroom, pulled the door shut, and locked it, placing the keys back on the key ring attached to his black leather belt. He strode along the hallway and descended the stairwell. Mr. Mendez also locked his classroom door and headed along the hallway to the stairwell nearest to his classroom. Ms. Vivehouse picked up her black-and-blue leather shoulder bag. She looped the strap across her right shoulder and left her room, locking it after her. It was lunchtime, and teachers made their way to the teachers' lunchroom in the basement. Some teachers were already sitting at tables eating lunch while others stood in line waiting to order and pay for their meal.

Seated next to Mrs. Baighman was Mr. Blair, who said, "I had a tough morning with class 806. Kenneth, Hector, and Merleen were off the wall. I couldn't get through with my lesson. They just talked and shouted throughout the lesson."

"I'm so upset. I got to call some homes tonight. Carlos, Woonin, Balram, and Renee were making it difficult for me to teach. They were out of their seats and carrying on at the back of the class, just talking and throwing things at other students who were trying to do work," complained Mrs. Baighman while she chewed on a chicken sandwich with lettuce and tomatoes and sipped a bottle of apple juice.

Joined in Ms. Vine, "I set up half the night preparing a chart and graphic organizers to do my lessons, and Jasmine, Derrick, Jack, Jaime, Mike, and Ortis just wrecked my class. They threw paper balls and books at each other. I called the dean and had them taken out of my class. Every time I have 704, there is a problem with these students. It's the same thing with 907. I had them during the first period, and Kenrick, Nuldun, Denny, and the few others ran wild around the classroom."

"And you call their parents, and they deny that they ever behave like this. Arrond's mom came up here on Monday because he repeatedly banged on the desk and cursed. He denied that he did anything," said Mrs. Baighman.

"His mother has to do something more in ensuring that he curbs his behavior. I agree, she comes up here, and he denies that he does anything wrong. He always claims it is somebody else or that somebody did him something that caused him to hit out or misbehave. His mother is here one day, and the next day he continues with his disruptive behavior. And he is not alone. Joseph behaves the same way. Even Jason, Rachel, Jasmine, and Kevin," complained Mr. Blair as he cut a piece of meat in his plate.

The aroma of food lingered at the table and the others at which teachers sat.

"I have it hard as well with those same students. You talk to them until you're tired. I brought in some nice, brightly colored pens, and I gave them, as an incentive, to students who worked. They felt good that I gave them something for their effort. I even gave pens to those who misbehave, on condition that they change their behavior. They promise they would change. As soon as they received the pens they continued misbehaving, shouting and running around the classroom," related Mr. Mendez while he ate baked chicken he cut from a chicken leg.

"Talking about that, I give rewards to my class. I give them silver and gold stars for improved and good performances in classwork, homework, and tests, also conduct. I also give extra credit, even pencils and pens, but what for? They continue to behave crazy. I told them I'm going to take them to the cinema, to see if it would work.

As usual, some of them pull themselves together. The others just don't care," stated Ms. Vivehouse, pulling on a straw as she drank a bottle of cold fruit punch after eating baked chicken, potatoes, and vegetable salad.

"And these students could do better. They could work if they settled down. I've known of instances where Alvin, Nuldun, Denny, Neisha, and many of the other students in class 907, performed well in my math class, in both classwork and tests I give," stated Mr. James, who sat at another table eating lunch he bought in the teachers' cafeteria.

"They're not stupid. They can work if they settled down and focused. Those same students, Nakon, Kevin, Jasmine, Jack, Jason, and the others in 704, performed well in the last two tests I gave. I was stern with them. I told them they would not be promoted. They got above eighty-five percent, each of them. And Derrick, he got a ninety. Normally, they don't care and they don't do the work. And by the way, they didn't sit together during those tests," declared Mrs. Hutchenson, as she finished chewing on a stem of steamed broccoli as she sat at the table with Mr. James.

Explained Mr. James, "These are not dumb students. They're not stupid. It's just that some of them don't mean to work. They want to play and disrupt your class. But if you get harsh with them and they know you're not playing, they work, but it's not easy to do, and not every teacher could get them to work. It has its toll on you after a while. When I get home I'm tired. I'm totally exhausted. It takes a lot out of you to get these students to work and not fool around in your class. There're those students who come in prepared to work, but the others, forget it. They are here to play, plain and simple, if they could get away with it. You got to be tough. It's not easy."

"You're right," answered Ms. Vine. "By the time I get home I'm exhausted. I could barely keep my eyes open."

"And it's not going to get better as we fast approach the summer holiday. Already, they're dressing as if they're going to a picnic or heading for the beach," remarked Mrs. Baighman.

"These students will run amok over the remaining few weeks before school closes for the summer," remarked Ms. Vine.

"I don't know what to say," said Mr. Mendez. "But the administration has to do something about this behavior."

"Well, with Mr. Cottle retiring at the end of the school year and with the appointment of a new principal, there should be some changes," stated Mrs. Baighman.

"What if they decided to retain his service for the new year?" asked Mr. Mendez. "The situation may well continue with all the indiscipline and problems we face daily."

"I don't think Mr. Cottle wants to stay on. He's tired and he wants to go. I think he had wanted to go even before he had reached his time for retirement. He's sixty-two now, and I think three years ago he had wanted to go but they asked him to stay on," mentioned Mrs. Baighman.

"Perhaps he has realized he was not up to it and had wanted to go before things got worse. It would have been better if they had allowed him to retire when he had wanted to. Look how things have deteriorated over the years," pointed out Mr. Mendez.

"I don't think he is mainly responsible for the decline in conditions here. Things have been sliding a long time ago, if you remember correctly, even before he was appointed as principal. The situation was almost the same when he was assistant principal. The directors thought he might have been able to fix it, but it's a rather difficult task. Also, parents have to become more involved, and this is not happening, in a very effective way, over the years. It's a sad situation, and something has to be done to correct this downward spiral," Mrs. Baighman suggested, looking at Mr. Mendez.

"This is definitely a problem that administration has to deal with, and they need to have a more proactive approach," indicated Mr. James, leaning forward in his chair as he had finished eating his lunch.

"An aggressive strategy has to be implemented if this situation is to be corrected and improvement realized for the new year," declared Mrs. Hutchenson. "It's not an impossible task to undertake."

At the same time, in the teachers' lounge, the air or atmosphere was charged. There was much frustration among faculty. Members hoped that something would be done to alleviate the eroding discipline situation that plagued the school for a protracted period of time and which has grossly impeded instruction and learning. Mrs. Gringburg sat at one of the large, wooden tables in the bare, drab lounge, with a stack of written work by students. Next to her sat Ms. Bishop, who leaned back in the chair marking a test she had given students the previous day.

Said she, "I had such a hard time giving this test. Students would not sit still and focus."

"I had the same problem last week. I had to shout like if I was going out of my mind to let them know it was a test and that they had to stop talking. Three or four of them still continued, and I had to move them to the back of the class. Apart from a few of them, the work wasn't good because they're not paying attention to the lesson. I call home, they come to school and quiet down for a while, and it's back to the same thing: talking and yelling and not doing much work," Mrs. Gringburg mentioned with disgust in her voice. "So we all have the same problem. It's nothing new, but it's irritating. The students who really want to learn can't do so."

"That's the reason why many of them are not doing well in their schoolwork because of the disruptive behavior," concurred Mr. Howard, whose eyes looked red and tired from the constant fatigue in trying to bring order to his classroom.

Joined in Ms. Langevine, with a stark grimace on her face, as she was clearly upset with the constant disruptions in her class, "Just this morning I had to prevent a fight from breaking out in class 704. Kevin told Nakon about his mother, and Nakon picked up a hardcover textbook and threw it at him. Luckily, he got out of the way and the book slammed into the wall. Look, I was so angry because I'd just started a new lesson. I dashed over to him and let him know that if that book had hit anyone he would have been in so much trouble. As usual, he talked back saying he didn't care because Kevin had no right to tell him about his mother. I let him know that he wasn't going to mess up my lesson. He started cursing, and I told him he's not staying in my class. I immediately got security and had him and Kevin taken to Ms. Piggot. I have some good students who want to learn, and I'm not going to allow Nakon and Kevin and the rest to prevent those students from learning."

"Kevin, Nakon, Jasmine, Jack, and the others should stay at home. I don't know why they're here," said Ms. Hatmil, as she calmed herself from a grueling third period.

"Their parents should keep them at home. They hardly do anything in class. Just making it difficult for me to conduct my lesson," uttered Mr. Mendez.

"Some of these students are downright out of control. The talking, screaming, and leaving their seats are unbelievable. I had class 605 and Mia, Ashlina, Jerome, and Arrond would not stop talking. I tried to model a lesson, and every time I had to stop and tell them to be quiet. I went to class 806 and it was worse. Kenneth, Makalia, Merleen, and William were out of their minds. It was crazy in those classrooms," declared Mr. Wren, who echoed similar sentiments as the other teachers at the table and the one nearby.

On the opposite side in the teachers' lounge, Mr. Reece said, "I had to stop my lesson in class 702 during the first period and call the homes of Alfreda, Romero, and Damian. They threw paper balls at each other. I told them to cut the crap. They still continued. The entire class began laughing. I whipped out my cell phone and called their homes. I put them on to talk to their parents. I know it ain't gonna be nice with them when they get home."

"But you know what, Mr. Reece, you call their parents, they talk to them or promise they're going to punish them in some way by denying them privileges, and after a day or two they come back and do the same things or worse. It isn't working," said Ms. Stein.

"You're right. They do the same things to disrupt your lesson and smash your classroom," declared Mr. Reece as he leaned forward in his chair.

"Two days ago I had a fight in class, class 606. Daren and Kori. Security came and took them out. Officer Pandang was on the floor nearby, and he heard the commotion. He came into the room and grabbed both of them and took them out. They were placed in in-house for the remainder of the day. Their parents came up, and they got suspended. They came back to school, and they're behaving the same way. It's ridiculous," said Ms. Langevine.

"At the last staff meeting, Mr. Howard and Mrs. Hutchenson got up and spoke strongly about the wave of indiscipline among students and urged the administration to do something about it, but the situation seems to have gotten worse," said Ms. Vine, as she feels the pain of fatigue.

"I know the deans and assistant principals are making efforts to curb this discipline problem, but more has to be done. Something drastic has to be done with those students who are constantly disruptive. It is an ongoing, perennial problem, and they have to take bolder measures to improve this situation, Ms. Vine," opined Mr. James, furrows forming on his forehead.

Said Ms. Langevine, "The students who come to school willing to learn are often hampered. It's pathetic."

"I asked Carleen and Kendell of 807 and Melissa, Nigel, Charles, and Lawerence of 803 why they come here to create havoc. Every time you tell them about their behavior, they deny they did anything wrong," declared Mr. Reece.

"I firmly believe that some of these students who do the same things every day to create confusion need professional help in the form of psychological evaluation and treatment. The admin has to speak with the guidance counselors, school psychologists, and social workers to address this problem. Parents and guardians have to be called in and the matter discussed seriously. If not, we'll be going through this malaise every day with no end in sight," expressed Ms. Vine seriously.

Teachers voiced their displeasure with the manner in which the discipline situation was affecting their instructions and the ability of students to learn in a way that is not inhibited by disrupted tendencies. On a daily basis, the topic is aired in the teachers' lounge and work chamber.

Edward sat with his face in his hands in class 1105. He propped his face in his hands as if he were weighed down with sorrow. His blue eyes looked blank. He turned his blue baseball cap backward, settled it on his shoulder-length turf of brown hair, and scratched the left side of his face with his ring finger. His neck and cheeks looked pink compared with the rest of his face. Sitting next to him was Carlos, who portrayed his ancestors with his long, shiny black hair held together in a ponytail.

"What up?" he said to Edward.

"I hate this place," said Edward expressionlessly.

"This place sucks, and every day you got to come here," concurred Carlos, knitting his brow.

"I gonna cut tomorrow. I goin' downtown. I wanna ask my girl to come with me," said Edward, curling his lips.

"Whose your girl?" Carlos seemed interested.

"She's in 1107, that stupid-ass class where everybody is running wild," answered Edward.

"We running wild here, too," reminded Carlos.

"We not as crazy as they," stated Edward.

"So who she is?" inquired Carlos, leaning forward not to miss what Edward was about to say.

"Kathlene," said Edward, slumping in his chair and tapping his fingers on the desk.

"That ugly gal with freckles on her face and dimple in her chin?"

"ha, ha, ha..." Carlos laughed. *Bang, bang*! He struck the desk with his right fist.

"Hey, don't mess with my woman. She ain't ugly," quarreled Edward, anger settling in his blue eyes. "I never dis your chick."

"Who you talking 'bout?" asked Carlos.

"Susan," blurted Edward, his face getting red.

"I don't hang with da chick no more."

"Fuh real."

"Yeah, she wanna f— control me, yo, tellin' me what to do, and what I shouldn't do. I couldn't deal with that. I couldn't handle that. You know me, I like to do as I feel, sh—t."

"She was a nice, heavy broad, yo. Who she goin' with now?"

"I ain't know, a don' care."

"Who you hooking up with? Which shorty?"

"I got a sweetie on my block."

"I know her?"

"Sh—t no, you don't know her. You don't live on muh block and wha' you wanna know her for? You white guys don't want Hispanic chicks."

"I'm one with a difference. I hook up with any chick, a don't care."

"You don't mean you want my woman?"

"Hey, f— outta here, I don't want yuh woman. I got mine. If I didn't have her, yes, I woulda hook up with any chick, white, black, Hispanic, Asian. It doesn't matter."

"You fuh real."

"I fuh real, my man."

Elizabeth, with her flowing blond hair nestled across her shoulders, left her seat and walked over to Edward and Carlos. Her faded denim jeans hugged her thighs, and her skimpy, light-green, long-sleeve jersey spanned her torso and arms. Her small, straight nose looked pink at the tip as if irritated by the persistent cold weather.

"Where're you going to, Elizabeth?" questioned the literature teacher, Mrs. Baighman, a slim teacher with long, brown hair and prominent veins in her thin arms and hands, veins that look blue.

"What? Mind your own business," Elizabeth answered the teacher.

"That deserves a call home," said Mrs. Baighman.

"Go ahead, I don't care. You treat us as though we're in f— sixth grade. We're juniors," lashed out Elizabeth, frowning her face.

Mrs. Baighman did not answer; she did not want to escalate a situation with Elizabeth, who could be very frantic at times.

Stopping at Edward's desk, she said, "What the two of you doin'?"

"Wha' you wanna know? You just come over here to show your stink ass forehead," blurted Edward, looking up at her and grabbing her hand.

"Who you talkin' to?" asked Elizabeth, pulling away her hand and stepping back.

"You, and you so wiry with that big ass forehead of yours," Edward rolled with laughter. "Ha, ha, ha . . ."

"I'll knock you out with it, and my man likes me the more with it," scowled Elizabeth, backing away.

"Get outta here. You ain't got no man," shot back Edward.

"You only think so," Elizabeth said, slapping him on the head and walking away.

"She so nosy sometimes," remarked Carlos. "Always wantin' to know wha' people talkin'."

"Nah, she cool, she my homie," said Edward.

In the opposite corner of the classroom, Wooning and Balram drew cartoons in their notebooks. They tried to see whose hulkman looked stronger and fiercer.

Said Mrs. Baighman, "I thought everyone was reading but some people are talking and doing all sorts of things except reading. Next Tuesday we'll have our biweekly test, and I hope all of you who are not reading would be knowledgeable about the chapters we're studying. We studied chapters 11 to 14 over the last two weeks, and everyone should be familiar with the role of the characters, the various plots, and the conflicts and how they were resolved. You were asked during the last twenty minutes of this period to do independent reading, but many of you are doing your own thing."

"Can you stop talking? You're giving me a headache. You already made your point," said a stocky, full-faced, female student sitting in the middle of the class.

"You're getting rather saucy, Renee. How dare you tell me to stop talking," the teacher remonstrated.

Said Wooning, who sat behind Renee, "She looks old like the north star."

Renee picked it up and bellowed, "You look old like the north star. I didn't say it, Wooning said it."

There was hilarious laughter in the class. "Ahhh, ha, ha, ha . . ."

"She must be a thousand years old, ha, ha, ha . . ." Balram laughed, his thick, black, shiny hair falling on his forehead just above his thick eyebrows.

"Balram said you must be a thousand years old," echoed Renee, her mouth agape in laughter.

"Ah, ha, ha, ha, ha, ha, you funny, yo," cracked up Wooning, swaying in his chair.

"Renee, you are very disrespectful, and I'm going to see to it that your parents are up here," Mrs. Baighman said, obviously disturbed by what Renee shouted out in the class.

"I didn't say it, they said it, the two of them, Wooning and Balram, grinning at the back there," Renee appealed.

"Even if they said it you had no reason to repeat it. That's disrespectful and disruptive," said the teacher.

"All those wrinkles and lines on her face, ha, ha, ha," Wooning poked.

"Hear him, Wooning. He said all those wrinkles and lines on your face, ha, ha, ha," Renee mocked.

"What da f— wrong with you. Why you calling my name, Renee?" Wooning yelled.

"'Cause you and Balram sayin' things 'bout Mrs. Baighman, and now she's gonna call my house," complained Renee.

"You didn't hear me say sh—t, and you should mind your own business," rebuked Balram, staring at Renee.

"I mind my own business, sucker," Renee fumed at Balram, bobbing her head.

"If you been minding your own damn business, you wonna hear what we're saying," Wooning sneered, his small, slanting eyes becoming smaller. He pushed back his long black hair from his face.

"Look who calling me sucker. You're more a sucker. You dumbass," charged Balram, gritting his teeth.

"Like yuh momma," lashed out Renee.

"You don't know my mama. She has class," said Balram.

"Are you going to stop that nonsense. The stupid argument. You are wasting time and you have work to do," uttered Mrs. Baighman, stepping toward Balram, Wooning, and Renee.

"She started it," said Balram, pointing at Renee.

Renee did not answer but shifted in her seat and stiffened her neck as she ignored Balram.

Chapter 11

Mr. Linsmun drove along the Belt on another dreary winter morning taking the same route to take his wife to work before heading in to school. He pondered what the day would be like. Erwin pulled the door behind him, turned around, locked it and put the keys in the side pocket of his backpack, and then made his way to the sidewalk. He headed alone to the bus stop, where he waited for some ten minutes before boarding the bus. Students were coming from every direction on their way to Jones High School. A large crowd had already built up in the schoolyard. The shouting and screaming among students of the lower or junior school was deafening. Since the weather was a little better compared with the previous days when it was bitterly cold, students were going berserk. Coupled with the amount of noise they made, the sixth to eighth graders dropped their bags and coats anywhere and ran wildly in chasing after their friends or playing heady games.

At the sound of the bell, they made their way into the building. It took about fifteen minutes for the yard to clear. In Mr. Russo's 704 art class, Nakon got up from his seat and headed to the door.

"Where are you going, young man?" Mr. Russo asked, pointing at him.

"You just gave me permission, you losing it," said Nakon.

"I didn't give you permission to leave the class," the teacher said.

"Yes, you did. Man, you really losing it," emphasized Nakon, watching the teacher with mock indifference, knowing he did not ask for permission.

"You better sit and focus on what you're supposed to do," advised Mr. Russo, moving around the class checking to see how students were designing, sketching, and coloring their particular work of choice.

"Valcom, what's the problem? Why do you have your head on the desk? Where is your work?" said Mr. Russo.

Valcom answered, "My brain swelled. I can't do any work today."

"Your brain swelled?" asked Mr. Russo.

"Yes it is. I can't work today," said Valcom, smiling.

"Valcom, I expect to see some effort from you in trying to complete that project. I must see some meaningful work before the period is up," the teacher demanded strongly.

"Okay, okay, I do my work," Valcom said, giving the teacher a thumbs up.

The teacher then checked the work of other students, some of whom were fooling around. Notwithstanding, there were those students at all grade levels who did work that revealed a high level of creativity. On the canvas, the young men and women used bold colors to produce striking landscapes and intriguing objects as well as geometrical patterns. Mr. Russo worked assiduously with his students in instructing them on the finer details of art. The art room was small and resources were limited, but in spite of the cramped space and shortage of art materials, the various classes that were taught produced fascinating works.

Mr. Reece, a new reading teacher who had recently joined the staff, was given a coverage of a special-needs tenth grade class so that the class teacher, Mrs. Wooley, could have her prep time.

"Mr. Reece, you have to be tough with these students. You can't smile with them," advised Mrs. Wooley, a plump, buxom teacher with eyebrows that almost joined together. Her tan body hue blended with her bronze-colored hair that flowed along her solid broad shoulders.

"Okay, I'll handle it. Everything will be all right," the young male teacher answered, his eyes widening as he eyed the small class of twelve from the corners of his hazel eyes as they sat in their seats looking steadfast at him while he faced the class teacher.

"I hope so, but I'm just letting you know upfront," Mrs. Wooley counseled, picking up her black shoulder-strap bag, a textbook, and a pile of papers with written work.

"Thanks for the briefing," Mr. Reece said with a glint in his eyes.

"You're welcome." Mrs. Wooley cracked a smile and walked off clad in her black long-sleeve jersey, white ankle-length woolen pants, and black shiny leather shoes.

As soon as she stepped through the door, the students sprang from their seats as if they had springs in their bodies. They dashed for the hallway and yelled, "Ahhhhhh, ahhhhh." "Yes, yes, yes! This is it, ahhhhh," one of them shouted as he leaped back and forth from the hallway. Two grabbed and wrestled each other down to the floor. Seven of them, male and female, scuttled in the hallway while two remained in their seats. "Get back in here," Mr. Reece yelled, his face becoming red. The seven rushed back into the classroom at the order of the covering teacher.

One student pushed another, and he responded by hitting out. Garry, the heavier student, charged after him. Garry and Kenan ran around the classroom. Ian tried to block Kenan. "Move out da f— way," shouted Kenan as he pushed Ian. Kenan pulled a desk behind him as he ran. Garry finally caught up with him and unleashed some blows to his abdomen. Kenan doubled over. Straightening up seconds after, he blurted, "You hurt my f— stomach, yo."

"What? You don't play with me or you get hurt," said Garry, grinning and panting.

Meanwhile, Frank and Michael tumbled on the floor blowing heavily. Frank put Michael in a headlock with his right arm. "Ahhhh, ahhhhh," Michael grunted. Mr. Reece moved toward them. "Stop it! Get off the floor and go to your seats," he barked. Michael was able to break loose from Frank's grip and ran toward the door and through it into the hallway. Garry, Kenan, Sean, and Sergio also dashed through the door into the hallway. "Hit him," "Kick him," "Throw him 'gainst da wall," and "Slam him" were the piercing shouts that came from the hallway as the students wrestled each other to the floor.

Ashton, another student, leapt to the door and shouted, "Yo, come inside."

Mr. Reece stepped to the door. The anger was marked on his face. He barked, "I'm going to get your parents up here if you don't get in here and stop jumping around and wrestling."

"Shut up," Kenan yelled.

"I'm calling your home," retorted Mr. Reece.

"I don't care! Call my home!" shouted back Kenan, wiping his forehead with the back of his hand.

"Okay, I'll do it. Young men, get in here," the teacher ordered.

They rushed into the classroom in a burst of laughter. "Ha, ha, ha-ha, ha, ha-ahhh, ha, ha, ha, yeah, yeah yeah."

"I whip you, Sean," uttered Sergio as he went to the window and pushed it up, allowing the cold air to rush in.

While they dashed through the doorway, back into the classroom, Garry bounced into Mr. Reece and threw him off balance. Mr. Reece staggered back and bawled, "What's the matter, young man! You want to knock me down?"

"You was in da way. How you expect me to pass?" growled Garry.

"You didn't have to rush in the room like that and kindly sit down," Mr. Reece shouted, a tinge of disdain in his voice.

The young men stood around the room for a while. Mr. Reece walked toward the front of the class and stood in the center.

"Sit down, please," he said, but the students did not budge. Ashton threw a paper ball at Sergio. Sergio turned around and, seeing a heavy hardcover textbook on the desk, grabbed it and hurled it through the air at Ashton. Ashton ducked and ran to escape the impact of the book. "Wha' wrong with you? Why you threw da heavy book, man?" Ashton shouted. Others dashed out of the way. The book slammed into a locker in the southern part of the room with a big bang. Mr. Reece was incensed.

He yelled, "Your parents going to be called this evening. This is totally insane behavior."

Sergio just grinned and walked to his desk where he stood. Garry, who stood at the back of the class with Kenan and Sean, pulled opened the door of one of the metal lockers. He looked inside as if searching for something. Not finding what he appeared to be looking for, he slammed the door. *Bang!* The noise echoed loudly in the classroom. He pulled the door opened again and slammed it. *Bang!* The door flew back. *Bang!* He slammed it again. *Bang!*

"Stop slamming that door, Garry," the teacher yelled as he wrote an activity on the board.

"He's going nuts," shouted Sean, grinning broadly.

But Garry slammed the metal door once more against the body of the metal locker. *Bang!*

"Stop it!" bawled Mr. Reece. "You're out of your mind or what?"

With that, Garry, who had now stepped closer to the lockers was joined by Sean. Together, they pulled opened the doors of two upper lockers and slammed them shut. *Bang!* They pulled the doors opened again and slammed them. *Bang!* The doors bounced back with the force. They slammed them, *bang,* and again, *bang.* Doors were slammed *bang, bang, bang, bang, bang, bang,* by Garry and Sean and Kenan and Sergio, who had now joined them. There was ruckus in the classroom. The loud noise was deafening. Unable to stand the tumult, Mr. Reece hurried to the door and looked up and down the hallway to get some assistance from either the dean or the security officer, but no one was in the hallway. Unfortunately, the intercom in that room did not work, so he could not get to the office. He remained at the door shaking his head in disgust as the students, in their opinion, continued to have fun. The doors of four upper lockers were slammed simultaneously and then consecutively.

"Hey, Sean, I'll slam harder than you," bawled Garry. Stepping back, he slammed the door, *bang, bang,* as it flew back.

"Nah, I gonna do mine harder than yours," said Sean, and he slammed his. *Bang!* The door flew open again. He laughed. "Ha, ha, ha, I pipped you."

The teacher from the next classroom was so disturbed that she left her class and dashed toward Mr. Reece's and asked, "What's going on with your class, Mr. Reece?"

"This is unbelievable. These kids are going out of their minds. They continuously slam the locker doors although I shouted at them to stop," Mr. Reece complained.

Yelled Mrs. Croft, "Stop slamming those doors. You're disturbing my class."

She had a good day today, as her students were not acting up as they usually do, so she was trying to get through with a lesson.

"This ain't your class. Wha' you doin' here?" said Sean with a scowl on his face. "Go back to your class. You can't even tell yuh students to be quiet when they start on you, shu."

"Don't tell me to go to my class. I'm going to get the dean, Mr. Reece," she said.

"Is he in his office? I don't know," Mr. Reece uttered.

"I'm going to send one of my students to get him," answered Mrs. Croft, leaving the classroom.

"Who cares if you get him," remarked Garry, walking away from the lockers.

"I don't care either," said Sean. "We was just having some fun."

The noise abated as Garry, Sean, Kenan, and Sergio walked from the lockers.

"This behavior is unbelievable and unacceptable. And you're going to be suspended," said the teacher.

"You can't get me suspended," shrieked Sergio.

"If he only call my mother, I'm gonna smack him," Sean growled, pulling the collar of his yellow-and-red jersey and wiping his chin with it.

"You're going to tell the dean that," stated Mr. Reece.

Mr. Reece walked back to the front of the room, leaving the door open. Mr. Eisenburg almost ran to the classroom.

"What the hell is going on here? I'm tired and disgusted with this nonsense," Mr. Eisenburg almost cursed out. "What da, what's happening in here? Tell me."

He pushed aside a desk as he moved toward the out-of-control students.

"Get to my office now," he bawled.

Sergio, Kenan, Sean, and Garry made for the door.

"Mr. Reece, write it up. Let me get it before you leave," Mr. Eisenburg said in disgust, his voice rising. "Every day is the same thing with you students. I'm sick and tired of it."

"We ain't do nothin'. We just had some fun," said Sergio.

"Stay home and have fun. Don't come here to disrupt this place," the dean fumed. Anger was printed on his face. He was clearly upset.

The students sauntered to his office.

"Hurry up and get to my office," ordered Mr. Eisenburg. "I'm going to get your parents up here, plus I'm going to suspend you for a number of days."

"I shoulda stay home. I came to school and I suffered," said Sergio.

"That's what school is all about. They make us suffer when we try to have some fun," concurred Garry, walking slowly along the hallway behind Sergio.

Mr. Eisenburg had the parents of the four students in his office during the course of the week explaining to them the violation of the rules by the students. Garry, Sean, Kenan, and Sergio were each given three days' suspension.

In the 703 science class, Mr. Mendez used a model of the human eye to explain its structure. Using various materials, each student created an object of the eye and did a write up of its function. Moving around to help students with their activity, he was very concerned that some students were not working as seriously as they should.

"Why aren't you working, Jamal?" asked Mr. Mendez.

"My head hurt," Jamal said.

"Why didn't you say your head hurt rather than sitting there all the time without saying anything?" said Mr. Mendez, stopping and looking down at Jamal, who placed his head on the desk.

"I donno," the youngster answered.

"You better get on with the work," the teacher warned.

"Aright."

The teacher approached the next student. "Where is your work?"

"Here is it," Arshald said.

Mr. Mendez looked at the work on the loose-leaf paper. He glanced at the date. It was the date of the previous day.

"This is work you finished yesterday. We just started a new topic, the eye, Arshald. Where is the work you started?"

"Wait, leh me search for it." Arshald flipped the pages in his folder. "I can't find it."

He continued flipping the pages.

"Did you do the work?"

"Yes, I did but I can't find it."

"Arshald, you better get that work done by the time I return. You sat there doing nothing," rebuked the science teacher.

"What! I did my work," shot back Arshald with a grimace.

"Well, get it," Mr. Mendez stated flatly. "You don't expect your grade to go up by behaving in that manner."

"I don't care." The student squirmed.

"You'll care later when your parents come up here," said the teacher, walking off to check another student's work.

"So," answered Arshald.

"What are you doing, Monica, and where is your work?" asked Mr. Mendez.

"I'm reading," she said.

"But that's a novel. We have a science lesson on the board," Mr. Mendez uttered.

"I don't want to do any science," replied Monica.

"You have to," Mr. Mendez said.

"But I don't want to," answered back Monica, shaking her head and staring at the teacher.

"Are you going to tell your parents that when I call home and when they come up here during open-school night?" asked Mr. Mendez

"You mean!" Monica smirked, delving into her backpack to get her materials, notebook, and textbook.

"You got to do your work," advised Mr. Mendez.

It took much effort on the part of the teacher to get students engaged in the lesson even though many were motivated to work and did begin their work without being told to do so by Mr. Mendez.

Chapter 12

It was halfway into the fourth period and the English coordinator of the upper or senior school, Mr. Studdard, who worked closely with and also assisted the assistant principal and chairman of the English department, Mr. Holden, stopped by in room 1005 on the third floor to discuss a matter with Ms. Dunn, a tenth grade English teacher. They spoke about the reading test held last week. Damian, a ninth grade student, arrived at the door.

Said he to the coordinator, "Sign this."

"Sign what?" asked Mr. Studdard, a heavyset male with deep eyes, thick bushy eyebrows, and a full nose.

"I said sign this. You have to sign it," demanded Damian, pulling up with his stocky right hand the back of his pants, which dropped below his waist.

"Are you really speaking to me? You better have some respect and learn how to speak to teachers," Mr. Studdard said firmly.

"You got to sign this form. And you better get some respect too. Almost every teacher sign da form," the student said, pushing the form at the teacher.

"Don't push that form at me," Mr. Studdard warned, his face becoming stern.

Damian pulled the form away and watched Mr. Studdard with widened eyes. His mouth opened and his lip hung.

"Let me see what this form is all about," said the coordinator, taking the form from the student.

It was a petition requesting a committee meeting to deal with an important matter involving some changes at the school.

The coordinator began reading the form and looked up, "Have you seen this?"

He turned to the English teacher.

"No, I haven't as yet. I have no idea what it's all about. And this student is very rude," said Ms. Dunn.

Replied Damian, "Cool yuh head. I wasn't talkin' to you. I was talkin' to him."

"Don't tell me to cool my head," Ms. Dunn rebutted.

Mr. Studdard read the form and gave it to Ms. Dunn, who read it.

"You not gonna sign da form?" asked Damian, folding his arms across his chest.

"I'll think about it before I sign," said Mr. Studdard, calmly.

"But Mr. Blair want it signed now," shouted Damian, who became angry.

"Look, take this form. I'm not signing it now," said Ms. Dunn, returning the form to Damian.

Furious, Damian grabbed the form from Ms. Dunn and walked away, using expletives under his breath.

"He's so obnoxious in his behavior. No respect. He just wants to do as he pleases and talk to adults anyhow," bemoaned Ms. Dunn, furrows spreading across the peach skin of her forehead below her red luster of hair.

"I don't know where his home training has gone to if he really has any," stated Mr. Studdard.

The two teachers continued their brief conversation before Mr. Studdard left Ms. Dunn's room as she was about to have a class.

Ms. Dunn put four topics on the board for students to write narratives on any of them.

Said she, "You're going to brainstorm. Write down every idea that comes to mind, then make your plan how you're going to write your essay. After you wrote your essays, we'll discuss the story elements, some of which we began yesterday."

Shouted a student from the back of the class, "Ms. Dunn, how many essays we have to write?"

"Only one essay on any of the topics," the teacher responded.

Said Kirk, "Ms. Dunn, I want to write about three essays. You know, my brain is a little slow."

There was an outburst of laughter in the class by some of the students.

Ms. Dunn smiled ruefully. "Kirk, if your brain is a little slow, how could you do three well-thought-out essays in one period? Let me see how far you've gone in your work."

The teacher walked toward Kirk's desk and looked at his paper.

Said she, "Kirk, we're twenty minutes into the period, and you've not even written a complete line. Tell me, how are you going to write three essays? Hurry up and write the one you've chosen."

"Okay, Ms. Dunn. I'll write only one and I'll be quick about it," answered Kirk, picking up his pen from the desk.

"I'll appreciate that, and stop fooling around, Kirk," said Ms. Dunn.

A few students had begun writing their essays while many talked, read comics, and drew cartoon figures in their notebooks, much to the disapproval of the teacher.

After a brief explanation to move students along in their work, Ms. Dunn said, "I've noticed that many of you are not doing what you're supposed to be doing right now."

She left the front of the class and moved around to see what students did since she instructed them on what they were required to do. She was a little startled when she got to the back of the room but not particularly surprised at the behavior of some of the students.

Said she, "Is this what your parents send you to school for? To fool around? Do you think your parents or the principal would like to know that you're lying on the floor and a male student is sitting on you? Get up! And you, get off of her! Let me call security."

The teacher was clearly incensed. Her lips tightened as she looked down on Carla, a heavy, big student with a full, round face with pimples and wide eyes. Her lips were parted in a wide smile as she lay on her back on the floor clad in black jeans and bright-blue jersey. Her solid, heavy arms pushed at Curtis, short but tough and hardy with bulging muscles and bulging veins on his arms and temples, as he sat on her. He restrained her heavy arms, but it did not take much effort as he was strong in his arms, with great upper body strength. A grin was on his face, his angular, sharp face.

"No, Ms. Dunn, let me tell you what happened," said Curtis.

"Get off of her, I said," shrieked Ms. Dunn.

Said Curtis, "She pushed me off the chair when you were not looking, and I fell on the floor, then she jumped on me, she sit on me, trying to mark me in my face with her pen, and I turned her over to prevent her from marking my skin."

"Yes," said Joel, another male student. "That's what she did. She was trying to mark him."

"Yes," said Elena, a short, stocky female student with dimples on her cheeks. "She started it, Ms. Dunn. She was trying to mark him."

Curtis released Carla's arms and got off of her. He stepped back and ran to the front of the class. Ms. Dunn shook her head in disbelief.

"I'm gonna stab you with this pen," yelled Carla, still lying on the floor at the back of the class.

"What?" shrieked Ms. Dunn, her eyes bulging behind her thin metal-framed glasses.

"Yes, I gonna stab da sh—t outta him," bellowed Carla.

She turned on her side and struggled to her feet under her heavy weight. She pouted her lips and walked away from Ms. Dunn. A grimace spread across the face of the teacher as Carla walked from next to her.

"Don't come near me," Curtis shouted.

"I gonna catch yuh," Carla said, as she sat in her seat.

Curtis stood next to the door.

"That's what you did to my class: disturbed the lesson. The assistant principal will deal with you," lamented Ms. Dunn.

Ms. Dunn walked to the front of the class, picked up the intercom, dialed 3919, and called the assistant principal responsible for the tenth grade. Mr. Holdon came to the classroom. His eyes glared at the students. His head bobbed and his face looked tense.

He yelled, "Carla and Curtis, go to my office now."

"What for?" Carla shouted, moving her body in her chair.

"Go to my office, I said," Mr. Holdon demanded, stepping to her desk.

"I ain't going to no office. I ain't do anything," rebutted Carla.

"I said, go to my office," ordered the assistant principal, standing next to Carla's desk with his radio in one hand and the other resting on the desk. His fingers tapped on the desk, indicating that he did not have time to waste and that she had to get up immediately. Carla sat down in a chair in the middle of the room.

Said she, "Curtis started it. He alone should go to your office."

Curtis was already heading to the door, but Carla seemed defiant as she sat in her chair.

"I'm not going to talk to you again. I said to go to my office," ordered the assistant principal sternly.

Carla reluctantly got to her feet and walked toward the door. The assistant principal followed her and Curtis as they departed the classroom.

Stepping to the front of the class and turning around, Ms. Dunn said, "Students, you have work on the board. Do it and stop all the playing around. I know some of you are working. I hope the others would stop playing and start working."

"Come here," Kevin said, beckoning to Nakon, with brimful of laughter as he stood at the door of class 704 in room 1-704. Nakon did not move immediately. "I gonna get you," Kevin shouted as he flexed his arms at Jason.

"Ahhhh, ha, ha." Jason laughed, running around a desk.

"Stop shouting and running around the class, students," shouted Ms. Langevine, the social studies teacher.

"Whack him," Nakon said, encouraging Kevin to jump on Jason, who was laughing at Kevin.

"Huh, huh, huh." Ortis laughed, dropping his bag on the floor.

"Oh sh—t," muttered Jason as Kevin pounced on him and slammed him on the floor. *Blop.*

The young female teacher, in hurrying across the room, bumped her thigh into a desk, and yelled, "Ouch," from the sudden, penetrating blunt pain. She got to the students on the floor. In pain, she snarled, "Stop it. Get off the floor and go to your seats."

The students showed stark indifference as if her presence was not there; they ignored her.

"Come on, son, come on," yelled Kevin, making a fist.

"Yeh, yeh," Jason said. He got to his feet and went after Kevin, catching him between two desks. Jason grabbed Kevin and collared him around the neck, tripped his legs and slammed him on the floor. *Blop.*

Students slammed one another on the floor. Jaime and Jasmine tumbled to the floor wrestling each other. *Bang, bang.* They threw a desk and chair on the floor and pushed other desks and chairs, disarranging the furniture in the class. As Jaime struggled to his feet, Jack grabbed him and threw him on the floor. Jaime pulled Jack down with him. Jasmine got up and jumped on the two of them. Ortis and Nakon ran and jumped on them. Kevin, breaking away from Jason, ran and jumped on the group lying on the floor. "Ah, ah, get off o' me, get off," "Ahhhh, oh sh—t, get off," and "Hey, hey, you hurting my arm," were some of the sounds emanating from the rumble. Jason grabbed the left leg of Kevin and yelled, "One, two, three. Yeahhhh." He brought Kevin down, tumbling him from the group onto the floor. Jasmine, Jack, Nakon, and Ortis got off of Jaime

"I won, I won," shouted Jack.

"You didn't win," Jaime complained. "All o' y'all was on me. That's not fair. I couldn't kick out.

In another part of the room, Mike yelled, "No, no, no," as Joseph tried to put him in a headlock.

"Yo, yo, yo, come, come on, hit him," the aggressive Joseph shouted to others.

"No, no, nnno, nnno, uh, uh." Mike coughed as his aggressor got his left arm around his neck.

"Everybody come. Jump him, smack him," Joseph yelled.

Rachel and Lakendra jumped from their seats and jumped on Mike and began smacking him. He bawled, "Hey, hey, stop."

Ms. Langevine was furious about the behavior of the students. She hollered, "I'm writing referrals. And I'm getting on to your homes."

Nobody was listening to her, and the lesson she painstakingly planned was not on the board yet. A sweat broke out on her face.

She scratched her hair to the side of her head. Her eyes widened as she looked down at the students who were making it to their feet in getting off the floor, some breathing heavily.

Said she, "Let me get the dean or security to stop this behavior in here."

She walked from among them, with a little limp in her stride, toward the intercom. She dialed extension 1-616. The phone rang. "Yes," a firm female voice answered at the other end of the line.

"Ms. Piggot, this is Ms. Langevine. A few students are wrestling and throwing themselves down on the floor in room 704. Could you come up, please. I think somebody may get hurt."

"Okay, I'll be there in a minute," the dean said, her voice sounding terse.

"You call the dean on us?" queried Jason

The teacher did not answer after she cradled the intercom.

"Yes, she call the dean on us like if we did somethin'," said Kevin.

"I ain't care. I ain't do nothin'," said Jason.

Footsteps echoed along the dark brown–tiled floor. They were quick but measured and sounded deliberate. The steps became louder, and then the door to room 1-704 was pushed open. Ms. Piggot stood in the threshold with a stone face. She did not flinch or blinked but looked straight at the group of students who had become familiar to her by now. "I'm not going to call names. I don't have time to waste. You know who you are. Out. Get to my office right now. It's the same thing with you every time and in every classroom," she said.

With Jason and Kevin bowing their heads they walked out the classroom followed by Jasmine, Jaime, Mike, Jack, Nakon, Ortis, Lakendra, Joseph, and Rachel.

Tuning to look at Ms. Langevine, Ms. Piggot said, "I'll take care of it."

The dean turned and walked away from the threshold where she stood without even bothering to go into the room. She had to pull the same students from the room two days ago when another teacher covered the class during Ms. Vine's prep period.

"Thank you, Ms. Piggot," said the young female teacher, who could not even get to start her lesson, and twenty minutes had elapsed.

Looking over her shoulder, Ms. Piggot said, "Any more problems, let me know."

"Thank you, miss, I will," answered the seventh grade teacher.

The sharp footsteps sounded again against the hard tile and soon faded. Back in her office, Ms. Piggot made phone calls to the homes of the students and those who were sent by teachers of other classrooms, as they made it difficult for the teachers to continue with their lessons in a meaningful and productive way. Ms. Piggot even tried to get on to parents at their workplaces. A few were given suspension letters for a day or two depending on the seriousness of the misdeeds. Unfortunately, it was the same students who invariably were sent to the deans' offices from all the grades on a regular basis. With some difficulty, Ms. Langevine was able to start her lesson and teach a portion of it.

Students threw books at each other in class 606 in room 1-606 while Ms. Bishop tried desperately to get her lesson going. One student grabbed a heavy hardcover math book and hurled it through the air at another. He ducked as the book swished past his head.

"What da f— yuh doin'," yelled Horace, a scowl growing on his face.

Another book zoomed past his head. Horace got up, grabbed a book from the desk next to his, and threw it with force at Daren. Daren ran to the back of the class, "Aye, aye," he muttered. About five other students began throwing books at each other and ducking and dashing out of the way. At the same time, Kori threw Thomas on the floor and wrestled with him as Camille pulled his sneakers off his left foot. The sneaker was thrown around the class by four other students, including Camille and Beatrice. Daren put the sneakers to his nose.

"Hey, this sneaker smells like sh—t," Daren shouted. He passed it to Camille.

"This sh—t smell nasty. You got to change yuh f— socks. His sock got a hole," screamed Camille.

"Ha, ha, ha, ha, ha, ahhh, ha, ha, ha," the class erupted in laughter.

"Chill, man, chill. Gimme my sneaker," Thomas appealed, walking around with his gray sock on one foot on the floor strewn with candy wrappers, empty plastic soda bottles, empty juice boxes, loose-leaf papers, broken pens and pencils, and even gum.

Ms. Bishop leaned against her desk and just watched disdainfully as the students ranted. She had already made up her mind that she wasn't going to constantly shout at those who were disruptive, and if she spoke, it would only be once as she already decided the action she would take and pursue after dismissal.

Thomas grabbed Kori as he threw his sneaker to Daren. Daren, noticing that Thomas held on to Kori, walked over to Thomas and pushed him. Thomas pushed back.

"I ain't scare o' you," blurted out Thomas with his fist raised.

"Get outta my face," growled Daren as he realized that Thomas was ready for a fight, as he became angry that they did not return his sneaker

"I'd beat da sh—t outta yuh," Thomas fumed.

Camille dropped the sneaker on the floor after it was thrown to her. Nadine, who sat next to Camille, picked up the sneaker from the floor and handed it to Thomas, who took it and walked to his seat.

"Peace out," said Nadine to Thomas before she sat.

"One love," replied Thomas, grinning at Nadine.

The students then sat, which enabled the teacher to continue the lesson uninterrupted for the remainder of the period.

Chapter 13

The hallways were crowded as students on the first and second floors made their way to the cafeteria. They immediately ran amok. The screams and yells were unsettling. The school aides' supervisor, Mrs. Mangel, belched an order at them, "Get to your seats." Everyone scampered momentarily to a seat but was off the benches in a second. The other aides made their way into the lunchroom from the first floor to take charge of the students who were utilizing every moment they had to indulge in a bit of roughhouse behavior. The lunchroom staff was irritated, frustrated that the same behavior they had to confront every day in the cafeteria. The shouts and screams rose. The "yeahs" and "ahhhhs" were searing. Mainly the sixth and seventh graders and some eighth graders were in their element. The youngsters were freaking out.

The chasing and hollering and the discordant sounds were unbelievable. The expletives and yells were annoying. "A gonna f— you up," "You's a f— sh—t head," "I gonna whop your ass," "You a punk," "Grab 'em," "Gimme" "Da card is mine," "Gimme my stuff," "Gimme my game," "Throw him on da floor," "Punch him in da stomach," and the mixture of sounds continued unabated as they dashed from one area of the lunchroom to another. "Sit down," Mrs. Mangel bawled. It was either the students did not hear her or they starkly ignored her. Some looked in the direction from where the sound came looked at Mrs. Mangel as if she did not exist.

Others dashed back and forth, some somersaulted or cartwheeled and wrestled each other to the floor.

"Go to your seats. Stop the nonsense on the floor. No wrestling and cartwheeling on the floor," Mrs. Mangel spewed, flailing her left arm as she held the bullhorn with the right hand.

Immediately, Ms. Coldern, one of the school aides, trotted over to the area where students wrestled and somersaulted. "Stop it. All o' y'all go to your seats now. You can't wrestle and somersault in here."

Another female staffer, Ms. Lashel, stepped across to where other students also wrestled. She yelled, "Get off the floor. Are you what? Ah, ah, you going crazy or what? Sit down. And don't get out of your seats. If not, you're not going outside."

A number of male and female sixth and seventh graders from each area hurried back to their seats grinning and baring teeth as they panted. It appeared as though they just cooled their feet for a few seconds. They sprinted again and slid, allowing themselves to fall on the floor. The tumult was horrendous. A short sixth grader in a light-blue jacket and light-blue peak cap yelled as he dashed from behind a post, "You jerk chicken, yuh momma is a crackhead."

A heavy, round-faced eleven-year-old with knock knees, clad in a tan jacket, trotted after his verbal attacker, "Who you talkin' to? I gonna dust you up."

Reaching a safe distance away from his huge pursuer, the lean frisky kid turned and said, with a wide grin that exposed most of his even ivory-colored teeth, "You got to dust yuh face up." He turned and ran again.

Another sixth grader with a red-and-green bonnet topee on his head dashed in front of the frisky student in the light-blue jacket, cutting him off. A seventh grade student in a black parka hotly pursued the sixth grader wearing the green-and-red topee.

"Grab him fuh me," the seventh grader shrieked, but the sixth grader was too fast on his feet to be stopped.

Meanwhile, the sixth grader in the tan jacket chased after his frisky verbal attacker, who darted among the others and hid behind a post. At the same time, the student with the green-and-red topee on his head looked over his shoulder and bawled, "Catch me if you can."

The seventh grader in the black parka shouted, "I gonna whop your ass."

"You wish you could," shot back the student who wore the topee.

"Swish, swish, swish, swish, swish," the jump rope sounded as it repeatedly and swiftly hit the tiled floor of the cafeteria. A number of sixth and seventh grade and a few eighth grade female students jumped rope in the southern area of the cafeteria. Eager females waited their turn to jump. "Ha, ha, ha, ha . . ." One of the onlookers laughed as one of the females did a funny piece, jumping on one foot.

"That's cool. She did that real good," her colleague, who stood nearby leaning on her shoulder, said.

"Yeah, yeah, she could really jump," another broad-shouldered female seventh grade student said. "You ain't see anythin' yet. She does some good moves."

As the females did their pieces quietly in the corner, others still raced up and down the cafeteria. A hefty seventh grader chased after another seventh grader, who wore red sneakers, caught him, threw him on the floor, and punched him in the stomach.

"Sh—t, man, you hurt me, " groaned the student wearing the red sneakers.

The tall, hefty seventh grader turned, looked at him on the floor, and dealt a kick in his rear end, and said, "I'm da boss."

"Hey, dog, you hurt my butt," the subdued student hollered as he rolled on the floor.

The heavy seventh grader in the blue sweatshirt repeated, "I'm da boss. Tell me whose da boss?" His opponent lay on the floor, his wide eyes rolled.

The heavy youngster roared, "Tell me who's da boss."

"You's da boss."

"Tell yuh."

"You a punk. You ain't no boss," taunted another student, who sat on the large eating table.

"I'll smack you in yuh face," the heavy student in blue said.

"I dare you. You know where you'll end up," the student on the desk shot back.

The student in blue walked away and disappeared within the crowd.

The furor in the lunchroom was disheartening particularly to the four aides and their supervisor. The pantry to the kitchen was not yet opened. And with the ruckus mounting, Mrs. Mangel, the supervisor, shouted through her bullhorn, "If you can't be seated and be quiet, I'll see to it that you have lunch late, and you wouldn't go outside. I mean it."

Students began to hop back to their seats.

"Sit down, be quiet," she bawled again through her bullhorn. But the students hardly heeded her apart from a few who figured they should listen.

Again, Mrs. Mangel yelled, "You're not going outside. You're gonna stay in here for the rest of the week if you don't sit and stop shouting."

Aides in other parts of the cafeteria tried to get the students in their seats. Mrs. Mangel's face was stonelike as she glared at the disruptive, indisciplined students who ran amok in the cafeteria. As she stood in the lunchroom, her eyes became discolored. She felt a heat in her face; her vision became momentarily blurred and then clear again. She leaned against the wall she stood near to. "I didn't take my blood pressure medication this morning. How could I forget it" Mrs. Mangel lamented quietly.

"You okay, Mrs. Mangel?" asked Mrs. Elviro, stepping across to where her supervisor stood.

"Yes, I'm okay, but my eyes just went blurred a while ago," related Mrs. Mangel, pushing back the wavy hair that got in her face.

"What? That is serious," interrupted Mrs. Elviro, putting her left arm around the shoulders of Mrs. Mangel.

"Yes, but I see better, now," uttered Mrs. Mangel, folding her arms across her chest with the bullhorn resting on her high stomach.

"We got to fret and fatigue every day with these students in the lunchroom. It's enough to make you sick," complained Mrs. Elviro.

"What happened is that I forgot to take my medication for the pressure this morning," said Mrs. Mangel.

"Damn!" grunted Mrs. Elviro, shaking her head.

"I don't know how it slipped me." Mrs. Mangel sighed, a deep breath gushing through her lips.

"It happens sometimes with all this stress. These students just running wild in here," bemoaned Mrs. Elviro.

A seventh grade student who was nearby overheard the conversation. She sneaked up to the two school aides with a look of concern on her face.

"She sick?" the wide-eyed student asked.

"Yes, she wasn't feeling well," Mrs. Elviro uttered. "But she's okay now."

"Y'all stop. Stop behaving like jerks. Mrs. Mangel ain't feeling well," the tall, medium-build female student shouted loudly.

"I'm all right now," Mrs. Mangel said, trying to remain calm.

Two female students ran over to Mrs. Mangel with much concern in their eyes. "You sick, Ms. Mangel?" they said together, looking at her steadfast in her eyes. One of them held Mrs. Mangel's right hand.

Erwin, Makalia, Merleen, and Salome hurried across to Mrs. Mangel. "You aright, Ms. Mangel?" Erwin asked, while the three females looked on.

"Yes, I'm okay," Mrs. Mangel said.

"Fuh real," Merleen asked, staring at the school aide supervisor.

"Yes, I'm okay now. A while ago my vision became blurred. I could hardly see anything, but I'm seeing well now. I forgot to take my medication," the supervisor explained.

Makalia turned around. "Yo, shut up and stop running," she bawled. "Mrs. Mangel wasn't feeling good. Stop shouting and behaving wild before you make her sick again."

Melissa, Hector, Nigel, Michelle, Donnete, Nickita, Jaime, Nakon, and a few other students gathered around her as well as the lunchroom aides.

"Wha' happen, Mrs. Mangel?" Mrs. Gardaway asked. She saw the crowd around the supervisor and decided to approach it.

"Girl, I stood here calling on these students to sit down as you heard me through the bullhorn, and just like that I couldn't see anything clear. I thought to myself, *What's happening to me?* and then a few seconds after, my eyes cleared up. I was like scared. I then remembered I didn't drink my blood pressure medication," Mrs. Mangel relayed calmly.

"I tell you, we go through all sorts of things on this job in trying to get these children in order in this lunchroom. Take it easy and don't miss those medication. Hypertension is serious," Mrs. Gardaway advised, rubbing the shoulder of her supervisor.

"I'm seeing okay now, thanks," Mrs. Mangel said.

"Gimme this bullhorn. Leh me get these students sitting," Mrs. Gardaway said, taking the loudspeaker from her supervisor.

"Feel good, Mrs. Mangel," "Don't shout at them," "Take your medication." These were the comforting words or advice of the concerned students who had gathered around Mrs. Mangel and were now returning to their seats while most of the others ran crazy in the cafeteria.

"Thank you, students. I will take my medication," Mrs. Mangel said to the youngsters.

Mrs. Mangel sat on one of the benches while her assistant belched into the bullhorn. "Sit down. No running around now. You don't sit down, you don't go outside."

A good number of students hurried to their seats while others continued screaming, bawling, and running.

"I ain't gonna talk to you again. I wanna see everybody sit in their seats, right now," Mrs. Gardaway bellowed through the megaphone held in front of her face.

Stepping up to her, a tall, male school aide howled, "Lend me da phone, Mrs. Gardaway. Leh me talk to these students who seem as if they're deaf."

Mrs. Gardaway gave him the bullhorn.

Taking it, he barked, "Leh me tell all o' y'all something. Sit down on the benches now. If not, you going back upstairs hungry, and you remaining in this lunchroom for the entire lunch period for the rest of the week and next week. You hear me? I ain't here to babysit you guys. Let your parents come in here and do that."

"Who he think he is," grumbled one student as he made his way to sit on the bench.

"He can't send us back to no classroom hungry. He crazy," said another student, getting back to his seat.

"He can't keep us in here fuh da whole week. I'll be goin' outside to play," Nakon said to Jack.

"Douglas believe he's my father. He ain't my father," a petite female student said.

A lot of mumbling occurred, and remarks, inclusive of expletives, were made as students dragged their feet back to their seats.

"And you got to hurry and get to your seats. I ain't playin'. I ain't got time for that," Mr. Douglas yelled through the bullhorn.

Within five minutes, everyone was seated according to his or her class.

Said Mr. Douglas, "When everyone is quiet, we gonna serve lunch."

An eerie silence descended upon the lunchroom with sulking faces behind the tables. Mr. Douglas then hurried over to the pantry. He knocked on the door, and soon the door was flung open. "I gonna line them up now," Mr. Douglas said.

"Okay, line them up," said Ms. Mouryea, a staff member of the kitchen. She then closed the kitchen

"Line up, 601. No running or talking," belched Mr. Douglas, a no-nonsense school aide. He sported a neatly lined beard and a head of hair that nestled on his shoulder. He was medium build and muscular. An athlete and ardent sports fan who pursued studies in communication and computer science to upgrade his position while he did a second job, was very stern with the students who were out of control, but he found time to play basketball and baseball with all students during his lunch break or for an hour after school some afternoons.

Students of class 601 rose from their seats and walked briskly to the door of the pantry and formed a line.

Said Mrs. Elviro, standing, rooted in her position in front of the pantry's door, "I want a straight line. I'm seeing two lines. I said I want one line."

"Hey, get in line," reiterated one heavy student. "She said she want one line."

The young sixth grader shuffled and stepped one pace to the right to get behind the person in front of him.

"You got to be quiet if you want your food. I'm gonna pull some of you out da line," balked Mrs. Elviro, decked in her close-fitting blue jeans and pink long-sleeve jersey.

"You standin' in front o' me," Yetti said.

"I'm in front of you," Polly answered.

"Yeah, Polly's in front of you," Jonah joined in. Polly stepped in front of Yetti.

"Leh me see your game card," a voice whispered.

"Wow, I like this one," the sixth grader said.

Craning his neck to look over the right shoulder of the student in front of him to get a glimpse of the card, another student said, "Where you buy that?"

"My brother bought it downtown for me," the student with the card said.

A light chatter emanated about where one was positioned in the line and where one got things from like game cards. Mrs. Elviro, who was normally assigned at the door, was somewhat satisfied after three to five minutes that the line was straight and quiet and gave the signal for the door to be opened. She whipped the radio from the leather strap and spoke, "They're ready." The cafeteria staff member who was standing in the pantry with her radio in hand heard the message. She immediately pushed the door open. "One, two, three, four, five, go," ordered Mrs. Elviro starkly. The five students moved off immediately without a sound and entered the pantry.

At the counter, two female staff, dressed in white uniforms, served them lunch of which they had a choice. Some students chose spaghetti and meatballs, salad, and onion rings; others had pepperoni pizza, fries and salad; and yet some were served cheeseburgers, fries and salad. Each student also had a choice of milk or juice and had fruit such as apple, orange, grapes and banana. Other days they had cantaloupe, pear, watermelon, and strawberries As the first five edged forward and were served, Mrs. Elviro, having looked into the pantry and saw only two remaining students at the counter, shouted and pointed to the students in the line, "One, two, three, four, five, go." The students strode into the pantry as she called the number to be served a healthy lunch, the aroma and steam of which swirled in the pantry and drifted in the large lunchroom. It was an aroma that stimulated the appetite.

"What do you want?" asked one of the counter staff.

A petite female student with sparkling eyes and a bright smile, who wore a yellow-and-blue sweater, said softly, "I'll take pizza, fries, and onion rings."

"Okay, you could have either fries or onion rings," said Ms. Mickson, a tall, slim staff member behind the counter.

"I'll have fries," the student said.

With the plastic tong in her right hand, the staffer gripped a whole, round, six-inch pizza and put it in the student's white plastic tray. She gripped fries and put them in the tray, also.

The small-build sixth grader, who was quite polite said, "Thank you." A smile spread across her face.

"You're welcome," Ms. Mickson answered with a smile in return, as many students just grabbed their trays and moved off without a word.

"You took pizza?" the female student who stood behind her in a red-and-black sweater asked.

"Yeh," she answered.

"Nah, I gonna take cheeseburger," the student behind her uttered.

The petite student edged forward with the pizza and fries in her tray and was served fresh vegetable salad, an orange, a banana, grapes, and a box of apple juice by two other kitchen staffers who worked the counter.

"Come on up," Ms. Mickson said. The student in the red-and-black sweater moved forward in front of her.

"What do you want?" the employed adult asked.

"I want a cheeseburger," Indira answered without expression. She was served a warm cheeseburger with fries and drifted down to the other counter staff for the rest of her food.

"Come on up," Ms. Mickson's voice echoed again.

An equally tall male student stepped in front of her and said, "I gonna take spaghetti and meatballs." He was served spaghetti and meatballs and edged down along the counter where he was served salad, a banana, an apple and grapes, and a box of cold chocolate milk. He, like the others before him, exited the pantry as the other students came forward to be served. With their trays, they made their way back to their seats in the section allotted in the lunchroom to class 601.

Barked Mr. Douglas, "602, join the line."

Students from class 602 dashed from their seats.

"No running. Walk," Mr. Douglas shouted.

The students immediately changed gear. They walked to the area and formed the lunch line. Mrs. Elviro eyed them keenly as they queued up and edged forward to get their lunch.

Chapter 14

Mrs. Mangel, who felt much better, moved around the cafeteria with her bullhorn in her right hand, after Mr. Douglas returned it to her since quelling the students. She observed how the students were behaving in the lunchroom. The talking was gradually rising, but the seventh and eighth graders remained in their seats along with those remaining sixth grade classes which were not yet called. The line was moving very quickly, and students returned to their seats to have a satisfying lunch.

Moving toward one of the long tables where students sit to eat, the displeasure was on the face of Mrs. Mangel. "You, get off the table. You don't sit on the table in here," Mrs. Mangel shrieked at a student. "Do you sit on your dinner table at home?"

"Yes, I sit anywhere I want," the male seventh grade student answered expressionlessly as he slid off the table. His eyes were locked with those of Mrs. Mangel.

"Well, you're not going to sit on the table in here," Mrs. Mangel warned, her supple face becoming stonelike. She walked away and continued moving around the lunchroom.

Most of class 602 were served lunch and had returned to their seats. The cafeteria aides worked diligently to keep order in the lunchroom. Mrs. Elviro and Mrs. Gardaway called on students to minimize the talking and shouting and urged them to remain in their seats when they were finished eating. Mr. Douglas, who stood with the students at the pantry door, called out loudly, "603, join the line." Within twenty to twenty-five minutes, the sixth, seventh, and eighth graders were served lunch and sat and talked while they ate.

"Sit down if you're finished eating," said Mrs. Elviro to a student who was out of his seat, jumping around. The student sat for a while, and as Mrs. Elviro moved away, he was out of his seat again.

"Where you going?" Mrs. Mangel accosted Monica of 703.

"I'm going to my friend there," the seventh grade student said.

"Get back to your seat. No walking around now," the lunchroom supervisor ordered.

Boomed Mr. Douglas, "Too much walking around taking place in here. Get to your seats." Students hurried back to their seats. Most of the students still ate especially the eighth graders who were served last.

"I ain't like this salad," remarked Raquel of 604, decked in a black sweater with circle designs.

"So why you take it? I ate mine. It's good with the dressing," said Simone, who sat next to her.

"They gave me. I didn't want it."

"Well, throw it out."

At another table, Camille, of 606, uttered, "I like this pizza. It taste juicy and soft. It's good." She pushed up her black-framed spectacles, which had slid down her nose.

"Leh me taste a piece," a broad-shouldered, full-faced sixth grade student who sat next to her said. She broke a piece and gave it to him.

"Um, this taste good. I shoulda take pizza, but this burger taste good, too," the male youngster, Thomas, said, chewing briskly on the piece of pizza.

"This apple sour, man. I can't eat no more of this," Wong, from the seventh grade, blurted out.

"Why you didn't take a banana. It's sweet. At least mine taste good. It's sweet," a female seventh grader, Felicia, with the hood of her gray sweater pulled over her head suggested.

Students commented as usual on how the food tasted. "Too many people are out of their seats and moving and running around. I want to see everybody seated," Mrs. Gardaway shouted. Some students waltzed back to their seats with a sulk on their faces.

"You like that meatballs?" questioned a heavyset female with a deep dimple on her chin.

"I'm eating it. I'm hungry. It taste okay fuh me. I gotta get something in my stomach, yo," the tall, narrow-faced seventh grader with pimples on his face said.

"The last time I ate it, the spaghetti didn't have no taste. It was yuck. I ate the meatballs and dumped the spaghetti," the female student said.

"I ain't dumping anything. This is okay with me," the male student remarked.

The talking went on unabated as students ate. The staff got a usually difficult time in trying to contain the sixth and seventh graders who slipped from their seats as they had finished eating lunch. Some eighth graders were out of their seats too.

"I need a large bottle of water to carry down this food," stated Adrian, a hefty eighth grader dressed in a gray heavy jacket.

"You gonna be running to the bathroom during classes with all that water you talking about," opined Nigel, another big-build eighth grader, in a black-and-red jacket.

"Nah, I usually drink a lot of water. Water is good for you, bro. Every chance I get I drink water. I don't go for soda that much," Adrian said.

"I drink water, too, but not that much, especially when the weather is cold like it is today," Nigel posited.

Sitting at another table nearby, Teddy of 806 said, "This is the first time the food taste so good, dog."

"Da spaghetti and meatball?" asked Hector.

"Yeah, it tastes good. I ain't eat this for a long time," declared Teddy, swallowing a piece of meatball, with its sauce, which he chewed.

"Da pizza I took is good, too. Da lady shoulda given two," stated Hector, wiping his mouth with a napkin.

Teddy put some spaghetti with a bit of sauce in his mouth. William put a big bite on his cheeseburger and moaned, "Ummm, this burger taste good." He passed his tongue over his top lip.

"They put a lot of salt on da chips," said Kenneth, as he placed a few chips in his mouth.

Merleen gulped a box of chocolate milk. It felt cold going down her stomach.

"You want that milk?" she asked Makalia.

"Yes, I want it," replied Makalia, holding the brown-and-white box. "I want something cold in my stomach. I ain't want no soda today, if not I woulda give you da milk."

"I could drink another box with this cheeseburger. It has fresh tomatoes, lettuce, and onions. Another milk would be just good fuh me," stated Merleen.

"Go ask them for a milk!" exclaimed Makalia.

"Nah," answered Merleen.

"I gonna get one fuh you," shouted Makalia, jumping from her seat. She darted to the pantry.

"Where you goin'?" asked Mrs. Elviro, staring at Makalia.

"I'm going to get a box of milk," replied Makalia, turning up her eyes, showing the white of her cornea.

"Hurry up and get back to your seat," Mrs. Elviro ordered sternly, looking at the student. Makalia quickened her steps. Entering the pantry, she said, "Can I have a milk, please."

"Take one," Ms. Mickson said calmly.

Makalia took the box of chocolate milk, exited the pantry, hurried back to her table, and said, "Look, see, I got one for you."

"Thank you," said Merleen, with a twinkle in her eyes and a smile on her lips.

Makalia looked at her and smiled.

Merleen popped the box open and put it to her mouth and gulped several mouthfuls of the cold chocolate beverage, "Umm, this is good. It's nice and cold."

At the next table where seventh graders sat, Paul had just finished eating a cheeseburger and picked up a red apple, which he bit and chewed deliberately to taste the sweetness of it. Sitting next to him was Mercedes, medium build, with her hair in a bun and a yellow bandana around her head and just below the hairline on her forehead. Next to her sat Rosa, who still ate her spaghetti and meatballs. Mercedes, who ate pizza, had just finished chewing the last piece of it. She reached for an orange, which lay on the table, and peeled it with her fingers. She bit the orange and chewed on a piece. The juice from it, with its acidity, tingled her. She yelled, "This sh—t sour."

"It sour?" asked Rosa.

"Yeah! This'll gimme burn stomach."

"You mean heartburn?"

"Yeh! You wan it?"

"Hell, no! I ain't want it. You said it's sour."

"Yeh, it's damn sour."

"So why you think I gonna wan it."

"Aright! Aright!"

Mercedes tossed the orange from one hand to the other then suddenly threw it with force, a distance of two tables away from where she sat. *Blop!* It slammed into the head of a heavyset, full-faced seventh grader and smashed to pieces with fragments falling to the floor. "Oh, oh." The class sighed.

"Ahhhh," the student yelled and spun around as the sudden pain gripped her. "Who hit me with that in my head?" She jumped up from her seat, holding her head where she was hit. Mercedes heard her when she yelled and turned her head in the opposite direction.

"Who throw it at me?" Camille demanded.

Students who sat next to her looked up wide-eyed at her.

Wendy, who sat near to Camille at the table, while she ate the last piece of her pizza pie, said, "Mercedes is the one who threw it at you."

"She did?" asked Camille, with anger in her voice.

"Yes! She threw it," Wendy said, nodding her head in confirming what she said.

Camille jumped from behind her table and dashed toward Mercedes. "You throw that sh—t which hit me in my head," demanded Camille.

Whack! Camille punched Mercedes in her head. She swung again and punched her in the face.

"I ain't throw anythin' at you," Mercedes shouted.

"Yes, you throw da orange which hit me in my head," Camille snarled.

Whack! Camille crossed again.

Mercedes struggled from her seat and fired a punch in Camille's stomach. Camille threw back a punch in Mercedes's stomach.

"Yeah, yeah, fight, fight," a student nearby shouted.

"Whip her, Camille," another student shouted; he ran from the table where Camille was sitting.

"You takin' da," Joseph said to Mercedes.

"Fight, yeah, whack her, Mercedes," shouted Damon, who ran across to the scene of the action.

"Wendy, you a snitch," said Tamika.

"I ain't no snitch," returned Wendy, turning her head from Tamika.

"Yes, you snitched on Mercedes," yelled Monet.

Having heard what Tamika and Monet said while she sat at the next table, Nellita left her seat and slipped to the table where Tamika and Monet sat and queried, "She snitched on Mercedes?"

"Yes, Wendy snitched on Mercedes. She told Camille that Mercedes threw the orange which hit her in her head," Tamika said.

"You a snitch," Nellita fumed and pushed Wendy's head in running off to the scene of the fight. Students circled the two female fighters and prodded them on.

"Kick her, Camille," a shrill female voice echoed above the rest.

"Throw her on da floor, Mercedes," a female friend of Mercedes, who wore a red-and-yellow waist-length jacket, bawled.

"Fight, girls, fight it out. Let's see who gonna whop who," a male eighth grader chuckled.

"Punch her, Mercedes. She can't beat you," yelled Nellita.

Camille punched Mercedes in the shoulder, and Mercedes punched back. Wild punches were thrown by both students. Camille grabbed Mercedes's hair. Mercedes grabbed Camille's hair. Both pulled and tugged at each other's hair. Each felt pain, but they landed punches on each other. Both students were ruffled now. The noise was loud, and roars and screams and yells were deafening as sixth and seventh graders and a number of eighth graders gathered around and pushed at each other to get closer to the warring students.

"Wendy snitched on Mercedes. She told Camille that Mercedes pelted her with an orange in her head," Nellita told Donna, the female student in the red-and-yellow waist-length jacket.

"She snitched on Mercedes?" asked Donna dubiously.

"Yes, she snitched on Mercedes and caused Camille to start the fight. Both of them gonna be suspended," declared Nellita.

"We gonna go after her after school," suggested Donna.

"Yes, we gonna get Rachel and Kay and go after her," Nellita agreed.

Moving and getting close to Rachel, who was in the crowd pushing to get near to the fighters, Nellita said, "Wendy of 705 snitched on Mercedes. We gonna go after her when school dismiss."

"She snitched on Mercedes?" asked Rachel, squinting her eyes.

"Yeah," answered Nellita.

"Yes, we gonna get her this afternoon. We gonna jump her," said Rachel with a bit of hilarity and anger.

With the commotion in the lunchroom, students ran from various tables to spectate the brawl. Hearing the noise and seeing students running to the middle of the cafeteria, Mrs. Elviro, Mrs. Mangel, and Mr. Douglas dashed to the area. Mrs. Elviro burrowed through the yelling crowd. Mr. Douglas burrowed through the yelling crowd too to get to the brawlers.

"Get to your seats," Mrs. Elviro shouted. Students drifted apart.

"Move, get out the way," Mr. Douglas bellowed as he moved through the crowd.

Students scurried as Mr. Douglas bawled and rushed at the two fighters with Mrs. Elviro and Mrs. Mangel close behind. He grabbed Camille by her wrist and pulled her away as Mercedes waded into her with two body punches. Mr. Douglas got between the two fighters.

"Back off, you," he yelled at Mercedes, using his body to prevent both fighters from getting at each other.

"She had no right to punch me," shrieked Mercedes. Mrs. Elviro moved in and collared Mercedes around the waist and swung her away from reaching Camille.

"You had no right to throw that orange at me," retorted Camille, breathing heavily.

"I didn't mean to do it," shouted Mercedes as strands of hair got into her face.

"Be quiet," Mr. Douglas barked. "Hold her, Mrs. Mangel." Mrs. Mangel took hold of Camille while Mr. Douglas whipped out his radio.

Said he, holding the radio set close to his mouth, "Security desk, we need two officers down here in the cafeteria. There was a fight."

Students were out of their seats and yelling.

"Camille, whack her," bawled a male seventh grader.

"Camille threw a punch in Mercedes's head. Ha, ha, ha," another male seventh grader said loudly.

"Mercedes look for that. Camille shoulda whack her some more," opined Rosa.

"Camille wasn't joking, yo. She meant business," was another view expressed by Mylan.

"These sixth and seventh grade students are always fighting and running wild," Lily lamented.

"We fight and run wild, too," Dana said as they stood around after the fight.

Within minutes, Officers Stanhope and Morgan were in the cafeteria.

Said Mrs. Mangel, "These two students were fighting. This student said that she threw an orange which hit her in her head. This is why the fight started. Take them away."

"I didn't mean to throw da orange at her and she came over and punched me," related Mercedes.

"Why you threw the orange in the first place?" asked Officer Stanhope, holding Mercedes by the wrist as Mrs. Elviro released her grip on her.

"I didn't want it. It was sour," said Mercedes with a scowl on her face.

"Then you should have thrown it in the garbage," advised Officer Morgan, who held the forearm of Camille as Mrs. Mangel removed her hands from her.

"She shouldn't have thrown that at me. I ain't do her anything," complained Camille.

"Okay, let's go. The dean will deal with both of you," said Officer Stanhope. The officers then escorted the two fighters from the cafeteria.

"Be quiet. Get to your seats. Stop running," Mrs. Mangel bawled at the students.

Some students scurried to their seats and got quiet for a while but started talking loudly shortly after. Walking around the cafeteria and observing that most students had finished eating lunch, Mrs. Mangel decided that students would not go outside because of their behavior and that they should clear the tables.

Said she, "Class 601, throw your plates in the garbage and return to your seats."

Students of class 601 rose to their feet, moved from the table with their plates, dumped the remaining food and plates in the garbage bin, and returned to their seats.

"602, throw your plates in the garbage and get back to your seats," Mrs. Mangel shouted again.

Students of class 602 rose, deposited their plates in the bin, and returned to their seats. Class 603 then cleared their table, followed by the other classes until all the tables were cleared and students sat and talked without seeing the yard.

"Be quiet! Too much talking and shouting going on in here," barked Mrs. Mangel through her bullhorn.

Said Abena, a saucy female sixth grader who wore a light-blue jacket and black jeans, "We're finish eating and she should let us go outside."

"She's not sending us outside because everybody was yelling and laughing," mentioned Jennifer from class 604.

"She's keeping us inside," agreed Betty from the same class, who sat next to Jennifer.

"Mrs. Mangel, we wanna go outside," shouted Natalie, decked in her hooded red coat with the hood over her head.

Mrs. Mangel did not answer her. She stood next to one of the pillars in the cafeteria with her bullhorn in her hand.

"Yes, Mrs. Mangel, let us go outside, pleeeease," begged Adrian, who stood up.

"Sit down, you're not going outside," Mrs. Mangel said flatly.

"Please, Mrs. Mangel," Adrian pleaded.

"Sit down, I said, and be quiet," Mrs. Mangel snapped. She moved off and continued issuing orders through her megaphone, "Be quiet. Remain in your seats."

"Too much shouting going on in here," Mr. Douglas said loudly.

It was a task keeping the students quiet, but the cafeteria aides and supervisor managed to keep them in their seats. Five minutes later, subject teachers began arriving in the lunchroom to collect their classes. Ms. Vine walked down the stairwell leading to the cafeteria. She entered the lunchroom, looked at her watch, and went to her class.

"Ms. Vine, you have us?" shrieked a female sixth grader.

"Yes, I have you, I have 602," Ms. Vine said, standing near one of the tables.

"Yes, she got us now. We have language arts," said Louisa of class 602.

"Oh, I didn't check my schedule," answered Amanda.

"Line up, 602," ordered Ms. Vine as she sized up the class.

A few students moved, but others appeared not to have heard her. Mr. Wren came into the cafeteria followed by Mr. Howard and Ms. Vivehouse to collect their classes.

Said Mr. Wren loudly, "Form two lines, 703. Hurry up and let's go."

Some of the students immediately rose to their feet and shuffled in forming the lines while others remained seated unmindful that the teacher had told them to form two lines.

Again, Mr. Wren bellowed, "Join the lines, 703."

Students lamely got to their feet and joined the lines.

Barked Mr. Howard, "Come on, guys, get in line."

No one seemed to have heard him. Mr. Howard waited for a while for the students to get in line.

Mr. Wren moved off with his class of students who pushed and jostled each other. It was a ragged line as students made their way through the door and up the stairwell. Ms. Vine moved off with her class with students who broke the lines and ran, talked, and laughed. Other teachers entered the cafeteria and attempted to get their classes in order to take them to their classrooms to begin the after lunch session. Mr. Howard, after much effort in shouting and threatening some students to call their homes, moved off with his eighth grade class, which had little semblance of being in order. After more than ten minutes, the cafeteria was cleared with students climbing the stairwell to their classrooms as the cafeteria staff and custodians cleaned the lunchroom in preparation to receive the upper or senior school to serve them lunch. The atmosphere was much milder with the older students apart from the chatter which took place.

Within thirty-five minutes the upper or senior school was in the yard, shooting basketball into hoops and throwing footballs while others just milled around until the end of the lunch period when they made their way back to the classroom where instructions and learning with intermittent disruption continued.

Chapter 15

School was dismissed at three o'clock. Throngs of students made their way down the stairwell and on to the sidewalk. Tamika, Monet, Nellita, Rachel, and Kay and a few other female students stood on the sidewalk with their eyes darting everywhere to spot Wendy. They moved from the exit to the main entrance and back again to the exit.

"Where she at?" yelled Nellita in an agitated mood.

"I ain't see her yet," responded Rachel, flailing her arms.

"I just wanna see da bitch, son," Kay said. "I gonna whop her ass. She made my homegirl get in trouble."

"Yes, and she made Camille punch her in her face," said Monet, who came up and joined the others.

"How hard da orange hit Camille that she left where she was sittin' and punched Mercedes in her face. If Wendy din tell her she wouldn't know who throw da orange at her, shu," Rachel fretted.

"I just wanna see her and she gonna get it real good," Kay furiously declared.

"That orange couldn't hit her that hard. She behaving as if she was hurt," lamented Nellita.

The female students ranted; their eyes were all over trying to see Camille or Wendy. Camille had left earlier, as arrangement had been made the previous day for her to be picked up before school dismissed. She was picked up by her aunt.

"She believe she gonna get away with it. If we gotta jump her we gonna do it," said Nellita.

Wendy, Ruth, Rozern, and Felicia walked down the stairwell in leaving their classroom.

"Nellita said she waiting fuh me. She wanna fight me," Wendy said with an expression of concern on her face.

"If she wanna fight you, fight her. You didn't do her anything. Her friend pelt da orange at Camille, and you tell Camille she did it. So what? If she had hit me in my head with da orange as she did to Camille I woulda punch her too," fumed Felicia.

"Look, you don't bother with her friend. She got a problem," remarked Ruth, settling her haversack properly on her back.

"If she got a problem or not she ain't gonna hit me and I take it. They only come to school looking for trouble. She had no right to throw that stuff at Camille. I told Camille she did it and now her friend wanna fight. I ain't gonna let her friend hit me. She hit Camille and now Camille is gonna be suspended," lamented Wendy as she and her friends made their way down the stairwell.

Ruth pushed the door, and out they went on to the sidewalk where the crowd was still thick as students lingered and showed little interest in getting home in a hurry. Tamika, Nellita, Monet, Rachel, Mercedes, and Kay angled their way through the crowd to locate Wendy, who squealed on Mercedes since they learned that Camille was picked up before dismissal, when suddenly Rachel yelled, "Look her there!" They burrowed toward Wendy. Wendy and her friends were still moving through the crowd. Looking ahead, she saw Mercedes and her colleagues angling toward her. Wendy stopped and steeled herself. Her friends stopped and stood next to her.

"You snitched on Mercedes and put her in trouble," yelled Rachel, charging at Wendy as Mercedes and her friends attempted to circle Wendy.

Rachel threw a punch, which landed on Wendy's shoulder. Wendy dropped her bag, which Ruth grabbed off the ground, and barged into

Rachel, throwing punches which connected to Rachel's body. "You bitch," Wendy yelled.

Rachel felt a pain in her stomach but returned punches as she belched, "I gonna whop your ass."

Ruth, Rozern, and Felicia circled and goaded Wendy. Yelled Ruth, "Punch her, Wendy. She ain't no bully."

"Kick her, Wendy," bawled Felicia, her head bobbing to see how Wendy was handling herself.

"Punch da bitch in her face," shouted Rozern with wild antics.

"Fight, fight. Those girls fighting," one of three male eighth graders who were passing nearby shouted. A number of students started running and yelling, "Who fightin'." "Come on, let's see what's going on." "Somebody getting whop." Students formed a circle around the fighters. Rachel punched Wendy in her stomach and yelled, "You f—er."

Wendy punched back, hitting Rachel in her face, and murmured, "You, bitch."

Wendy grabbed Rachel's hair and pulled. Rachel threw her right arm around Wendy's neck in attempting to throw her on the road, but Wendy held on to Rachel's hair and tugged. "Ah, ah, ahhhhh," Rachel yelled in pain. Wendy's grip on Rachel's hair slackened, and Rachel pulled her head free while Wendy worked herself free from the headlock that Rachel had her in. They freed themselves from each other and then rushed and held on to each other and threw inside-body punches and kicked each other. "Yes, punch da bitch in da stomach," Nellita bawled, circling the students who brawled.

"Punch her in da stomach, Rachel," Tamika shouted, prodding her colleague on.

"Don't take that from her, Wendy. Beat her real good," Ruth spurred on the fight.

Students who stood nearby ran toward the crowd that encircled the two fighters.

"A fight goin' on there," a thin, tall seventh grade male student burst out in a loud voice and ran toward the scene.

Another male student hollered, "Let's go, a fight down there." And he bolted up the sidewalk. And yet another student, Jasmine, shrieked, "Somebody fightin' there." In a haste she took off.

"Come on, Nioki, a fight takin' place," said Jessica.

"Oh, yeh," responded Nioki, and together they dashed toward the fight.

"Punch her, Wendy," a voice rang out as Wendy landed a punch in the shoulder of Rachel. Rachel threw a flailing blow at Wendy and kicked her in her knee. And the punching and kicking prevailed. Their friends urged them on. Again, Wendy grabbed Rachel's hair. Rachel angled herself and also grabbed Wendy's hair and punched with her left hand. Wendy punched back with her right hand. They seemed like two wrestlers.

The noise rose and the security officer at the main exit noticed the build-up of students at the further end of the block and felt something was going on. He called for backup and dashed from his position. By the time he had realized what was happening the fighters and the crowd drifted from the sidewalk onto the road. "Beat her, Rachel," one of Rachel's friends shouted above the noise. "Beat da girl," Rozern blurted, encouraging Wendy. Wendy and Rachel scrambled and pushed and punched each other as they ended up on the roadway just as a car came barreling down the road.

The crowd was now in the middle of the road. The driver, realizing what was suddenly happening in front of him, in that the crowd had now spread across the road, slammed on his brakes, and the vehicle skidded but straightened up and came to a screeching halt yards away from the crowd. Another car that traveled in the opposite direction came to a sudden stop as the driver pressed heavily on his brakes. The drivers of other vehicles which traveled down the road at a reasonable speed pumped their brakes as the crowd of disorderly students paid no attention to the traffic. Traffic actually came to a halt.

Sergeant Grogan, who hurried out from the first floor on to the sidewalk after receiving the message on his radio set, heard the noise and, looking up, saw the commotion up the street and students running in the direction of it.

"What's going on down there? Another fight?" Sergeant Grogan asked Officer Stanhope, who joined him after a quick dash from the western part of the sidewalk.

"I guess there's some fight taking place with all that noise," suggested Officer Stanhope.

"Let's see what's going on there," Sergeant Crogan said, breaking into a sprint with Officer Stanhope at his aide.

Hearing the loud noise too, Mr. Linsmun said, "Students are fighting down there, I bet."

"Oh no, I thought they were just standing around there. Not another fight this afternoon," Ms. Cort fumed, moving off with Mr. Linsmun in the direction where students ran and shouted.

Mr. Delph, who stood on the western part of the sidewalk urging students to go home, sensed that something was wrong as there was a backup in traffic with drivers honking their horns as students ran between the now-stationary cars and in front of oncoming cars causing drivers to slam their brakes and swear.

"What the hell wrong with these kids? They want to get us in trouble," swore one irritated driver. *Screech!* The tires of a car traveling from the opposite direction heading west burned, leaving heavy black marks on the road as the driver slammed his brakes.

"What's happening with these children?" he yelled.

A passenger in the front seat said, "Every day is the same thing with these students running across the road as if they don't care about their lives."

"If they don't stop, one of them is going to get hit on the road," complained the driver.

"Yes, a car is going to hit one of them. They don't care about the traffic, and this is a busy street. I bet it is a fight taking place up the road," suggested the female passenger.

"You live around here?" asked the driver.

"Yes, I live a few blocks up the road, and I see how they run wild if there is a fight after school is over," the female passenger pointed out.

"I ply this route, and you got to be careful when school is dismissed, and just as you said, if there's a fight you're stalled for a good five minutes until the security appears on the scene and breaks up the crowd and takes away the fighters if they catch them. I try not to pass here at three o'clock, but sometimes you take a chance," the driver stated with his foot on the brakes while he waited for the children to get off the road and on to the sidewalk.

"Grogan and Stanhope comin'," a female seventh grader yelled.

Looking over her shoulder another female shouted, "Linsmun and Cort comin'."

And they made a dash for the sidewalk and darted for the next corner. Their shouts were loud enough to alert the other onlookers or spectators that staff and security officers were after them. Many scampered toward the sidewalk. Students now pushed and jostled each other to disappear from school officials. "Get out da way," a medium-build male tenth grader barked as he tried to make a distance between himself and Sergeant Grogan and Officer Stanhope, who were closing in on the crowd. Rachel unleashed two punches on Wendy. Wendy countered with a punch to Rachel's stomach. Another student yelled, "Look, Grogan!" And the crowd moved faster. A shrill voice echoed, "Cort and Linsmun comin' up da road."

Rachel dashed across the road and ran on the sidewalk. Her friends and supporters darted across the road for the sidewalk, which they speedily made their way along. They turned the corner with Rachel and together headed south on the pavement. Wendy, too, dashed for the sidewalk with her colleagues and supporters, hurried along it, and rounded the corner. They made a run for it. They sprinted down the sidewalk heading north. Within seconds the crowd vanished. A few students were still walking on both sidewalks in going home. They appeared not to be interested in the brawl.

Having reached the students who walked on the northern sidewalk, Officer Morgan asked the three of them, "Do you know the students who were fighting on the road and blocking traffic?"

"I aint know, we wasn't in any fight," said Bliny, one of the three eighth grade students.

"We goin' home. We didn't see who was fighting. We ain't interested in no fight," replied Erwin.

"Okay," Officer Morgan said and moved ahead.

"Why he asked us if we know who was fighting?" remarked Salome, the female eighth grader.

"He wants us to snitch," stated Bliny.

On the southern sidewalk, Sergeant Grogan approached a group of students who went in the same direction. "Who was fighting on the road?" he asked a male ninth grade student who wore a red jacket and black beret.

"Wha' you askin' me? I ain't know nothin'," the young man grumbled.

"You ain't know?" the sergeant asked, as if in doubt with the answer the student gave.

"I ain't know, don't ask me," the student protested.

Looking at another student clad in a black coat, black pants, and red cap, the security supervisor asked, "You see what happened?"

"I ain't no snitch. I ain't know wha' happen," the student retorted.

"Why are you talking about being a snitch or not? All I wanted to know was what happened and who were the fighters, youngster," related Sergeant Grogan. The student did not answer.

"What's happening out here? Don't tell me it's another fight," remarked Ms. Cort, her eyes darting in every direction and her brows knitted. She was clearly angry with the repulsive behavior that took place on the road and which had become a regular embarrassment to the school and the administration.

"It's another fight," stated Sergeant Grogan. "I tried to get here to nab the fighters, but they saw me coming and everybody ran up the road and turned the corner. It's so disgusting."

"I'm so annoyed with this kind of behavior, and no one is going to say who were fighting. That's the horrible part of it," said Ms. Cort, turning and looking around. "We're going to find out who were the people fighting out here and affecting traffic."

"It's almost becoming a daily occurrence when school dismisses. You suspend them and they return to school and do the same thing again," complained Mr. Linsmun, shaking his head.

"It's, indeed, horrible that we have to go through this so often," fumed Ms. Cort, pulling back a few strands of graying hair from her face.

"We're going to find out who were the people fighting," Mr. Linsmun said flatly.

"Yes, we got to do something before somebody gets injured on the road and they put drivers in trouble unnecessarily," suggested Sergeant Grogan, as he walked back to the building with the deans while Officers Morgan and Stanhope remained standing on the sidewalk at the corner to ensure no further infraction of the rules of the school took place. With the sidewalk cleared as students headed home, the deans and security officer entered the building.

The next morning, the deans pulled a few students and tried to find out who were the fighters, but they had little or no success in their endeavor, as students would not disclose who the fighters were. Indeed, some students who were pulled definitely did not know that there was a fight and who the fighters were. But the problem was serious and was of much concern to the administration since the obstruction of traffic and running in front of moving vehicles have the possibility of creating serious accidents that could result in casualties. The administration decided that it would put more security and supervising staff on the sidewalk at dismissal so that the problem could be alleviated or completely stamped out.

Later in the day, Mr. Blair maneuvered his way among students in heading to a class. A student from within the cluster on the floor shouted, "Mr. Blair." Mr. Blair looked in the direction from where the sound came. A male student burrowed his way through to him. Said he to the teacher, who is African-American, "Mr. Blair, where you from? China?"

Said Mr. Blair, "If you feel so."

"Ha, ha, ha." A student who walked nearby laughed. "He's asking Mr. Blair if he's from China. He sick, yo," said the student, turning to his friend.

Said the friend, "He dumb, son. He ain't see Mr. Blair is African-American."

In class 907, Alvin, a tall, slim male student, walked to the front of the room. He pulled the hood of his sweater over his head. He banged on the desk where Martin had just rested his head. "What's wrong with you? Why you messing with me?" Martin said, raising his head from the desk.

"Wake up, you sleepy head," said Alvin with a grin on his narrow face.

"Who you calling sleepy head, you long streak o' misery," Martin said, sitting up.

Alvin was offended and grabbed Martin's shirt. "Who you talkin' to?"

Martin retaliated by grabbing Alvin's sweater. "I'm talkin' to you." They faced off each other as Martin got to his feet. There was a brief struggle, and the teacher separated them.

"I gonna f— you up," fumed Alvin.

"I gonna f— you up too," shot back Martin, arching his shoulders.

"Cut it. Stop the nonsense," said Mr. Mendez.

Kenrick, a slightly muscular student with a full nose, whose ears were pierced and fitted with gold-and-silver earrings, like many of the other male students in the upper school, left his seat, walked up to Alvin, and punched him in his right shoulder.

"Why you punched me, yo?" demanded Alvin glaringly.

"You always's telling people sh—t," said Kenrick.

Answered Alvin, "I ain't tell you anything."

Kenrick threw a punch into Alvin's jaw. Alvin winced in pain. He yelled, "Wha' you punched me for?"

Kenrick then connected another right cross to Alvin's face and Alvin cried, "Ahhh, ahhh . . ." Tears rolled down his face, making two parallel streams.

Mr. Mendez could not move fast enough to stop the physical outburst by Kenrick.

Said Mr. Mendez, moving among the desks, "I'm going to get the dean. Stand over here, Kenrick."

Kenrick ignored Mr. Mendez and made a move toward Alvin with his fists raised. Alvin backed away still sobbing from the pain he felt in his face. Mr. Mendez finally got between Kenrick and Alvin and attempted to push Alvin out of the way and from the reach of Kenrick.

"Why you beating up on Alvin?" yelled Nuldun, a heavyset, muscular, athletic student.

He moved toward Kenrick. Denny, medium-build and tough, followed him. Together they slammed into Kenrick. Kenrick drifted backward. Nuldun pushed him and crossed to his chest. "What da f— you think you doin', beating up on Alvin," Nuldun growled.

Before Mr. Mendez could have turned and pulled Nuldun away, he threw another punch at Kenrick. Kenrick fell backward. He fell to the floor, hitting the back of his head on the edge of a desk as he went down.

"Ahhhh," he yelled in pain.

"He got whack," "Nuldun whack 'em," "Wow! Wow! Da was a punch," "Whop his ass, son. Why he beating Alvin," were some of the shouts that came from the class.

Kenrick writhed in pain. He rolled over and got up in a rage. He cried, "A gonna f— you up."

"No, no, you're not going to do anything. The dean going to deal with this," barked Mr. Mendez, stretching out his arm and grabbing Kenrick.

"A gonna f— him up," Kenrick blurted out, trying to pull away from the strong grip of the teacher.

"Neisha, call the dean," Mr. Mendez said, still holding on to Kenrick.

Neisha got up and left for the dean's office. Blood ran down the neck of Kenrick. He was wounded by the impact on the back of his head from the desk.

"You got to go to the nurse. One of the students will take you. You got a small cut on the back of your head," said Mr. Mendez, looking at the cut and the trickle of blood.

"I ain't going to no f— nurse," Kenrick yelled as the warm blood oozed down his neck while he tried to break away from the grip of the teacher.

"You got to go to the nurse," said Mr. Mendez, tightening his grip. "Travis, come. Take him to the nurse."

"Me?" Travis asked.

"Yes," answered the teacher.

Travis got up from his seat and made his way to the teacher.

Nuldun and Denny stepped away and stood near the window closest to the front of the class. Nuldun heaved his chest and leaned against the window. Denny folded his arms across his chest.

Said Nuldun, "He thinks he's bad. Alvin made a lil' joke by bangin' on the desk, and all Martin did was curse and grab his sweater after Alvin grabbed his shirt and da was all. But he just got up and start punchin' away at Alvin like if he was sittin' at da desk when Alvin bang on it. He bang on da desk when other people got their head on the desk, too, sh—t, and nobody punch him."

"He believes he is big and bad. Likes to take advantage on those he could mess with. He doesn't mess wid us 'cause he know wha' he gonna get," concurred Denny.

The dean hurriedly arrived in the class with Neisha behind him. "What's happening here? What kind of stupidity is taking place," roared Mr. Delph.

"There was a fight," said Mr. Mendez, facing Mr. Delph.

"Who were involved?" questioned the dean, folding his arms across his heaved chest. His face looked stern and hard.

"Alvin, Kenrick, Nuldun, and Denny. Kenrick got cut on his head after he fell hitting his head on a desk from a punch by Nuldun," explained Mr. Mendez.

"All of you, go to my office! You, go to the nurse. Take him to the nurse, young man. When you're finished with the nurse, let me see you in my office," shrieked the dean. "Write it up, Mr. Mendez, and let me get it in my office."

The four young men edged their way to the door. Travis held Kenrick's arm as he accompanied him to the nurse's office to get treatment for his wound. The dean turned and faced the class. He gazed at the students who sat, some of them without a book in front of them. Others who had books in front of them had them closed. Some slouched in their seats while a few had their heads on the desks.

"Mr. Mendez, is this your official class? Oh, sorry, I know whose it is," said the dean.

Mr. Mendez did not bother to answer. The dean paced the floor in front of the class. He then turned and faced the class. Said he, "Sit up." The class sat up.

He then said, "This is a ninth grade class, and almost every day I have to come up to this class whether Mr. Mendez has it or not. Regardless of who the teacher is, I have to constantly be in here.

Let me tell you, I'm tired of seeing your faces for the same things over and over again. Let me see your faces for something positive. Something that could do you, the school, and your parents good. Not some stupid fight, running around the room, throwing books at each other. Your parents didn't send you to school to do that. You're here to learn, to get an education, and all you do, except some of you, is to fool around, horseplay, every day. You sit and do nothing. That's how your parents' money is used: for you to do nothing. If within another week I don't see improvement in your conduct, I'm going to have the parents of each of you up here, maybe with a few exceptions. I'm tired of this behavior. Get your books in front of you, get them open."

The dean turned and walked through the door after they complied with his order.

"Who he thinks he talkin' to?" said Martin, sucking his teeth.

"He could give us a break," uttered Philipia.

"They only comin' here fuh lecture to us 'bout how we must behave," Martin howled.

"I don't give a sh—t what he and the others say. I just wonna get outta here. I'm tired with this sh—t," said Carlton, scratching his head. And the conversation continued.

"This behavior is totally disgusting," said Mr. Mendez. "It is keeping this class back." He tried to do some work, but hardly anyone was listening.

Chapter 16

Early Monday morning, students entered their classrooms, and the loud talking began. They related the weekend's experience. They talked about cinema shows, parties, visits to friends and relatives, eating out at restaurants, and visits to other states. There was ruckus in the classrooms. Students were told to put their coats in the closets. Some did it willingly while others just ignored the instructions. There was much laughter and yelling by many. It took some fifteen minutes before most of the classes settled down.

Mr. Nishum, a short, heavyset male with thick arms covered with thick tan-colored hair, began his science lesson in class 1002. It was a feature of his to wear suspenders, as his pants settled below a bulging paunch he had developed. After a "Do Now" and the collection of homework from only a few students, the lesson began on the topic of photosynthesis. Students were told to read the first paragraph on page 197 in the biology textbook, which dealt with photosynthesis. About half of the class began reading and continued. Mr. Nishum, who wore square metal-framed glasses and portrayed a tense facial expression, partly followed in the text. About ten students, six females and four males, did not read but whispered in carrying on their own conversation. The teacher eyed the inattentive students. He looked over his glasses. The students did not notice him. At the end of the reading, he said, "Class, what is photosynthesis?" Nobody answered. There were blank stares. Mr. Nishum then pointed to Greg, one of the students in the group at the back.

Said he flatly, "Greg, what is photosynthesis?"

Greg looked up; he looked at the teacher with some surprise. He did not say anything. He curled his lips, leaned his head to one side then said, "Photo what?"

"Photosynthesis. Tell us what you know or learned about it from our reading," the teacher uttered, looking steadfast at Greg.

Greg looked at him and said, "I ain't no photographer. What you asking me about that for. I'm a sinner." The class burst out in laughter.

Said Joshin, another student, "That's your idea about photosynthesis?"

Replied Greg, "I don't give a sh—t 'bout that."

Said Mr. Nishum, "Joshin, tell us about photosynthesis?"

"I don't know anything about that. Don't ask me," Joshin said.

The teacher was about to explain what is meant by photosynthesis when a heavy hardcover textbook flew through the air and landed in front of him, a foot away.

"Who threw that book?" he questioned.

"I don't know. Don't look at me," Peter said, leaning back in his chair with a textbook and notebook opened in front of him on the desk.

"If another book is thrown again everybody at the back is going to be in serious trouble," stated Mr. Nishum. The class became somewhat attentive and the teacher was able to continue with the lesson.

Sitting in the middle of the class, Denine volunteered, "It means sunlight on the chlorophyll in the cells of plants is able to produce carbohydrates from carbon dioxide and hydrogen."

"Very good, Denine," remarked the teacher. Denine lips parted in a warm smile as she leaned forward placing her arms on the desk.

Mr. Nishum asked students a few more questions and then indicated that the class would use the microscope to examine the cells in leaves and observe the composition of the cells. He then instructed the class that each student would write up a report on his or her observation in his or her log. The lesson continued with hardly any other distraction.

The sixth-period class, class 701, was in disarray. The teacher shouted at them to be seated and stop talking. Two plump female students who closely resembled each other conversed. To the teacher's amazement, the bigger girl jumped up and then the other. Amanda, the heavier one, with braided hair, grabbed the other, Nioki, and pushed her against the closet. Holding Nioki's hands and spreading her arms apart, Amanda faced off with her against the wall.

"Don't you mess with my mother," yelled Amanda.

"I ain't say anythin' 'bout your mother," pleaded Nioki, with her arms pushed against the closet by Amanda.

"Next time I'm gonna smack you," said Amanda. She then released Nioki.

Nioki took her seat and then blurted out, "F— me up, f— me up, you think you big and bad."

"I'd f— you up the next time you tell me anythin' 'bout my mother," shouted Amanda, leaning over to Nioki.

Ms. Dennison walked up to the desk where both of them sat and said, "What kind of foul mouth the two of you have?"

"I ain't got no foul mouth," Nioki answered, bobbing her head and tightening her lips.

Said Amanda, "She told me 'bout my mother."

"Why you did that, Nioki?" questioned Ms. Dennison.

"I ain't tell her anythin' 'bout her mother," replied Nioki, turning away her head with her hair styled in a bun.

"Yes, she did," burst out Amanda.

"Okay, cut that. Do your work which is on the board," Ms. Dennison ordered.

Students would talk in a friendly manner, and in a jiffy, they would start cursing out each other and were ready to fight. It is funny how they trip so easily and are at each other's throat.

Three students sat on desks in the class while Ms. Dennison taught the lesson. Joking with each other, Rashad said to Donald, "You have vampire teeth, ha, ha, ha."

"You got a crocodile potato head, ha, ha, ha," Rashad reacted, pointing his finger at Donald.

Donald faked a stern angry face. Said Rashad, faking an angry face, too, "You got a beef with me, uh, you got a beef with me?"

Answered Donald, "I ain't got no beef wid you."

"'Cause I'll smack you in da face." Rashad faked with raised fists.

"Ha, ha, ha, ha." The two of them laughed.

"You funny, son," said Donald, patting Rashad on his back.

"You funny, too, yo," Rashad chuckled, giving his friend a fist bump. Donald reciprocated.

"So what's the lowdown for this afternoon," asked Rashad.

Donald shrugged his medium-sized, curved shoulders. "I ain't got anything new."

"Cool, but we could play some ball in da yard," suggested Rashad.

"No problem," agreed Donald.

Said Rashad to Romero, "You's a nut."

Answered Romero, full-faced with dimpled cheeks, "How come you callin' me a nut?"

Said Rashad, "'Cause you look like a nut."

"I ain't no nut. I'm too hyper to be a nut," returned Romero, lifting his arms and flexing his muscles.

"That's what I mean," stressed Rashad, his cheekbone appearing more prominent.

"I ain't no nut though," countered Romero.

"You got money," asked Rashad, looking at Romero.

"I ain't got no money," answered Romero flatly.

"If you ain't got no money, you ain't got no woman, no homie, and you ain't got no love," uttered Rashad, pointing at Romero.

"I got my woman, she loves me. Nobody can't mess wid her," Romero bounced back.

"Don't feign, you ain't got nothin', 'cause you ain't got no money, and you can't get a chick like I got. Get outta here, Romero. You a punk," blasted Rashad.

"You's a pu—y," Romero charged back, seeming a bit angry at what Rashad was saying about him.

"You ain't talkin' to me, son," demanded Rashad.

"I talkin' to you, yes, and wha' you gonna do 'bout it," Romero snarled, his full brown eyes widening.

"You a nut, man. I ain't gonna waste time talkin' to you." Rashad smirked.

Romero leaned back in his chair and folded his arms across his chest.

Said Ms. Dennison, "I've been hearing a lot of idle talk going on there. I hope when I come to check your work I'm going to see evidence of it."

"I'm not talking so I hope she not referring to me," said Gail, looking up from what she was writing in her notebook.

"She ain't talking to me either," whispered Matilda, a tall, big-build female with penetrating eyes and red hair.

A few classrooms away from 701, down the hallway in the east wing, on the same floor, the noise boomed against the wall in class 706. Furniture was pushed in every direction as students, boys and girls, jumped from floor to desk and to the floor again, elbowing each other. "Stop!" the young, small-build female teacher bawled from the top of her lungs. Her blue eyes dilated. They mirrored anguish. Agril pushed Damon. Damon, a hefty student, fell on the floor. Nellita jumped on him and elbowed him in the back. "Ahhhh," Damon hollered.

"Give him another," shouted Darozel, a slim, diminutive boy with lanky hands who cracked up with laughter. "Ha, ha, ha, ha, ha . . ."

And Nellita landed two more elbows in his back. "Ahhhhhh, ahhhhh," Damon bawled, turning over on his side. Nellita jumped up and darted; a minute or two after, Damon turned on his side and struggled to his feet.

Standing and rubbing his back, he said, "I gon catch you."

Nellita laughed and did a little jig.

"Jump her, jump Nellita," shouted Paul, a medium-build youngster with tough hands.

Damon and Harry then chased Nellita. "Stop!" Ms. Stein shouted again but to no avail. No one listened. They caught Nellita at the back of the room against the closet. Damon grabbed her on her shoulder and brought her down. She fell on her side and ended up on her stomach. Damon seized the opportunity and came down on the floor, elbowing her in her back. "Ahhhh," she yelled. Damon quickly got to his feet. Harry then jumped on her, elbowing her in the back once, then twice. "Ahhhh, no, no," Nellita shouted as the boys jumped on her and elbowed her in the back. She thought Harry was going to elbow her again.

"No, no," she shouted, but Harry got up.

Said he, "We're champions."

Another group of four wrestled on the floor. Donna and Kay jumped on Justin and Searon. "Huh, huh, get off of me," shouted Searon as he received body blows.

"I'm calling the dean. Stop this playing," yelled the teacher. "Stop this nonsense in the classroom." She walked to the door in the hope of seeing the dean or one of the security officers. No one was there apart from a number of students who walked the hallway, apparently cutting class. She turned around and headed to the intercom. She hesitated, looked at the class, and shouted, "Stop." Nellita, Damon, and Harry rushed back to their seats. But Paul and now Agril continued rolling on the floor. "Yeah, yeah, I got you, I got you, ooh, ooh, oooh," Agril grunted as he pummeled Paul.

"Ahhhh, ahhhh, I gonna get yuh, I gonna whop yuh," Paul moaned.

Shouted Damon, "The dean comin'." Paul and Agril scampered to their seats.

"I can't believe this," Ms. Stein shouted. "You students are totally out of control. Your behavior is downright disruptive. And you have so much work to do. I'm going to report all of you to Ms. Piggot."

"Who cares," shouted Nellita. "She needs reporting herself. She doesn't do anything. All she does is sit in her musky office."

The flustered teacher shook her head. Nellita then looked down at her black-and-green sneakers.

"Oh sh—t, my sneakers got dirty," she said to Donna. Raising her right hand, she licked her index and middle fingers and rubbed the tips or toes of her sneakers. Placing the two same fingers in her mouth, she moistened them with saliva and rubbed the toes of her sneakers again. She did the same thing again the third time. She then admired the sneakers, which looked clean. "My sneakers look cool now."

"My toes are sweating. They feel damp," said Donna. Donna slipped off her sneakers, the laces of which were untied.

"Why you take off those smelly sneakers?" said Nellita.

"My sneakers not smelly," said Donna, putting one sneaker to her nose.

"Gimme da sneaker," Nellita yelled. She grabbed it from Donna and placed it to her nose.

"Your f— sneaker smells," bellowed Nellita and dropped it on the floor.

Donna picked it up and put it again to her nose. She said, "It only smells a little."

"It smells a damn lot," bawled Nellita.

Donna did not say anything; she put on her sneakers and delved into her bag where she retrieved a comb and began combing her hair.

"Ladies, you have work to do. Open your books," said Ms. Stein with a stern expression on her face.

"Relax, Ms. Stein," shrieked Nellita, getting up and sitting on the desk.

"Cool down, Ms. Stein, we gonna work just now," shouted Donna, still combing her hair.

Nellita then grabbed the comb from Donna. Said she to Donna, "Leh me give you a good style. I gonna give you a minsee."

"What's that?" asked Donna, looking up at Nellita, who got off the desk, stood, and began passing her fingers through Donna's hair.

"You don't know 'bout minsee. It's the style where you bring down some of the hair to your forehead just above the eyebrows. It makes you look nice," Nellita explained, looking at Donna straight in her eyes.

"Fuh real?" asked Donna

"Fuh real," Nellita answered, combing out her hair

"Ohh, yeh, I know that style. My cousin who is older than me use to use it. It look nice on her," remarked Donna, turning her head and looking up at Nellita.

"She don't use it no more?" questioned Nellita, stretching out the hair.

"The last time I see her she had a bun. Maybe she decided to change. But that use to look good on her. I remember."

"I gonna give you one so you could look pretty like her."

"Wha' you mean? I got my looks. I'm damn cute."

"I'm damn cute too and more cute than you."

Donna pulled away her head and looked up at Nellita. "Since when you more cute than me?"

"I ain't sayin' anythin'. Come leh me fix your head."

Donna relaxed and Nellita began grooming her hair much to the consternation of Ms. Stein, who refused to bother with those who were not working. She wrote the names in a book and said, "Some homes would be called tonight."

"She ain't calling my home," murmured Nellita.

Nellita continued grooming Donna's hair as if they were in a salon while Damon and Harry romped at the back of the class as a few others sat without even attempting to open their books.

It was eight o'clock, and Mr. Richmond was at the dinner table having dinner with his wife and three children. It was cold and raining, and the rain had felt icy on his face on his way home. It was a bleak day from the prolonged rainfall, interrupted by a few breaks in the downpour, and a dark windy night when Mr. Richmond arrived home from work. He and his family ate baked chicken, candied sweet potato, peas and rice, and a tomato gravy after he had sipped a cup of hot mint tea. Everyone was still sitting at the table when the phone rang. Neola ran and grabbed the phone. "Hello," she said.

The voice at the other end of the line said, "Good night, can I speak to Mr. Richmond?"

"Dad, the phone for you," the ten-year-old said.

Mr. Richmond rose from his seat at the dinner table and stepped into the living room where he took the phone from his daughter.

"Hello, Mr. Richmond here," answered Mr. Richmond, clad in a blue short-sleeve shirt and brown-and-white plaid, loose-fitting, pajama-like cotton pants.

"Good night, Mr. Richmond. This is Ms. Stein, Nellita's language arts teacher. I'm calling to complain that Nellita was out of control in class today," stated Ms. Stein calmly and politely.

"Out of control. She was out of control you're saying," interrupted Mr. Richmond with a raspiness in his voice.

"Yes, she was wrestling with some male students, elbowing them in the back, and they elbowing her in her back as well," explained Ms. Stein candidly.

"No, miss, you're not talking 'bout my daughter. You made a mistake. You're on to the wrong home. My daughter don't behave like that," Mr. Richmond interrupted again.

"I'm talking about Nellita Richmond. Apart from wrestling, she cursed in class and began combing and grooming another students' hair. She refused to sit in her seat but instead sat on the desk before engaging in wrestling on the floor," Ms. Stein further explained.

"Ms. Stein, I'm not going to accept this. I can't believe this. This is unbelievable that my daughter, a polite and well-behaved child, is behaving like this in your class. Are you sure you're talking about the right student? Let me put my wife on the phone to hear what you're saying about our daughter," said Mr. Richmond, somewhat upset. "Lily, come here. Listen what this teacher is saying 'bout our baby, Nellita."

Mr. Richmond gave his wife the phone. She put the receiver to her ear. "Hello," she said, "This is Mrs. Richmond. What is it with Nellita?"

"Good evening, Mrs. Richmond. I'm Ms. Stein" said the teacher politely.

"Good evening, Ms. Stein," Mrs. Richmond answered with a little irritation in her voice.

"I was just saying to Mr. Richmond that Nellita was out of control in class today. She ran around the class, wrestled with male students on the floor. She elbowed them in the back, and they in turn elbowed her in the back. It was horrible and she would not listen. She cursed also. She then sat on the desk and later got off and began grooming another female student's hair although I told her to stop," explained Ms. Stein.

"This is unbelievable. Are you talking about Nellita Richmond?" Mrs. Richmond inquired.

"Absolutely, I'm talking about her, and as I have said, her behavior was most unacceptable. I would like you to have a serious talk with her so that her behavior and participation in class could be improved. If possible, you could come into the school so we can discuss her conduct," related Ms. Stein.

"I'm going to find out from Nellita what kind of behavior she displayed in class. She doesn't behave like that at home, and that's the reason why I asked you if it's the same child you're talking about or if you didn't make a mistake. I'm terribly surprised and upset," stated Nellita's mother with much disappointment in her heart.

"It's Nellita I'm calling about, and her behavior is very unacceptable," emphasized Ms. Stein firmly.

"I definitely have to look into this matter," said Mrs. Richmond.

"Thank you," said Ms. Stein, feeling a bit relieved that some action would be taken.

"You're welcome and thank you for calling. Good night," said Mrs. Richmond.

"Good night, Mrs. Richmond," replied Ms. Stein. The phones were hung up.

Mrs. Richmond looked at her husband; he looked at her. Both were dumbfounded. They walked back to the dinner table and sat. Both no longer felt like eating.

Nellita sat at the table looking innocent and quiet as she overheard what her parents were saying.

Said Mrs. Richmond, "Nellita, Ms. Stein just called to say how you behaved out of control in class today; that you ran around the class chasing after male students, you wrestled with them on the floor, elbowed them in the back, and that they elbowed you in the back. She said you cursed and then sat on a desk and combed another student's hair. What kind of behavior is that, Nellita? Is that the way you behave in class? I can't believe it for a moment. At home your behavior is so pleasant and ladylike. I don't know how to take this. We send you to school to learn, Nellita. We didn't send you to behave in that way."

Nellita remained quiet.

"I don't know what to say. Nellita, that is not the way we brought you up. I never thought you would behave like that in school. I'm surprised, I'm embarrassed," said Mr. Richmond, feeling despondent, shaking his head in disbelief at the table. Part of his dinner remained in front of him. The other siblings looked on but said nothing as they tried to finish their dinner.

An expression of sadness formed on Nellita's face, as she could not find the words to answer her parents, who were very disappointed. Tears streamed down her worried face. Nellita had almost finished her dinner. Her parents then decided to go and sit in the chairs in the living room.

Said Mr. Richmond, in a voice that racked with heaviness, "Nellita, finish your dinner, then come over here, please."

Sitting on the brown sofa next to her husband, Mrs. Richmond said, "I can't believe our baby is behaving like that. I'm stunned."

"This one floored me. Cursing, running, and doing all the other crazy thing. This really punched me hard," said Nellita's father, propping his chin with his right hand.

"I feel just the same," Mrs. Richmond told her husband.

Nellita ate her dinner. She swallowed the last mouthful of tea, wiped her hands with tissue, and got up from the table. She edged to the living room and stood in front of her parents

"Sit, Nellita," her mother said, somewhat despondently. Nellita sat in an armchair opposite her parents.

Said her mother pointedly, "Nellita, why did you behave like that in Ms. Stein's class? I want to know."

Nellita bowed her head and thought. Her mother waited on her. She looked at her parents then looked away.

"Do you have an answer as yet," Mrs. Richmond asked with a calm voice as Mr. Richmond looked on and leaned back in the sofa.

Nellita finally answered after some three minutes of thinking. Said she, "Mom, some of the children were running around the class. The teacher wasn't controlling the class." Nellita paused. Her parents waited. They were patient. After a while, her mother asked, "What happened next?"

Nellita pursed her lips and said, "After they started wrestling and chasing each other I got up and joined them. We wrestled. I elbowed them and they elbowed me. We were just having some fun."

"Nellita, we didn't send you to school to wrestle with other students and elbow them, causing them to elbow you. You are there to learn, and even if the others are running around, chasing each other and wrestling, that doesn't mean you have to do it, that doesn't mean you have to join them," advised Mrs. Richmond, looking steadfast at Nellita.

"Even if they are running, chasing each other, and wrestling and rolling on the floor, you have no right to join them. Your purpose in class is to listen to your teacher, become engaged in the lesson, and do whatever activity she instructs you to do even if the others are not paying attention. Do not follow what other people do negatively. Don't follow what the other students are doing in a destructive way," Mr. Richmond said in a firm but counseling voice.

Interrupted Nellita, "But nobody wasn't learning anything. Many of the students were running around and playing and wrestling. She wasn't teaching."

"Students have to allow the teacher to teach. If they run around the class and wrestle, rather than sit in their seats and be ready to learn what the teacher has to teach, does not mean you have to do the same thing," cautioned her mother.

"If everybody is seated and ready to learn, then the teacher would be able to teach. Nellita, I expect you to listen to your teacher. If the others want to run wild, that's their choice and it's regrettable. You don't have to do the negative things that they do. And don't do it. Don't be a follower. When you follow people, and in this case, students, who do negative and unacceptable things, you get in trouble along with them. Sometimes, while they go free, while they get away with it, you are the only one who gets into trouble. Don't be a follower. Be a leader in doing the right thing, in doing something positive," declared Mr. Richmond in a firm and clear voice. Nellita listened, sitting and looking very meek.

"Nellita, I don't want ever again to hear that you are involved in wrestling, cursing, and combing other student's hair in class. That's not what you're in class for, do you hear me?" her father said. "If you follow people, follow people who do the right things, people who do positive things, people who do things which are uplifting and that can make you a better person. Follow what your teachers do. They are doing things which are positive. The work they do with you in the classroom is positive."

"Yes, Dad," answered Nellita quietly and almost piously.

"You made us feel embarrassed. You're not going to follow others again, in that negative way. Nellita, is there another reason for joining in and running around and playing in the class while your teacher is trying to calm the class and teach a lesson?" Mrs. Richmond asked, trying to get to the bottom of the matter as to why her daughter behaved in that manner.

"No, Mom. I was just trying to have some fun with my friends," said Nellita.

"That's not the time and place to have fun, Nellita. The classroom is a place to learn and to get fun from learning something meaningful and constructive. You don't get fun from disrupting a class and preventing others from learning and the teacher from teaching. It is a negative, disruptive form of behavior, and I don't want you to be involved in that kind of behavior. Do you understand me?" Mrs. Richmond asked her daughter.

"Yes, Mom, I understand you," responded Nellita.

"Do you behave like that in other classes?" asked Mr. Richmond calmly.

"No, Dad, I don't behave like that in other classes. I do my work," replied Nellita, looking in the direction of her parent but without eye contact.

"Because of breaking the rules of your class you would suffer some consequences. Your pocket money is forfeited for the week, no TV, no games, and for the next two weeks, no friends would be allowed over," said Mrs. Richmond. "Further, your father and I would examine your classwork closer to see what you're doing in each class. Also, we'll check your homework more than twice a week. I think I'm going to go to the school to find out more about your performance and conduct in other classes," Nellita's mother said.

Nellita did not answer or made any remarks about the punishment her mother imposed on her. Her parents scolded her and further discussed the complaint with her to get to the root of her behavior and bring about change before her conduct further deteriorated.

Chapter 17

The bell rang for the beginning of the fourth period. The crowd was still in the hallway, and no one seemed to budge since the bell rang. Ms. Cort was still in her office; she was on the phone attending to an important matter, and the seventh grade dean had two parents in his office trying to resolve a dispute between two seventh grade students who were involved in a fight the day before. With the absence of the deans in the hallway, a considerable number of students was congregating in the east wing where they tried to hang out on the first floor. There was a shortage of security officers on that day, as four of them did not report for duty as the daily struggle to get students out of the halls and under control was taking its toll on the officers and faculty.

Noting that no security personnel was on the first floor, the sixth and seventh graders took advantage of it to remain in the hallway of the east wing. The chatter, shouts, screams, and laughter grew. It became incessant and flowed through the main hallway. It caught the attention of Ms. Cort. She asked the person on the line to excuse her for a while. She bolted out of her office and started yelling in order to get the crowd out of the east wing and also the main hall where the main office was located. Students scampered. Ms. Piggot also broke out of her meeting and hurried into the hallway heading toward the east wing to assist Ms. Cort in clearing the floor and getting students into their classrooms.

Twenty minutes into the period and all students were still not in their rooms. With effort on the part of the deans and the assistance of a few teachers, the hall was finally cleared. Students dashed into Ms. Vine's 705 language arts class. The same manner in which they entered by running, they continued running and jumping in the class. Some gathered at the back of the class. Girls began wrestling with boys, and so the boys wrestled with them. The noise level was at its peak. Students shouted and laughed. Some ran around the classroom. Ms. Vine yelled and cautioned them, calling on the disruptive students to be quiet and to take their seats but to no avail. She tried to summon the assistance of the dean to bring order to the class by calling on the phone, but Ms. Cort had left her office for the main office and could not be reached by Ms. Vine. Disgust was printed on her face.

Turning to a student who sat in a group in the front section of the class, Ms. Vine said, "Calvin, go get the dean or security for me."

"Who, me?" Calvin said, with a smirk on his face. "No way, I ain't goin'. You go."

Ms. Vine's eyes widened with surprise since she thought Calvin would go, as he was one of the students who assisted her with any errands within the building.

"Calvin!" she said.

"What?" Calvin barked.

Ms. Vine knitted her brow, wiped her forehead with her bare hand, bobbed her head, and turned around to face the board. She then walked away to the door, looked up and down the hall of the east wing, and then pulled back into the classroom.

Said Tamika, an obese but kind-hearted student with a lovely smile, "Ms. Vine, you want me to get security?"

Before the teacher could have answered, another heavy female student, who sat two desks away, blurted, "You fat overgrown pig, you getting security on us?"

"You fat jerk chicken, yes," Tamika shot back, her face contorting, incensed by what Deanna said. The class burst out in hilarious laughter. "Yeah, yeah, yeah . . ." *Bang, bang, bang, bang!* The class banged wildly on the desks.

"You speakin' to me?" asked Deanna, her face puffing with anger, as it did not take the student long to become angry.

"Yes, you, I'm talking to," Tamika railed.

"Fuh real?" Deanna questioned, her face tightening.

"Fuh real," Tamika answered, rising from her seat as Deanna rose from her seat.

"Where you going?" said Ms. Vine, walking over and standing next to Deanna.

"Get outta my way," Deanna shouted, angling around the teacher.

"Don't you push me," said Ms. Vine, as Deanna was very close to her almost without any body space between them.

"I ain't pushin' you but get outta my f— way," Deanna yelled at the teacher.

She stared at Ms. Vine; Ms. Vine stared back at her. Deanna was fuming as if she wanted to face off with the teacher.

Said Andrew, "Deanna, sit yuh fat ass down."

Deanna spun around and faced Andrew, "You on my case too, you on my case."

"Sit yuh fat ass down, Deanna. Wha' you could do to anybody? You can't even breathe good, shu," shouted Andrew, a muscular, broad-shouldered youth with solid arms, the veins bulging in his muscles.

Deanna was flush with embarrassment, and water welled up in her squinting, slanting eyes that looked as if they could hardly open. "Ahhhhhhh," she screamed and flung herself on the floor. "Ahhhhhhh, this ain't gon end here. I gonna bring my brother on you. He gonna whack your ass, Andrew. I gonna whop you when we get outside, Tamika." Deanna cried, the tears rolling down her full round face. The twelve-year-old seventh grader ambled herself to her feet and with a now-shy face trudged to her seat.

Shouted Andrew, "Tamika, you ain't gettin' no security nor dean on us, aaight."

"Nah, nah, nah," Tamika smiled and took her seat

"Yuh know you my homie," said Andrew.

"Yeah," Tamika's smile widened, baring some beautiful white teeth.

Ms. Vine was abandoned by Tamika, as her homeboy urged her not to seek assistance for the teacher. In a flustered state, Ms. Vine knew that her woes for the period were not over. She thought, *Why am I doing this job? Isn't there something else I can do to earn a living? Why do I have to go through this every day? I prepare and I can't get to do my work. I want to work with my students. I want to help them.* She got herself together and focused on her task. But she was not alone. Other teachers were going through the same thing on a daily basis despite the fact that homes were called and parents came up to the school. Teachers became burnt out from the daily melee, which made it difficult for them to do what they were required to do.

Ms. Vine stood in the center of the class and tried to model a lesson after struggling to get some reading done; suddenly there was an outburst of laughter at the back of the classroom. Students jumped from their seats and ran around the room. "Stop the running!" Ms. Vine screamed as she seemed to be losing it now from the persistent horseplay in the class. Ms. Vine's class, like ninety percent of the classes at Jones High School, was multiracial and multicultural. There were students who hailed from or whose parents came from every continent. In the class she was now teaching, there were blacks, whites, Asians, and Hispanics as in every other class, and they all did the same things that were disruptive to effective teaching and learning. She no longer was appalled as students punched and threw paper balls at each other. Miguel bent over and grabbed a sneaker off Felicia's foot and threw it at Marzin, a tall, dark-skinned, small-framed student with long dreadlocks which reached about his waist. Marzin caught it. "Hey." He grinned.

"What da f— you doin'? Gimme my sneaker," shouted Felicia.

Marzin shouted, "Movell!"

Movell, a tall, heavy white student with red hair looked over at Marzin and raised his hands. Marzin threw the sneaker, and Movell caught it and ran. Rajendra, a medium-build, long-haired East Indian student, was already out of his seat and shouting, "Movell, here." Movell threw the pink-and-white sneaker at Rajendra, who caught it and hurled it through the air at Rozern, a brown-skinned African-American student, who grabbed it. Jumping from her seat, Monet, a slim Hispanic student, almost tumbled over her desk in stretching forth her hands as she called, "Rozern, to me, c'mon." Rozern pelted the sneaker at Monet, who caught it, but it slipped through her hands and fell on the desk. She immediately scooped it up before anyone could get it; she looked around to see whom she should throw it to as the others yelled, "Me, me." With her head dancing from side to side, she threw it to Marzin. Marzin caught it and stabbed it in the air in a form of victory over the others and then looked at Kemchand, another student with roots from the Asian continent. He hurled it to Kemchand, who coolly caught it and fired it to Wong, a medium-build Chinese student with a crew cut and tiny eyes and a little goatee. He caught it and without hesitation shot it to Harry, another white, tall but slim student, who grinned broadly as he received the sneaker.

"I got to get my sh—t," yelled Felicia as she hopped around the class in one white sock and one sneaker.

As soon as she uttered those words, Harry flicked the sneaker to Rozern, who grabbed it, but it fell from his hands. Felicia was closing on him. As the sneaker fell to the floor, she wrestled with Rozern and grabbed her sneaker from the floor. A bright smile masked her face. "Shu, I hada get my sneaker."

"Mannn," Rozern squealed, flailing his arms as he lost the sneaker.

"You a punk?" asked Rajendra, as he passed by Rozern. "You let her get da sneaker."

"It fell, son. It fell," said Rozern.

"He got grease in his hand, son," declared Movell.

"He messed up," said Miguel, who took a seat on a desk.

"We had a good time and he screw up everything," said Wong.

Ms. Vine was on the phone trying to contact Ms. Cort, but she was still not in her office. Meanwhile, Marzin, Miguel and Kemchand milled around the room trying to see whose sneakers they could grab from their feet while the others sat on the desks and put their feet on the chairs. Unfortunately, no security personnel was in the hallway of the east wing. Ms. Vine felt fatigued from the persistent shouts in trying to bring some degree of order to her classroom and to somehow initiate some form of instruction. She knew it was a daily ordeal for her, and she became heavy in spirit.

Still walking around the room and eyeing other students who sat and bantered, Marzin sneaked up behind Kathleen, a broad-shouldered white student with full, solid arms who sat at her desk talking to Yunda, a dark-complexioned, small-build, black female student. They always talked about something or shared something in the form of candies, snacks, or sodas. As Kathleen sat with her feet under her chair and the toes of her sneakers goring the floor, Marzin stealthily crawled on his knees, held her right ankle, and pulled her white Nike sneaker off her foot. "Who da f— hold my ankle and pulled my sneaker off my damn foot," Kathleen yelled as if the words were typed at a hundred words a minute, looking over her shoulder. Marzin scampered to his feet. "Yeah, we got it," he bawled.

"Hu, hu hu," Movell and Kemchand huffed with glee on their faces.

"Movell," Marzin shouted and threw the sneaker at him. Movell caught it.

"Leh me get my sneaker. I ain't into this sh—t," Kathleen blurted, getting out of her seat and going after Movell, who now held her sneaker.

With a broad smile, Movell shouted, "Rajendra." Rajendra held his arms open and caught the object as it was fired at him. The students now ran around the room throwing Kathleen's sneaker, as she moved toward one student after the other to get her footwear. Marzin ran, and so did Movell, Rozern, Wong, Monet, Rajendra, Kemchand, Chung, Ruth, and Miguel and a number of others who had now joined the band.

Again Ms. Vine shouted, "Stop! Go to your seats and do your work." It all fell on deaf ears as the boys and girls ran around the room. Miguel tripped and fell, and Movell, who was close behind, stumbled and fell on him. Marzin also tripped and fell on both Miguel and Movell. "Yeah, yeah . . ." was the loud laughter as they fell, and other students also fell to the floor as they collided with each other. The sneaker fell on the floor, and in the confusion, Kathleen moved in and grabbed her sneaker from the floor.

Two doors away, in class 707, Ms. Hatmill a young brown-skinned African-American teacher who had recently joined the staff, was having the works trying to bring her class under control and get some work done. She tried to read a passage from a social studies book, but the students were not with her. Miguelina, a medium-build Hispanic student, repeatedly slapped a white student in his back. Hardy returned a punch, and they started wrestling. She fell on the floor, and Hardy, Paul, and Ramirez hit and fake-kicked her. She got up and hit out at them. They ran up and down the classroom. As Miguelina and the others wrestled and ran around the class, a black male student whose parents hailed from Africa ran around the class. He punched a Hispanic student in the back. A white student whose parents hailed from Europe joined in and pummeled the Hispanic student. Two students, a Chinese and an East Indian, joined in and punched others. They grabbed at them, and soon they all were on the floor tumbling and rolling and yelling.

An obese Chinese male student, two male Hispanics, and a white male student joined the melee and punched at each other. Three black students and two East Indians sprang from their seats, being excited by the wild frenzy, and headed toward the bunch of grinning, hilarious students. They struck out in mock anger. Half the class now railed and jumped around. Desks and chairs were tossed about, *Bang, bang*, was the loud noise as some fell on the floor. The classroom was smashed. Posters were deliberately, not accidentally, ripped from the walls as the students went on a rampage.

The teacher looked diminutive among some of the students, eleven and twelve years old, who were almost six feet in height. Ms. Hatmill stood in front of the class with her hands on her hips. She bawled, "I'm not going to take this. This ain't no crazy house with you students running around as if you're out of your minds." They did not look at her. She began calling, "Hardy, Ramirez, Paul, Miguelina, Leon . . ." as she took a notepad from her desk and wrote the names of the students who were out of their seats. A few of the timid ones hurried to their seats, but the more aggressive and tough youngsters continued the rampage in the classroom.

Said Ms. Hatmill, in a somewhat furious manner, "Expect a call and expect your parents up here tomorrow."

Said one student, "Who she talkin' to. Not me at least. I diggin' fun. I don't care."

Echoed another, "She pompin' a scene. She ain't calling nobody house. And my mom not comin' to this place."

Pointing to the students, Ms. Hatmill said, "I'm going to stay back here this afternoon and write up referrals."

"She ain't giving me no referral," grumbled Miguelina, slumping in her seat.

"She wanna get us suspended like if we do somethin'," Hardy grumbled too, still standing in the classroom.

Said Ramirez, sitting on his desk, "I ain't takin' no referral, shu. I ain't do sh—t."

Some students still shouted and ran about the room. A few students who remained in their seats had their textbooks open. In spite of the loud noise, they read a passage from the text and worked on an assignment handed out to them, which involved the factors responsible for rapid population growth in some parts of the world and the slow growth rate in other parts and what measures could be taken to correct the imbalance. Their faces were the essence of frustration, as they were disappointed with the behavior of their colleagues.

As the students ran around in a frenzy, about four of them leapt on desks and chairs as they tried to escape the attacks of their colleagues, who charged in hot pursuit as they swarmed around the class.

"What da f— yuh doin'," blurted out Filond, who pulled his head out of the way as Leon flew past on the desk. "Why you don't sit down and do some work?"

Leon skipped on some four desks and had students leaning backward to avoid hitting them in the head with his feet. He then jumped to the floor, unmindful that Filond chided him for his recalcitrant behavior. Two students, one following the other, stood in two chairs and raised their outstretched arms in the air. Bawled the bigger, heavier student, "Ahhhhh, ahhhh." He stabbed the air with his fist and jumped to the floor. The other student then jumped to the floor. Together, they walked to the back of the room and leaned against the wall breathing heavily.

Dessin, a student involved in the melee, pushed the head of a female student, who also jumped around the class. She immediately climbed on her desk.

She shouted, "Dessin, I'm comin' after you. You better look out; it ain't gonna be nice." She jumped from her desk and charged after Dessin. Akashia caught Dessin at the door and kicked and punched away at him. He pulled away. Mercedes, Rosa and Akashia charged and attacked Dessin, in their usual mock offensive. They hurled expletives galore as they unleashed a barrage of punches and kicked him as he backed up against the wall.

Lam, Afredo, Wendell, as well as Jorend and Martuk, all black, white, Asian, and Hispanic students, rushed at the girls, who were of similar ethnicity, and hit them. The girls struck back wildly, screaming and laughing as they enjoyed the commotion. In an effort to ward off the tugs, pushes, kicks, and punches lodged on them, Dessin and Akashia, overbalanced, slid and fell on the floor. Mercedes, Rosa, and Lam lost their balance too and fell on her. She screamed and cursed, "Get the f— off o' me. You're hurting my arm." Elation had now turned to anger and was further aggravated when Leon, who ran toward the group, stumbled and fell onto her chest, sending severe pain in her entire chest and abdomen. Akashia became violent and very angry. She kicked repeatedly at the boys as she lay on the floor.

Ms. Hatmill moved in toward the group and howled at them, "Get off the floor and get to your seats. It's horrible what you girls are doing following these boys."

It was disgusting and repulsive to see female students behave so horribly. The students rose to their feet. Akashia struggled to her feet frantically as Dessin, Mizzeal, Lam, and Jorend backed away, laughing and gesturing. She launched at Dessin. He ran. She darted after him. He ran to the front of the class. Akashia cursed as she chased him. Dessin ran to the back of the class, pulling and pushing chairs and desks. Akashia picked up a chair and continued chasing after him. He ran out of the classroom and into the hallway. She went after him with the chair. The other male and female students rushed to the doors laughing. It was a show of stark indiscipline. Dessin dashed down the hallway.

"Remove from the doors, take your seats," shouted the teacher. Some of the students returned to their seats, but others ran into the hall behind Akashia. They soon headed back to the classroom with Akashia leading the way, cursing loudly, "I' gonna f— you up." Passing the threshold, she threw the chair on the floor. *Bang!* There was no end as the commotion continued.

The situation was no different in class 704. Students threw paper balls at each other. Girls, black, white, Hispanics, and Asians threw paper balls at boys, white, blacks, Hispanics, and Asians. Some of the male students romped with each other. A white student, medium build, threw a pencil at a medium-build Hispanic student. The pencil hit him in the chest. "Why the hell you throw that at me?" Ortis yelled.

"We're playin'," retorted Billy, whose cheek was red from romping with the others.

"I ain't playin'," shouted Ortis as he advanced toward Billy. He pushed Billy, Billy pushed him back. They confronted each other. They glared at each other. Ortis pushed Billy. Billy grabbed him, spun him around, and threw him on the floor before Ms. Bland could part them. She grabbed Billy's hand and pulled him away. As Ortis fell to the floor, the back of his head struck the edge of a chair. *Bang.* Ortis winced as he felt the impact. "Ahhhhh, ahhhhh, huh, huh, ahhhhhh," he cried from the sudden severe pain that gripped him. He turned on his side and curled up. The teacher moved toward him to find out if he was badly hurt.

Said she, "I know you're feeling pain, Ortis. Get up. I'll get someone to take you to the nurse."

The young man got on his knees and belched at the teacher, "What da f— you tellin' me? Move from me."

The teacher was taken aback, surprised at the outburst by Ortis.

Still in pain, he rose to his feet and confronted the teacher. "You see him throw me on da floor and cause me to hit my head on da chair and now you tellin' me I'm in pain. You ain't do nothin' when he threw me down."

The teacher looked hard at Ortis. Said she, "You know you're not supposed to be fighting in class."

"But he started it. He threw a pencil at me. I ain't do him nothin'," protested Ortis, rubbing his head as he turned around and went to his seat.

"Take the pass and go to the nurse so she could look at where you got hurt. Go with him, Jaime. I'm going to send Billy to the dean. I'm going to write a referral right now, and I'm going to call his house," said Ms. Bland, walking to the front of the class.

"You not gonna call my house. I ain't do him nothin'. He started it," said Billy, standing next to the front window.

Ms. Bland picked up a card from her desk and began writing up a referral for Billy.

"What yuh doin'," shouted Billy, stabbing the air with his fist.

"I'm writing a referral for all those who were disrupting this class. I'm going to continue it at lunch and give it to Ms. Cort," said the teacher.

Despite the fact that the teacher wrote up a combined referral, students left their seats and wrestled again and threw each other on the floor. A few girls left their seats and ran the length and breadth of the room. They sparred and hit each other. "Get to your seat," was the sound that rang out from the teacher. "There is still work to be done in this class." A few students did some amount of work. One female ran around, climbed on a desk, and shouted, "Those nerds are working."

"Who you calling nerd?" one of the hardworking youngsters said.

"You I calling nerd. You and the others workin' while we havin' fun. Join us," she said.

"You could yell and run around, but we're gonna work. You call us what you will. We're gonna learn something," said one of the students, looking up from the book he was reading.

Still wreaking havoc in Ms. Vine's 705 class were Marzin, Michael, Kemchand, and the rest. Their actions seemed not to have abated to any extent although Ms. Vine threatened to have their parents come up to the school to meet with the dean and perhaps the assistant principal of the department. She struck her desk with a hardcover textbook to get the attention of the students, but the disruptive students of her class did not listen to her but continued running and jumping, laughing, and screaming. Ms. Vine was on the intercom again. She did not get in touch with Ms. Cort, who was still out of her office dealing with a matter in the main office. Ms. Vine left the front of the classroom and walked to the back where she took out her keys and locked the backdoor so that it could not be opened from the inside or outside.

Said Kemchand, "Why she locked the door?"

"She locked the door?" asked Marzin, who now stood leaning against the wall at the back of the room.

"Yeah," answered Kemchand, pulling a chair from behind a desk and sitting astride it with his arms resting on the back of the chair. Marzin turned his blue baseball cap around and started rubbing the tip of his left index finger. Ms. Vine walked back to the front of the classroom and toward the front door. She stood in front of the closed front door, which was unlocked. With three minutes before lunch and with some students still out of their seats, Ms. Vine said calmly and loud enough for everyone to hear, "We're going to stay in for lunch. Twenty minutes—"

"What!" a few students shouted together, interrupting the teacher.

"We're not staying in here fuh lunch," yelled Marzin, who rose from his seat and sat on a desk.

"I'm hungry. I gotta go to lunch," shouted Movell.

Continued Ms. Vine, still in a calm manner, "Twenty minutes of your lunchtime you'll spend in here. Nobody is leaving."

"We gotta go to lunch, man," fumed Rozern, leaning back in his chair.

Cling, cling, cling-cling, cling, cling! The bell rang, ending the fourth period and signaling the beginning of lunch for the sixth, seventh, and eighth graders.

Most of the class jumped to their feet and grabbed their bags.

"Stay in your seats, students. We're not going anywhere, not right now," Ms. Vine said, standing in front of the door with her body blocking the lock and door handle.

Some of the students made for the backdoor not realizing it was locked. Others moved to the front door, looking at Ms. Vine as if to tell her to move out of the way. She bit her bottom lip as she looked at the students now standing in front of her and mumbling. Wendy, Felicia, Wong, Andrew, Marzin, Miguel, and others stood in front of Ms. Vine.

"I'm hungry, Ms. Vine," Felicia complained, dropping her bag on the floor.

"I need food. Leh me go," said Marzin, folding his arms across his chest. The teacher did not answer. She stood her ground.

"We're hungry, Ms. Vine. Could you let us go?" begged Marzin, leaning his head on one side.

"I want all of you to go to your seats," uttered Ms. Vine, taking most of her weight on her left leg.

"How long we gotta stay here?" Wendy asked. The teacher did not answer.

"She wouldn't say nothin'," said Miguel.

The few who had rushed to the backdoor thinking it was open joined the group standing in front of Ms. Vine.

"Ms. Vine, could you move from the door so we could leave? I'm mad hungry," appealed Andrew, but the teacher did not budge.

"Unless you return to your seats we're not leaving here," the teacher said flatly.

"Let's sit down, son," shouted Felicia, picking up her bag from the floor.

"Come on, let's sit," encouraged Tamika, stepping off with her bag on her back.

"She gettin' tough on us," said Wong, taking his seat with some of the others.

"We gotta stay here for da full twenty minutes?" asked Kemchand, putting his bag on the desk.

"I'll decide on that. Some people are yet to be seated," the teacher stated.

"Sit, y'all," belched Rozern, whose facial muscles tensed.

Students began sitting until the entire class was seated, but some talked squeakily. Ms. Vine made her point. Said she, "Some people are still talking. This class has to be quiet before you leave here."

"I wanna get outta here. I'm hungry, yo. I need to get my food," said Rozern, frowning.

"Stop talking, you idiot," Felicia growled; her face looked rigid and stony.

"You callin' me idiot," shrieked Rozern, pointing at Felicia.

"You wouldn't stop talkin' so we could leave this lousy place," replied Felicia.

"Calm down, yo, calm down, I wanna eat. I got da cramps. My stomach is churning," barked Andrew, turning the peak of his red-and-blue cap to the back of his head.

The class calmed down somewhat after ten minutes had passed. Ms. Vine remained in her position at the door. She looked at her watch a while after. Fifteen minutes had passed. They were fairly quiet, but she maintained her stance. After twenty minutes she said, "You may go." She stepped away from the door. A few students were relieved and a weak smile came across their faces. A number did vent their anger. "Ahhhhh, ahhhhh," they shouted. *Bang, bang, bang.*

They tumbled desks and chairs on the floor followed by expletives as they stormed out the classroom.

"Pick up those chairs and desks," Ms. Vine shouted, moving toward the students.

"I didn't throw down anythin'," said one student.

"I ain't picking up nothin'. I didn't do it," said Miguel, looking up at the teacher as he walked by, leaving the room.

Ms. Vine shook her head and thought aloud, *I should've kept them for twenty-five minutes.* She picked up the desks and chairs but felt in some way she was able to let them know there were consequences for their disruptive behavior. She fixed her class and swept the floor littered with paper, snack food packets, plastic bottles, broken pens and pencils, and candy wrappers. The teacher then headed to her locker, where she removed her bag, took out her purse, locked her locker, and walked out of her room pulling the door behind her, locking it shut. She made her way down to the basement to the teachers' cafeteria.

Chapter 18

Mr. Linsmun pulled his chair, sat, and arranged a few documents on his desk. He thought, *I have to see Mr. James and Mrs. Hutchenson to find out what they're going to discuss at the disciplinary committee meeting tomorrow.* He read two referrals which lay on his desk. Picking up a red ink ballpoint pen, he carefully underlined three statements or sentences in the referrals. He put a weight, a disk-like polished wooden object, on the two forms. He pulled a yellow folder in front of him from the in-tray and opened it. Mr. Linsmun sorted the letters in the folder while he glanced at the contents of some of them. There was a knock on his door. "Come in," said Mr. Linsmun.

"Hi, Mark, how is it? I didn't see you yesterday," said Mr. Eisenburg, who walked into the office and stood in front of the desk.

"I'm good. Only thing, I had it up to my neck yesterday. I've seen so many parents and students, it's unbelievable," replied Mr. Linsmun, looking over his bronze-colored, metal-framed spectacles in speaking with his colleague.

"I know how it goes. Some days could be darn hectic. I see so many of them some days, I want to pull my hair out" concurred Mr. Eisenburg, pushing his hands in his pockets.

"You tell me!" replied Mr. Linsmun, briefly touching his right cheek before settling his arms on his desk.

"I've had a busy day too. Hope it's less busy today," remarked Mr. Eisenburg, cracking a weak smile.

"Well, you know how things could turn in this place."

"I know. Every day there's some fight or problem in the classroom, among these kids."

"The frustration is that you call up parents and guardians and you discuss the matter and make recommendations, and a few days after the students are right in your office again. It's unbelievable."

"It's very agonizing and it's not getting better."

"Makes it tough on us."

"I know. Anyway, see you later."

"Okay, Paul. Thanks for dropping by."

"Don't mention," said Mr. Eisenburg with his matted brown hair. He walked through the door and headed for his office.

Mr. Linsmun glanced at his watch; it was 8:15 a.m. He closed the folder, rose from his seat, put on his coat, reached for the megaphone that stood on a low file cabinet, and made his way through the doorway, pulling the door shut behind him. It was quiet on his floor. He walked along the hallway, came to the exit, and descended the stairs. Reaching the first floor, he pushed the heavy metal door open and entered the yard. The wind was brisk, and the cold was biting, yet the yard was crowded. He pulled up the collar of his coat to cover his neck and pushed his left hand in his coat pocket. He stood close to the building and watched the scene as it unfolded. Other members of staff, including security personnel, had entered the yard from other exits and observed the hub of activities taking place. About five minutes after, Mr. Linsmun moved off. No one gave him any attention.

Cling, cling, cling-cling, cling, cling-cling, cling, cling was the loud sound that came from the building. The football still continued, as did the basketball, baseball, jump rope, and the running around, the hollering, and sitting on the cold concrete and wooden benches. Students still tried to get the balls in the several baskets, others tried to deliver a home run, and still some attempted to get the final jumps on the jump rope.

Mr. Linsmun bellowed into his bullhorn, "It's time to go." A few students began moving toward the building. "Let's move it," shouted Mr. Eisenburg. Many students did not heed the call; they still sauntered, apparently unmindful to leave the yard. In the eastern part of the yard, Mr. Lany shouted into his megaphone, "It's time to go, keep moving." He repeated the same order over and over, but some students were clearly adamant. Assistant Principals Pearson, Tillock, and Ascowitz gave similar orders in other parts of the yard. Some teachers who were in the yard seized the balls and bats from students who ignored the calls to get into the building. In the southern section of the yard, Mrs. Browman had it no easier trying to get the students out of the yard and into the building even though it was a cold and windy morning. It appeared as if the weather did not bother them though the temperature was in the low thirties, just a degree or two above freezing. It took some twelve minutes before the schoolyard was cleared, and the deans and assistant principals began making their way into the building to clear the hallways.

There were disruptions as usual in many classrooms, but the morning went fairly calm with no major upheavals. During the fifth period, Mrs. Hutchenson was informed that she had a seventh-period coverage in class 806 on the second floor. Before the beginning of that period, she left the barely furnished teachers' lounge and made her way to the classroom. As she approached the door, she realized it was not locked but just pulled in and a little ajar. She thought the door should have been locked by the previous teacher or by a teacher with a key to the door. Mrs. Hutchenson pushed the door and entered the classroom. She walked toward the desk, but then she jumped as she turned her head and noticed someone, a male student, whom she figured was a sixth grader from his small stature, though she seldom came to that conclusion in determining a student's grade based on his or her size or build.

Mrs. Hutchenson stopped. Said she, "Why are you here?"

"I came to get my bag. I forgot somethin' in it," answered the short, frail student.

"But this is not your class, and you're not supposed to be in this classroom. How come your bag is here?" the teacher asked, being much concerned that he was alone in the room.

The student walked along the aisle near the closet in approaching the teacher. She looked to see what he had in his hand. It was a bag of chips. Mrs. Hutchenson then approached a partly enclosed area next to the last closet after she noticed a light-blue material about sixteen inches above the floor. She stepped up to the partly enclosed area where teaching materials, books, and equipment were stored and, to her surprise, saw a female student, who appeared to be a sixth grader, sitting in a chair. Said the teacher, with alarm, "What are you doing here, young lady? What the two of you are doing in here?"

With surprise and fear in her eyes, she got up and got out of the partly enclosed area and stood momentarily in front of the teacher and stepped off and walked along the southern passageway alongside the desks and chairs. Mrs. Hutchenson started walking to the door.

Said she, glaring at both students, "Come, let's go to the dean. Which class are you in?"

"I'm in the sixth grade," the female student said. The male student did not answer.

"I asked which class are you in?" the teacher demanded as they got closer to the door. Neither student answered.

As the teacher approached the doorway and entered the hallway with the two students near to her she turned, pulled the door shut, and locked it with her key. She moved off with the two students at her side; suddenly the boy dashed for the stairwell and the girl dashed after him, and they both ran down the stairs. Mrs. Hutchenson ran behind them but abruptly stopped. She said aloud, "I'm not going to run behind you."

A female teacher who just came out of her room to go to the computer lab asked, "What happened? Why you're running?"

Mrs. Hutchenson explained to her that two students were in a classroom that was unlocked and she was taking them to the office when they ran. She went immediately to the sixth grade assistant principal, Mr. Lany, and made a report. He instructed her to make a written report after her seventh-period class and to return to his office so they could find out who were the students. With five minutes to go before the end of the sixth period, Mrs. Hutchenson went to Ms. Cort and explained what occurred. Ms. Cort said she would get behind the matter to locate the two students. After Mrs. Hutchenson's seventh-period coverage, she wrote a report but did not complete it. She then joined Mr. Lany, the sixth grade assistant principal, and Ms. Cort, the sixth grade dean, in conducting a search of all the sixth grade classes. The door of class 601 was opened and the party entered. "Excuse me, Ms. Dunn, we're checking for two students who were out of their classroom during the sixth period," said Mr. Lany.

"Go ahead and check," said the teacher.

Mrs. Hutchenson looked at the students.

Turning to Mrs. Hutchenson, the assistant principal asked, "Have you seen them?"

Mrs. Hutchenson looked around the class, carefully watching the young faces. "No. I haven't seen any of them."

"Okay, thank you, Ms. Dunn. We haven't seen them. And sorry to interrupt your lesson," said Mr. Lany.

"That's okay" answered Ms. Dunn. The three teachers left the class and went over to the next class that was in session but was much disrupted.

Said Mr. Lany, "Sorry to disturb your class, Mrs. Baighman, but we are searching for two students who were out of their class during the sixth period." Students immediately became quiet, and those who were walking around dashed for their seats.

"Go ahead, sir" answered Mrs. Baighman. The assistant principal and the dean stood by the door while the teacher looked into the face of every boy and girl. Meanwhile, the security on the floor was asked to search every area where students who were cutting may be found loitering. Two officers, a male and female, executed the search. They checked stairwells and bathrooms on the first and second floors and had students scurrying out of stairwells. Sixth, seventh, and eighth graders who were in the bathrooms without passes were taken to the deans' offices.

The AP, the dean, and the teacher completed their search, thanked Mrs. Baighman, and left the class without finding the students. They walked from the west along the hallway to the eastern wing, where classes 603 to 607 were located. They entered class 603, asked the teacher's permission, and conducted a search, which left them empty-handed. Thanking the teacher for the permission granted, they exited the room. The party walked over to class 604. Mr. Lany explained that they were searching for two students and that he requested the teacher's permission to conduct the search. The teacher gave the green light, and the search by Mrs. Hutchenson began. She finally saw the two students and indicated that to Mr. Lany.

Said Mr. Lany, as Ms. Cort looked on, "Mrs. Gringburg, we're going to take these two students whom Mrs. Hutchenson identified."

The class was bright-eyed, with heads turning and bobbing, as they wanted to know what was happening.

"Okay, Mr. Lany," responded Mrs. Gringburg. The assistant principal then ordered the two students to leave with them.

Having checked the two students' schedule of classes, Mr. Lany communicated with the teacher of the sixth-period math class, Ms. Austin. Said he, "Ms. Austin, this is Mr. Lany. Kindly come to the office of the sixth grade dean."

"Okay, Mr. Lany" answered Ms. Austin. She cradled the phone and went to Ms. Cort's office.

Said Mr. Lany, "Ms. Austin, could you tell me why Marcelle and Dunley were out of your class?"

Explained Ms. Austin, in a calm tone of voice, "Fifteen minutes before the end of the period Marcelle said she wanted to go to the bathroom, and I gave her permission to go. About three minutes after, Dunley said he wanted to get some water, and I told him no. He then said that his throat was dry and like he was having an asthma attack and wanted water. In becoming concerned I allowed him to get water. Those were the reasons for the students leaving my math class."

"Okay," the assistant principal nodded.

Ms. Austin clasped her hands in front of her as she stood next to Mrs. Hutchenson.

Turning to the students, Mr. Lany said to Dunley, "Do you suffer from asthma?"

"My throat was dry, and I thought I was going to have an asthma attack," replied Dunley without expression.

"Did you ever have an asthma attack before," questioned the assistant principal, looking steadfast at Dunley.

"No, I never had, but I thought I was going to have one," Dunley answered.

"I'm not going to dwell on the health issue right now. Why did you go into room 806?" Mr. Lany asked Dunley.

Dunley answered, "I saw her went into the room, and I went in to see what she was doing."

"Why did you go into that room?" asked Mr. Lany, in questioning Marcelle.

Said she, "I didn't wanna stay in the math class because I felt tired and didn't understand what the teacher was teaching."

"Why were you tired?" asked Ms. Cort, keenly.

"I hada get up to look after my baby sister during da night 'cause she was crying. She would wake up and start cryin' and I would wake up and start shaking her back to sleep. Then she would get up again. Me and my brother took turns," Marcelle said, looking a bit apprehensive.

"Where was your mother?" asked Ms. Cort as she sensed something.

"She hada go to work," Marcelle said in a soft but cracking tone of voice.

"Dunley, stand in the hallway for a moment," said Ms. Cort as she followed him to the door. "Don't you move from there." Dunley did not answer but stood in the hall. The hallway was clear except for the presence of a security officer who had just arrived on the floor to do duty.

Said Ms. Cort politely, "Officer Pandang, could you have an eye on him for me. I'm attending to a matter in here."

Replied Officer Pandang, "Certainly. I'll take care of him. He wouldn't leave here."

"Thank you," Ms. Cort said with a brief smile.

"You're welcome," the officer said. He watched Dunley. Dunley watched him. The officer moved off.

Ms. Cort turned, closed the door behind her, and walked back to where she previously stood. Officer Pandang paced the main hall.

"Where does your mother work?" asked the assistant principal as Mrs. Hutchenson and Ms. Austin listened to the questioning.

"She look after an old person in Queens," she said.

"Where is your father?" asked Mr. Lany, tilting his head toward his right shoulder.

The student hesitated then said in a low-key tone, "I don't know. He left."

"Do you know how long?" asked the AP, trying to assess the home situation.

She looked to the ceiling, pursed her lips, and then said, "Long now, 'bout a year."

"I see," uttered the assistant principal, nodding his head.

"How old is your brother?" asked the dean with much concern.

"He's sixteen," Marcelle said, passing her right hand over her hair, tied in a pony.

"And he helps you with your baby sister when your mother is at work during the night?" asked the dean, her hazel eyes fixed on the student.

"Yeah. He sleeps deep. I gotta call him or go over to da next bedroom and push him before he wakes. Then he would come over and pick up the baby and shake her to sleep. Sometimes he don't come over and I gotta shake her 'cause she cries loud," said the student.

"Okay, young lady," said the dean.

"We got to get her mother up here," remarked the AP. "We have to refer her to the counselor and social worker, and they would take it from there. I would monitor how things unfold."

"Definitely," concurred the dean as she walked to the door. She pushed it open.

"Come in," she ordered Dunley, who leaned against the wall with a worried expression on his face. He looked up at the dean and stepped off into her office.

Looking up the hallway, she said, "Thank you, Officer Pandang."

"Don't mention, Ms. Cort," Officer Pandang answered. She waved at him, turned, and walked back to where she stood

Turning to the male student, the assistant principal said, "Why did you follow her into the room?"

With fear in his eyes, Dunley said, "I wanted to know why she went into the room so I pushed it and went in too."

"What did you tell her when you got in the room?" asked the assistant principal with his eyes fixed on those of Dunley.

"I ain't tell her nothin'. All I did was look and see her sitting with her hands to her head," said the student.

"What you did after that?" questioned Ms. Cort, looking at him steadfast.

"I walk away and started eating my chips which I took from my pocket," said Dunley, knitting his brow.

"Did he tell you anything?" the dean asked the young lady.

"No. I just looked up and saw him and I continue holdin' my head," Marcelle said, meekly.

"Do you have a headache?" asked Mr. Lany.

"Just a little," Marcelle answered. "My head hurt me sometimes when I don't get to sleep much."

"I'll send you to the nurse shortly," said Mr. Lany.

"So why did you tell me you came to get your bag because you forgot something in it?" asked Mrs. Hutchenson, watching keenly at the male student.

"'Cause I didn't know what to say and I was scared," answered Dunley, holding his hands behind his back.

"Then you ran and she ran after you when I told you we were going to the dean," stated the teacher.

"I didn't wanna get in trouble," Dunley uttered, looking scared.

"Now you're in more trouble," said Mrs. Hutchenson, removing her spectacles from her face.

"No, I didn't do anythin'," he lamented, turning away from facing the teacher.

Said the assistant principal, "We're going to give both of you two days of in-house suspension for entering an unoccupied classroom without being authorized to do so. You had no right to be in that room. I'm going to have the parents of both of you up here tomorrow. Marcelle, if you didn't feel well and could not concentrate on your work because you lacked sleep, you should've asked your teacher to go to the nurse. You just can't walk into a vacant classroom like that. Suppose one of the older and aggressive students had seen you walk into that vacant room and had walked in after you and hurt you, then you would have put the school into a lot of trouble. You cannot do that, young lady. You ought not to be in any unsupervised classroom alone. And, Dunley, those instructions apply to you, too. You cannot enter a vacant classroom. I have to see your parents up here."

"No, my parents can't come. They at work." retorted Dunley.

"They have to come," said the dean with a sternness in her voice.

"Damnnn," shouted the young man, jerking his head.

"Don't 'damn' in here," said Ms. Cort flatly.

"Marcelle, go to the nurse and return when she is finished with you," instructed Mr. Lany. Marcelle left for the nurse's office.

Said the AP, "Mrs. Hutchenson, you would complete the report by including their names."

"Yes, I'll do that," replied Mrs. Hutchenson.

Mr. Lany then said, "Ms. Austin, thank you, and you may return to your class."

"Thank you," Ms. Austin said and left the dean's office where the matter was investigated.

Turning to Mrs. Hutchenson, the assistant principal mentioned, "We definitely have to keep a keen eye on these students. Thanks for your help in this matter, and I'll collect the report before you leave."

"You're welcome, Mr. Lany, and I'll work on it right away," replied Mrs. Hutchenson as she turned and headed for the door of the dean's office.

"Ms. Cort, you're going to take care of the rest, and let me know how things unfold when the parents come up to see you tomorrow. I'll possibly sit in on the meetings if I'm not otherwise occupied," mentioned the assistant principal affably.

"I'll handle the matter," said Ms. Cort with a faint smile.

"Okay," answered Mr. Lany as he walked through the door. "Young man, sit in that chair until the dean is ready for you." Dunley moved toward one of the chairs and sat, placing his backpack on his thighs.

Ms. Cort finished signing off on some forms in a file. She stamped them with the school stamp before reaching for the intercom on her desk. Said she to the student while he sat in the chair, "Is your mother or father at home now?"

"No. They at work," answered Dunley, shaking his head.

Ms. Cort called the office and asked one of the two office assistants to bring up the emergency cards for class 604. Within a few minutes, the cards were delivered to the dean. Ms. Cort sorted through the cards and took out those belonging to Dunley and Marcelle. She read the information on the two cards and then picked up the phone and dialed a contact number. She got on to the workplace of Dunley's mother. Someone answered the phone, "Hello, how can I help you?"

"Good morning, can you put me on to Mrs. Meckford," said Ms. Cort, in a soft but firm tone of voice.

"Hold on, just a second," the person at the other end of the line said.

Seconds after, a clear and penetrating voice said, "Good morning, this is Mrs. Meckford. How can I help you?"

"Good morning, Mrs. Meckford. This is Ms. Cort, the sixth grade dean of Jones High School, and I'm calling about a matter pertaining to your son, Dunley," said Ms. Cort firmly.

"What happened?" inquired Mrs. Meckford with concern in her voice.

"Your son, Dunley, was out of his class and found himself in a classroom that he was not authorized to be—" said the dean.

"Did he leave his class without telling his teacher or asking permission?" interrupted Mrs. Meckford, her voice becoming softer.

"He got permission but another matter resulted. He was not supposed to be in an unoccupied classroom," stated Ms. Cort courtly.

"Oh my goodness, what happened!" exclaimed Dunley's mother, wanting to know what transpired.

"I would therefore like you to come into the school tomorrow to discuss the seriousness of this matter," said the dean.

"I'll come up there in the morning," Mrs. Meckford agreed.

"Thank you," said Ms. Cort. She cradled the phone. She flipped the cards and placed Marcelle's emergency card in front of her. She checked the number and called Marcelle's home. Fortunately, her mother was at home. The dean explained the reason for the call and invited her to come to the school the next day. Ms. Canter said that she would come to the school during the afternoon session, to which the dean agreed. Ms. Cort hung up the phone and said, "Young man, kindly go to in-house. Take this form." Dunley took the form from her.

"Your mother will be up here tomorrow," uttered Ms. Cort.

"Whyyy? Why you call my mother?" Dunley grumbled, picking up his bag.

"Go to in-house," the dean firmly instructed.

Dunley frowned and left the office bound for in-house. Quite a while after Dunley had left, Marcelle arrived in Ms. Cort's office after spending some time in the nurse's office.

Said the dean to Marcelle, "I called your mother and she would be here tomorrow. Kindly go to in-house. Give this form to the teacher who is there."

The young lady took the form, turned, and walked out of the office, bound for in-house. During the remainder of the last period, Mrs. Hutchenson completed the report and handed it to Mr. Lany in his office.

Chapter 19

Mr. Linsmun and the other deans and APs were having it a bit quiet for the afternoon since they were not called for any major incidents. It appeared that many students were sitting peacefully or were trying to do some work or yet were engaged in doing something of interest to them, though not necessarily schoolwork, but did it in a subdued manner. It seemed as if it took forever before the bell rang dismissing school at 3:00 p.m. As usual, there was the mad rush by many to get out of the classroom but not the hallways where they congregate to meet their friends and engage in light banter, spilling expletives indiscriminately without regard for anyone or authority. Some days it was more hectic than others to clear the hallways, and it placed a mighty strain on the security personnel and administration to clear the building. But the building was cleared quickly, and Mr. Linsmun and his counterparts breathed a sigh of relief at the end of the day.

With the chairs on desks, Ms. Hatmill exited the building, got to her car, and drove to Queens; she took the Brooklyn–Queens Expressway. The traffic flowed, but she felt very heavy in heart as she drove. She thought about the tough day she had at work, the way her students had behaved that taxed her physically. She felt drained from the constant problems in her classroom and her being unable to teach a lesson and teach it effectively without disruption. Within an hour she was home. She parked her gray car, picked up her bags with books and papers, and headed to the door of her home. Weighed down with emotion, she entered the living room, dropped her bags on the floor, and slumped in a soft cushioned armchair. Her oval face with high cheekbones was drawn.

"Good night, Mom," Ms. Hatmill said as her mother, a plump, short, brown-skinned lady with long wavy hair, came into the living room from the kitchen, where she was preparing dinner.

"Good night, honey," Mrs. Joyce Hatmill said, leaning over to hug her distraught daughter. "How was your day? You look so worn and tired."

"It wasn't easy, Mom. It was one of my worst days. The students would not sit, they would not stop running around, they would not work. It was unbelievable."

"They were so terrible today? None of them did any work, Joanann?" asked Mrs. Hatmill, standing in front of her daughter.

"About half the class did work. The others were just out of control. I can't take this anymore, oooh, oooh, oooh . . ." Joanann cried, tears rolling down her dark, smooth cheeks.

Her mother sat beside her and placed her arm around her shoulder as she sobbed, overcome by sadness over the way her working life was going.

"Don't take it personal, Joanann. Talk to your colleagues and ask them to help. Talk to your students and let them know what they are doing is not right. Do things differently, get them more involved, and try to give them some bit of reward, some form of incentive for things they do and do well. I know it is hard, my child, but try different methods and see if things would be better. I'm not in the business of teaching, but I was a parent of school-age children. Talk to their parents. Get them involved, and I'm sure conditions in your classroom would be better. Don't give up on what you're doing, on what you really wanted to do and studied and trained for. It's going to be hard but just persevere. Just hang in there."

Joanann wiped away the tears with her bare hands. Said she, "Okay, Mom, I'm going to try harder and get some help. Thanks,

Mom." Mrs. Hatmill squeezed her daughter's shoulder and touched her face lightly in giving her assurance.

"Come, eat some dinner. Your father would be in shortly. He called just before you came in," encouraged Mrs. Hatmill.

"I'll go have a shower, by which time Dad would be home, and we'll have dinner together," Joanann answered, rising from the wooden armchair. She headed for her bedroom. Joanann was the youngest of four siblings. The twenty-three-year-old had recently joined the staff of the school. Mr. Hatmill arrived home, and Joanann sat with her parents and ate a tasty and satisfying dinner over which she related some of her difficulties to her father.

"The day was so difficult. Half the class was out of control. They were running and jumping and fighting. The students would not listen. It was so difficult to teach my lessons," Ms. Hatmill described.

Her father comforted and encouraged her. Said Mr. Hatmill, reassuringly, "Joanna, I know it's tough. These children could pose a real problem but be strong. Don't let them force you out of what you're being called to do. You're going to be constantly in my prayers."

"Thank you, Dad," said Joanna, looking over at her father, a man with strong faith and a believer in change for the better.

"Things would change, things would be better, and you will enjoy it right at that school," her father said prophetically.

Ms. Vine drove to her Staten Island home. She crossed the Verrazano Bridge and made her way along the Staten Island Expressway and exited on Victory Boulevard. She felt so irritated and frustrated as she drove. The disgust was seen on her face as she could not resist thinking about the horrible day she had at school. Parking her car in the driveway behind that of her sister's, she grabbed her two bags with teaching material and partly marked papers in addition to her personal effects and hurried to the door. She inserted the keys and stumbled through the door. She placed her bags on a nearby small table, kicked off her shoes, and headed for the sofa. A feeling of exhaustion overcame her. She needed to relax for a few minutes.

She shared the one-family home with an older sister who has owned the premises for almost ten years. Her sister, Betty, had just come downstairs after having a nap since she was on two weeks of vacation leave and had decided to remain home and rest rather than travel as she had done over the years. Betty emerged from the kitchen and saw Nia lying on the burgundy sofa.

"What happened? You look so drained like you had an awful day," Betty said, looking down at her sister.

Nia shook her head and said, "It was another awful day. The kids were out of their minds. They were off the wall. I could hardly get through half the lesson much less to finish it."

"Didn't you get some help, maybe, from the dean or a supervisor to bring some order to the class?" asked Betty, putting her hand to her face.

"That's not working. As soon as they leave the students start again," said Nia as she turned her head to look at her sister.

"Then you have to find a way to deal with that situation. It's wearing you down. Your face looks haggard and you're losing weight. You set up late at nights doing work and hardly getting much rest and then have to go through all of that fatigue during the day. It's not good for you. You got to devise some way to reach out to the kids. Get them more involved in what you're doing," stated Betty.

"I do all of that. I give them incentives. I allow them to be more engaged. But it's a few of them who start the disruption, and then the others join in," interrupted Nia. "It's getting to me. I'm so exhausted. You shout until you're tired. I'm even losing my voice."

"Talk with some of the other teachers, and see what tips they could give you so you could control the class better. It's frustrating to do all of that work at weekends, preparing your lesson plans for the week and all the other things you do and then you cannot get through with your work. It could be disappointing. And I imagine how you feel," Betty empathized.

Water settled in Nia's eyes. She rubbed her nose and sniffed. She put her head on one of the cushions and pushed back the auburn hair that fell on her face. The tears trickled down her gaunt cheeks, and she pursed her thin lips, which did not even have on the veil of lipstick that she colored them with when she left for work.

"I'm sorry. Take some rest and compose yourself. I know it's difficult. It's a hard job. There's no doubt about that," Betty said and turned away. "Your dinner is still hot. I cooked before taking a nap."

Nia did not answer but scratched her right temple. She leaned over, pulled a piece of tissue from her bag, and wiped her eyes. She turned and curled up on the sofa. She was too tired to even get up; she just wanted to relax on the sofa for another thirty minutes or more before going to her room with her bags.

Her sister returned and said, "My job is hectic but I don't go through what you have to deal with every day. And I guess you're not the only one who goes through that ordeal every day."

"No, there're other teachers who experience similar situations every day as well. They have to constantly call security to take some of the students to the dean for fighting in the class, playing in the classroom or taking the things of other students," related Nia.

"I understand. Take a little rest right there and revive yourself. I'm going up to my room. When you're finished taking dinner, you could join me in my room if you feel like," said Betty, rubbing her younger sister's shoulder before walking off and climbing the stairs to her bedroom.

"Okay," Nia murmured. She soon fell into a deep sleep.

The parents of Dunley and Marcelle arrived at school the next day. Mrs. Meckford arrived at 9:00 a.m. with her son at her side. She signed in with security at the front desk, was given a visitor's pass, and directed to the main office from where she made her way to the dean's office across the hallway. She knocked on the door. "Come in," was the voice that came from the room. She stepped into the office. "Good morning," said Mrs. Meckford, swallowing very hard. "I'm Mrs. Meckford, Dunley's mother."

"Good morning, Mrs. Meckford. I'm Ms. Cort and I'm the sixth grade dean. Pleased to meet you," said Ms. Cort, stretching forth her hand and shaking that of her visitor.

"Pleased to meet you, too," answered Mrs. Meckford, with Dunley standing next to her.

"You may have a seat," offered Ms. Cort, gesturing to one of the two chairs in front of her desk.

"Thank you," said Mrs. Meckford.

"You're welcome," said the dean.

Her visitor weakly smiled.

"I did not want to inconvenience you to come up here to see me. I could have dealt with the matter without you being present, but in all fairness to both parents, though the other parent would not be aware of your visit to the school, I decided to summon you to a meeting since the matter relates to both students. Your son was out of the classroom. He told the teacher he wanted water, that his throat was dry, and that he was about to have an asthma attack. He ended up in an unoccupied classroom following a female student who had gone in there because she said she was not feeling well and had a headache. Do you know of your son having an asthma condition?" asked Ms. Cort, leaning forward in her chair and placing her elbows on the light-brown desk, stained with coffee spills and ink marks.

"No, he has no asthma condition. Why did you lie to the teacher?" his mother asked, looking at him straight in his eyes.

"She didn't want me to get water. I was thirsty," Dunley said, his eyes widening.

"But you don't lie to your teacher, and you had no right to go into that room behind the girl," Mrs. Meckford scolded, pressing her lips tightly together.

"I ain't tell her nothin'. I just wanted to see what she was goin' in there for. If to take anybody's thing," Dunley uttered.

"You had no right," his mother said firmly.

"Let me just say, firstly, that Dunley lied to get out of the classroom and secondly, he should not have gone into an unoccupied classroom with a female student or behind a female student. We do not allow students to be in classrooms by themselves unsupervised. Because of his actions he's given two days of in-house suspension," the dean said, shaking her head to underscore her point.

Mr. Lany, who sat nearby, said, "We strictly do not allow students to remain unsupervised in any classroom. Anything could happen negatively, that could put the school in such an unpleasant situation, that it does not want to be in."

"I understand what you're saying, sir, and I'm totally annoyed with Dunley. Where would he be during the in-house, and would he have any work to do and homework?" questioned Mrs. Meckford, concerned about the instruction and learning opportunity provided to her son while in that environment.

"He would be in a special room that is used for that purpose. And, of course, he would have work to do and would be given homework. Current work would be provided by his teachers," Ms. Cort said.

"I really feel upset by what Dunley did," said his mother, looking at her son with pain in her eyes.

Said Ms. Cort, "Thank you for coming, Mrs. Meckford, and I'd like you to have a serious talk with Dunley. He cannot lie to teachers to gain permission to leave the classroom. Also being in a vacant classroom is a serious matter. Anything could happen when he's there that could create lots of problems for us. I do not expect a recurrence of his action. Any further disregard for the rules would result in heavier punishment. Again, thanks for coming."

"Thank you, Ms. Cort," Mrs. Meckford said, rising from her seat, shaking the dean's hand, and leaving her office.

Ms. Cort wrote a note and gave it to Dunley. She instructed him to take it to the in-house suspension room and give it to the teacher in charge of that unit.

Marcelle's mother did not arrive at the school until after one o'clock. She checked in with security, stopped in the main office, and was directed to the dean's office. She introduced herself and was offered a seat by the sixth grade dean. Mr. Lany had a meeting and could not be present for the second meeting with the parent.

Said Ms. Cort, "Ms. Canter, your daughter was out of her class. She claimed she wanted to go to the bathroom but instead entered an unoccupied classroom and sat there. A male student from her class entered after her, claiming he wanted to see what she was doing or going to do. It is unauthorized for students to do that. Students are prohibited from being in classrooms without a teacher. If another older and aggressive student had seen her alone in there and had gone in there and hurt her, then she would have put the school in problems."

"Why you did that, Marcelle? Why?" asked her mother, becoming agitated.

"I didn't feel well," answered Marcelle, looking at her mother with distended eyes.

"But if you didn't feel well, why didn't you let your teacher know?" Ms. Canter questioned.

Marcelle's face looked blank and she did not answer.

Said Ms. Cort, "She further said she had to babysit her baby sister during the nights while you were away at work."

"Yes, I have to work. I work at nights sometimes. It's hard. I know I have to leave them alone, but I don't have any choice. I don't have anyone to stay with them." The mother broke down and cried. "Oooh, oooh, oooh, hu, hu . . ."

The dean felt concerned. "I understand," she said.

After the mother had composed herself from a bout of sobbing, she said, "Their father had become aggressive. He'd drink heavily especially when he got pay at weekend. He cursed me out, even the children, when he gets drunk. He gives me no money. I have to work hard to pay the school fees, the rent, and upkeep them."

Marcelle bowed her head as her mother cried and talked about the behavior of her father. She did not dislike her father. She thought of him much and wished she could see him even as her mother was angry with him.

Said Ms. Cort, "She said her father left. How long now and where did he go?"

"Yes, he left about a year ago. I heard he was in Florida, then a relative said she saw him in California. He hasn't supported the children since he left," uttered Ms. Canter. "Oooh, oooh . . ." She cried again. The dean pulled tissue from a box on her desk, reached over, and offered it to Ms. Canter, who wiped her eyes.

"Okay, Ms. Canter, I'll refer Marcelle to the counselor and social worker. I'm going to seek some further advice as to how you could get help. However, Marcelle will spend two days in in-house suspension for going into that unoccupied room without permission. It's a serious matter for students, especially females, to go into a classroom that is vacant. I'll advise you to have a serious talk with her. We are definitely against students being in unoccupied and unsupervised classrooms. Marcelle cannot break the rules. Any further disregard for the rules on her part will result in her being given a heavier punishment," Ms. Cort stated, interlocking her fingers as her arms rested on her desk.

"I understand," responded Ms. Canter, biting her lips. Marcelle remained mute.

"I would shortly contact the counselor and social worker, who would look into this domestic situation, okay," Ms. Cort said, leaning back in her chair.

"Aright," Marcelle's mother said, shaking her head, drying her eyes, and wiping her cheeks with the tissue.

"They'll let you know what progress is made in getting you information so you'd know where to go to get help," the dean told Marcelle's mother. "That's all for now. You'll hear from us with regards to help and talk to Marcelle so she'll know that certain things she cannot do. Okay, thanks."

"Thank you," Ms. Canter said, rising from her seat and zipping up her black, hooded jacket, her nails short and clipped and manicured with a natural nail polish that began to flake.

"You're welcome," replied Ms. Cort, an expression of concern covered her full face with a slight double chin which began to show recently, perhaps an indication that she was gaining weight, which she resented but seemed to do nothing about over a considerable length of time.

"Bye," Ms. Canter said, dragging her feet as she slowly left the office with a look of deep thought on her face.

"Bye," answered Ms. Cort, picking up a blue-barreled, black-ink ballpoint pen with which she wrote a referral for two days of in-house suspension.

Marcelle sat meekly in the chair without a word uttered. She twirled a colored pencil with artificial colored feathers between her fingers and bobbed her head as if she were listening to some pop music.

"Take this to Mr. Bergen. You'll spend two days in in-house," the dean stretched forth her hand in giving Marcelle the referral. She got up from the chair, took the paper, and briskly walked out the dean's office in her close-fitting blue jeans, white sneakers, and gray hooded sweater, bound for her destination. Ms. Cort then wrote in a file and logbook the nature of the discussions with both parents and the time of occurrence.

Chapter 20

In the teachers' lounge, teachers sat and marked papers, prepared lesson plans, prepared projects, or just relaxed from a hectic and tumultuous period in the classroom. They voiced their disapproval that the discipline problem at the school seems to prolong unabated.

"I'm so upset," said Ms. Hatmil, scratching her head for no apparent reason. "Miguelina threw a book that hit Hardy in his back. Hardy picked up the book and hurled it at Miguelina, who luckily got out of the way. If not, it would have caught her. Miguelina rushed Hardy, and they started punching and headlocking each other. I got Officer Morgan to take them out of my room and take them to the dean's office. Like everybody else, I'm tired and disgusted with their behavior. Your lesson would be going fine, and suddenly Miguelina and Hardy would start acting up. If it's not the two of them, it's Filond, Dessin, Mercedes, and Lam, and if it's not them it's Jorend, Marjo, and Akashia."

Opined Mr. Wren, "It seems like this is not going to end anytime soon. It's the same students every time. A parent called me to find out what is happening with discipline at the school, as her son is encountering problems with students in his class. I told her we have some students who create problems every day. I said if her son is having problems with any of the students, she should come in to the school and discuss the matter with the dean or assistant principal."

"To deal with this problem I think parents have to be involved. It's only when there's a problem that you see them up here," voiced Ms. Vine, shaking her head.

"It's quite a while since we haven't had a parent–teacher's meeting to discuss this escalating problem," said Ms. Vivehouse, looking up from the paper she was marking.

Joined in Ms. Dunn, "Is the PTA still in operation? I haven't heard anything about it for more than a year now."

"But when there's a meeting, just a few parents turn up. This school has over a thousand students and less than fifty parents, far less, arrive at the meetings," stated Mr. Howard, turning the newspapers in front of him.

"If we had those meetings, I figure more parents would be aware of what's taking place in school, how these students behave, and something might have been done about it," said Ms. Dunn.

"I think we need new leadership in the parent–teacher association so that different measures could be put in place, um, implemented so that this problem of indiscipline is rectified," uttered Ms. Vivehouse, propping her chin with her right hand.

"Some new approaches should be undertaken to get parents to come out in large numbers. Put an ad, an advertisement, on the TV stressing the urgency and importance of the meeting. At least we'll be reaching many more parents," expressed Mr. Wren, clasping his hands.

"Do you think that would work? Would it be effective?" asked Mrs. Baighman, who sat at another table nearby. She, too, was severely affected by the adverse behavior of students in the classroom.

"Yes, I think it would work. It would be very effective since many more parents would be reached, and the word would pass around and get to those who didn't see the ad. Parents do know each other from the neighborhood, and they would tell each other. Also, they should continue to give students letters to take home, urging parents to come out to such meetings," declared Mr. Wren, cracking his fingers.

"Most of the students don't take the letters home, you know that. Only a few of them do. You find the letters and other notices given to them in the compartments under their desks and on the floor. You see it, Mr. Wren. They litter the floor with the handouts and even make paper balls and pelt each other with them," retorted Mrs. Baighman to the suggestion of sending letters home to parents. "Some parents don't even look at the TV channels.

"We have to start somewhere, Mrs. Baighman," exclaimed Mr. Wren.

"Yes, we have to start somewhere, but I think the administration ought to be more aggressive in dealing with the issue, which is getting out of control. Mr. Cottle has to be aggressive and hold both students and parents accountable for what is going on in the school," said Mrs. Baighman, as she sorted some marked papers in front of her

"I understand what you're saying, but this matter was brought up at previous staff meetings. Teachers spoke out about what is happening in the school: the disruptive behavior of some students in each class, from grades six to twelve, and the difficulty of teaching a lesson uninterruptedly, but what has come of it? The same behavior continues to plague us," said Mr. Wren, who glanced at his watch, noted the time, and gathered his papers, books, and pen. "See you later in class 603. Don't forget we have staff development session after school."

"Oh, yes, I almost forgotten," answered Mrs. Baighman, laughing briefly.

Cling, cling, cling . . . The bell rang. Teachers who had homeroom made their way to their classrooms. The hallway was teeming with traffic again. Students slowly proceeded to their homerooms. After ten minutes, the bell rang again, and students bailed out the classrooms as if they were late for an appointment. Shortly after, teachers and administrative staff hurried to class 603. Mr. Cottle addressed the faculty, and minutes later, the session began. Mrs. Browman conducted the session that dealt with planning and curricula.

At around 9:15 a.m., a student of Mr. Russo's 904 art class arrived and gave him a late pass collected from the security officer at the desk at the main door. Mr. Russo read it while he checked artwork hurriedly done by two female students. He returned the work to both students, pointing out their flaws so they could improve the quality of work they presented. Looking around the class, he noticed that other students were busy working on their art projects. Returning to his desk with the late pass, he changed the mark on the class attendance form from absence to late. Seconds after, a female student, Abigail, arrived late and gave the late pass to the teacher, who made the changes on the attendance form. Just as he was finished, a female student approached the desk and submitted her artwork. He took the work, glanced at it, and made some suggestions about the way she could enhance her painting by using oil paint; he then returned the work to her. No sooner than Shaney moved away from the desk, another female student, Camleta, arrived late. It was 9:20 a.m. when she arrived and gave the teacher the late pass.

"Why are you so late, young lady," Mr. Russo asked, looking up at her from his desk.

"I woke up late and I missed the bus. I had to wait another fifteen minutes before another bus came," Camleta replied with a weak smile.

"You have to get up early," advised the teacher.

"I got up early but I fell back to sleep," Camleta answered, walking toward her seat.

Picking up the attendance from his desk, he checked for the student's name and made the change from absence to late when he heard a sudden yell. Looking up, he saw about eight students sitting in a circle hitting a paper ball from one person to the other. Each student tried eagerly to hit the paper ball to the next student. There was much laughter as the ball was hit around the circle. "To me, hit it to me, Allan," called out Terence in glee.

"Over here," Cleopatra shouted, her arms flailing in the air. Mandy struck the paper ball, and it zoomed past to Wanda. She struck it with force, "Ply" and "Swish!" It fled to Gerald.

"Wow," Wanda shrieked, pumping her arms above her shoulders.

"Over here," Terence shouted. Gerald hit the paper ball, and it went to Terence. Terence slammed it to Cleopatra. She hit and missed.

"No, damn," Cleopatra yelled as the ball fell on the floor. Allan scrambled for the ball as Cleopatra tried to grab it from the floor. Allan had the ball.

"Cut it!" Mr. Russo snarled. "I made a note of those who're not working. I'm not going to talk to you again. I hope you're thinking about your grades."

"I got it," Allan laughed broadly. He hit it to Mandy, who struck it to Gerald.

"Yes," Mandy yelled, rocking her shoulders in a sort of jig. The hitting of the paper ball continued for a while, and the behavior became uncontrollable whereby the students began throwing or pelting the paper ball at each other. Another two or three students joined in, and the paper throwing became more aggressive. Students ripped loose-leaf paper from their binders and yanked pages from their notebooks, crumpled them into balls, and hurled them at each other.

Allan opened his binder and pulled two pages from it.

"Gimme a page," shouted Gerald, his body nimble with excitement. He grabbed the page, crumpled it, and threw it at Mandy. "Yeah, yeah," he shouted.

Turning around, Mandy said, "Sh—t."

A paper ball hit Terence in his head as he tore pages from his notebook. "Hey," he yelled as he crumpled the pages in his hand into a ball. He hurled it at Cleopatra. It hit her in her head. She sneered at Terence, "You bitch." She ripped pages from her binder and charged after Terence while crumpling them into a ball. Terence ran among desks and chairs in the art room with Cleopatra pursuing him. She unleashed her missile. It struck Terence in his back. "Yeah, I gotcha," Cleopatra bellowed with a wide grin.

With many notebooks ripped apart and binders left void of pages, Terence rushed to a nearby closet. He pulled some old newspapers from it, crushed them into a ball, and blasted Octavia, another student, with it. "Sh—t, son," Octavia hollered. Wanda, Mandy, and Gerald dashed to the closet. They pulled newspapers and magazines from it, rolled them into balls, and threw them at the others. A section of the floor was a mess with paper balls, newspapers, and magazines strewn all over.

Barked Mr. Russo, his eyes bulging, "You're not going to wreck this room with those paper balls. You know what, I'm going to call some homes right now."

He whipped his cell phone from the case attached to the belt around his waist and edged back to his desk where he collected a list with names and phone numbers. Phone numbers of homes and workplaces. Immediately, he began calling parents.

Said he, as he reached the home of Terence, "Good morning, are you Ms. Elliot."

"Yes, I am, and who's calling?" Ms. Elliot asked, her voice serene and polite.

"I'm Mr. Russo, your son's art teacher of Jones High School. I'm calling to complain that Terence is very much out of control. He's out of his seat, he did no work, and he's throwing paper balls at other students and running in the room right now. He pulled newspapers and magazines from a closet, crushed them into paper balls, and hurled them at other students. He is not listening. He is off the wall, and his behavior is quite unacceptable."

"That's what Terence is doing in your class, sir?" asked Ms. Elliot, somewhat dubiously.

"Yes, that's what he's doing right now. I spoke to the students, including Terence, who are running and jumping and throwing paper balls at each other," explained the teacher.

"I can't believe this. Could you put him on the phone, please," Ms. Elliot asked.

"Yes, I could," Mr. Russo answered. "Terence, come here. Your mother is on the phone."

"You call my mom?" questioned Terence, staring at Mr. Russo.

"Yes," Mr. Russo said, firmly

"Why?" asked Terence, quite upset.

"She wants to talk to you," uttered Mr. Russo, giving the phone to Terence.

Terence took the phone and put it to his ear. "Yes," he said.

"Terence, that is what you're doing in class, throwing paper balls at other students, pulling newspapers and magazines from closets, crumpling them into paper balls and throwing them at others, and not doing any work. This is what I send you to school for? To play in class and waste your time. Behaving as if you're crazy. I'm going to deal with you when you come home. All privileges cut," Ms. Elliot railed.

"But it wasn't I alone throwing paper balls. They throw it at me, and I throw it back," Terence related, frowning.

"If you were working, no one would throw anything at you," said his mother courtly.

"It wasn't my fault," Terence appealed.

"I'm finished talking to you. Let me talk to your teacher," Ms. Elliot said, feeling very irritable.

"Here, she wants to talk to you," Terence said, returning the phone to Mr. Russo.

"Yes, Ms. Elliot," answered Mr. Russo.

"I spoke to him, and I'm going to deal with him when he gets home," stated Ms. Elliot somewhat apologetically.

"Thank you, Ms. Elliot," said Mr. Russo, feeling a bit satisfied that he got through to a parent.

He looked at the paper on the desk and dialed another number. He spoke to four more parents, three at home and one at work, and left messages on the answering services of those whom he did not contact. Some he failed to reach because their phones were disconnected. As a result of the calls he made, the tone of the class immediately changed. Students took their seats and began working. There was some amount of quiet talk among the students, but the horseplay promptly ceased, making it possible for instruction to take place.

Mariam worked on her language arts, completed the book the class was required to read, did the factorization in math, studied the pulmonary system in life science, and sharpened her skills in computers despite the great amount of disruption in the classes involving fights among students and incessant talking and yelling. The last period in her class was hectic with all the noise and distraction from students as the teacher made a great effort to get the class engaged in work.

With the sound of the bell at three o'clock, at the end of homeroom, Mariam grabbed her bag and made her way to the door. She hurried down the stairwell and darted through the door. She stopped momentarily on the sidewalk, made an about-face, and looked at the door, expecting to see her cousin leaving the building. Students rushed out the building. Some made their way to the yard shortly after, mainly the male students from the junior school, and some from the senior school to play basketball and baseball.

As Mariam edged along the sidewalk, looking over her shoulder a few times to see her cousin, making her way to the bus stop, a silver sports car pulled up on the block next to the school. Two young men in their early twenties got out of the vehicle. The driver closed his door, but the passenger side door remained open. The driver walked to the back and on to the sidewalk. He and his friend sported colorful baseball caps: the driver a red. his friend a green. The driver wore a brown, hip-length leather coat while his friend wore a black. Gold chains hung around their necks with the oval and star pendulum resting on their chests. Gold nugget rings adorned almost each finger. Baggy jeans sagged below their hips. One wore a tan construction boots while the other wore blue sneakers. Heavy pulsating music blared from the cabin and trunk of the car. It was a popular hip-hop tune. One of the young men sat on the bonnet of the sporty car while the other leaned against the front of the vehicle. They moved their upper body to the rhythm of the music and in particular the beat.

Students walked along the sidewalk. Mariam increased her stride as she expected to get the bus soon. She pulled her jacket closer to her and zipped it as she felt the cold air. She looked back once more and thought, *Has Shureen left already?* She stood for about two minutes, and Shureen did not appear. Mariam settled her backpack on her back and walked off. She hurried to the bus stop.

Another shiny sports car, a hot red, pulled up with a *screeech* on the block obliquely opposite the school, and three young men between the ages of twenty and twenty-five disembarked the vehicle. The taller of the three, who appeared to be the youngest, wore a heavy black coat, with a mixture of brown and tan fur around the collar, which fit him just below the waist. A blue sweater he wore under his open coat. Close-fitting blue jeans, with a boot cut, he donned and walked with a swagger in his black sneakers to the back of the car. He leaned against the trunk of the automobile. He pulled a packet of Benson and Hedges from the pocket of his coat and flicked a stalk in his mouth. The lower part of his tan or peach index and middle fingers were brown from constantly holding the butt of the cigarettes he smoked. The oldest of the group sported a brown leather jacket and tan denim jeans with tan construction boots. He too swayed to the back of the sports car and gave his counterpart a high-five. "Son, there's a lot of shorties passing dis afternoon," said the older guy with a floss of red hair falling on his square shoulders.

"You wanna hook up with one?" asked the youngest.

"You bet. These chicks look good," replied the eldest.

Eleventh and twelfth graders passed by. Many of them, the young ladies, donned close-fitting black and blue jeans. Some wore their jackets open, beneath which were colorful jerseys and sweaters in blue, purple, orange, green, yellow, pink, and red. The young ladies passed; they were blacks, whites, Hispanics, and Asians of various hues and sizes. Mariam also passed by, and she was brisk in her steps as she had wanted to get home early.

Some of the females sauntered along the sidewalk while many stood bantering with each other in a haze of hilarious laughter and wild touching and gesturing that portrayed the femininity of the young. The other young male, who leaned against the front of the car with his cell phone in his hand text-messaging a friend, stepped over to his two hunchos. A black-and-white-flowered scarf covered his head with a tied knot at the back. He also was decked out in a black leather coat, straight-leg jeans, and a high top, pointed-toe boots. "Wha' happen? You ain't hook up with any of da chicks yet?" Bob asked.

"Nah, we just diggin' da scene. Checkin' out da sweeties," the youngest replied.

Just then, a slim brunette with bright hazel eyes strutted along the sidewalk. The young, square-jawed, straight- and narrow-nosed youngster eyed the female twelfth grader as she headed in his direction. Their eyes met. She recognized him. A smile beamed across her face, which flushed with a rose pink hue. A sparkle glinted from her even ivory teeth.

"Hey, Bob, wha' you doin' here?" she said, as she lunged into his wide-open arms. "I ain't see you fuh a while since you left."

"Me and my homies just come around here fishing," said Bob, using the normal street lingo.

"You fishing? Fishing fuh what?" Kathy asked him as they released each other after a good hug.

"We just checking on da chicks to see who we could hook up with," said Bob with a big grin. "Wha' you up to?"

"I'm going home," she uttered.

"How was school?" asked Bob.

"I hate that place but I still gotta go. I wanna graduate this year," Kathy announced flatly.

"Good," remarked Bob, patting her shoulder.

"Good," said the oldest one, with the tan construction boots, leaning against the car. "That's your girl, Bob? She looks great."

"You don't know her? She was a cheerleader in the tenth grade when we were seniors there," announced Bob.

"Oh, yeh, I remember her. How ya doin'?" asked Ronald, the eldest of the group.

"Yuh still cheerleading?" ask Bob, kindly before Kathy could have answered Ronald.

"I'm good. No, I'm too busy now to be in cheerleading. Too much work to graduate," Kathy related, shifting the strap of her black canvas bag firmly on her right shoulder with books and other accoutrement.

"You too big fuh da now," said Ronald.

Kathy shrugged. "Not really. I got to catch up with my work."

Ronald shook his head.

Angling along the crowded sidewalk, two hefty blondes in brown and black down coats headed in the direction of the trio. "Hey, shorties," Ronald hailed. One of the young ladies smiled, the taller and heavier of the two.

"Leh me talk to you for a minute," said Oscar, putting on a brave smile in response to that of the female twelfth grader.

"What you wanna talk to me 'bout?" she asked, decked in her black coat as her lips, with a dark, chocolate-colored glossy lipstick, parted in a canny smile.

"You know I wanted to talk to you since last month. I'd been watchin' you since then, and couldn't let today pass by without reaching out and talking to you," he lied, his face portraying an expression of sincerity in what he said.

"Really?" questioned the senior, somewhat taken in by what she heard, as her medium-build friend in the brown coat walked a few steps away from earshot.

"Yeah, I really wanted to talk to you," he stressed, pushing both hands in his side pockets and arching his shoulders as his coat hung loose with the front opened and whipped by the light afternoon breeze.

Ronald then approached the friend, who was blushing and laughing. "You're a senior too?" he asked casually.

"I'm a junior," the young lady answered, looking at him with slanting eyes.

"So you hangin' with da seniors," he joked.

"Not really. We live on the same block," she replied.

"I got it. She's your pal, your homegirl," Ronald remarked, baring a smile.

"Correct. We go places together," said the junior, smiling reciprocatingly.

The conversation continued with Ronald and the junior and Oscar and the senior while Bob and Kathy indulged in their bit of talk. Much smiles and oohs, ahhhs, and laughter passed as the banter became deeper. A few yards away, a silver Honda Lxi pulled up with a zoom as the engine throttled to a halt. Two young men cavalierly got out and left the doors open after parking the automobile at a forty-five-degree angle. Hip-hop music blasted with heavy rhythm and base. They donned red and blue baseball caps, blue name-brand jeans, and Adidas and Nike sneakers. The leaner of the two, Kurt, sported a black waist-length leather jacket while his colleague wore a similar brown suede jacket. They called out at some of the older females as they passed by.

Said the slim one as two females walked by, "Hi, bonita." The young ladies kept their heads straight. About half the crowd on the sidewalk was moving while the rest stood by. Another three young ladies made their way in the same direction. The stockier young man, Carlos, called out, "Hi, sweets."

The three young ladies giggled. "Who he calling sweets?" said the slimmest of the three.

"I think it's you he calling at," stated the female student in a green knee-length jacket.

"Who, me?" questioned the female student, who wore a yellow-and-blue coat, with her dark hair in a bun at the top of her head.

Carlos then beckoned with his right hand.

"Yes, look, he's pointing at you," reiterated the slim girl in the green jacket, black denim jeans, and high knee-length black boots with stiletto heels.

Said the student in the yellow-and-blue coat, "Leh me go over to him and find out who he's calling at." She maneuvered through the moving and stationary crowd on the sidewalk and edged to the caller.

Said she, brazenly, "You callin' me?"

"I sure do, baby," he replied, baring teeth with a gap in the two front incisors. He sported a tattoo of a mermaid on the side of his neck, which looked pink from the constant chafing of the cold wind.

"Wha' you calling me for," she asked, eyeing him from the corners of her eyes.

"You look like a chick I could click with," he said with a straight face.

"I ain't no chick you could click with," she said and began walking away.

"Look, I didn't mean it that way," he stated, shifting and moving his body.

"So what you mean," the student asked, her eyes rolling, revealing the complete white around the pupil.

"I mean you look like such a nice, sweet young lady that I would like to talk to, and um, ah, I would like to see," Carlos said, with a swagger in his walk.

"Is that so? It sounds so funny," she said, turning and looking over her shoulder, as she suddenly stopped.

"I could do so much fuh you."

"You can't do nothin' fuh me."

"You won't believe it, but there's much I could do fuh you."

The conversation moved from one level to the next between Carlos and the twelfth grader in the yellow-and-blue coat; the conversations among the other young men and female seniors and juniors took a different tone and form.

In less than half an hour, the engine of the red sports car roared, the doors slammed shut, and it backed up from its parking area. It screeched burning its tires as it gunned along the road with Bob, Ronald, Oscar, Kathy, and the taller and heavier of the two blondes. They laughed and yelled as the automobile drove away from the proximity of the school. Shortly after the shiny silver sports car drove off with two female students, one an acquaintance and the other a senior whom they met for the first time. Minutes after, the Honda backed up with Carlos, Kurt, the student in the yellow-and-blue coat, and her two female friends from the senior school. It roared as it sped down the road, leaving the area of the institution of learning.

Within minutes, another shiny car pulled into the space from which the red sports car pulled out. It was a sleek black Camry Avalon. Two young men alighted from the vehicle. One wore a multicolored cap while the other wore black. Both were attired in black leather jackets and blue jeans. It was a daily feature of cars driven by young men pulling up on the block opposite or obliquely opposite the school. The young men talked to and cajoled many of the young ladies in the twelfth grade and some from the eleventh, the majority of whom were eighteen and nineteen years or months short of eighteen. Some of the female students were seventeen. Nonetheless, many of them looked forward to seeing the young men in their shiny automobiles and willingly talk to them without any reservation.

Chapter 21

Mariam got to the bus stop, where she boarded the bus that had just pulled up. She made her way to the middle of the bus since she told herself she could not take the noise, yells, and curses that went on at the back. Mariam stood in the middle and held on to the handrail as the bus pulled off. Minutes after, she felt a bit of tiredness in her eyes. Her eyes felt heavy, and drowsiness overcame her even as she stood. Her head bobbed, and she straightened up herself and held on to the bar firmer before she lost her balance.

At the back, students cursed and yelled for no particular reason. Said Mariam to herself, in a whisper, "They would impregnate the air with the profanity they use." Adults were in the bus, and the sixth to eighth graders showed no regard for the women and men who could be their parents and grandparents. Said one seventh grader, whom Mariam recognized, "I gonna f— him up. He took my game card from off my desk and didn't give it back to me."

"If it was me I'd f— him up right away," said another at the top of his lungs.

One adult woman looked up at them. Disdain was on her face. The youngsters carried on with the expletives jumping from their mouths with ease. Mariam continued to hang on to the crossbar and tightened her grip when the bus swerved or made a turn. It made several swerves to pass vehicles which double-parked and many turns around corners before Miriam disembarked. She wanted to get home eagerly to rest for an hour or two before getting up to do her homework and read a book she had started two days ago which she borrowed from the library a few blocks from her home.

The persistent cursing and yelling by students from her school really annoyed her. She was one of the students who was focused and had particular goals for the future and guarded herself against being distracted by some of the things that went on in school and outside of it. The bus stopped, and an elderly woman got up from the seat near the spot where Mariam stood. Mariam slipped the bag from her back and sat in the seat. Said the lady next to whom she sat, "You're a different student. Hear how those children are behaving at the back with all that cursing and shouting." Mariam looked at the lady and slightly smiled.

"Do they go to your school?" the lady asked, looking at Mariam.

"Yes, most of them go to my school," replied Mariam, gripping the strap of her bag to prevent it from sliding to the floor of the bus.

"Is that the way they behave in school?" the elderly woman asked with much concern on her face.

"Most of them behave like that because they follow a few of them who're always acting up," stated Mariam.

"They must be giving the teachers a hard time,"

"Yes, they do."

"I'm sorry for those teachers."

Mariam smiled shyly.

"You seem to be such a different person," the lady emphasized. Suddenly, there was a ruckus at the back of the bus. "Ahhhh, Ahhhh." Then a student bawled, "Gimme my sh—t."

Another yelled, "This sh—t ain't yours."

"This sh—t is mine," the first voice rang out.

"You see what I'm saying. These children have no regard for anyone. I hate to travel on the bus at this time when school is dismissed," the lady said to Mariam.

"I don't know why they behave like that. They do it every day," Mariam mentioned. The ranting went on unabated.

"Shut up. You're hurting my head," a young female voice sounded at the back.

Turning and looking over her shoulder, Mariam noted that it was Patricia who shouted at the foul-mouthed students whom she sat among. Mariam straightened up and looked ahead.

"I hope they would come to their senses and start behaving like decent young people," the lady said. The yells and curses continued among the eight or nine students, male and female, in the back of the bus. The bus covered two more blocks and then came to a stop. "Good night," Mariam said, upped her bag, and got up.

"Good night, young lady, and stay strong," the elderly woman said to Mariam. Mariam smiled again; she moved along the aisle and descended the stairs of the bus. She hurried along the sidewalk since it was still cold and turned the corner. Minutes later she was in the comfort and warmth of her home. She placed her bag next to the writing desk, spoke with her sister and brother, who had already arrived home and were eating, before she also had dinner and two hours of sleep to revive herself from the drowsiness she felt. She expected her parents to be home from work by six-thirty.

The bus continued on its journey, making stops to put off and take on passengers. Patricia pulled the hood of her black down coat over her head to muffle the noise her colleagues made. Sixth graders were taunting each other.

"You know they call him jelly belly. His belly got marks like jelly beans," one sixth grader, who wore a red-and-yellow coat, told another, who sat on his right in a blue coat. He pointed to the student whom he referred to, who sat on his left in a black coat, as they hit each other while they sat at the back of the bus.

"At least I can't fly with my ears," responded the friend in the black coat, "Look at the size of your ears."

"Stop hitting and talking about each other like that," Patricia, an older female student who sat with them, said. The two nine-year-old-looking students, the one in the yellow-and-red coat and the other in the black coat, slapped each other on the hands and shoulders.

"Stop, stop, I said. You think it's funny," Patricia yelled, leaning over from her seat and punching both young men in the arms and shoulders to get them to stop hitting each other.

The two quieted down for a while and then started slapping each other. The student in the yellow-and-red coat, the slimmer of the two, stood and then backed up so as to prevent the other, in the black coat, from hitting him.

Yelled Patricia, "You putting your butt in the lady's face."

"No, I'm not," responded the youngster. The lady looked at him sternly but said nothing. The behavior of the students was unpleasant, much to the disdain of the adult passengers.

The bus drove for another twenty minutes and turned several corners. It stopped at several bus stops putting off students and adult passengers. Finally, all the students disembarked before Patricia came off at her stop. She walked a block and a half before she came to her apartment building, entered the lobby, and got to the elevator, which took her to the fifth floor. She pushed the brown, heavy metal door of the elevator and stepped from it into the hallway. Whipping the keys from her backpack, she inserted them, turned the locks, and entered her home. She was taken aback. "Mom, Mom, I came home and you're drunk on da floor," Patricia complained.

"What, what da f— you want? Get to f— outta here," her mother said in her drunken stupor.

"Ahhh, ahhh, ahhhh, hu, hu, hu, hu, ahhh, hu, hu," Patricia cried. "Mom, you tell me you gonna stop getting drunk, that you gonna stop drinking."

"Whaa, what yuh want, eh, eh," the mother grunted, lying on the floor.

"You said you gonna stop and still you don't, ahhhh, hu, hu, hu, ahhh, hu, hu, hu…" Patricia cried aloud.

"I ain't tell you sh—t. Wha' yuh want, wha' yuh want with meh?" she questioned in her drunkenness.

Patricia's mother, Helena, lay on her stomach in faded blue denim jeans, long-sleeve red jersey, and gray socks on the light brown carpeted floor. Her bronze-colored hair was disheveled. Her tan-complexioned face was pudgy, and the white of her eyes had the color of blood. With much effort, Helena turned her head and looked up at Patricia. Everything she saw was sort of spinning. She was disoriented. She recognized Patricia was in the house, but it appeared she was seeing two of Patricia in motion and could not say exactly in which part of the house she was. She tried to get her bearing, but her head was a mess. She could not figure out where she was as everything whirled. "Patricia, Patricia, Patricia," she called.

Patricia had gone to the bathroom to wash her face after dropping her bag on the floor. She thought, *Why is she drinking this much?* With the bathroom door closed and the chilled water running in the sink, making a hissing noise of its own, Patricia splashed water on her face to get a grip of herself and to remove the salty tear stains from her cheeks. She felt the coldness on her face and a slight exhilaration. She allowed the water and the feel of it to sink in on her skin. Feeling a little better, she turned off the tap and opened the door to hear her mother shouting her name. "Patricia," she called out.

"Yes, Mom, I'm here," Patricia answered, wiping her face with a hand towel.

She walked across to where her mother lay on the floor. She bent over almost to the floor and slid her hands under the bosom of her mother and tried to turn her over on her back. She managed to turn her mother on her back. At that moment, the door lock turned, the door was pushed open, and Richard entered. He exclaimed, "What! She drunk again. Mom, what's wrong with you?" Still bending over, Patricia slid her right arm under the upper torso of her mother and held her mother's right arm with her left hand. Seeing the effort his sister was making, Richard said, "What you doin'?"

"I'm putting her to sit so I could get her in her bed," Patricia said, watching up at her brother, who was older than her and much bigger in size and height. Patricia is tall and big, a hefty young lady when compared with her mother, who is medium build. Cognizant of what his sister was doing, he stepped across, bent, placed his hands under his mother's arms, and pulled her up into a sitting position with the help of Patricia.

"What, what?" Helena mumbled, the scent of strong alcoholic beverage was heavy on her breath.

"We're trying to help you sit so we can put you in your bed, Mom," said Patricia as she and her strong-armed, muscular brother got their mother to sit. Richard then got behind his mother, gripped her under her arms again, and raised her to her feet. Realizing that her legs were wobbly, he lowered her back into a sitting position. Said Richard, "Patricia, hold her legs and we gonna lift her and put her in bed." Patricia held her mother's legs, and she and her brother lifted and took their mother into her bedroom and put her in her bed.

"I don't understand why she is still drinking," complained Richard.

"I started cryin' when I came in and saw her drunk on the floor. I don't know what's wrong with her," Patricia riled.

"She got to stop drinking. Most times she's off duty she gone to the liquor store and buy some sh—t. She know she can't drink. The other day she poured a shot and started drinking. By the time she got to the third shot, she was high like a kite. She got to stop drinking that piss, mannnn. I feel bad to come home and see her in that state," the tall, big, eighteen-year-old Richard, who sported a goatee, said. He bowed his head in frustration that his mom seemed unable to kick the habit of drinking.

"I'm so upset when I see her drinking. She drinks so much sometimes she can't even go to work," lamented Patricia, standing by the door of her mother's bedroom.

"But she doesn't drink that much and she gets drunk. Whatever problem is bothering her, she should get some help. I know our father left her. He walked out on her, but she got to forget about that and move on. She has a life, and she can't waste it by thinking of him, the things he did her, and drinking as if that gonna change anything or solve da problem. I'm sure Dad not thinking 'bout her and drinking himself to death. If she continues like that she gonna get sick," remarked Richard, pacing the northern part of the living room next to the windows.

"If she lose her job, wha' gonna happen with us?" questioned Patricia, putting her right hand to her head.

"I don't know. All I'm concerned 'bout is that she stops drinking," fretted Richard, leaning against the window.

Patricia's mother lay on her back stone in her bed. She did not call any of them; she could not as she lost all awareness of what was happening around her. She fell into a deep sleep.

"She didn't even cook anythin'. I gonna buy some Chinese food," said Patricia.

"Bring some fuh me," Richard begged. "You have enough money?"

"Yeah. I got enough money," answered Patricia, as she opened the door and left for the restaurant on the next block. Richard slumped in a chair and waited for his sister to return with the food. Minutes after, she returned and they had an afternoon meal.

Mr. Miller came into the eighth grade classroom, room 2-802, as Ms. Vivehouse stood in front of the class. Said Mr. Miller, "I'm here to check on some students to see if they're cutting class."

"Okay," replied Ms. Vivehouse.

A female student who sat in front said to Mr. Miller, "Get out! You don't belong here."

Answered Mr. Miller, with a stern facial expression, "Is that the way you speak to your father?"

"You don't know my father, so don't tell me 'bout my father. If you call him, I'll come back here tomorrow and whop your ass," Dana blurted, staring with wide eyes at the teacher who stood in front of the class, not really surprised.

"Dana, show some respect, that's a teacher you're talking to," cautioned Ms. Vivehouse.

"I don't care. He doesn't belong here. Say he comin' checkin' fuh students who cuttin'," Dana riled.

"She's lacking in self-respect. If she had any for herself, she would have respect for others," said Mr. Miller, leaving the room after seeing two of the students he was looking for at the back of the class.

"You ought to be respectful, Dana. You cannot talk to adults in that manner and especially a teacher."

"He ain't my father so I can tell him what I want," retorted Dana furiously.

"But you will find yourself in trouble by telling people what you like," the teacher advised.

"So?" Dana answered defiantly, pulling a bag with candy from her haversack that lay on the desk.

"You're not going to eat that candy in here," ordered Ms. Vivehouse, looking sternly at Dana.

"Why? I need to freshen my breath. Her breath need to freshen, too," uttered Dana, turning squarely to watch Lily in her eyes. Lily smiled but did not answer.

"Lily, leh me smell your breath," said Dana, leaning toward Lily.

Lily tightened her face and turned up her eyes showing much of the white cornea beneath the blue pupil.

"Dana, I've had enough of this. I said you cannot eat in this class and I mean it. One more word and you'll stand in front of this class for the rest of the period," Ms. Vivehouse roared, her pale face becoming pink in the cheeks. Dana stopped talking.

Said Ms. Vivehouse, "We're going to continue with the adding of integers. What did we say about adding positive numbers?" She looked around the classroom. The students in front sat attentively and were involved in the lesson. A number of them who sat at the back talked quietly; they paid no attention.

"Carl, what did we say about adding integers?" Ms. Vivehouse asked as she turned sideways and placed her right hand, with the piece of chalk, against the board ready to write the response given by Carl.

Replied Carl, rubbing his chin, "We said the sum of positive numbers give a positive result."

"Good, very good," remarked Ms. Vivehouse, as she began writing the response on the board. "And Nella, what was said about negative numbers?"

Nella answered loudly, "The sum of negative numbers give a negative result."

"Fine!" Ms. Vivehouse said, nodding her head in approval as she turned and wrote on the board again. Facing the class once more, she said, "We'll do some exercises on integers. Turn to page 192 in your text."

The teacher walked away from the chalkboard and headed to the back of the class where some five or six students sat engaged in idle talk. One of them pushed the peak of his cap to the side of his head and slouched in his chair. Another male student put his head on the desk and closed his eyes.

Ordered Ms. Vivehouse, with a grim face, "Take out your pens and begin the work."

Said Albert, grinning broadly, "We did that already."

"No, we did not, Albert. It's time you get started. And I want to see all of you sitting here start your work," the math teacher said.

Some students took out pens and pencils from their bags and started writing in their notebooks. Ms. Vivehouse then turned about and went back to the front of the class. As soon as she left the back of the class, Albert and Mylan got up from their seats. Albert grabbed Mylan and threw his right arm around his neck as Mylan struggled to set free himself. Albert then half-spun Mylan and threw him on the floor. *Blop!* Mylan sprawled as he landed on his back. Albert then fired two kicks in the legs of Mylan. "Ahhhh, you a punk, Mylan," Albert said and then jumped on him, landing an elbow in his chest. Mylan groaned, "Ohhh, ohhh." Albert jumped up. Mylan got to his knees, then his feet and chased Albert. He caught him against the wall and crashed his right shoulder into Albert's chest. Albert moaned, "Ahhh."

Onris left his seat and ran and clobbered Albert in his left shoulder. The punches stung and Albert winced in pain. He clobbered him again, about the body. "Hey, hey, hey," Albert muttered, drifting against the wall. Onris then turned on Nijwel, who left his seat and joined the fray. Onris rushed Nijwel and launched some body shots at him. "No, no, no," Nijwel appealed, raising his arms to block the punches, which got through to his body. Onris then grabbed Nijwel around the waist, lifted him way off the floor, and slammed him down on the dark-brown tiled floor. Nijwel grimaced, "Ahhhh," and rolled over on his side. The pain was evident in his face.

Patrick, a tall and heavier student who was standing nearby, grabbed Onris around the neck and tumbled him on the floor. *Bang.* Onris went down hitting his left arm on the edge of a desk.

"I'm the champ here," Patrick shouted, raising his strong, muscular arms in the air. He kicked Onris in his side.

"Ouch, ouch, ouch, ouch," Onris hollered with each kick he received.

Patrick gasped and fired more kicks at him.

"Chill, chill, chill, mannnn," Onris begged as Patrick's size-twelve-sneaker-clad foot landed in his ribs.

Jaywun then jumped on Onris landing on his stomach.

"Ahhh, ahhh, ahhhh," Onris balked, rolling on the floor.

"Let's jump him," Jaywun shouted at Patrick.

Mylan, who was standing nearby, rushed and jumped on Onris's chest. Albert jumped on him. "Yeah, yeah," Albert yelled as his elbow pounded Onris.

"Ease, ease, mannnn. You hurtin' me," Onris cried as he lay defenseless on the floor.

Agitated by the fistic fury, Louis, a short, slim, narrow-faced, square-chin student, eased out of his seat and pummeled Onris in his side and back. Manuel jumped on him and began punching him. Chung also left his seat and fired two kicks in the legs of Onris.

"Okay, leave him now, we whop him, good," said Mylan, brandishing his fists above his head.

They got off of him. Grimacing, Onris rose to his feet and immediately threw punches at Albert, he then turned on Mylan. Albert instantly punched Patrick, Patrick punched back; Manuel punched Chung, and Chung hit back. Now each was punching the other. It was a melee.

"Enough of this bloody nonsense! I'm sick and tired of it. Are you going out of your minds or what? Cut the crap," Ms. Vivehouse bawled at them. Her face became red with anger. She pulled back her graying hair from her face. Her lips quivered as she stared at them.

"Son, this was fun," Patrick said as he backed away to his seat. "Let's cool it, guys. Sit down."

Listening to Patrick rather than the teacher, Nijwel, Mylan, Albert, Manuel, Chung, and Onris returned to their seats. Some quiet prevailed for a while before some of them were up again behaving in a disruptive manner. It was a day when that type of behavior dominated most of the classes in the lower school and some in the upper school especially among the ninth and tenth graders.

Students showed much indifference to instruction in class 604 on that sunny but brisk, windy Friday afternoon. Sitting at their desk, students verbally attacked each other. Ms. Stein was teaching the class when Ryan, who paid no attention, said to Simone, "Your ears is so big you could use them as a parachute."

"Shut up! You like five people in one body, you five-in-one fat pig," Simone blurted out to the chunky youngster.

"You funky, yo," Ryan snarled at her. And only a while ago they were laughing together.

With a smirk, Simone said, "I funky? You stink, mannnn. Go wash your body."

"F— you," Ryan belched at Simone.

"Move from here, you dumb d—ck," Simone hurled.

"You a bitch," Ryan echoed.

"Like yuh fat momma," Simone hit back at him. Ms. Stein shook her head in disgust since she had to tell students, daily, to desist from the profanity they engaged in while attacking each other verbally for no particular reason.

Barbara got up from her seat, took the window pole, and tried to open the window. It did not open. She replaced the pole in its position. She walked back to her seat but tripped. Ryan put his right foot in the way. She turned and dealt him several blows in his back. "You fat-ass turkey," Barbara yelled. "I'll punch you out next time." Ryan shook off the punches and smiled.

Said Ms. Stein, in a disturbed mood, "I'm watching you at the back there. Keep on idling and see how far you'll get. We'll be having a test in another week."

Some of them did not hear what she said. They were busy with their infraction. Some of them yanked loose-leaf paper from their binders, crumpled them into paper balls, and threw them at others. Cyrus threw a paper ball. It hit Raquel.

"Don't throw paper at me," she said, baring her teeth. She had previously done an extraction. She extracted one of her incisors, which was irreparable because of a cavity and exposed nerve that dealt her excruciating pain

Said Cyrus, "That grandma lost her teeth since World War II."

"Who you talking to?" blurted out Raquel, offended by the remark.

"You," said Cyrus, leaning over and away from Raquel, who threw two punches at him.

There seemed no end to the foolhardiness of the students. Sitting next to the wall and right up front, Nicholas rose from his seat, stood in his chair, and attempted to stand on the back of the chair. "Get off that chair now, Nicholas," squealed Ms. Stein.

"I'm an acrobat." Nicholas giggled trying to get on the chair back.

"I want you to sit in your seat," ordered the teacher.

"I'm going to be a famous acrobat when I grow up. Aren't you going to watch me on TV?" Nicholas inquired from the teacher; his eyes brightened as he spoke.

"I want to watch you do your work right now, and stop the nonsense you're doing," Ms. Stein said with graveness in her voice.

Indiscipline prevailed in class 805 as well. Two slim girls hit each other in a fake fight. The girl in the red jacket said to the one in the yellow sweater, "You so bony, your hands hurt me."

Answered the girl in the yellow sweater, "You bony too. Look at your knuckles. Look how they big. You could break a wall with them."

The girl in the red jacket was offended and countered. "But I have shape, though."

Retorted the student in the sweater, "But you smell like onion."

Fired back the one in the red jacket, "You smell like hot ass."

And the class erupted, "Ha, ha, ha, ah, ha, ha, ha . . ." The girls and boys in the little group of detractors rolled with laughter.

The folly in the classrooms was so pervasive and protracted that it impeded effective instruction and learning, as some individual students or group of students would blurt out something that halted the learning process and create hilarity. Class 904 was affected by such distraction during the afternoon session while Mr. Blair taught a lesson when a student barged into his room and said in a loud but raspy voice, "Teacher, I got something important to say."

"What is it?" Mr. Blair asked, being interrupted in conducting his lesson.

"Something important, man," answered the student, who stood in front of the class.

"What is it?" Mr. Blair asked again, somewhat perturbed, from the grimace on his face, that the student had disturbed his lesson.

The student shouted loudly, "Anybody got white-out?"

"Is that the important thing you have to say?" asked the teacher, a bit exasperated, his eyes blinking rapidly as he thought of what to say to the student.

"Hey, Travis, come here," said Allan, who sat in the second row of seats.

"What?" asked Travis.

"Come here, motherf—r," howled Allan. "Here, I have white-out."

Travis grabbed the small bottle and shrieked, "Thanks." He dashed for the hallway.

"Bring my sh—t back when you finish," shouted Allan, zipping his bag.

Next door, the idle banter was no different as some seemed bent in engaging in types of activity which was not beneficial to any of them.

Mandy said, "Take off that mask. You're scaring me. Where you got that face from? An alien spaceship?"

"You're more an alien. Look at those twisted teeth," Terence hit back.

"Cut it, cut it. Stop that idle talk," said Ms. Bland, trying to move ahead with the lesson.

Wanda, who sat in another group at the back, questioned, "Why your foot is in the chair? Don't you have any manners or training?"

"I'd kick yuh in yuh face," the lanky Terence said, flailing his long slender arms.

"I dare you," snarled Wanda, a fairly hardworking student.

It was not unusual that students acted cavalier. Alice was no exception as she sat in class 804, with her foot on a short, brown wooden stool. She drew a design of a dress in her black hardcover notebook while she had her hair combed by a friend who sat nearby. Monique pulled the comb through Alice's thick mane, but Alice moved her head intermittently, making it hard for Monique to comb it even though the teacher cautioned her to desist from engaging in such activity.

Said Alice, "My cousin went with us to California last week, and he ate like a pig."

"Ha, ha, ha." Monique laughed, pulling the brown plastic comb through Alice's hair.

"When everybody took one patty, he took two. When my sister and me had a pizza each, he took three . . ." said Alice.

"He was greedy," interjected Monique.

"Yes, he was greedy. When everyone had two pieces of chicken, he ate four. He ate so much when we came back to New York, he was big as a house," said Alice with glee on her face.

"Ha, ha, ha, I like that," uttered Monique, her lips spreading widely.

As the two female students spoke and carried on with their inattentive behavior, Aprel, Uldeen, and others idled at the back of the class. Shouted Aprel, who wore a pair of round earrings in his ear, "You hear what this boy is sayin' 'bout me?"

"Wha' he's sayin'?" asked Uldeen, decked in a red baseball cap and red hooded sweater.

Before Aprel could have answered, Tacta, who tied his head with a black durag, blurted out, "He's deaf in the right ear and hard of hearing in the left."

The others laughed.

"You see what I mean. He's dissing me," complained Aprel, shaking his head.

"You know I sayin' da truth," said Tacta.

And the barrage of unseemliness, likewise, went on unabated. It went on unabated in room 3-905. Sitting in the center of the class, Kathrin slapped Orin in his face. "Ouch! Why you slap me? I ain't do you nothin'," cried Orin, rubbing his face. "I gonna tell the dean."

"Who cares," remarked Kathrin.

Stacey said, "You gonna get in trouble, get suspended, Kathrin. He's crying."

"I don't get into trouble. You ever see me in trouble?" asked Kathrin, a grin spreading across her narrow face with high, zygomatic bones.

"Yes, I see you in trouble before," said Harlon.

"No, I don't get into trouble," said Kathrin as the grin faded from her face.

"Because you've been in this school for twenty years," yelled Harlon.

"Yeah, yeah, ha, ha, ha." The small group of inattentive students laughed.

"You dumb. I ain't been in this school for twenty years. I'm not even twenty years," Kathrin frowned.

Class 1007 saw similar distractions on that Friday afternoon that was typical of Friday afternoons at Jones High, when a male student with long brown hair walked around the classroom asking other students for loose-leaf paper to do his work. "Yo, yuh got loose leaf?" he asked.

"Nah," the first student he asked answered.

"Bro, yuh got loose leaf," he asked, another student.

The second student flipped through his binder. "I ain't got any."

He went to yet another student. "Leh me get some loose leaf."

"I only got a notebook," the third student answered.

The long-haired student gave up after he did not get any loose-leaf paper from the three students he asked. He ended up at the back of the classroom in front of a sink and mirror. He turned on the tap and allowed the water to run on his hands. He then smoothed his long, flowing hair. He put his hands under the running water and smoothed his hair twice before leaving the sink.

"Hey, shorty," the long-haired student said, referring to a big-build, almost six-foot-tall, female redhead student with slight freckles on her arms. "You got loose leaf."

"Who you callin' shorty? You want me to smack you?" she said, showing a stern face while cutting her eyes.

"Nah, nah." He smiled.

Ruby whipped out two sheets of paper from her folder and gave it to the male student, who returned to his seat and began doing some work. Soon after, Preta, with a fair length of shiny black hair, left her seat and stepped up to the mirror on the wall at the back of the class. Plucking a black plastic comb from the back pocket of her faded denim blue jeans, she combed her already neat head of hair. Mrs. Baighman approached her and said, "Young lady, you cannot comb your hair in the classroom."

Answered Preta, "I have to look good for the boys."

"Oh, so," replied Mrs. Baighman. "Please take your seat and begin your work which is on the board." Preta returned to her seat and attempted to do some work.

Students in both the seventh and eighth grades opened the barricaded windows above the normal safety level. The teachers closed the windows. The students complained about the heat in the classrooms and opened the windows again way above the safety level. The teachers lowered the windows to the safety level. The students raised the windows. Assistant Principals Pearson and Tillock were called at different times to deal with the situation. The windows were lowered. That behavior continued among the seventh and eighth grade classes situated on the first and second floors, respectively.

The bell rang signaling the end of the sixth period. A few minutes after, it rang again, even louder, it appeared. *Cling, cling, cling-cling, cling, cling.* The seventh period started, and students gradually edged to their classrooms. It took some time before the hallways on all the floors were cleared. Mr. Linsmun, Mr. Eisenburg, Ms. Cort, Mr. Delph, Mr. Holdon, Mr. Azcowitz, Mr. Tillock, and Mrs. Browman and the remaining deans and assistant principals were in force on the floors with security personnel to move students along. It took more time, it appeared, for everyone to get into his or her class. The disgust was stark on the faces of the administrative and supervisory staff and security personnel.

The din soared and it took a while for classes to settle. Rather than sit in their seats, some students moved to the windows in two or three of the classrooms. They complained that the rooms were hot, and so they raised the windows to an unsafe level. The teachers told them to lower the windows. They refused and looked out. One female student then sat on one of the window sills. She seemed unconcerned about her safety. The teacher ordered her to get off the sill, and she blatantly refused. The security officer who patrolled the hallway on the second floor was called, and the female student was rebuked about the dangers of sitting on the sill. She was then escorted to the dean's office from where she was sent to in-house. The remaining students who stood next to the windows were ordered to their seats and scolded about their behavior and the dangers of having the windows opened above the safety level.

Chapter 22

Ms. Langevine moved around the class in room 3-1005 checking and observing how students did the "Do Now" on the board. Some students were already writing in their notebooks and folders and had completed some portion of the work.

"Many of you are not working as yet, and I'm going to stop the class shortly so we could move on with the lesson," Ms. Langevine said.

A few who had not started before headed her instruction and began working. Looking around, she saw those who idled. Said she to Kerdel, who sat in the second row of seats, "Take out your notebook, young man. You have a 'Do Now.' Several times I told the class about this."

"I don't feel like doin' nothin'. I'm tired," said Kerdel, resting his head on his backpack, which he placed on his desk.

"I hear this every day, Kerdel," said Ms. Langevine, looking at him with concern.

"Don't stare at me. I'll tell my mother. Nobody in my family stare at me. Only my little cousin I allow to stare at me."

"What I want you to do is begin your work, Kerdel. Every day I have to put up with this. It's not right. You're here to learn," said the teacher.

"I don't wanna learn sh—t," yelled Kerdel.

"This is very sad, Kerdel," said the teacher.

"I ain't care," lashed out Kerdel.

"I'm going to call your mother," Ms. Langevine warned, feeling somewhat disgusted.

"Good," answered Kerdel, scratching the back of his head.

A few doors away, class 1001 had a similar experience. Mittle got up from his seat while the class was working on a science project. The class was on the computers in the computer lab researching on the earth's magnetic field. Mr. Mendez, the science teacher, said, "Student, why are you standing?"

"Because I have legs," replied Mittle.

"I want you to sit and carry on with what you're doing on the computer," Mr. Mendez said sternly.

"But my legs are telling me to stand," replied Mittle with a silly smile.

"You heard me," the teacher barked.

"Okay, okay," Mittle answered and sat in his seat behind a computer and attempted to get up some vital data.

Another student was unable to maintain his focus and began talking to the student next to him, who seemed to hardly listen to what was said. Mr. Mendez spotted him and said, "Stop talking, Marjo." Marjo continued talking.

"Didn't you hear me say stop?" Mr. Mendez's voice pitched.

"No. I'm deaf in my right ear. I have wax, much of it, in my left. And it's hard," replied Marjo without an expression on his face.

"Ha, ha, ha, ah, ha, ha, ha, ah, ha, ha, ha." The class rolled with laughter.

"If you're deaf, how come you heard me?" the teacher questioned.

"I don't know," said Marjo.

"Then you need to be in a school for the deaf," Mr. Mendez hit back.

And the class cracked up with more laughter. "Ha, ha, ha, ah, ha, ha, ha . . ."

Disruption appeared to be contagious during the afternoon session on Fridays just after lunch. Things just happened without notice. A female student suddenly burst out in a tantrum, crying and then screaming at the top of her lungs in class 702. She fell on the floor and rolled. Ms. Bishop and students gathered around her, and the security officer who did duty in the hall came into the room. The teacher and two female students lifted her to her feet and helped her to a chair. "What's wrong, Josefina?" Ms. Bishop asked, leaning toward her.

"Ahhhhhhhhh, ahhhhhhh," she screamed, doubling over with her hair falling into her peach, oval face.

"What's the matter, Josefina?" Ms. Bishop questioned, but the student bawled.

She calmed down, and minutes after, she started screaming again, lashing out at other students with her slender hands. Officer Pandang finally managed to take her out of the room and escorted her to the nurse's office. Shortly after she was taken out of the classroom, Alfreda pulled the pen cover from her pen and put it in her mouth. She chewed on it. Ms. Bishop spotted her and ordered, "Take that pen cover from your mouth. And why are you chewing on it?"

"Because I have no candy," she replied with a weak smile.

"You dumb, son. Chewing on that for candy," spilled Damian, who sat next to her.

"Who you callin' dumb?" Alfreda smirked, but her male counterpart did not respond.

It was almost the middle of the seventh period, and students were restless. From their body language and speech, it was clear they wanted to get out, but teachers were still pressing on with the work despite the disruptions. Mr. Niles, who taught a lesson in class 802, walked around the class checking students' work and assisting them with the problems they encountered. Mr. Niles approached a student who was out of his seat, having pleasure in distracting those who did their class assignments. Mr. Niles pointed his index finger to his own head as he approached Mylan and asked, "What's wrong with your head, Mylan?"

Said Mylan with a plain face, "It gone out of power."

"You're probably right. If not, you wouldn't be behaving like that," Mr. Niles stated.

Mylan then delved into his blue-and-black haversack and pulled out a banana. He threw it in the air and caught it. Mr. Niles was explaining something to another student. Leaning over the desk, he turned his head and said, "Mylan, kindly sit down." Ignoring what the teacher said, Mylan walked to the front of the class, turned his head, looked at the students, and began regurgitating food, the color of yellow, into the garbage bin. He continued looking at them as some squirmed at his action, which appeared as if he was vomiting. Mr. Niles shouted at him, "Mylan, what are you doing?" Mylan spat the yellow stuff in the bin, emptied his mouth, and walked back to his seat. The teacher realized that Mylan had chewed the banana and kept it in his mouth before he spat it in the garbage. Some students really thought he puked and hid their faces. Others seemed upset and looked as if they too had wanted to vomit. Uttered Mr. Niles, walking up to Mylan, who now sat in his seat, "Mylan, this kind of behavior requires a call home."

"No, no, mannn. Chill, Mr. Niles. We cool, you my homie," stated Mylan, looking up at Mr. Niles.

"We're not cool, and it's not cool for you to be behaving like this in class," Mr. Niles scolded, turning away to help another student with his work.

The crassness during that afternoon did not end. A sixth grade female student walked up to Mr. Blair while he sat at his desk making entries in a ledger as students worked. Said she, "Mister, do you live alone?" Mr. Blair was taken aback by the sudden, unusual question, his eyes widened, and furrows formed in his forehead.

Mr. Blair responded, "Why do you ask me that question?"

Said she, smiling, "I just want to know."

"Why?" Mr. Blair questioned, his face looking sterner.

"Because my mother live with us alone," she said.

"Really?" remarked the teacher, looking at the seriousness on the face of the student.

"Yes," said the student, the smile having faded a while ago. "My father left my mother. He walked out on her. I hate him."

"Ohhh, I'm sorry to hear that," Mr. Blair said, shaking his head.

"So tell me, you left your wife?" the sixth grader asked pointedly, her eyes squinting.

"No," answered Mr. Blair.

"Do you still live with her?" she asked, emphasizing what she asked before.

"Yes," said the teacher.

"Good. I just wanted to know," said the student as she walked back to her seat, leaving the teacher thinking of the psychological trauma she is going through to have the pluck to ask him such a personal question and airing what her father did to his family. It appeared that she was very upset and worried that her father had left the home. There was a silence that settled in the class.

Suddenly, someone yelled, "Why it's so quiet?"

And the tumult began with a surge. Talking soared in every area of the room.

Said one female student with a red scarf tied around her head, "You goin' with Kori from 606?"

"Don't mess with me," said her friend in a blue sweater.

"My bad," said the student with the red scarf around her head.

"You diss me, man, gimme my sh—t" the female in the blue sweater fretted.

"You a rake, man,"

"You're more rake than me. Why you askin' me if I goin' with him?"

Walking to the middle of the class, Mr. Blair said, "Young lady, sit down. There's still work to complete."

"No, I can't sit down until I find a quarter," the student replied, clad in her black-and-gray coat.

"Where do you expect to find a quarter?" asked Mr. Blair with disbelief.

"Somewhere, somewhere, somewhere," she squeaked and returned to her seat.

Ms. Bland, who had recently joined the staff, had a coverage in class 707, but she found it difficult to get the students to remain in their seats. In the middle of the class, Troy grabbed Filond around his neck and pulled him down, dropping him on the floor. Leon jumped to his feet, grabbed Filond by his neck as Filond struggled to his feet, and pulled him down, dropping him to the floor once more. Hardy and Alfredo toyed with each other, arms flailing, each trying to gain the advantage of grabbing and headlocking each other. "Come on, come on, come on, you sucker," growled Hardy, a big, heavy student with dimples in the cheeks of his full, round face.

"I comin', I gonna get yuh," howled Alfredo, an even bigger and taller student with a thick, robust neck. Alfredo maneuvered, flailing his arms, and grabbed Hardy, throwing his left arm around his neck. He then pulled and dropped Hardy on the floor with a deep thud. In her soft feminine voice, the teacher said, "Boys, stop. You can't do this. This is a classroom. It's not the yard." The young men soundly ignored her. Lam and Dessin pawed at each other's neck. Lam finally threw Dessin on the floor, jumped on him, and dealt an elbow in his side. "Ahhh, ahhhh, ahhhh." Dessin gasped.

"Tell yuh, I'm da boss, the champion. Respect me," Lam yelled, kicking him in the side.

"Hey, hey, stop. It hurt," cried out Dessin, lying on the floor.

Ms. Bland raised her voice, which was hardly much above her normal pitch. "Stop the foolishness in the middle there. Go to your seats."

About ten students grabbed each other's neck and threw them on the floor. They were practicing wrestling stunts when they should be learning. Some willingly allowed others to grip them around the waist, lift them and hurl them to the floor. "Ah, ah, ah," "Okay, you got me," "Come on," "Whack him," and "I gonna smack yuh" were some of the yells that came from the students, who were wild in performing their stunts.

"You're going to hurt yourselves. I'm calling the dean in here," Ms. Bland said.

A slim, dark, female student in a gray-and-red hooded sweater asked the teacher, "Why don't you shout at them?"

"Does one have to shout for you to sit and do your work?" the teacher said rhetorically.

"Yes, some of the other teachers shout and scream at them," said Gail, a hefty white student in a black jacket and black headband just above her brown hairline.

"Is that the only way you understand, by the teacher shouting and yelling at you?" Ms. Bland inquired.

"Yes, they don't listen. You got to shout at them," Victorina said, her long dark hair pulled together in one with a huge yellow plastic clip.

"Okay, but you're not even listening, too. You're out of your seat," rebuked Ms. Bland.

"Aright, aright, I'm goin' to my seat," Victorina said, hurrying off to take her seat.

"Students, stop wrestling in the classroom and return to your seats," Ms. Bland ordered firmly. A few of them responded by going back to their seats while Ms. Bland continued with the lesson as some refused to pay attention.

It was a bright Monday morning but windy and chill, and many students had settled down to work. Some did research on specific projects, others worked on assignments while many paid attention as teachers modelled lessons. About fifteen minutes into the third period, in class 805, Nicholas got up from his seat and started behaving in a very disruptive manner. He shouted, cursed, and walked around the room. Ms. Vivehouse cautioned, "Nicholas, your behavior is unacceptable. You cannot walk around here cursing and shouting. I'll put you out of this class." Nicholas persisted. He cursed louder. He then grabbed an empty chair and threw it across the room at another student who was busy about the classroom. Ms. Vivehouse charged after him and grabbed him by the arm. She backed him up against the wall. "What the hell you think you're doing throwing a chair in my class. Are you darn crazy?" she yelled in anger as her hands tightened around his upper arms."

"Take yuh hands off me," Nicholas squealed, making a scowl.

"No! You're not going to throw another chair in this class," Ms. Vivehouse yelled as her muscles became taut.

"You hurting me," Nicholas complained, gazing at the teacher.

"Get security for me, Juneann," Ms. Vivehouse said, looking over her shoulder at the female student.

Juneann dashed from her front-row seat and bounced into the hallway bound for the security desk, as no security officer did duty in the hall.

"Let go my arms, you squeezing me," Nicholas growled, wriggling and resisting the teacher's hold on him in order to set himself free.

"You're not going to stay in here," Ms. Vivehouse said, releasing her grip on his arms. Nicholas slipped sideways and got out of the reach of the teacher.

"Ha, ha, ha." Nicholas laughed, moving to the side of the room. "You holding me. You ain't my mother. My mom don't hold me like that." He seemed quite indifferent to what Ms. Vivehouse said and shortly continued his tirade, his unpleasant behavior. "Leave this class, Nicholas. Get out!" Ms. Vivehouse yelled.

"F— outta here. You ain't my mother. Say you holding me," Nicholas cursed.

He yelled at some of the male and female students who focused on their work. He then grabbed a heavy hardcover textbook from the counter, at the side of the class, and hurled it at another student across the room. The student quickly got out of the way and picked up a book to throw it back as Nicholas quickly snatched another book. Ms. Vivehouse sensed that someone was likely to get injured by the books thrown, and so she hurried to the door to get the security officer who patrolled the hallway. Mr. Tillock, assistant principal, eighth grade, was in the hallway, just having left his office. "Mr. Tillock, come please," called out Ms. Vivehouse, peering into the hallway. Mr. Tillock approached the door. Ms. Vivehouse pulled back into the class and saw Nicholas leaving the classroom through the backdoor. She promptly leapt through the front door into the hall and pointed him out to the assistant principal. Said she, "He's trying to leave the classroom. He threw a chair and books at students and pushed back at me when I held him."

"Come here, young man," the assistant principal roared, his voice filling the hallway.

Nicholas turned and walked toward Mr. Tillock, a burly six-foot, muscular administrator. Said Nicholas, his eyes squinting, "What?"

"You're answering me in that manner and throwing furniture and books at other students?" the assistant principal questioned, looking at him sternly.

"I aint do nothin'," Nicholas denied.

Said Mr. Tillock unhesitatingly, "Go to the dean's office and let me see you when I get there."

Asked Nicholas, "What I do? I ain't do nothin'."

"The teacher said you threw a chair across the room at another student and that you threw a book too. Go to the dean's office," Mr. Tillock ordered.

Nicholas turned and walked toward the dean's office. Ms. Vivehouse stepped back into her classroom. Shortly after, the bell rang ending the period. She picked up her bag, left the classroom, and headed along the hallway for the teachers' lounge. Near the middle exit she saw Nicholas. He approached her in a very threatening manner. Said he, "You call da AP on me, yo. When other students curse and fight you don't do nothin'."

Ms. Vivehouse looked at him but said nothing.

After lunch, Ms. Vivehouse went to class 703. She sat at her desk checking some folders while the class spent a few minutes answering a "Do Now." Said Nathaniel, "Olene, you got a pen?"

"Yeah," Olene answered and dug into her black backpack, which she picked up from the floor and put on the desk. Finding a pen, she threw it at Nathaniel. The pen flew past the teacher's desk and hit the lower wall beneath the chalkboard.

Said Olene, "Miss, pass me that pen on the floor."

Ms. Vivehouse looked at her with a stern expression on her face.

"You hear me. Pass that pen for me," Olene's voice raised.

Ms. Vivehouse did not budge but continued to check her folders until the class was finished with the four minute activity.

"Shut up, you retard, you ain't see she ain't listenin' to you," shouted Kim.

"Who you callin' retard?" fumed Olene, spinning around to face Kim.

"You! Who you think I talkin' to?" replied Kim

"I ain't no damn retard," said Olene before the teacher intervened to put an end to the exchange.

Using the projector and transparencies and her laptop, which sat on her desk, to access the Internet to provide students with additional information as she developed her lesson, Ms. Vivehouse saw a female student get out of her seat and begin moving around the classroom. "Young lady, have a seat. And have you started your work?" the teacher asked.

"No. I can't see clearly what's on the board," Matilda said.

"Sit down and hurry up with what you are told to do," Ms. Vivehouse ordered, her voice rising slightly.

Walking over to another student, Ms. Vivehouse said, "Vevin, why haven't you started your work?"

"I can't see on the board. You write too small," said Vevin, drawing a bike on the desk with his blue-ink ballpen. The desk, like many others in the class and the school, was filled with drawings and ink marks.

"Vevin, I think I write big enough for you to see what's on the board. You never raised that question before, so I know you're fooling around," cautioned the teacher, looking over her narrow metal-framed glasses.

And Dariand, who sat next to Vevin, said, "I can't see on the board either. Can I borrow your glasses?"

"Young man, please. Do get on with your work," said Ms. Vivehouse as she walked around the class checking the work of students.

Said Delray, a thin youngster, with deep-set brown eyes and clad in a black waist-length coat, "Want to hear somethin'?"

Before Nathaniel, who sat next to him, could have answered, a sharp sound was emitted. "Brrrrrrrrrrrrr." Delray flatulated. "You awful. You farted right here," cried out Nathaniel as he hurried to get out of his seat and head for the window. Kim, who sat close by, darted from her seat as well, saying, "You're a stink ass. You have no manners. Yuh mom didn't train you."

"What! You behavin' as if you don't do that. I didn't mean to do it. It just slipped out." Delray grinned.

Three other students who sat behind and a few nearby dashed from their seats as well and hurled expletives at Delray. The air in the classroom became fetid. The students who moved to the windows pushed them up beyond the six-inch safety level.

Ms. Vivehouse was in the student's face. "You don't upset things in my class with your nasty behavior. Smell this class. It stinks. Tell your mother to get your colon clean. Flush out. Take some laxative, some colon cleanser. Get me the air freshener." She beckoned to one of the students who sat in front. The student left her seat and reached for the can of air spray which sat on a small table with books, papers, and teaching aids next to the teacher's desk and gave it to Ms. Vivehouse. She shook the can and sprayed. *Shaaaaaaaaa.* Seconds after, a nice aroma filled the just-fetid room. A scent of roses, peaches, and cherries floated in every corner of the classroom and refreshed the atmosphere. Everybody then breathed with ease, and students returned to their seats and continued with their tasks.

Said Ms. Vivehouse, "I don't speak to students so harshly, but when you deliberately disrespect me and my class and disrupt my work, then you open yourself to be spoken to with disrespect. And your action warrants a call home." Ms. Vivehouse resumed checking and assisting students with their class activity.

Chapter 23

On the second floor, a student ran into class 807. "I cut my finger. Look the blood. It's bleeding. You have band aid?" he yelled at Mr. Hanner.

"No, I don't have any. Go to the nurse quickly. She'll take care of it," Mr. Hanner said, sitting at his desk marking assignments during his prep period.

"You don't have any?" the student asked, leaning on the teacher's desk with his hand with the bleeding finger on the desk.

"No, no, I don't have any. The nurse will take care of it. Go to her," the teacher advised, looking up from the assignments he marked.

Samuel writhed; he gaped, baring even, off-white teeth. He straightened up, saying, "It's bleeding more." He brought the finger with the bubble of blood on it closer to the teacher, his hand held over the desk.

"No, Samuel, you got to go now. You got to see the nurse. Let's go," Mr. Hanner ordered, rising from his seat.

Samuel then wagged his finger, which he held a few inches from Mr. Hanner's face, and giggled. Mr. Hanner was on his feet. Samuel backed away and laughed. "I got you. It's dye from a marker. Ha, ha, ha. You fall for it." Mr. Hanner was incensed mainly because the student disturbed and deceived him with a stupid prank when he had much work to do in compiling grades. With a smirk on his face, the teacher said, "Leave. Don't come back here. And don't you have a class?" Samuel did not answer but turned, gave a thumb's up, and entered the hallway. Mr. Hanner closed his door to prevent any other student from intruding and disturbing him.

Mr. Hanner's fourth-period class began and was in progress when Natalie hit and pushed Ahul, Davenand, and Chin. They got up from their seats. Paulette struck out at Davenand, and he reciprocated; he punched her in her right shoulder. It was a rough form of play although they were cautioned to stop. "Stop playing," Mr. Hanner shouted. Natalie left her seat behind her desk, ran and jumped on Ahul's back, throwing her entire weight on him, and choked him while Paulette hit out at him. Natalie seemed very hyperactive; she would not sit still for a moment and frequently hit out and choked Ahul. He in turn squeezed her arms and hand in stopping her from hitting him. Mr. Hanner frequently warned them. It seemed she was constantly hitting Ahul.

As Mr. Hanner tried to bring some order to his class and get as many students as he could to engage in the learning activity, Shardon, Obin, and Tyrell hit Gambert, a quiet student, and took his things when the teacher was not looking in their direction. They punched him and hit him on the head with books. He told them to stop hitting him and taking his things, but they persisted. In most of Mr. Hanner's classes, they hit him and took his things. They jumped him, and he fought back at times. He was tough and muscular but did not interfere with anyone. He was willing to learn, but Jones High was a place he abhorred. He complained to his parents, and both his mother and father decided to visit the school to see the principal. They wanted to make a strong complaint about the constant attacks their son experienced at the hands of mainly the three students in the class. The students seemingly made it their duty to tell him something repulsive, throw things at him, or take his supplies.

The Friday before his parents visited the school, Gambert was again attacked by the three students in Mr. Hanner's class. Shardon picked up Gambert's marker from the desk. Gambert barely saw when the marker was taken.

"Gimme my marker," Gambert said, turning toward Shardon.

"I ain't got no marker fuh you," shouted Shardon, his eyes widening.

"Look, you got my marker under your notebook," Gambert blurted and banged on the desk in anger.

"I ain't got nothin' fuh you," snarled Shardon, pushing at Gambert's books and bag, which lay on the desk.

"Don't push my stuff, man," Gambert said, circling his arms around his things.

"I mad knock this wimp out. He sayin' I take his thing. I don't want his stuff," protested Shardon, looking over at Tyrell, who sat nearby.

"Wha' you tellin' my homeboy?" asked Tyrell, throwing a punch in Gambert's left shoulder.

"Why you hitting me?" Gambert reacted. He gritted his teeth and thought seriously whether he should retaliate.

Shardon came around from the other side and threw a punch in the other shoulder of Gambert and pushed his bag and stuff off the desk.

Gambert winced and then yelled, "Don't punch me. I didn't do you anything."

Gambert had the strength but did not have the heart to strike back as constantly at Shardon and Tyrell. He bore his anger. Shardon tramped on his bookbag and kicked his books. Gambert got out of his seat and picked up his bag and books as the disgust seethed within him. Gambert was taunted and harassed almost daily by Shardon, Tyrell, and Obin. Teachers in other classes rebuked them mainly about bothering or hitting Gambert and even wrote referrals and had them placed in in-house. If one day passed and they did not bother him, it was certain they would take or threw his belongings on the floor or punch him the next day. Gambert complained to his parents when he got home that Friday afternoon.

His parents arrived at school early Monday morning and waited in the office to see Mr. Cottle to lodge a complaint about what was happening to their son. Gambert sat in the chair next to his father. Mr. Ramos was very angry and his voice resonated. The school's secretary told him to wait, as the principal was in a meeting with two assistant principals.

Said the secretary, Mrs. Caldwell, "Can I have your name?"

"I'm Mr. Ramos," said Gambert's father with a serious expression.

"And that's your son?" Mrs. Caldwell asked, pointing to the youngster who sat with his red-and-blue backpack on his thighs. Gambert wore a heavy black coat and blue jeans like his father.

"Yes, that's my son. His name is Gambert Ramos, and he's in class 806," said Mr. Ramos, quite upset and agitated.

"Thank you," Mrs. Caldwell said as she returned to her seat behind the monitor of a computer.

The boy's father fumed. The lividness was ripe on his face. It was more pronounced when his huge walrus moustache quivered when he talked to his wife, a full-figured buxom woman. Redness showed on her face and neck.

"This nonsense must stop. They can't be hitting him every day. He doesn't have anything for them," Mr. Ramos declared in a tense manner. "I told him to complain to the teachers, and nothing seemed to happen. No action was taken as they kept bothering and fighting him. He gonna have to fight back if they're bullies and nothing is done. I pay money just as their parents do, and we don't have to put up with this crap almost daily. A week doesn't pass and there isn't a problem. It has to finish today. My son is a quiet kid. And I'm sure he could deal with any of them. I'm tired of it."

"We're definitely tired with it, and I hope Mr. Cottle would do something serious about it. I don't want to come here again for this matter," said Mrs. Ramos, quite upset.

"In coming here I must come for something positive. Something that makes sense and that would help my boy," Mr. Ramos stated firmly.

"Mr. Cottle would deal real good with this matter," his wife said with worry on her face

"He better do because I ain't want to be here for this matter again. This is school and these are kids. Why they got to be fighting and cursing each other in the class and in the building. I know how hard it is on teachers. Having to teach and have to deal with this disruptive behavior, it ain't good and it ain't funny. They're here to learn, and I want our son to learn. I know the teachers are making an effort so they could learn, but some of these children, huh, I don't know what to call them. They must be giving their parents hell," Mr. Ramos strongly declared.

"The parents probably can't control some of them. Look how they behave on the buses and trains when school dismisses in the afternoon and they're with their friends. I don't want to travel at that time. Last week, I was out and I decided to pick up Teddy since I was near his school, and we joined the bus. The children from his school behaved horrible. Adults were on the bus, and they were cursing, yelling, and even wanted to fight each other. It was a shame. Their behavior was outrageous," Gambert's mother explained.

"Some parents got to do more in controlling their children. They cannot allow them to run wild," his father said as both parents waited on the principal to finish his meeting and have an audience with them.

Two other parents arrived at the school to see assistant principals and deans. And yet more parents and guardians came in to see some of the administrators. At the end of the meeting with the assistant principals, who left through a door leading to the hallway, Mrs. Caldwell knocked on the principal's door and entered his office. Standing next to the door, which became ajar, she said, "Mr. Cottle, the parents of a student are here to see you about an important matter concerning their son."

"Let them in," Mr. Cottle said, putting away a file which lay on his desk.

Turning around, the school secretary made her way to the counter and said to both parents, "You may go in to see him."

"Thank you," said Mr. Ramos. He and his wife and son rose from their seats and walked into the office area behind the counter and headed to the principal's office. He knocked on the door and entered the principal's office. Mr. Cottle was seated behind a medium-sized desk with a host of files and papers and other stuff. The desk looked cluttered. He sat in a black, low-back swivel chair which appeared to be uncomfortable for a man of his size and six feet three inches in height.

"Good morning, sir," said Mr. Ramos, stretching forth his hands and shaking that of the principal's.

"Good morning, sir," answered Mr. Cottle.

"Good morning, sir," uttered Mrs. Ramos, holding the strap of her bag, which slung over her right shoulder.

"Good morning, miss," replied Mr. Cottle, reaching out and shaking the hand of Mrs. Ramos. "You may be seated." Mr. and Mrs. Ramos sat in two of the three chairs placed in front of the mahogany desk. Gambert sat next to his father.

"How can I help you, Mr. Ramos and Mrs. Ramos?" asked Mr. Cottle, leaning forward in his chair.

"My son Gambert is beaten by three students in his class, almost every day. They punch him and kick him and take his things. They demand stuff from him, and when he doesn't give them, they push his bag and books on the floor. He keeps complaining to us, and we tell him to tell the teachers to see if they would do something about it. I don't like coming up here, but nothing seems to have been done. They're still hitting him and taking his things. I'm tired of it. I send my son to school to learn, not to be bullied by others every day. If nothing is done, my son gonna have to fight back. He could handle himself, but he's not brought up that way to be fighting in school," said Mr. Ramos, who was clearly incensed as he sat and shifted in his chair momentarily.

"Yes, he would complain to me when he gets home in the afternoons about these three boys mainly and sometimes others who would punch him in the shoulders and head and take his things. He tells me the teacher normally sends them to the dean or writes referrals for them to be placed in in-house, but when they return the next day or two, they do the same things to him. They punch him and take his things. He is clearly upset when he comes home. He even told me that he doesn't like the school and wants to go to another school. He doesn't want to come to school in the morning knowing what happens when he gets here. He's so frustrated, and I'm frustrated by what is happening to my son. We're all upset, especially knowing we have to pay such a hefty fee for our child's education, and then he's being punched and bullied in the classroom. I can't believe that they continue to do this even after they're punished by the school. I think that something more serious has to be done so that my son could feel safe coming to school," Mrs. Ramos interjected and related in disgust. Gambert sat still in the chair.

Mr. Cottle listened intently to what both parents said without interruption. He took a deep breath and then said, "This is definitely a serious matter. Mr. Ramos, Mrs. Ramos, I share your concern. This matter should have been solved long ago, and I would see to it that it is redressed. Gambert, who are the students that constantly beat up on you?"

"Umm, umm," Gambert cleared his throat. "Tyrell and Shardon from class 807. Sometimes Obin would hit me, but it is mainly Tyrell and Shardon who hit me and take my things," Gambert explained in a soft voice.

"Okay, let me get these students down here," said the principal. He picked up the intercom and called the office aide. Ms. Coorame knocked and entered his office. He instructed her to check the schedule of class 807 and to call the subject teacher and inform him or her to send the three students to his office. The office aide complied with the instructions by the principal in calling the subject teacher on the classroom intercom instead of using the public address system, and soon had the three students in the office. A grimace was on the face of each student as they seemed worried that they were called to the office to see the principal.

"You are the three students from class 807?" asked Ms. Coorame as the three medium-build young men entered the main office.

"Yeah," Tyrell said.

"Okay, knock and go into the principal's office," said Ms. Coorame firmly.

"What! Wha' happen?" Shardon asked, seeming a bit apprehensive.

"The principal wants to see you," the office aide said.

"Wants to see the three of us?" Obin asked as he appeared worried.

"Yes," answered Ms. Coorame.

Shardon bobbed his head while Obin and Tyrell pursed their lips and walked off to the principal's office. They knocked and the principal answered. "Come in." They entered the office and were starkly surprised to see Gambert and his parents sitting there. Their countenances changed. Their faces dropped; they became wide-eyed.

"Give me your names," said Mr. Cottle flatly.

"Obin," said the taller of the three students.

"Shardon," answered the next.

"Tyrell," the third student answered, frowning.

The principal took his pen from the desk and wrote the names on a white writing pad.

Said Mr. Cottle, sitting up in his chair, "This young man's parents are here and have made a complaint that you constantly attack him and take his things—"

"I ain't attack him or take his things," interjected Obin, his brown eyes glaring.

"Neither me," said Tyrell, pursing his lips.

"Kindly listen. I'm speaking," Mr. Cottle ordered, sternly. His eyes did not blink. The student ceased talking.

Continued Mr. Cottle, "Gambert complained to his parents that you constantly harassed him by punching him, taking his pens and pencils, and when you did not get what you want, you threw his backpack and books on the floor. This is a form of bullying, and it appears that you bully this young man. He frequently tells his parents about the matter. He said, according to what they told me, that he tells the teacher what you normally do to him, and even though you're being sent to in-house for a few days, you come to class and continue to attack him. What is your response to the complaints Gambert made to his parents? Let me hear what each of you has to say."

Obin frowned. "I ain't do this guy nothin'."

"Haven't you punched him and took his things from him on Friday or recently?" asked Mr. Cottle, looking at Obin with a stern face, the pupil of his eyes dilating somewhat.

"No, I ain't punch him and took anything from him on Friday," objected Obin, his eyes rolling from one corner to the next.

"If you didn't do it on Friday, you did it before and recently," said Mr. Cottle, still looking steadfastly at Obin.

"He takes my things too," growled Obin with a smirk on his face.

Joined in Gambert, "I don't take his things. When I don't lend them my pens and pencils and give them loose-leaf paper, they would punch me and take anything I have. Obin, Tyrell, and Shardon, they all punch me and take things from me, but those who do it the most are Tyrell and Shardon."

"Gambert said that all three of you attack him and take his things," the principal reiterated.

Tyrell and Shardon shook their heads in denial that they ever attacked Gambert.

"What you have to say about the complaints made by Gambert? Let me hear you, Tyrell?" Mr. Cottle ordered firmly.

"He's lying on me. I never punched or took nothin' from him. He takes my pens and pencils, and when he ain't give me back when I ask him for them, that's the only time I would punch him. He punch me, too," Tyrell said, bowing his head.

Jumped in Mr. Ramos, "My son wouldn't take anything from you. He wouldn't punch you so what you're saying is just not true. Gambert is not that person who would take your things."

"Yes, he takes our things and he punches us too," Shardon joined in.

"You students seem not to be telling me the truth. I'm going to have a full investigation into this matter so that the three of you do not attack this student as he alleges. I'm going to refer this matter to the dean so that he deals with it and gives me a full report of the outcome. This kind of situation must stop. Gambert's parents came up here to have this matter resolved because they are much worried about his safety owing to the constant complaints he makes to them. You denied that you punched him on Friday or even recently. If it is found that you have been attacking this student on a regular basis, you would receive the full punishment that this misconduct deserves. I'm going to instruct the dean to thoroughly deal with this matter. Mr. Ramos and Mrs. Ramos, I would assure you that your son would not be subject to this kind of harassment again. It is something that we do not tolerate. I'll call Mr. Linsmun, the dean responsible for the eighth grade, who would investigate this matter. I'll give him clear instructions. Your son would subsequently come to school without fear that he would be attacked or bullied. Let me get on to the dean right away," Mr. Cottle uttered. He leaned forward, reached for the intercom, and dialed the dean's office number. The phone was picked up at the other end of the line.

Said Mr. Cottle, "Mr. Linsmun, can you come to my office? I have an important matter I would like you to deal with." The principal then cradled the phone. In minutes, Mr. Linsmun was in the principal's office. Mr. Cottle explained to him the situation and instructed him to conduct a full investigation and mete out the full penalty that the infraction deserves.

Turning to Mr. and Mrs. Ramos, who sat a bit tense in the chairs in front of the principal, expecting a solution to the problem their son was experiencing, Mr. Linsmun politely said, "Mr. and Mrs.

Ramos, you may kindly come with me. Young men, kindly come to my office."

Gambert's parents rose from their seats. Said Mr. Ramos, reaching out and shaking the principal's hand, "Thank you, sir, for looking into this matter."

"You're welcome, Mr. Ramos, and I can assure you that your son would not be attacked by these three students again," the principal said confidently. Releasing the principal's hand, Mr. Ramos then stepped off.

Looking at the principal, Mrs. Ramos said, "Thank you, Mr. Cottle, and thanks for the assurance that this kind of attack on my son would end."

"You're welcome, Mrs. Ramos. The attacks would surely end and thanks again for coming," Mr. Cottle said reassuringly, shaking the hand of Mrs. Ramos.

Mr. Ramos and his wife moved off with Gambert at the side of his mother. The three students walked behind Mr. Linsmun as the dean made his way to his office on the second floor. Mr. Linsmun stopped and told the three students to continue on to his office as he joined the Ramos's and walked beside Mr. Ramos, pointing out to him that he will thoroughly investigate the matter so that his son could have some peace and focus on his schoolwork.

Mr. Linsmun climbed the stairwell to the second floor, preceded by Gambert and the three misbehaved students, while the parents ascended alongside him. He unlocked the door and entered his office. The parents and students entered after him. Immediately, Mr. Linsmun began to find out what happened. Gambert told the dean what occurred over a period of time and last Friday. His parents then spoke about the complaints by their son. Subsequently, the three students were called on to explain their part in response to the complaints lodged against them. They objected to the allegations. Witnesses were called; five of them indicated that they did not see anything perhaps out of fear of snitching. Three students, two female and one male, supported what Gambert said. After thoroughly and carefully weighing the situation and the statements made by the witnesses, the dean came to the conclusion that the three students indeed beat up on Gambert, seized his things, and threw his bag and books on the floor. Tyrell, Obin, and Shardon were each given three days of suspension in the presence of Mr. and Mrs. Ramos and were warned that they faced heavier penalties if the misdeed recurred. Mr. and Mrs. Ramos thanked the dean for bringing a settlement to the problem their son continuously experienced at the hands of those three students. Henceforth, Gambert came to school without being bothered by his former attackers. They do not even look in his direction now. Gambert was able to concentrate on his studies and improve his performance.

Chapter 24

Upstairs on the fourth floor, students hung out in the hallway while Assistant Principals Browman, Holdon, Ascowitz, and McCurdy and Deans Walcott and Harding met with many parents in their offices throughout the day, three days or more in the week. Being aware that the administrators and supervisory staff were rather busy, some students from the eleventh and twelfth grades gathered and played dice on the platform of the stairwell leading up from the third to the fourth floor. It was now the eighth period, and students have swarmed the hallways and lined the stairwells since the first period. Five young men, some of whom appeared grown and somewhat older than seventeen and eighteen years of age, stood together. With a pair of glassy red dice in his right hand Harojd bent over low, shook, and then rolled them on the gray metal platform. They ended up showing the numbers three and six. "Damn! I thought I got double six," Harojd squeaked, glaring at the two dice on the surface.

 A thin, tall student with a sort of hump, who wore a light-green waist-length jacket, said, in giving support, "Roll again, Harojd." He watched as Harojd, once again, rolled the pair of dice feverishly in his folded hand as if they were on fire and threw them on the floor of the metal platform between the third and fourth floors. The two cubes rolled and stopped. They showed the numbers one and two. "Sh—t," Harojd snarled and gritted his teeth. "I say I got it now." He straightened up leaving two dollar bills on the floor.

 Martol, who had his temples and the back of his head cleanly shaven, with a deep part in the middle of his hair which fell back on both sides, scooped up the dice. It was his turn to play. He shook them and let them go. A four and a three appeared on the upper sides of the dice. "Huh," he sighed. His palms felt a little clammy as he placed his hopes on walking away with the bets. "Shake, Martol," an anxious colleague said. Martol turned his head, looked up at him, and nodded. Martol's hand moved back and forth as he rattled the twin glassy objects in his folded right hand. Two other students stood around with one-dollar bills in their hands. "Hit it, Martol," the stockier one said and Martol threw the dice after shaking them two more times. The dice rolled and ended up on the sides, which showed double six. "Yeah!" Martol yelped.

"Yes, we did it," his homeboy said with a big smile on his face. Martol then grabbed four dollars, pocketed two and held two in his hand. A short, medium-build student with braids, a black jacket, and full, baggy blue jeans retrieved the dice. He shook them and let them roll from his hand. He got one and four. He frowned. The others bent over and watched keenly.

Meanwhile, on the fourth floor, an unusual number of eleventh and twelfth graders stood in the hallway of the east wing. Midway two groups, each with about six or seven students, did the same as those in the stairwell. They shook and, in this case, threw their dice against the lower marble-tiled wall of the hallway. The dice ricocheted to the floor and ended up showing various numbers with each throw. Some were pocketing money; others were dishing it out.

Here and there along the hallways, the corridors, of both the east and west wings, students sauntered. Some claimed they didn't have any subject during a particular period; others said their teacher for the subject was absent. Consequently, they didn't want to stay in the room with a teacher who was covering the class. Hence, various pockets or groups of students, both male and female, assembled within the halls; they mingled and bantered. Some sat on the brown tiled floor in their baggy and close-fitting denim jeans and loose-fitting track pants and sneakers and tan, black, and assorted-colored, high-topped, combat-looking, construction-looking, boots. Walkman, CD players, and iPods with their varying headsets were stacked against their ears, and the devices held in swaying, moving hands; they feasted on their various brands or genres of music.

With their backs against the walls of the halls, male students, black, white, Hispanic, and Asian held female students, petite and heavyset, in their arms in a close embrace. Young women, black, white, Hispanic, and Asian, nestled cozily against young men, and young men snuggled up against young women. Eleventh and twelfth graders Rubina, Ragnauth, Esther, Li, Jenevieve, Jerard, Sherryl, Narine, Quing, Chendu, Maniram, Wonke, Annabelle, Balinda, Isaac, Jameisha, Xinhua, Xangtu, Edward, Carlos, Elizabeth, Woonin, Balram, Renee, Susan, Jiang, Ninyang, Angelina, Millicent, Andrew, Renwick, Kalia, Veoni, Shana, Zarena, Irma, Clyvern, Lucas, Minera, Fay, Yavette, Hardat, Hund, and Kathlene, among others, nestled and snuggled against each other.

Students who did some level of work in the classrooms worked, some in earnest, others with a weak spirit. Those who remained in the hallways frolicked. Back in the stairwell, the five students shook and rolled dice and passed dollar bills around. They stooped and at times bent over to see the numbers the dice showed. Again, Martol shook his dice and rolled them on the platform. *Click!* He snapped his right thumb and middle finger as if to indicate he may get the numbers he wanted. A scowl masked his face as he got low numbers. "Shake again, Martol," his buddy told him. Martol upped the dice and shook them vigorously.

"I'm going to see what's happening up there," a loud, coarse voice broke in the lower part of the stairwell.

"Grogan! Grogan comin'!" Harojd squeaked. *Bram, bram, bram . . .* was the instant thunderous sound as feet clobbered against the metal steps of the stairwell as the dice players scampered up to the fourth floor. "What's happening up there?" Sergeant Grogan shouted, running up the stairwell.

"Grogan comin'," Martol yelled, and the students who played dice in the hallway stopped, straightened up, and walked around. Before the supervising security officer got to the fourth floor, the recalcitrant students from the stairwell had disappeared and blended in with those who malingered in the hallway, those talking, laughing, holding, embracing, and walking. Reaching the fourth floor, Sergeant Grogan pushed the door, entered the hallway, and barked, "Who just ran up here from the stairwell?" Eyes rolled and darted from one direction to another, but no one answered.

"You're not going to answer me?" the sergeant bellowed, walking among the groups.

A big-build, round-faced young lady, decked in red knee-length jacket with a fur collar, and wrapped and cuddled in the arms of a big, stocky youngster, looked up in his face and said, "Are you gonna snitch?"

He looked down into her sparkling brown eyes and asked, "Do I look like a snitch. Hell, no. I ain't snitchin' on nobody." His homegirl snuggled up to him and lay her head on his chest. He held her closer.

Bawled a loud-mouthed student, tall and muscular, with a slight beard on his face, "We ain't snitchin', you know that. You wanna know, sneak up yourself or send your guys. But we ain't snitchin'."

Sergeant Grogan pursed his lips as he twisted and turned among the juniors and seniors who were very resistant and had staked out a turf on the fourth floor. Mr. Ascowitz and Ms. McCurdy, the assistant principals for the eleventh and twelfth grades, respectively, came into the hallway of the east wing, where most of the students harbored during sessions.

Said Sergeant Grogan, approaching the two assistant principals, "Ms. McCurdy and Mr. Ascowitz, I think some of the students from here were gambling in the stairwell. I heard a stampede as I was in the stairwell coming up here to see how things were getting on. The noise was loud as they fled the stairwell. It's only when they're playing in the stairwell, and they know I'm coming that they make that noise in fleeing."

"I don't know why so many of them are in the hallway," said the twelfth grade assistant principal.

"You know why we're out here. Either we don't have a subject, or we don't have a teacher. Come on, now. We're juniors and seniors," said Jerard, who looked as if he were twenty.

"You could go to the library, read, research, study. Do something," suggested Ms. McCurdy, holding her black-framed spectacles in her right hand while rubbing the jacket of her pale sky-blue pantsuit with the other. A narrow gold band blended in well with her tan-colored arm.

Wei, a full-faced female Chinese twelfth grader, clad in a tan waist-length coat, said, "We're always out here when we don't have a subject or a teacher. We do work out here. We study, we do homework right here. Why you wanna take away our space when we always been out here?"

"Yeh, yeh, why tell us to move after all this time?" joined in Lucas, a white twelfth grader, decked in a long black coat.

"After all these years students been out here. You kissin' up to Grogan to move us outta here," Zareena, another female twelfth grader of East Indian descent, said.

"We gonna stay right here when we don't have a teacher or a subject," Shana, a female African-American twelfth grader, declared.

Suggested Mr. Ascowitz, "Students, all we're saying is that you could use the library as an alternative where more work could be done."

"Who wants more work? We cool right out here," Juan, a male Hispanic twelfth grade student, broke in.

"But you can't be playing and gaming out here when work is done in other classes," Mr. Ascowitz emphasized, straightening his red-and-blue striped tie that matched with his dark-blue business suit and black square-toe leather shoes.

"We do work out here," Judyann, a thin, blond-haired, white female student, said.

"We're going to leave it at that," said Ms. McCurdy, raising her hand as if she succumbed to defeat. "Mr. Grogan, that's about it, but we're going to keep an eye out for those who want to do other things apart from sitting and doing some peaceful work out here when a teacher is absent or they do not have a subject."

"Yes, this is our space," shouted Jenevieve, a petite African-American, from class 1102, as she embraced Jerard, from the same class.

"We're not moving from here. We ain't bothering anybody," Jerard supported.

"We ain't want to be in no boring classroom when we have a coverage," Phulmattie, from class 1103, mentioned, as she snuggled in the arms of Maniram, from the same class.

"Everybody do work out here even though we talk and laugh sometimes," Azura, a medium-build Chinese female from class 1104, mentioned, as she nestled with Chu, from 1104 as well.

"They seem adamant about moving from here where they claim they do their work apart from talking and laughing a bit. The ones who engage in other unacceptable activities we're going to look for," stated Ms. McCurdy, shaking her head.

"Okay, Ms. McCurdy," said the security officer, moving off and making his way to the exit and down the stairwell. The assistant principals went back to their individual offices. *Cling, cling, cling . . .* the bell rang twenty minutes after to dismiss school at 3:00 p.m. Students now bailed out of classrooms as if it were a stampede and plummeted on the stairwell for the yard and sidewalk, where they congregated.

After clearing the hallways and the number 3 stairwell leading from the second floor to the first, Mr. Linsmun returned to his office where he began some paperwork he did not get the time to do earlier in the day. As he perused one of the several files on his desk, he heard a loud noise coming from the yard. He got up from his seat and looked through the window overlooking the yard. He saw a mob circling two male students who punched away at each other. He bolted from the window, grabbed his bullhorn, and sped down the stairs and out the door. Rushing into the yard, he darted toward the group while he pulled out his radio and called for backup security. A voice then rang out, "Linsmum comin'." Everybody scampered and ran for the southern gate with Mr. Linsmun in hot pursuit. In a jiffy, Officers Stanhope, Morgan, Pandang, and Pamela Kurt were in the yard dashing after the mob of students who showed their heels bolting through the gate. They sprinted up the sidewalk and across the road and disappeared, but the officers and Mr. Linsmun did not give up the chase. They rounded the corner after the students to ensure the crowd was fully dispersed.

"These kids would not go home right away after school is dismissed," protested Officer Kurt, blowing heavily after the chase.

"No, they want to head for the schoolyard and start a fight. They have issues to settle. Trumped up issues with no reasonable grounds. Someone may say something that he or she doesn't like, and they want to fight over that. It's insane and it's the same thing every day," balked Officer Morgan, shaking his head.

"I'm going to find out who those fighters are and deal with them in the morning," said Mr. Linsmun, moving his bullhorn from his right hand to his left.

"You know you're not going to get very far with that, Mr. Linsmun. Nobody is going to say anything," opined Officer Pandang.

"It so frustrating to get these students to say anything," Mr. Linsmun uttered in a very upset mood since he was disturbed from doing the work he had started. The dean and security officers walked back to the school building venting their displeasure about the soaring indiscipline.

Like every day, the next day, Tuesday, a similar scene unfolded with twelfth graders and most eleventh graders malingering in the hallway, mainly in the east wing with a few in the west wing. They continued to show resistance to security and administration, who were not too happy with their presence in the hallways, a feature that occurred over the years. Seniors and juniors were unwilling to move from their turf where they socialized and did some amount of work during the periods when they did not have a subject or a teacher was absent. They became elated with the absence of teachers. They became equally elated when they did not have a subject for a period or two. It appeared to be an occasion of revelry and frolic.

Teachers kept their doors closed to keep the noise out, to enable students in their classrooms to work. Some students who were viewed as nerds by their colleagues sat on the brown tile floor and studied when they did not have a subject or a teacher was absent. Sergeant Grogan and some of his subordinate staff constantly rushed to the fourth floor to keep an eye on what the seniors and juniors were doing. Dice playing had become a problem for security personnel. Known students were suspended for playing dice in the hallways and the platforms of the three stairwells. Security looked out for the recalcitrant, but they were often elusive, and their fellow juniors and seniors, both male and female, refused to point them out to school officials and security.

Additionally, many seniors and juniors looked for camaraderie or comfort from the opposite gender. It seemed as if they sought the company of each other with a passion and fierceness which indicated that something was missing or absent within their domicile. It looked like desperation for togetherness. Leaning against the walls of the hallway, they cling to each other; they snuggled, nestled against each other. Perhaps they sought out their identity or direction. Plump and heavyset young ladies constantly embraced slim young men. Yavette, Minera, Judyann, Irma, and Veoni, among many others were constantly embraced by Clyvern, Li, Andrew, Hardat, and Jose, among many other young men. And faculty and other staff seemed unable to do anything about it. When they rebuked or cautioned students, the students in turn cursed them. It was a tight rope and thin line for faculty and staff, knowing full well that turning a blind eye and allowing students to indulge has serious consequences for students and the image of the school.

Plump and heavy young women hugged and caressed stocky, heavy young men. Slim young women found themselves in the arms of or being cuddled by big, heavy young men. Esther, Rubina, Annabelle, Balinda, and Millicent, among many others, were in the arms of or being cuddled by Enrique, Xinhua, Narine, Isaac, and Ajadu, among many others. And slim young men hugged and cuddled big, heavyset young women. Slim young women also embraced slim young men. It was a mosaic of the human form and spirit. A portrayal or picture of male–female connection. A trend entrenched within the senior school that exuded a feeling of happiness and strength as was expressed by many who found it absent within the domiciliary environment. Students let teachers know that they had endearing friendships with other students of the opposite gender.

Even in the classrooms, when the twelfth graders were not sauntering in the halls of the fourth floor, they cuddly sat and worked. Working together, daily, when they had classes and were in the mood to work, they sat and leaned over to each other, cooed in each other's ears, held each other's hands, and threw their arms around each other's shoulders as they engaged in some learning activities. Among those who had forged strong relationships, holding and hugging each other on a daily basis had become the norm in and out the classroom.

It was since the last semester of their junior year that Veoni and Andrew had developed a friendship which grew steadily. They, obviously, were not the first and were not alone in having a relationship at school. Over the past years, males and females in their senior years had formed some tightly knit friendships that persisted even after they had left school.

It was approaching spring, and the weather was still bleak on many days and snow still fell, making the weather even colder, with the frozen ice on the ground and roofs of houses. Using the cold days as a reason, the young men and women wrapped arms around each other while clothed in their warm jackets. Veoni and Andrew nestled as did Renee and Ragnauth, Rowti and Olatundi, Xho and Pablo, Rosalina and Quing, and Sherryl and Lucas, among a host of other students. They did so in the hallways on the fourth floor, where they hung out in the absence of a subject teacher or if they did not have a subject during a given period.

During lunchtime, Veoni waited for Andrew as they went to the cafeteria. Other seniors and juniors of the opposite gender waited for each other in going from the classroom to the science lab, from the classroom to the language lab, from the classroom to the computer lab, the arts and crafts room, or the auditorium. The cafeteria was an area mainly where they went holding each other's hands or with arms around each other. Veoni normally said to Andrew when he was in the hallway before her, "You wasn't going and leave me here?"

Andrew normally replied even though he knew it was not so, "I was waiting for you."

"You wasn't. You was with your friends," Veoni fretted, grabbing him around the shoulder or waist. "Let's go," she would squeak. She would then smile and bubbly walk off with Andrew.

When Andrew played basketball with his friends some afternoons in the schoolyard, Veoni sat on one of the benches and waited for him, many times cheering him on when he scored. She could have gone home with some female friends from class 1203 or 1204 like Shana, Zarena, Irma, Fay, and Yavette, who traveled in the same direction, or she could have walked home alone, but she was so attached to Andrew that she did not mind waiting for him for an hour or more while he played ball when the weather was cold.

After playing a game of basketball on any given day after school, Veoni and Andrew, in the company of other school friends, would walk down the sidewalk holding hands in heading home. He followed her as far as the block on which she lived and then continued on to his home by getting on the bus. Sometimes, a block away from Veoni's block, they stopped and talked for about twenty or thirty minutes, just to be in each other's company, before they parted and went their separate ways. Both Andrew and Veoni were quite elated in being with each other, but it seemed that Veoni was more than overcome with emotion in seeing Andrew or just hearing his voice when they met or spoke on the phone. Those were moments she did not want to lose.

Some female and male students told teachers they were going to start serious relations with each other when they finished school, which meant either graduating or dropping out of school. Some were thinking of living together later on in life to see how things would work out. The clinging and embracing among some students were irresistible. It was a source of endearment, of emboldenment among the adolescents, those approaching adulthood, and it shed, according to many, the sense and feeling of being forlorn. Notwithstanding, in the spirit of companionship and togetherness, many of the young adults, in the eleventh and twelfth grades, employed the closeness in a positive way. At times, some left the hallway hand in hand and headed to the library or computer lab to embark, collaboratively, on a project or an assignment that was shortly due.

It was not unusual even for some of the junior school pupils to make their way to the fourth floor to catch a glimpse of what their bigger brothers and sisters or older student body were engaged in, in the hallways. In asking for permission to go to the bathroom, Erwin climbed the stairwell and entered the hallway of the fourth floor to have a look at the older ones locked in warm embrace. He was in full glee but he was not alone; Ortis, too, hurried up the stairs to the fourth floor. Jaime did the same as did Fatima and Makalia, Carleen, Nuldun, Blinny, Nakon, Pedro, Ingram, Kemchand, Avery, Curtis,

Hemwattie, Chung, Deonarine, Lawrence, Dana, Barbara, and many others. Whether they thought of imitating the same or not, they got delight from seeing their seniors locked in arms.

"What you doing on this floor?" Officer Stanhope challenged Erwin.

"I went to the bathroom," answered Erwin, his eyes glaring.

"But your bathroom is not on this floor," said Officer Stanhope, his face tightening.

"They locked the bathroom on the second floor," Erwin appealed, scared that he would be sent to the dean and placed in in-house.

"Get off this floor right now," the officer barked at Erwin. He dashed for the stairwell. Hearing Officer Stanhope's voice, Ortis darted; he burrowed among the seniors and juniors and dashed down the stairwell. Fatima angled her way among the older students in trying to escape the eyes of the officer. "Oh gosh, Stanhope on da floor," she muttered. Reaching the exit, she pushed the door and skidded down the flight of stairs. So did Carleen, Pedro, Ingram, and the rest, who sauntered in prohibited territory, the fourth floor, after asking permission to go to the bathroom. The students from the junior school, who got permission to leave the class and those who cut class, all scampered in recognizing the presence of the officer.

Officer Stanhope looked with disdain at some of the older students who embraced each other. Veoni hugged Andrew. Wearing a short-sleeve, round-neck, pink-and-white stripe jersey despite the cold weather, she threw her full arms around his shoulders as he leaned against the wall, decked in a black jersey, black coat, and black baggy denim jeans. His arms, enclosed in the full sleeve of his coat, circled her gently around her waist. Veoni, who groomed her hair in a bun, rested her head against Andrew's chest.

Standing close to Veoni was Esther, whom Luciano lightly held. She pawed his face while they engaged in a light chat. Gloria, a junior, wrapped her pal, Hernandez, around his waist. He reciprocated with his arms around her round tapered shoulders, outlined by the thin stretched fabric of the white jersey she wore. Savatrie hugged Vibert. He held her around the waist. Ping wrapped his arms around Zareena. Others hugged, caressed each other, and bantered. Officer Stanhope looked at them. He frowned but did not say anything. Veoni and Andrew bantered like the others. As they did, she took her index finger and touched him on his lips. He smiled while they shared a bit of light talk. Veoni snuggled with Andrew. She told him something and then punched him in his side. "Chill, man. What you doin'," Andrew squealed.

"You think I can't give you a good punch?" she said, stepping back and looking in his eyes.

"I know you could," uttered Andrew, with his arms now at his side.

Said Veoni, "I'm not coming to school tomorrow."

"Why? Wha' happen? You got somewhere to go?" Andrew asked, his right arm gliding around her waist. She nestled up to him.

"No. I just feel like staying home," said Veoni, looking up in Andrew's face.

"That's whack when you could come to school and be among your friends. At least I could get to see yuh," Andrew suggested.

"Nah, I don't wanna come here tomorrow," Veoni stated, gripping Andrew around his shoulders and pulling him closer to her.

"Well, do as you please," said Andrew. "I'm in school tomorrow. I'll see you the next day."

"You're not coming to school tomorrow either," mentioned Veoni, gliding her full arms down Andrew's side and squeezing him.

"Ahhhh," Andrew croaked, as her arms closed in against his torso. "What! I coming to school tomorrow."

Despite Andrew's tendency to hang out in the hallway as most twelfth graders and eleventh graders did when they did not have a class or a teacher was absent and a substitute was present, he was mindful to focus on his schoolwork, as his parents were very serious about his performance in school. He had tremendous respect for them and wanted to do well. The seniors and juniors were less restless than the ninth and tenth graders and, in particular, the junior school. They did not run around the class and fight. They cursed, as usual, but if a student was not interested in a subject, he or she would either sit quietly, walk out the class, or cut that class and hang out in the hallway with friends. This was the usual behavior among recalcitrant eleventh and twelfth graders. Students at those levels who were not interested in schoolwork simply dropped out, but Andrew was a serious student and had a different approach to school.

Veoni and Andrew still had an interest in schoolwork. They ensured they showed up each day but it was surprising that Veoni was not inclined to be at school one day.

"You're coming to my house 'cause I'm not coming to school," insisted Veoni as she bobbed her head, still making her point about Andrew not coming to school the next day.

"So 'cause you ain't comin' to school I gotta come to your house? No. I don't wanna come to your house. I'm coming to school." Andrew was adamant.

The bell rang ending the period, and students hurried out the classrooms into the hallway. Students who hung out began drifting into classrooms as they had subjects during that sixth period.

"I goin' to math now. I got Mr. James. What you got now?" Andrew asked, moving off.

"I got accounts with Mr. Howard," answered Veoni, looking intently at Andrew.

"I'll meet you outside after three. I got a double science after math," Andrew told Veoni.

"Aright," Veoni replied. She started off in the opposite direction and then turned and ran back and grabbed Andrew around the waist before he could have entered his classroom, room 1201, at the end of the main hall. He turned in surprise, wanting to know who grabbed him, as he thought Veoni had gone. She threw her arms around him, hugged him, and reached up and smooched him on the cheek. Andrew threw his arms around her and smiled.

"See you later," Veoni smiled, removing her arms from around him. Rubbing his head, Andrew entered the classroom to have math with Mr. James as Veoni walked down to the east wing to have class in room 1206 with Mr. Howard. Mr. James continued a topic in geometry. Andrew and Richard sat nearby and worked together, discussing a geometrical problem as Mr. James guided them along. In his accounting class, Mr. Howard reviewed entries in the ledger and procedures related to receipts and payments. At the end of the sixth period, Veoni moved to a seventh-period English class with Ms. Dunn, where the emphasis was placed on grammar and essay writing. Andrew headed to a science class with Mr. Blair, where the class used a model of the brain and spinal column in examining and studying the central nervous system of the human body. Much interaction took place between the teachers and students.

Chapter 25

The bell rang at 3:00 p.m. School was dismissed, and students exit the classrooms and made their way down the various stairwells to the yard and sidewalk. Veoni had already hopped down the stairwell and now stood on the sidewalk waiting for Andrew. She was becoming a bit agitated that he was not out of the building or had gone and left her standing there even though she had indicated she would be waiting for him outside after dismissal as she normally did or he would normally do. Her eyes darted here and there to discern Andrew in the crowd. She did not see him and so began walking along the sidewalk. She thought, *I don't think Andrew left already. He said he gonna meet me out here. Leh me see if he's in the schoolyard playing ball.* Veoni walked to the western entrance to the yard and looked to see who were playing there.

A few students played ball, basketball. She scanned the area but did not see him. She sighed, turned away, and walked along the sidewalk, making her way among the crowd of students. She went back to the main entrance to see if he was waiting somewhere around there for her. She did not see him. She thought again, *Where is Andrew? Is he still in the building? I don't think he has left. I told him I would be waiting here for him.* She shook her head.

Students were still leaving the building. Her eyes were steadfast on the students who came through the door. She pursed her lips and knitted her brows, as she did not see Andrew. "Where is Andrew?" she said aloud. She moved off and headed to the next door. Students were still rushing out the building. Most of them stood on the sidewalk creating much congestion.

"Who you waiting on?" her friend Elesha asked, walking up to her.

"I'm waiting on Andrew," answered Veoni, pulling up the zipper on her coat.

"He must be in there," suggested Elesha, turning and looking at the door from which students exit the building.

"I've been waiting on him for nearly fifteen minutes now," Veoni fretted.

As she became agitated, Andrew worked in Mr. Blair's class on a science project.

"How are you getting on with your research, Andrew?" asked Mr. Blair, glancing at the work Andrew was doing. Andrew did research on a project that dealt with the neurological system of the human body and was just about to complete the work he did for the day.

"I'm getting on good. Getting a grip of how the synapses and neurons function," replied Andrew as he wrote the last bit of data for the afternoon in his log.

"Have you looked at the various studies I discussed in previous lessons?" inquired Mr. Blair as he scanned a science manual.

"Yes, I did," Andrew replied, packing his books and putting them in his bag.

"Okay," the teacher answered.

Slightly turning to his right, Mr. Blair said to another student, "Oscar, are you getting any relevant material for your project?"

"Yes, I am. I'm working on it," Oscar responded.

"And what about you, Onyx? I suppose you're finished with your research," queried Mr. Blair, with much interest in the way students worked.

"No, I ain't finish as yet. I'm still reading on my topic and gathering data," Onyx replied, curtly, without a blink.

"All right, you have your material. Continue doing your research and I'll see all of you tomorrow. Good night," Mr. Blair said, removing his glasses from his eyes.

"Good night, Mr. Blair," Andrew said as he slung his bag over his shoulder and walked out of the classroom.

"Good night, Mr. Blair," Oscar echoed as he slung his backpack on his back and headed for the door.

"Good night, Oscar," Mr. Blair answered.

"Bye, Mr. Blair," uttered Onyx as she and two other students left the science classroom.

"Bye, students," the teacher replied as he stood in front of the classroom.

Andrew and Oscar skidded down the stairs from the fourth floor and made their way through the northeastern exit on the first floor. Walking on to the sidewalk, they headed east. Said Andrew, "I still have more reading to do for my project. When I get home I got to get down to it. What I don't understand I'll ask Mr. Blair to explain it."

"I, too, got a lot of reading and note-takin' to do. I just want to finish with this project, man. It's a lot of work," stated Oscar, settling his backpack properly on his back.

The two young men continued talking about their projects as they walked down the sidewalk to the cross street adjacent to the school. Veoni's eyes were still darting in every direction, and she was becoming more annoyed that she did not see Andrew. She thought he might be somewhere near the school with his friends and had forgotten that she was waiting on him. She had just walked away from the northwestern exit and was making her way eastward after Elesha had departed. Focusing ahead of her, in an effort to discern Andrew if he were in the crowd, as students stood and talked on the sidewalk or pavement, she increased her pace. She then noticed a coat with a familiar color. She began running and maneuvering within the crowd. "Andrew!" she shouted from about ten yards away. Andrew looked around in recognizing the voice. He stopped. Oscar also stopped. Andrew saw it was Veoni.

"Where you went to?" Veoni spurted as a scowl took shape on her face.

"I was in class," said Andrew expressionlessly.

"You were in class?" Veoni questioned, her eyes dilating.

"Yeah. We just left Mr. Blair's science class. I was working on my project. He was working on his project, too," Andrew explained.

"Yes, we were working on our projects," Oscar agreed. "We just came downstairs from Mr. Blair's class."

"Where you going now?" Veoni asked Andrew.

"I going home," Andrew mentioned, looking at Veoni.

"I thought you had gone and leave me here. I was lookin' all over da place fuh you," Veoni declared, shaking her head.

Andrew did not answer. He and Oscar continued talking about their projects. They later switched the conversation to basketball. Veoni joined in from time to time, as she looks at the game frequently and is a supporter of certain stars. After covering four blocks, Oscar said, "Guys, see you tomorrow."

"Later, Oscar," Andrew said, as they knocked fists in giving each other a pound.

Oscar turned the corner and made his way home.

"I was standing on the sidewalk for nearly fifteen minutes. I was thinking whether you gone home and leave me standing out here. I told you I was gonna wait fuh you after school. So when I didn't see you, it was like, wait a minute, he couldn't go and leave me here," mentioned Veoni.

"I was in class," declared Andrew.

"As I told you at lunchtime, I'm not comin' to school tomorrow. I want you to come to my house," said Veoni, reaching out and holding Andrew's hand.

"I can't. I got this project I'm working on for my science class. It's a part of my test grade," uttered Andrew in a serious tone of voice.

"You could still come by me. It wouldn't prevent you from working on your project."

"Yes, I got some serious research to do, and I can't miss any days. Gordon and I working on da same topic, and we share ideas. I don't want to miss out on anything and affect my work."

"You could still come and see me, Andrew. I don't want to stay home alone."

"But you could come to school. You don't have to stay home."

"But I don't want to come to school tomorrow. And I'm not coming to school tomorrow. If you don't come by me tomorrow, I don't want to see you again. Don't ever talk to me or come near me and I mean it."

"I'll think about it."

"You betta think about it or this friendship is over."

Andrew did not respond.

"You come by my house tomorrow, and I'll cook something for us to eat. I could make a cheeseburger or some macaroni and cheese. We could listen to some music, play some video games, and relax rather than coming to school every day. I need a day to chill from schoolwork."

Andrew remained mute. He was thinking hard; his mind raced. He thought about his project and the amount of research he had to do. He really wanted to attend school every day.

"Why you so quiet on me?" Veoni eyed him and threw her arm around his waist.

"Nothing. I just thinking 'bout the work I have to do."

"You could still do your work the next day." Veoni and Andrew continued walking and talking until they came to her block.

"Listen," she said. "I got to go. You could call me later if you want, but I'm looking out to see you at my home in the morning. Remember, no school. I ain't going and you ain't going, too." Veoni words were very precise and demanding.

Andrew tilted his head to one side and looked at Veoni.

"Wha' happen? Why you lookin' at me like that," she questioned.

"Nothin' and I ain't lookin' at you any way different," he said with a heavy mind.

"Okay, son, see you tomorrow at my crib," Veoni stated firmly. She threw both arms around him and hugged him.

"Aright," Andrew said reluctantly.

She released him and they parted. "Bye, Andrew." She patted him on his back.

"Bye, Veoni," Andrew replied. She went to her home, and he strode off in the opposite direction.

He was not really pleased that Veoni wanted him to stay away from school, but at the same time, he did not want to upset her. He wanted to get home and decide what to do. He was very fond of Veoni, and she had a passion for him. She liked to see him every day. She was a serious student as he was, but she could become distracted, especially when she thought deeply about him.

Andrew walked down the sidewalk at a fairly moderate pace, with steady, even steps. He covered a number of blocks and turned a few corners and walked another five blocks in going to his home. A block away from where he lived, he saw a friend. "My man, what up?" Dorven asked.

"I'm good," responded Andrew as they fist-bumped each other and hugged.

"Where you off to?" Andrew asked, arching his shoulders against the chill wind.

"I goin' home. I'm just from school," Dorven answered.

The two of them turned the corner and headed up the road. They talked on their way home. They did not bother to take the bus.

Andrew then said, "My girl wants me to go to her crib tomorrow."

"Yeh, she want you to?"

"Yeh, but I got a project I'm working on and much research to do," related Andrew, looking over at Dorven.

"I'd be over there in a blink, my man."

"I told her I can't come."

"You kidding. Your girl wanna see you and you tellin' her you can't go."

"I gotta work on my science project."

"So? I'd be over there. I'd be at her crib chillin' with her. If she needs your company, check her out. Forget about school for a day."

"I'll think about it."

"You ain't gotta think 'bout it. Just go. Be with your woman for a day," Dorven suggested.

"Son, tell you da truth, I don't wanna go to her home tomorrow. My place is in school," Andrew countered.

"Look, a day away from school wouldn't hurt."

"Well, I really got to think about this tonight."

Andrew and Dorven talked for a while longer as they walked along the various sidewalks in going home. They soon parted and went their separate ways.

Andrew arrived home. His three sisters and brother were already home. They were eating supper. He later joined them. They bantered and played some video games before everyone settled down to homework. Their mother arrived home about seven-thirty and, as usual, had a light conversation with them. Much laughter ensued. Mr. Gussburn was home at around nine. He greeted everyone. There were smiles and laughter, and light talk among them heightened. The siblings went back to work after a while. At around eleven o'clock, Andrew decided to retire. He packed his books in his backpack and headed for the bedroom, which he and his younger brother shared. Lying in bed, he tossed, as his mind was filled with thoughts of Veoni and her wanting to see him tomorrow. He wanted to go to school, but he knew if he did not visit Veoni's home, the friendship would abruptly end as she threatened. Whether she meant it or not, he did not know. He soon fell to sleep.

It was six-thirty when Andrew awakened. He went to the bathroom and then the kitchen. He saw his mom. She sipped a cup of coffee.

"Good morning, Mom," Andrew said, his voice a little coarse.

"Good morning, Andrew. You had a good rest?" Mrs. Gussburn uttered, a faint smile forming on her supple round face.

"Yeh, I had a good rest," Andrew answered, rubbing his eyes.

Mr. Gussburn entered the kitchen, ready for work in his dark slacks, black shoes, and blue long-sleeve shirt.

Said Andrew, in his raspy voice, "Good morning, Dad."

"Good morning, son. You look as if you didn't have much sleep," Mr. Gussburn said, sitting at the table to have a light breakfast.

"I had much sleep. I gonna prepare now for school. Have a good day at work, Mom. Have a good day at work, Dad," said Andrew, walking off to prepare for school. "Thanks, son," his parents answered together. He headed to the bathroom again, where he brushed his teeth and tongue and gargled with mouthwash. He had an exhilarating bath. Andrew dressed, had breakfast, and spoke to his brother and sisters, who were now up and had begun preparing for school. His parents had already left for work. Andrew put on his black-and-yellow jacket, placed his backpack on his back, and headed through the door.

He walked to the bus stop as the early October wind and chill brushed against his face. The hood of his jacket he had already placed over his head. He waited at the bus stop. A few workers and students attending other schools waited on the bus. In ten minutes it arrived. Andrew climbed the stairs, made his way to the back, and held the overhead bar. The bus was fairly crowded. It pulled off, making stops at each bus stop along the route to put off and take on passengers, many of whom were mainly students.

Andrew got off a block away from Veoni's block. He did that most mornings and walked to her building, where he waited for her. Together, they headed to school, sometimes meeting friends along the way. Instead of making his way to school since Veoni decided not to attend school, he headed to her home. As he walked along the street to her home, he thought, *Should I go to her home or go to school?* The thought gripped him. He stopped. He thought hard; he wrestled with it. He looked up at the building in front of which he stood. It was the building before the one in which Veoni lived. He looked down and thought of making an about-face and heading to school. He bit his bottom lip and edged forward. He looked around and continued to move forward. He finally ended up in front of the main door to the four-family brick home. He pressed the buzzer to the second floor. A familiar voice answered, "Who is it?"

"Andrew," he said. The buzzer sounded. He pushed the door and went in. His respiration increased a bit. His heart pounded stronger. He knew he never visited Veoni during schooltime. He only did so on Saturdays, after lunch, and not very often. He climbed the stairs and got to the second floor. He tried to compose himself not to appear timid. He pressed the bell on the wall near the door. The door gradually opened, and a bright smile greeted him.

"Come in, good morning," said Veoni, her smile becoming broader.

"Good morning," Andrew said and walked into the home. Veoni closed the door. She turned and hugged him. He hugged her. The living room was somewhat dim with only one table lamp on. The dark, heavy curtains flowed to the floor and prevented the entry of any daylight.

"Good to see you. I feel good that you did come," Veoni said, releasing Andrew. He removed his arms from around her.

"Yes," Andrew said, looking around the living room.

"Remove your bag and take off your coat," Veoni said, still smiling. She wore a gray hooded sweater, gray sweatpants, and pink bedroom slippers.

Andrew removed his black backpack and took off his black-and-yellow jacket which Veoni took from him and placed in the closet.

"Sit wherever you want," she said, tapping him on the back. He remained expressionless.

"Your parents home?" Andrew asked out of concern.

Veoni knitted her brow and then said, "Absolutely not. They left for work about an hour ago. They not gonna be home 'til six or seven o'clock. Don't worry." Her older sister was away at college.

Andrew sat in a long, solid brown sofa.

Standing in front of him, she said, "Doesn't it feel good to be away from school for a day?"

"I ain't know," mumbled Andrew with a worried look on his face.

"Of course, you know it feels good," said Veoni with an unusual brightness in her eyes.

Veoni then sat next to Andrew on the sofa. Quietly, they looked at a TV show. At the end of it, she said, "Let's play a game of monopoly. I like this game." She giggled and rose from her seat. She walked to a bookshelf from which she retrieved the game. She returned and placed it on the sofa, and together she and Andrew played the game of monopoly. After a good hour of playing and since Andrew won most of the games, Veoni mentioned, "I promised I gonna do some cooking."

"Wha' you gonna cook?" asked Andrew, looking over at Veoni as she sat a foot or two away from him, with the game in the middle.

"I gonna make you a nice juicy cheeseburger with lettuce and tomatoes. We have some baked chicken. I'll make us a chicken salad. Then we'll have some cold fruit drink. How that sounds?" Veoni asked, moving the game, edging closer and throwing her arms around Andrew.

"That sounds good. At least I'll fill my belly." Andrew chuckled.

"Hope your belly don't burst," laughed Veoni, rising from the sofa.

It was near eleven o'clock. She patted Andrew on the shoulder and walked to the kitchen. "I'm going to get this food together," Veoni uttered.

She opened the refrigerator, took out the meat, and added some seasoning while Andrew sat on the sofa and looked at a movie.

About ten minutes after Veoni busied herself in the kitchen, seasoning the four raw beef patties, she said, "Come over here, Andrew. Come see what I'm doing."

"I'm looking at this movie," answered Andrew.

"I want you to see how I'm cooking," pleaded Veoni, looking over her left shoulder.

"Okay," Andrew said. He got up from the sofa, pulled the waist of his jeans, which sagged just below his waist, and walked to the kitchen.

"It's nice for you to be next to me, seeing what I'm doing," Veoni said with a quick wink and a smile.

Andrew smiled. "You making a salad too?" he asked, not feeling as tense and out of place as before. "Yeh." Veoni nodded.

He helped her, and together they prepared juicy cheeseburgers and a bowl of chicken salad. It took them about an hour to prepare the food. Together, they sat on the sofa and heartily ate the cheeseburgers and salad. As they ate, they drank the ice-cold fruit punch while watching another movie. It was approaching half past one when they finished eating.

Veoni got up, went to the bathroom, and washed her hands and mouth. She returned to the living room. "I'm going to wash my hands and mouth too," said Andrew, having enjoyed the meal and felt satisfied like Veoni. He rose to his feet, pulled up his jeans, and edged to the bathroom. Within minutes, he was back in the living room, relaxing on the sofa next to Veoni. She snuggled up to him and leaned her head against his chest as she placed her feet on the coffee table. Andrew placed his left arm on the back of the sofa. He curved his arm at the elbow and passed his fingers on the top of Veoni's long, black hair. She looked up at him. He looked down at her. Their eyes locked. Veoni reached up and smooched him on his left cheek. He smiled. His body tingled. He brought his arm down and lightly held her shoulder. She leaned more on him and then said, "I'm feeling warm in this sweatpants and sweater. I'll be with you in a minute."

She got to her feet and walked to her bedroom. Soon after, she returned wearing a white T-shirt and a medium-length, red-and-blue flowered skirt. She sat and cuddled up to Andrew. He turned and kissed her on her right cheek and then her lips. She sighed. Andrew felt a little tense, as he thought that he should not be there at that time of day. He knew he had cut school and that momentarily bothered him, but he quickly dashed the idea as he closely held Veoni and passionately kissed her. He then relaxed his grasp around her shoulder. She got to her feet, grabbed his right hand, pulled him to his feet, and led him to her room. He meekly followed as a passion soared within him as it did within her.

It was three-thirty when Andrew stood at the door. "I'll see you tomorrow at school," said he.

"Yes, I'll see you tomorrow," Veoni answered. They hugged each other, and she gave him a kiss on his cheek. He did the same and walked through the door. Andrew thought about his visit during school time. He had visited her home at weekends on a few occasions, especially Saturdays. He thought many times about this particular visit. And again, Veoni encouraged him to visit her on three more occasions during school days.

It was December, and Veoni appeared as if she was gaining weight. Her face looked fuller, and her shoulders and hips became larger. She was heavyset and became even heavier over the last few months. She had started wearing fuller and looser clothes and they made her look bigger than her normal heavy size. Veoni constantly thought of her situation, and she frequently imparted her feelings and thoughts to Andrew. He also thought hard about her. As usual, they arrived at school on time, and as the days went by, she even became closer to him. She continued to wait for him during lunchtime and at dismissal at three o'clock, and he also did the same. In class, she tried to focus on her work though at times she felt a little uneasy.

"You're putting on weight, Veoni, or is it the full clothes you're wearing that's making you look bigger?" asked Judyann from class 1205.

"Yeh, I putting on a little weight," answered Veoni casually.

"She may be eating a lot of food. Your appetite must have doubled," remarked Nadira, rubbing Veoni's stomach. Nadira was on her way to her class in room 1202 when she saw Judyann, and both of them stopped to talk with Veoni.

"I ain't eating all that much," responded Veoni. Other students asked her similar questions.

She just told them she was putting on a little weight. She talked to two or three of her very close friends about her weight gain, and they showed much empathy for her. Andrew also told two of his friends about Veoni's situation in gaining weight. They understood and rallied around him.

Veoni did her work and made efforts to complete her assignments to get the requisite number of credits to graduate. Andrew appeared to be more focused. He had completed his project and submitted it on time. His friend Oscar had submitted his project as well, and his teammate Gordon, who did a similar project, had also presented his to Mr. Blair. Andrew, like his two close friends, continued research in science and worked hard on his math. He was doing good in class although he was a little distracted. He was one of the hardworking students, and his parents depended on him to do well in his studies. They took a keen interest in his work. Even as Andrew worked hard, he did not at all times look jolly and upbeat as before, but he managed to submit his projects and other assignments on time.

Chapter 26

Veoni parents also expected her to do well, and they gave all the encouragement she needed. They saw to it that she had everything she needed for school. Both parents talked with her about the conditions at school and the fact that she was still performing well. They were careful about what she ate since she was rather plump. Nevertheless, her parents noticed the weight gain but just thought she was eating more and wearing the loose garment to cover her weight. Veoni worked hard on her assignments and did the necessary studies in the school library and at home. Both she and Andrew had wanted to graduate on time, and although they were enamored by each other, they managed to put in hours of study.

As the months slipped by, Veoni looked even fuller and continued to wear even looser clothing. She became more attached to Andrew. Every spare moment she had at school, she wanted to be with him, but that was not possible, as he had much work to do, and he made the effort to do so. She frequently talked over things with her close friends. Andrew even did the same. As the month of April approached, Veoni found herself taking a day off or two from school. When questioned by her mom about her staying away from school, she said they did not have a teacher or a subject.

Veoni did not go to school one morning during the spring season of May, as she did not feel well. Her stomach pained. She felt muscle pain. It was a sunny Thursday morning, and a mild breeze swept the surroundings. She looked through the window from the living room and saw the bright sunlight. It was close to ten o'clock, and her mother was sorting some important documents in her bedroom. The door was slightly ajar. Veoni turned from the window and noticed the door was not closed.

She thought of going in to see what her mom was doing and to have a light conversation with her since they just greeted each other for the morning and did not have any lengthy talk, but just as she stepped away from the widow she felt a lancing pain in her abdomen and so decided to go to the bathroom. The pain became more intense while she stood for a brief moment. She wrung her hands as the pain bit her. Her face twitched. She gritted her teeth as there was no letting up in the pain. She realized that water flowed along her legs and instantly decided to enter the bathtub. With the pain, she did not even feel the coldness from the floor of the tub. The water flowed more, wetting her thighs, nightdress, and floor of the tub. The water was discolored. And the pain almost wracked her stomach. She could not stand any longer and decided to sit. The pain became unbearable, and Veoni screamed, "Ahhhhh, ahhhhhh, ahhhhhhh . . ."

The bathroom door was not fully closed, and her mother, who sat in the nearby bedroom, heard the loud cry and dashed for the living room. She did not see Veoni. She rushed to the bathroom. "Ahhhhhh," the mother yelled. She saw Veoni lying in the bathtub and a baby, covered in blood and mucous with the umbilical cord attached, on the cold and wet floor of the bathtub. "Veoni, you were pregnant? Why didn't you tell me, why Veoni?" Mrs. Vendura cried, the tears streaming down her surprised and shocked face as she leaned over the tub, looking fleetingly at her daughter who was almost knocked out and the baby who bawled, "Ahhhhh," at the top of his lungs as he felt the hands of his grandmother, who touched him. Instantly, Mrs. Vendura dashed for a towel, bent over, and wrapped the baby in it. She placed it on Veoni's stomach and told her to hold the newborn. She tried to keep her head on as she was much confused, not expecting to see what she saw. Her heart was pounding. With the baby on Veoni's stomach and Veoni masked with a grimace on her due to the severe pain, she lamely raised her arm and held the child lying on her.

Rushing from the bathroom, Mrs. Vendura grabbed the phone in the living room and dialed 911. In five minutes, the ambulance and paramedics were at her front door. They entered with a stretcher and other equipment. They hurried to the bathroom where they briefly attended to the baby and mother. Shortly after, they were wheeling Veoni and her baby through the living room to the elevator. They were rushed, along with Mrs. Vendura, to the nearest hospital. Veoni was taken to the emergency room and then admitted to the maternity unit, where she and her baby did fine.

Mrs. Vendura, still confused and startled, had forgotten her cell phone, but through a payphone at one of the booths on the floor, she managed to get through a call to her husband. "What you said? I don't think I heard you clearly. You're not serious," Mr. Vendura answered as if something dealt him a blow in his stomach.

"Yes, I am. She's in the hospital," Mrs. Vendura emphasized, with her voice cracking.

"You're serious or you're passing one on me—" Mr. Vendura said, trying to decipher what his wife was really saying to him.

"Oh, Alridge, I'm serious," Mrs. Vendura interrupted and began crying aloud.

Instantly, Mr. Vendura felt as if his stomach was tearing apart. His pressure rose immediately, and he felt dizzy. He couldn't catch himself. It was as if his world was spinning and spinning out of control. He tried to calm himself by taking some deep breaths. Moments after, he went to his boss, knocked on his door, and entered his office. He explained to him that an emergency had developed at home and that he wanted to leave and, if possible, he would be back for the afternoon session. The manager was considerate, knowing that he was a dependable and committed worker who gave his best to ensure that the company remained vibrant and competitive in the marketplace. The manager allowed Mr. Vendura to leave. He left and headed to the nearest subway and made his way to the hospital. He decided which train he would need to transfer to in order to reach his destination. His head felt heavy, and his temples felt as if they were pounded with a sledgehammer. He was in a state of shock, but he journeyed to his location.

Within an hour, he got to the hospital. His wife saw him and broke down. He tried and composed himself and attempted to console her though he felt the pain both physically and emotionally. They were not allowed into the unit, as the doctor and other health-care providers were in attendance to ensure that the baby was fine as well as the mother since she was not under the care of an obstetrician and gynecologist during her prenatal period of pregnancy to give her any advice and treatment. They had wanted to determine if there were any risk factors involved. After a thorough examination of both mother and child and a determination of the prognosis of the delivery, visitation was allowed. Both parents stood at the bedside looking at the newborn baby and their daughter whom they did not observe was pregnant. They were dumbfounded. They did not know what to say to each other or to their daughter. Veoni did not know what to say to her parents also. She lay in bed as though she was lost.

Two days later, she was discharged from the hospital. Prior to her leaving the hospital, Mrs. Vendura, with the assistance of her husband, checked various children and baby stores where she purchased baby clothing and accessories for her grandson and attire for her daughter and new mother. Everything had changed for the

Vendura family. The parents felt deceived and hurt, but they gave support to their daughter; Veoni's brother and sister also supported her mutually and physically.

Upon her discharge, Veoni communicated with Andrew. She broke the news that she gave birth to a seven-pound, nine-ounce baby, a boy. It was bittersweet for Andrew. He was glad that she had a safe delivery and that he had a son since he knew she was expecting but did not tell his parents. To him, it was the last thing on their mind and the last thing they wanted to hear. When he broke the silence and told them that Veoni gave birth a few days ago and that he now fathered a son, he was greeted with both outrage and empathy. His parents were so disappointed that they remained home for a few days to get themselves together. Mrs. Gussburn suffered a spell of depression, but with the support of her husband and medication prescribed by their family doctor, she was able to overcome the brief illness. Finally, they came to grips with reality and gave Veoni and their son the necessary support they needed in the upbringing of the young child and their grandson. Both Veoni and Andrew continued at school for the remaining months until they graduated and moved on with their lives, having realized the mistake they made as two young people.

Chapter 27

Disruption continued to be a repulsive element of classroom delivery and learning. It would abate. It quells for a moment, then spirals to the next. The moment students arrive, there is the possibility that some unpleasant scenario would erupt, whether mild or grave. With the sound of the bell, Tamara waltzed into room 3-1003 flailing her arms while having her bag slung across her shoulder. She moved toward her desk, put her backpack on it, and headed toward the radiator. She turned, heaved herself, and sat on the warm radiator. It was "passing," just after the bell, and the teacher who stood at the door observing students as they passed by looked into the classroom as students entered. Her eyes caught the female student. She ordered, in a roaring voice, "Young lady, get off that radiator. Why are you sitting there?"

Tamara replied, "I'm just warming up."

"What!" Mrs. Gringburg exclaimed in surprise.

Smiling, Tamara said, "I trying to get some heat."

"Young lady, kindly get off the radiator," Mrs. Gringburg belched again. The student finally came off the radiator.

The business lesson began after the class entered and sat, with students reading material on how the stock market works and how investors invest their money. They were advised to focus on the difference between investing in stock and investing in bonds and how the market unfolds on any particular day. After reading two articles, much discussion began among students, and Mrs. Gringburg guided the talks. She then explained a point on stocks.

Said Terence to Mrs. Gringburg, "Could you stop talking? You're hurting my head."

"You're rude, young man. I'm instructing the class, and you're telling me to stop talking," Mrs. Gringburg rebuked.

"Yes, you're too loud," retorted the abrasive student as he crouched over his desk. The teacher grimaced and shook her head in disbelief. She then continued with her instructions. The lesson went peacefully until there was a sudden bang. A desk was overturned. Promptly Mrs. Gringburg walked to the side of the class.

"Who threw that desk on the floor?" she questioned, her face becoming tight.

Blurted out Mark, "Keil did it."

With deeply set eyes in his narrow face, Keil said, "Kirk was fooling around. I told him to stop touching my things and hitting me."

"But that doesn't mean you have to overturn the desk. Raise your hand and make a complaint," said Mrs. Gringburg, looking intently at Keil.

"He was touching my stuff. I'm not gonna let anybody interfere with my things," said Keil, pouting.

"Kirk, stop touching his things. And Keil, you're not going to be throwing desks on the floor because someone touched your things. Let me know and I'll deal with it," Mrs. Gringburg said firmly.

Keil made a stern face that showed anger. The teacher continued with the lesson. Students were then given a class activity to work on and were allowed to share ideas. Mrs. Gringburg interacted with them until the end of the period to have an assessment of what was learned. The bell rang, and students rushed into the hallway apparently relieved that the period was over and that they could walk around cavalierly for a minute or two.

Students hollered and yelled in the hallway while they travelled to their next class. A bird flew into the hallway on the first floor and like a flash of lightning, hysteria broke out. Students ran and shouted,

"Ahhhh," "Da bird gonna pick," "Hell no, get out da way," "Where da sh—t come from," "Move, move," were the loud noises as they pushed each other to get to their classrooms. Teachers were perplexed at the way the sixth and seventh graders reacted.

Said Mr. Blair, "What's the big fuss or scare about? It's just a bird!"

Said Ms. Langevine, "Why you students are running and pushing your way into the classroom?"

"A bird's in the hallway," shrieked a female student, quite agitated.

Stepping to the threshold of the classroom, Ms. Langevine saw the bird flapping its wings close to the ceiling. She commented, "You students should be ashamed of yourselves. Don't tell me you're afraid and running from a bird. And it's a beautiful bird at that. You are sixth and seventh grade students. What's wrong with you?" The students were in an uproar at the sight of the bird in the hallway.

"Wha' you gonna do if the bird bite us?" a female sixth grade student asked after she ran into the room.

"Those birds don't bite anyone. And they don't pick anyone too," explained Ms. Langevine.

"It could pick me in my eye. I don't wanna get blind like that. That's why we running," another female student said. The teacher did not prolong the exchange.

The stress that teachers felt daily from managing the classes was wearing down many of them to the point where there were absences among them every day. The administrative assistant called many substitute teachers to fill the gap when regular staff members could not make it to work. A female substitute teacher, among others, was called in to cover a class since several teachers were absent from work that day. The professional-looking young woman decked herself in a black pantsuit and white shirt, the collar of which rested on the lapels of her jacket and gave her that extra poise for a corporate environment. With well-manicured hands and well-done makeup and mild accessories, she reported to Jones High School very optimistic that she would have a very productive day in teaching a lesson in earth science. In the main office, she was given her schedule; she read it and walked off graciously in her black pointed-toe heeled shoes. *Clix, clax, clix, clax* was the sound that rose from the tiled floor.

She proceeded to room 1-602. Mr. Howard performed the official routine of class 602 during homeroom. The young substitute teacher entered and spoke with him. The eyes of every student widened in anticipation. Asked a student who sat in the front row, "You're our teacher for today?"

"Yes," the medium-build and gracious-looking teacher said.

"Ahhhhhh, yeahhhh, ahhhhhh . . ." was the explosive, electrifying outcry.

The young woman was taken aback; she was jolted by the suddenness of the eruption.

"Why all of this loud noise? It's uncalled for," Mr. Howard barked and glared at the class.

"Hu, hu, hu . . ." some of them hooted.

Turning to the sub teacher, Mr. Howard said, "I don't know what to say about some of these students. I hope you manage and have a good day."

"Thank you. I hope so," said the substitute teacher, as the veteran teacher walked to the door and entered the hallway.

"Yeah, yeah, yeah . . " the class bellowed again. Students rose from their seats. Others jumped on desks in moving from one part of the room to another. Some wrestled on the floor, and yet others rushed into the hallway and back into the classroom. Garbage bins were overturned. They hurled paper balls, crayons, pens, and books in the air at each other. The floor became a mess. Confusion reigned in the class for the rest of the period much to the bewilderment of the substitute teacher.

With the absence of many teachers on all the floors, students appeared to have a cavalier attitude in the stairwell, the bathroom, the east wing on the other floors, the east and west wings on the fourth floor, and even the classrooms. On the second floor, Shardon, from class 807, rushed into the hallway and saw two of his friends running around. Said he, "What yuh doin'? You're not goin' to classes?"

"We're going to the guidance counselor," said Carla, dragging her haversack on the littered floor of the hallway, strewn with loose-leaf paper, paper bags, plastic bags, plastic bottles, broken pencils, busted pens, markers without covers, candy wrappers, gum that stick to the soles of footwear, and remnants of food which attracted rodents. It was surprising how quickly the hallway was littered during passing at the end of class after custodial staff had diligently swept and removed litter and mopped spillage of juices, soda, and milk, which were prohibited from being brought into the hallway and classroom, but students had a way of sneaking in food and drink in their backpacks and eating and drinking them in those two areas.

Added Kathlene, "He has to sign this letter for us to have additional reading classes."

"You need extra reading classes?" asked Shardon.

"They say we have to get it," Carla replied.

Shardon then pulled a toy teddy bear tied on Carla's bag, and she yelled, "Don't pull it."

Shardon playfully pulled it again and stepped back grinning.

Carla shrieked, "Don't pull my teddy bear."

Shardon pulled it once more, and she lashed out at him with a book in her right hand. "I said don't pull it."

Shardon drifted back, turned, and ran as Carla chased after him, dropping her bag on the littered floor. She caught up with him, cornered him against the wall, and, with flailing hands, dealt him several blows about his body. With a flailed right hand, Shardon returned light punches at her while he held a bottle of soda in his left.

Tyrell darted into the hallway from his classroom chanting the lyrics of a popular hip-hop tune.

Shardon shouted, "Hold muh soda fuh me." Tyrell reached out and held the soda while Shardon and Carla playfully traded light punches at each other. She hit Shardon, and it appeared as if a button broke from his shirt. Shardon looked down at his shirt, but it was the zipper that slid down. Thinking that his zipper might have broken, Carla turned and ran away, picking up her bag from the floor, as Kathlene, who stood a distance away, said, "Let's go, man. I want this form to get signed."

"Okedokee," uttered Carla quickly as they ran down the hallway. Shardon pulled up the zipper of his jacket.

Walking toward Tyrell, who held the green bottle of soda, Shardon said, "You drink my sh—t?"

"I ain't drink yuh sh—t," answered Tyrell.

"Gimme," Shardon snapped, snatching the bottle from Tyrell's hand.

"Don't diss me, man," rebutted Tyrell, knitting his brow.

"I ain't diss you," replied Shardon, putting the bottle to his mouth and gulping his soda. The two young men walked back to their classroom. At the threshold, Ms. Dennison accosted them, "Why did you leave the classroom?"

"Move out da way, I wanna pass," Shardon belched.

"No. Don't tell me to move out the way because you want to pass. I didn't send you outside," the teacher scolded.

"So," answered Shardon.

"You're so disrespectful. For that matter, I'm going to call your home," said the teacher.

"Do as you please, call it," Shardon shot back.

"You're going to talk something else tonight," said the teacher.

"Whatever," snorted Shardon, as he slipped past the teacher and moved toward his seat. He sat down, slouching in the chair. The teacher then turned and approached Tyrell, who had slipped into the class and into his seat as the teacher accosted Shardon.

"Where is your work, Tyrell?" the teacher asked.

"You sent me to the bathroom," reminded Tyrell although he did not reach the bathroom.

"Yes, but where is the work you did before going to the bathroom?" the teacher asked.

Tyrell started flipping through the pages of his binder and responded, "I'm searching for it."

"What! Do you have to search for your work when it ought to be in your notebook in front of you?"

"I wrote on loose-leaf paper and put it in my binder," Tyrell declared.

"You better get it by the time I get back to you. You just kept talking and talking," the teacher warned.

Obin, the next student in the row, did some of his work. Asked Ms. Dennison, "Why haven't you finished your work?

"I did it," replied Obin, eyeing the teacher through his metal-framed glasses.

"But it's not finished. I saw you carrying on a conversation with Nicole. And she hasn't even started as yet," said the teacher, glancing at Nicole's notebook.

"Wait a minute. Haven't you seen me started my work?" blurted out Nicole.

"But all you've done is wrote the aim, and we're twenty minutes into the period," remarked the teacher.

"I started my work if you didn't know," Nicole fumed at the teacher.

The teacher did not prolong the exchange but moved around checking the work of other students and assisting them in solving the problems.

Erwin had asked to go to the bathroom and was given permission to go. As he walked along the hallway on the second floor, he looked into some of the classrooms. He looked into a room and said, "That room is thrashed." The classroom was untidy with newspapers strewn and textbooks scattered on the floor. Students emptied trash from their desks on the floor. Candy wrappers, book bags, plastic bags, paper bags, plastic bottles, broken pencils and pens, loose-leaf paper, and magazines and colored coats were all over the floor. It was a mess. Desks were overturned, and chairs were tumbled on the floor. Two desks were pushed near the wall, another four in the center, three were disarranged near the blackboard. Another few desks were lying near the backdoor and chairs were all around in classroom 1-705 as students came in but did not settle down so that the teacher could begin the lesson.

Many of them in the room shouted, laughed, and screamed at each other. Some, as usual, jumped and ran around the classroom. A little while after, a group of female students and two or three males moved toward the window and looked out. They pointed and shouted through the window at a number of young men, who were way beyond school age, perhaps in their early and mid-twenties, but played basketball in the yard. The female students in particular hailed. Bawled Felicia, leaning through the window, "Hi!"

"Come to the fence leh me talk to you," Ruth shouted, her hazel eyes twinkling.

And yet another female, Camille, hailed, "Hi, Falecia, say she wanna talk to yuh."

One of the young men in a gray hooded sweater looked over to where the young ladies were at the window. "You wanna talk to me or him," asked the young man, pointing to a colleague in a red-and-white jacket, who bounced the ball on the court and fired a shot at the basket.

"I wanna talk to you," Felicia shouted.

Yelled Ruth, "She doesn't wanna talk to you, I do."

The teacher barged to the students and howled, "Away from that window now. And close it."

"What's wrong with you? We're trying to make friends," said Felicia. "You don't make friends?"

"Remove from the window, now," the teacher ordered, her eyes glaring and steadfast.

Reluctantly, the young ladies moved away from the window. The male students who had briefly looked through the window and watched for a moment the young men playing basketball had removed and had returned to their seats where they malingered unwilling to do any work. The teacher hurried back to the middle of the class and continued her lesson with half of the class not paying attention.

In returning from the bathroom, Erwin was curious to know what was going on in some of the classes. He was amused by the way lots of his colleagues behaved in the classrooms though he refrained from behaving in that manner inasmuch as he giggled and laughed at the way some of his friends conducted themselves. Erwin peered into a few rooms as he walked close to the wall in the hallway on the first floor and saw the disruption that took place.

Fumbling in her black-and-red bag for tissue, Abena, who sat next to where Mr. Mendez stood, said, "Mister, soda spilled on my skirt and wet it. Could I go to the dean and call my father? He will bring a dress for me."

"Where's your father?" asked Mr. Mendez.

"He's at work," said the petite student. "And he's gonna bring a skirt for me."

Said the teacher, "Is your father going to leave work to bring a skirt for you?"

"Yes," said the student, her eyes widening as her mouth remained open.

"You cannot go to the dean," said the teacher, shaking his head.

The student began to cry. She wailed. Mr. Mendez ignored the tantrum. Suddenly she stopped and started laughing with her friends.

The teacher went around the room, checking the work of students. Said he, "Hello, young man, have you started your work?"

"I'm doing my work in my hand," answered Daren boldly. "I don't like to waste my paper."

"You better waste it. Get your work done," Mr. Mendez ordered sternly.

"Aight, aight, we cool, mannn. I gonna do your work," Daren replied.

"You better do," the teacher uttered.

Disruption continued during the remainder of the week. Students pounded on desks and chanted rap lyrics in creating a ruckus with their rhythm and loud noise. Hardly any work was done; they just wrote the questions without any answers and claimed they did their work, while they sat in small groups talking, laughing, and cursing.

Elonz, who paced near the windows of his class, coughed and spat on the floor. Mrs. Baighman saw him and hurriedly approached him. Said she, "Why did you spit on the floor? You cannot do that."

Elonz coughed and spat on the floor again.

"Did you hear what I said? You cannot spit on the floor. It's nasty and unhygienic," Mrs. Baighman warned in a pitching voice.

"I got asthma," Elonz said, putting his hand to his throat as he coughed, "Ah hum, ah hum."

"Take the pass and go to the nurse," the teacher ordered.

"I ain't goin' to no nurse. I ain't need no tablet," said Elonz, walking away and then turning around. "You want me to clean it?"

Elonz grabbed a newspaper from the desk, bent over, and wiped the floor in a wild manner.

"You smearing that sh—t all over da floor," a plump, full-faced female student said loudly.

Straightening up, Elonz said to the teacher, "You satisfy now."

The teacher glared at him but did not say anything. She walked back to the front of the class. The intercom rang. A staff member from the office called but before Mrs. Baighman could have gotten to it a student who sat nearby leapt from his chair, grabbed the receiver, and said "This is Cliff's Restaurant. Can I take your order?"

"What? shrieked Ms. Ellis from the main office.

"What happened?" asked Mrs. Caldwell

"Some student answered the intercom and said, 'This is Cliff's Restaurant. Can I take your order?' What's going on with these students in this place. I called to speak to the teacher," Ms. Ellis fretted.

"Ha, ha, ha, these children are out of their minds. I don't know what is happening," Mrs. Caldwell said.

Ms. Ellis called again, and this time the teacher answered the phone.

Shortly after the teacher spoke with the office staff, Mr. Ascowitz, assistant principal, brought a folder to the classroom and instantly cautioned students to be quiet. Said he, to one of the talkative and often disruptive students, "This is your binder. It was found in the hallway. Do your work." He put the binder, with the student's full name and class, on the desk in front of him.

The student glanced up at the assistant principal and said, "That is not mine. I don't want it."

"It's yours. Your name is in it and your work," said the assistant principal.

"I said it's not mine. I don't want it," he yelled. The student then leaned over to his side and threw the binder in the garbage bin.

The AP looked at him with stark disbelief and shook his head.

Said the student, "Wha' you lookin' at me for?"

The assistant principal walked to the door and exited into the hallway closing the door behind him.

Chapter 28

"Students, you have thirty minutes in which to do the quiz," said Mr. Aaron, standing in front of the class.

Mr. Aaron walked from the front of the chalkboard and moved around the room. He collected the handouts and written work from students, most of whom had finished the quiz before the thirty minutes had elapsed. They were given additional work while the six remaining students who were not finished were allowed to continue working until the bell rang. It was a fairly good day for Mr. Aaron as he conducted quizzes in five classes, sixth and seventh grades, and was able to properly monitor the classes, ensuring that students worked in a quiet atmosphere.

The students in all five classes did cooperate with Mr. Aaron, who substituted for Mr. Glick, a veteran teacher of almost thirty years at Jones High, who was out sick for more than a month. The noise level was low, and hardly anyone spoke as students tried to do their best, focusing on the assignment, the quiz. At 2:50 p.m., the bell rang signaling the end of the eighth period. Mr. Aaron walked to each of the remaining six students who still worked and collected the quiz and the handout as the rest of the class sat and did some assigned work which he said he would continue the next day. He then walked back to his desk on which he put the papers.

A pleasant thought filled Mr. Aaron's mind, *No doubt it was a good day.* He breathed a sigh of relief, knowing it was Friday and the end of the working week. A sudden bang on the door from the hallway echoed, and chirpy, high-pitched voices rattled.

"Can we leave now, Mr. Aaron?" asked a student who sat in the front row.

"Yes, all of you may leave. You've already given me your papers," replied the teacher.

The students rose from their seats, headed for the door, and opened it. In rushed a group of sixth grade students pushing and yelling at the top of their lungs even before the class could leave. Mr. Aaron looked with disbelief as the students shoved through the doorway and into his classroom.

"Allow the class to leave the room," said Mr. Aaron, his voice somewhat elevated.

But the sixth graders, 605, pushed their way in, preventing the seventh graders from leaving without pushing and easing their way through the throng. Inside the classroom, the sixth grade students stumbled into chairs and desks, hitting them over.

"Stop pushing and be quiet," Mr. Aaron barked. The students ignored him and surged toward the closet to retrieve their coats. About half the class had surprisingly placed their coats in it. Mr. Aaron had earlier opened the closet and the students stormed it, wrenching their coats from it.

"Young ladies, young men, sit down," shouted Mr. Aaron, his face contorted. Over the intercom, the principal had begun his announcements, but the ruckus was so intense that no one, even the teacher, heard what he said. Students cursed, pushed each other, jumped around, and screamed without a cause.

"Be seated," the teacher shouted again.

"Shut up," a voice rang out from among the students.

Instantly, a few of them lifted up chairs and slammed them on the desks. *Bang, bang, bang* was the loud, deafening noise that rose from the desks and chairs. A few chairs slipped off the desks and crashed to the floor, *bang, bang, bang*, as students in their wild frenzy bumped into them. Others turned and picked up the chairs from the floor. Mr. Aaron shouted for the students to be quiet, but they were deeply involved in their acts of indiscipline.

Then suddenly, Kassima, medium-build and daring, darted from among the roaring group and stopped inches away from Mr. Aaron, who now stood at the door and ordered and beckoned the students to get in line. "Form two straight lines. I want to see two straight lines. You cannot leave the classroom in this disorderly manner," he said. Kassima looked up at him straight in his face and said flatly, "Let me outta here."

Mr. Aaron was taken aback and replied, "Kassima, join the line."

Kassima did not budge. She curled her lips and snarled, "Let me outta here. I gotta go."

"No. You join the line. You must join the line," ordered Mr. Aaron, now standing against the closed door.

"I want to go, let me out," Kassima shouted.

"Join the line. I must have two straight lines," Mr. Aaron insisted.

Kassima stretched her hand to grab the doorknob but the teacher shifted his body, preventing her from reaching it.

Some of the students began shouting even louder, "We gotta go. We wanna get out," "We gotta go home," "It's already three o'clock," "We gonna be late for da bus," "I gotta pick up my sister," "I gotta pick up my brother." It was 2:55 p.m. The disruptive students began pushing each other toward the door. Mr. Aaron, now exasperated, made a slight turn, held the doorknob and slightly opened the door, enough to peer into the hallway to summon the assistance of the dean or assistant principal. He made a glance, but none of the floor supervisors or security officers was there. Pulling back into the classroom, he felt a jerk as someone pulled the door even before he could have turned fully to face the class. Sophia, who stood in front of the line, pulled the door.

"What's wrong with you, young lady?" said Mr. Aaron sternly.

"We wanna go," she bawled.

Thereupon, a brazen female student from the middle of the girls' line marched to the front and grabbed the door, which was slightly ajar, and began pulling it.

"What's the matter with you? Leave the door," the teacher ordered.

"Get to f— outta my face. Leh me go," Cynthia yelled, tugging at the door.

"Are you speaking to me, Cynthia? You'll have to talk to the dean and your parents," Mr. Aaron said.

Cynthia pulled the door again, but the strong hand and body of the teacher kept it firmly, making it difficult for it to open wide. Cynthia now fumed. "I wanna f— go. Get outta my f— face. I wanna f— go. F—, leh me go."

Some of the more cautious and well-mannered students seemed aghast while others giggled and laughed as Cynthia cursed and tugged at the door. Mr. Aaron's eyes widened with shock and disbelief at Cynthia's outburst with expletives. Realizing that she was becoming rather aggressive, Mr. Aaron released the doorknob and shifted his body. Cynthia then pulled the door, pulling it open with a force. She stormed out the classroom and into the hallway with long strides, lifting her feet high above the floor. Kassima, Ashlina, Cina, Philipi, Rupert, Jerome, and a few others surged, pushing Mr. Aaron into the hallway. "Ha, ha, ha . . ." They laughed and yelled. A frown masked Mr. Aaron's face. He felt totally humiliated and disgusted.

Said he, to the students who remained in the classroom, "I'm going to report her and the others who left."

Declared one student, "Mr. Aaron, it's not me. I remain in class."

Joined in another student, Arrond, "We are here. We didn't do anything. We didn't behave like the others."

"I know," answered Mr. Aaron.

Lashanda said, representing the others, "Mr. Aaron, you know who did it. You can't report us."

"Yes, I know who did it, and they are going to be seriously punished," Mr. Aaron said as he pursed his lips. The remaining students looked at him as he stood next to the chalkboard.

Uttered Mr. Aaron dejectedly, "The rest of you may leave."

"Good afternoon, Mr. Aaron," said Quanisha with wide-open eyes.

"Good afternoon, students," Mr. Aaron answered, taking a deep breath.

"Good afternoon, Mr. Aaron," another female student, Sophia, said.

"Good afternoon," Mr. Aaron replied.

A few more students paid their respects to Mr. Aaron as they left the classroom with their haversacks slung on their shoulders or on their backs. Mr. Aaron walked back to his desk with heaviness in his heart. He sat in his chair for a few moments to compose himself. He thought, as he placed the quiz in a folder and settled it in his brown leather bag, *I can't believe this. Such a good day turned ugly in an instant.* About five minutes after, he got up from his seat, went to his locker at the back of the class, unlocked it, and removed a dustpan and a long-handle broom. He walked back to the front of the classroom where he leaned the broom and long-handle dustpan against his desk. Mr. Aaron then picked up the chairs and desks, which the disrespectful students tumbled on the floor when they rushed out of the classroom. Taking the broom and dustpan, he swept the floor, sweeping the candy wrappers, papers, and empty plastic bottles, which they threw on the floor, into the green dustpan. The seventh grade class was not very untidy during the eighth period since they did the quiz and did not behave out of control as they normally did.

Having rearranged the desks and chairs, Mr. Aaron sat at his desk and wrote a list. Checking it to see that he had the required names on it, he left the classroom and pulled the door behind him. He then turned and locked the door before making his way along the hallway.

Mr. Aaron went to the teacher's lounge with the list of names of the students who were disorderly in coming into the room during homeroom and the female student who cursed him grossly, pulled the door, and walked out along with the others who followed her in leaving without being dismissed by him. He checked off the home and work numbers of those parents or guardians whom he was about to call. Positioning himself at the small table where the phone was placed, he picked up the receiver and touched the numbers. The phone rang at the other end. A strong male voice answered, "Hello." Mr. Aaron felt good that at least he had gotten through to an adult who was at home. "Are you the parent of Cynthia Gonzales?"

"Yes. Who is this?" the voice boomed through the receiver.

"I'm Mr. Aaron, Cynthia's earth science teacher. And your name is?" asked Mr. Aaron.

"I'm Raul Gonzales," his voice thundered.

"I'm calling to complain that Cynthia was very disrespectful to me during homeroom. Her class came rushing into the room even before the seventh grade class that I had was able to fully leave the room. After Cynthia and the rest of the students collected their coats, I told the class to form two straight lines so they could leave in an orderly manner. The students were getting in line when Cynthia left the line and came up to me and told me to let her out the room. I told her that she had to join the line. Using the four-letter word, she demanded that I let her go and that I get out of her face. She repeatedly cursed me with that word and pulled at the door. When I realized that she was getting very aggressive, I let go the door and she stormed out of the classroom with others following her. It was very disturbing and disrespectful."

"That's what she did, teacher?" asked Mr. Gonzales

"Yes! That's what she did!" said Mr. Aaron pointedly.

"I'm goin' to, gosh, deal with this girl. Every day I'm gettin' a damn call about her behavior. I'm dead sick with this. I can't settle my head. I donno what's wrong with her these last days," lamented Mr. Gonzales.

"She was cursing and carrying on at the top of her lungs. It was disgusting. Unbelievable. Something has to be done so that this behavior does not repeat itself," said Mr. Aaron.

"Sir, it's not going to happen again. She has no right to disrespect you. No right to curse you out and pull the door when you're holding it and trying to get the class in line. I gonna deal with her when she comes in. There would be no more problems, sir," Mr. Gonzales assured.

"Thank you, Mr. Gonzales," Mr. Aaron said.

"Thanks for calling and let me know what's happenin' anytime she's in class," Mr. Gonzales said and hung up the phone.

Mr. Aaron then hung up, checked the list, and dialed the home of Kassima, who pulled at the door and shouted. "Yes, good evening," was the voice on the other end of the line.

Feeling relieved that he was getting through to parents, Mr. Aaron said, "Good afternoon. Are you the parent of Kassima Redman?"

"Yes, I am. I'm her mom. How can I help you?" Mrs. Redman inquired.

"I'm Mr. Aaron, and I'm Kassima's earth science teacher, and I'm calling to complain that Kassima was disrespectful to me during homeroom before I dismissed the class," explained Mr. Aaron, looking at the list in his hand.

Mrs. Redman, who stood in her living room with her left hand on her hip and her eyes rolling as the teacher spoke, joined in, "What did she do?"

"She refused to follow instructions and left the class without being dismissed. At dismissal I told the class to form two straight lines since I was not going to dismiss a disorderly class. She broke the line, came up to me at the front, and said she wants to go. I told her no. I ordered her to join the line, but she refused to budge. She stood there saying she wants to leave although I insisted that she must join the line. She reached for the doorknob to pull the door open, but I shifted my body and prevented her from reaching it. Her behavior was very disrespectful. Kassima stood in front of me and would not move. When another student behaved in a very aggressive manner and walked out the room, after I removed from the door, Kassima followed her and left the room as well. Kassima's behavior was very disrespectful and unacceptable . . ."

"Oh, my goodness, I can't believe that Kassima behaved like that. Being disrespectful to her teacher. Refusing to join the line and trying to pull the door when you're standing in front of it and leaving the classroom without being dismissed. I can't believe this. Kassima did that?" Mrs. Redman almost doubted.

"Yes, she did, and even though I spoke to her she refused to follow my instructions. When the other young lady began pulling at the door and was becoming aggressive and I let go of the door, Kassima was the first one to storm out the classroom after the girl. Kassima's behavior was very disrespectful."

"I'm sorry her father is not here to hear what you're saying. Kassima never behaves like that. I'm so peeved, Mr. Aaron. I, I, like I don't know what to say. Her father and I keep telling her not to follow those students who're disrespectful and mischievous. Now here is it, she is following them."

"I'll ask you to have a serious talk with her so that she would improve her behavior."

"I'll definitely talk to her. Her father would do so, too. If possible I'll come up to the school tomorrow since I'm off duty to find out what's really happening with Kassima when she's at school. I'll talk to her when she gets in. And thanks for calling."

"Thank you," Mr. Aaron said and cradled the phone.

He made a number of other calls; some of the parents or guardians he did not reach at home. He called their places of work and spoke to a few. Others he was unable to reach and promised to call from his home later in the evening. Mr. Aaron left the teachers' lounge and walked back to his classroom feeling somewhat relieved that he had spoken to a number of parents.

It was after four o'clock, and most of the staff had left since it was the end of the working week and a very sunny day although it was cold but had warmed up from the previous days when it was at freezing point. Mr. Aaron put a book, some written work, handouts, and two folders in his brown leather bag with a shoulder strap. He walked to his closet, unlocked it, removed his black down coat, locked the closet, and walked back to his desk. Resting the coat on the back of the chair, he headed to the chalkboard and erased written work. He then dusted off his hands by rubbing his palms together. Turning around, he upped his coat, swung it, and pushed his left arm through the sleeve followed by the right through the next sleeve. Zipping his waist-length coat, he gripped his bag and walked toward the door. He stopped momentarily, switched off the lights, and closed the door behind him. He then turned and locked it. Looking up, he saw one of the custodians sweeping the hallway. He hailed, "Have a pleasant weekend."

With a broad grin, the tall muscular-build custodian answered, "Thanks. You have a good one too."

Mr. Aaron stepped into the main office and removed his card. He placed it in the out-slot on the attendance board. He noticed that the principal was still in his office, as the phone rang, and the principal's voice sounded as he answered it. Mr. Aaron left the office, hopped down the stairs, hit the sidewalk, and got to his car. He pulled off in a hurry and soon disappeared from the vicinity of the school. He felt downright tired when he arrived home. His wife was already home. She stopped at the sitter and collected their only child, Nitty. "Hi, honey, you're home," Ulsleen, his wife, said, stepping forward and greeting him with a hug. "Yeah, honey, I'm home," Mr. Aaron replied as he threw his arms around his wife, hugging her warmly. Releasing her as she did the same, he said, "Where's Nitty."

"You know she's asleep. Since she had her snack, she ended up on the couch sleeping," Mrs. Aaron related. "You look tired."

"I'm not so tired today as I'm upset," replied Nestor.

"What happened?" his wife asked, resting her hand on his shoulder.

"The day went pretty smoothly until dismissal when the sixth graders barged into the room, grabbed their coats, with some of them actually refusing to join the line before I dismiss the class. Then two female students were so disrespectful to me. They pulled the door and cursed to get out of the room. One of the two cursed me to my face using the four-letter word. It was so disgusting," Nestor explained to his wife, and her jaws dropped. He does not normally relate the day's disruption to his wife. He may just hint that the students did not behave well, but today he was totally upset by the behavior of

Cynthia and Kassima in particular and the others in general, whose actions were deplorable.

"I know how hard it is in dealing with those students. It could be so frustrating. Why not talk to the principal about it?" Ulsleen comforted her husband.

"I called the parents of a number of them. They said they're going to seriously rebuke them or punish them by taking away privileges," said Nestor.

"I hope there is some improvement in their behavior," said Ulsleen in a soothing voice.

"Let's hope so. I expect to see some of it in their conduct as from next week," uttered Nestor.

"I know it's tough but this is Friday evening. Take a hot bath, not to burn yourself, and let us have dinner. I cooked something nice, and let's have a tall drink of wine after," said Mrs. Aaron, throwing her arm around her husband as they sat in the burgundy sofa.

"That sounds good. It'll cause me to forget the ill behavior of some of these kids," uttered Nestor, rising from his seat.

By the time Mr. Aaron returned to the living room and headed to the dining area, Nitty had awakened. "Hi, Dad," six-year-old Nitty said as she lunged into her father's arms.

"Hi, Nitty," Mr. Aaron beamed as he hugged and kissed his daughter on her smooth, soft cheeks.

"Did you have a good day, Daddy?" she asked, looking into his eyes.

"It was good throughout the day, but at the end of it, things did not turn out well," he said. "But it's okay, I dealt with it."

"Good, Daddy," little Nitty said, with her arms around her father's neck.

"We're going to have a nice dinner," Nitty's mom said as they sat at the dinner table.

Mr. Aaron and his family dined and enjoyed the rest of the evening.

Monday was a cold but sunny day, and Mr. Aaron arrived at work very early. He thought that the day would be a good one but challenging as always. With charts on the board and transparencies under the light of the projector, he was ready for the morning's class after homeroom. Class 604 came rushing into the classroom at the beginning of the second period.

"Hold it. You're not coming in here in that disorderly manner and with all that noise," said Mr. Aaron as he stood at the door while the sixth graders entered. Mr. Aaron then walked into the room.

Students, girls and boys, pushed and tugged at each other. Hands flailed. Daren, Arlon, and Malessa pushed Noel through the door. They laughed. Noel turned around and pushed the door to get back into the classroom. Daren, Arlon, Malessa, and Betty leaned against the door. Mr. Aaron, who was now standing next to the window, barked, "Remove from the door and take your seats." The teacher's words fizzled away. The students yelled so loudly they did not hear a word he said. Standing in the hallway, Noel, a medium-build student, pushed the door with much force, and the door came ajar. Daren, Arlon, Malessa, and Betty pushed back, closing the door in Noel's face. A big-build, heavy student from an eighth grade class was walking along the hallway.

Said Noel, "Son, help me push this door open. They push me out."

The tall eighth grader shook his head in agreement and walked up to the door. He placed his broad, square shoulder against the door and, together with Noel, pushed the door; it flew open, tumbling the others forward. Noel and the eighth grader lurched forward. The eighth grader steadied himself, hopped from the classroom, and trodded along the hallway while Noel balanced himself, made a few steps forward into the room, and started punching away at the others who pushed him out the class. Noel scrambled Arlon; Arlon punched him. Malessa threw two jabs in Noel's ribs and he winced. Betty dealt him two punches in his back. Noel broke loose and ran. "Sit down. Go to your seats," Mr. Aaron yelled, moving toward the group. In a skelter, Arlon, Daren, and Malessa scrambled Ryan and pushed him out of the room. Turning in a mad scramble, they grabbed Iftikar, rushed him to the door, and pushed him into the hallway as he appealed to them to let him go. They also pushed Louisa, who was standing next to the door, out of the classroom. Standing in the hallway, Ryan and Iftikar banged on the door and yelled.

"Let us in," Iftikar shouted and kicked the door. "Ouch!" He felt the pain in his toes as his foot slammed against the door.

"Move from the door and let us in," Ryan bawled.

"I'm not gonna bang on no door to hurt my hand. They're knuckleheads. They don't mean to stop playin' around, and the teacher told them to stop. I ain't playin' with them, and they push me out da room," Louisa said in disgust as she was in no mood to play.

She had wanted to get on with her work and was much upset, but did not show much of it. On the other side of the door, Daren, Arlon, Malessa, and Betty giggled and laughed while they leaned against the door to prevent Louisa, Ryan, and Iftikar from getting back into the room. Jennifer rose from her seat and joined them in forming a barricade against the door. They prevented Mr. Aaron from getting to the door. "Remove from the door. Take your seats," Mr. Aaron shouted, but they ignored him. They pushed against the door. After repeated shouts by the teacher, they opened it. Louisa, Iftikar, and

Ryan stormed into the room and began punching those who blocked their entry back into the classroom.

Arlon and the four others struck back. Being upset, Louisa wrestled with Arlon, who lifted her up and was about to throw her on the floor, but she held his head and punched it viciously. He let her go and ran. She charged after him. "You sissy," she screamed. She pushed a boy out of the way. She scrambled Daren and pounded him in his chest. He punched her back and ran. Yvonne and Petalina joined with Louisa and began hitting Malessa, Arlon, Daren, and Betty. Jennifer had rushed back to her seat after a brief foray. The punching and running continued for a while around the class. The teacher was disgusted.

In the back of the room, six girls stamped and tramped on the floor, *bam, bam, bam-bam, bam, bam*, while playing a game. "Cut it. Not in here. No playing. It's time for work," the teacher yelled. But they clapped their hands loudly and chanted as they went through the paces of the game. They clapped, bent their knees, clapped low, then high, then low again, did a foot movement, then clapped and stamped repeatedly with a rhythm. "Stop that noise," Mr. Aaron barked. "A class is below us, and you're disturbing it."

"Wha' wrong with you? We can't play?" a brazen, hardy female student asked, folding her arms in front of her.

"This is not the yard. You can't play in here. It's a classroom and there is work to do," said Mr. Aaron. While the teacher talked to the girls who played the game, others in front and the middle of the class jumped from one desk to another. Seven or eight of them jumped on desks. They upturned tables and chairs in chasing each other around the class. They pulled and tossed furniture around. Daren overturned a long narrow desk with books, magazines, and handouts. On the go again, Arlon, Malessa, Jennifer, Ryan, Betty, and Nayi were definitely hyper as they behaved totally out of control. Daren grabbed a solid, heavy textbook and tossed it at Arlon. He ducked, and the book slammed into the door of the wooden closet with a loud bang. Daren turned around, grabbed another heavy textbook, and threw it at Arlon, who now headed for the door. Nayi and Malessa grabbed books and hurled them across the room at Daren. Arlon dashed back into the room. He grabbed a book and threw it at Malessa. They were all throwing books at each other.

"Stop! Stop! Stop this nonsense! What do you think you're doing?" Mr. Aaron shouted, his head involuntarily shaking as he tried desperately to stop the fracas. But his words went unheeded. The running, shouting, jumping on each other, and slugging it out at each other persisted. After a good five or seven minutes, some of them pulled chairs and sat down breathing heavily.

"Son, this was fun. I whop his ass. Noel ain't get me. I throw him on da floor," muttered Arlon.

"Huh, I slammed Nayi on the floor." Daren giggled.

"Oooh, my arm is hurting. I fell on it when he slammed me," Nayi said as he sat slumped in a chair.

Said Malessa, "I grab 'im in a headlock and beat da sh—t outta 'im."

"Dog, this was some fun," said Ryan, who normally wore a pair of round metal-framed glasses which he took off and placed in his backpack. He wiped his face with a piece of tan paper towel and pitched it on the floor and then delved in his backpack for his glasses which he put on. Ryan looked over it as it rested on his nose. He pulled it from his face and placed it on the defaced desk with blotches from the ink of markers and pens. Iftikar, who sat opposite him, picked up the spectacles and put it on.

"I can't see with this sh—t. How you see with this?" he asked Ryan.

"I see okay with it. I been wearing this all da time," Ryan replied. As some of the students talked and did no work, others thought of other things.

Arlon, Daren, and Nayi, who sat on desks, got up and walked to a book closet at the back of the room. Daren opened the door of the closet, which was built attached to the wall, and they climbed the shelves of the locker built within the closet and got to the top of the locker where they sat. Their heads reached the ceiling of the closet, which caused them to bend their necks. Their feet dangled. They raised them and placed them on the inner anterior part of the closet just above the door. Four other students joined them. They sat cramped at the top. Mr. Aaron left the board on which he wrote and ordered them to leave the closet. "We're reading," Arlon said. They could hardly see each other's faces as they sat in the dim closet without any light. The teacher sighed.

"I'm going to get the assistant principal or the dean if you don't come down and get out of there," he ordered.

"We're reading," Daren shouted.

"We're not botherin' you," Nayi uttered.

"But I want you out of there," Mr. Aaron said flatly. He moved to the door and looked into the hallway. No security officer was on the floor at the time. He pulled back into the room. The intercom in his room did not work. The connecting cord to the receiver was removed. The phone was dead.

Malessa, Ryan, and Noel rose from their seats and started wrestling, punching each other and putting one another in headlocks. Turning around, Mr. Aaron barked at them, "Cut this nonsense right now." His voice was thunderous. The muscles in his face tightened. The three students scurried back to their seats.

Walking back to the closet, he roared, "Get down and get out of there, now."

Sensing that Mr. Aaron was in an angry mood, Nayi twisted his body, turned, and crawled down the shelves from the top of the locker in the closet. And one by one, the students crawled down from the top of the locker and made their way out of the dim closet. They seemed bent on acting out of order and creating difficulty for Mr. Aaron. Arlon and Daren barged from their seats and dashed to a metal cabinet at the side of the room. *Bang, bang*, was the metallic sound from the cabinet as they beat on it. "Yeah, yeah," they chanted. *Bang, bang.* "Yeah, yeah." *Bang, bang*. Then Arlon belted out some lyrics, "I love muh money and muh honey, gimme muh money and I get muh honey. Don't step in my way, 'cause I'll lose muh away. My girl is on her way."

Dashing to the back of the classroom, Mr. Aaron shouted to the top of his voice, "Cut that. Go to your seats."

"Ha, ha, ha, ha, ha." The students laughed and walked to their seats. The day was not only difficult for Mr. Aaron.

Chapter 29

Other teachers had a similar fate on that day. Many grappled with the students' behavior and survived the tumult. Many students walked the hallway and pushed open classroom doors. One tall frail student in a green long-sleeve jersey pushed a classroom door open on the third floor. He shouted as he saw some students working, "Hey, those nerds workin'."

The teacher turned and roared, "Get out the hallway. Go to your class."

The student turned and said to his pal, "He kiddin'. Go to which class."

"My class sucks. I ain't going there," the shorter student said.

They strolled along the hallway. Three other students who walked the hallway also pushed doors open. "Ah ha, ha." One of them laughed, pointing his index finger at the teacher, who leapt to the door but said nothing. He just shook his head in disdain. A group of tenth graders, five of them all together, male and female, who cut class, walked behind the three others and threw paper balls and broken pencils into the classroom as the teacher pulled back into the room. As the paper balls and pencils landed on the floor, the teacher spun around and dashed to the door.

"You throw stuff in here again, and I'll have you in the dean's office," the teacher shouted as the group hurried down the hallway.

"Why in hell they throw da sh—t in here?" a female student who was working on a science assignment blurted out. She rushed to the door where her teacher stood and looked out. She saw the students making their way toward the main hall on the third floor.

"You throw garbage in here again and we gonna get you," the young lady yelled, bobbing her head.

One from the group, a young man, looked over his shoulder and showed a fist, "She bounced out the room like she wanna fight."

"Who's that ugly girl from 1002. She want a good whopping," one of the females from the group concurred. They later turned into the main hallway and disappeared. The east wing was cleared for a moment. The student and her teacher walked back into the classroom. Said the teacher, "Those students don't want to learn. They'll someday regret it."

In the class in room 3-905, students ripped pages from their notebooks and crumpled and formed them into paper balls. In the presence of Ms. Bishop, who came from another class to cover 905, they threw them at each other. They got out of their seats.

"Stop throwing paper balls. Sit in your assigned seats. No one should be standing or walking around the class," Ms. Bishop shouted from the middle of the class. Students hurried to their seats. Shortly after, they were out of their seats again, aiming and throwing paper balls into the garbage bin.

"Move out da way leh me throw," yelled Victor. He threw the paper ball at the bin and missed. "Damn."

Bawled Elonz, pumping his arms in the air, "You a wimp. Can't even score."

Victor ran toward the bin and grabbed the paper ball that fell next to it. Hurrying back to where Elonz stood he waited for Elonz to throw his paper ball. He aimed and threw the paper ball. *Tut*. It entered the bin. "Yeah, yeah, I'm da champ," Elonz yelled, jumping around.

"Watch me do it," shrieked Victor. He threw the paper ball and again he missed. His face fell as the grin instantly disappeared.

"Go to your seats now. Hurry," squeaked Ms. Bishop, darting in front of Victor and Elonz.

"What?" Victor yelled, frowning his narrow face with full brown eyes.

"No more of that in here," the teacher ordered, gesturing with her hands.

While Ms. Bishop cautioned Victor and Elonz, two other students argued over money.

"Where my quarter?" demanded Mohan, watching Francis stark in his face.

"I ain't got your quarta," fretted Francis, pushing his hands in his pockets.

"I had it on da desk near you," said Mohan, his face becoming drawn.

"I ain't got yuh quarta," denied Francis.

Mohan pulled Francis's backpack as they sat in their seats.

"Don't pull my bag," shouted Francis, pulling his bag away from Mohan. Mohan pushed Francis on his shoulder.

"Don't push me, man," Francis barked, pushing back at Mohan.

"You takin' that. Got da punk pushin' yuh," said Denny, inciting Mohan.

"Wha' sh—t wrong with da two o' you? Goin' wild over a quarta?" shrieked Mandy, a tall, medium-build student with short brown hair who donned dark shades.

Mohan punched Francis in his right shoulder.

"Wha' you punched me for?" asked Francis, furrows forming on his forehead.

Mohan punched Francis in his shoulder again. Francis turned and punched Mohan in the chest. Mohan connected to Francis's chest and both started punching each other while they managed to get to their feet.

Students who stood nearby drifted toward the brawl.

"Yeah, yeah, yeah, fight, fight," some four students yelled.

"What's going on there?" barked Ms. Bishop, hurrying over to where Mohan and Francis slugged it out.

"Punch him, Francis, whop his ass," a colleague of Francis hollered.

"Come on, Mohan, punch him," a female student shouted, trying to get close to the brawlers. Mohan and Francis held on to each other. Francis now pushed Mohan against a desk. Other desks and chairs were pushed by the bodies of the two fighters and those students who tried to get close to them in prodding them on.

"Fight, fight," Stacey jumped on a desk and yelled.

"Break it up, come on, break it up," shouted Ms. Bishop as she jostled among the students in trying to get to the two brawlers. A desk tumbled, and both Mohan and Francis fell on the floor. Still grabbing each other, they continued punching each other. Mohan slammed a punch in the stomach of Francis. Francis countered with a punch to Mohan's. They now held on to each other with each trying to put the other in a headlock.

"Come on, Mohan, you could whip him," Shantel's voice rang out above the din.

Ms. Bishop got to them and grabbed Francis's arm and pulled him with all the force she could muster. Francis' grip on Mohan loosened, and Mohan fired a punch that caught Francis in his chest. Francis kicked out and caught Mohan in his left leg. Ms. Bishop finally got Francis on his feet and pulled him away.

Harlon, decked in a plaid hooded sweater, dashed out the room and ran down the hallway. Kathrin dashed after him. Harlon darted into Mr. Delph's office. He shouted, "Fight in Ms. Bishop's class, Mr. Delph."

"What!" Mr. Delph said, looking up at the student who entered suddenly and swiftly.

"Two students fighting in the class," Harlon said breathlessly.

Rising from his seat, Mr. Delph said, "Okay."

Before he could have moved from behind his desk, Kathrin rushed into his office. She hollered, "Mr. Delph, fight in class 905. Mohan and Francis fighting."

Mr. Delph was out of his office.

As Ms. Bishop held on to Francis's arm and backed him away, Mohan rose to his feet and advanced toward Francis.

"You better stop right there," yelled Ms. Bishop as she now stood between the two warring students.

"He started it," muttered Francis, panting for breath. "I ain't do him nothin'."

Orin, a good Samaritan who was hardy and muscular, moved in and grabbed Mohan.

"Get off o' me. It ain't finish," said Mohan, a swelling rising just above his right eye.

"Cool yuh head," growled Orin as he held on to Mohan, who tried to pull himself away from the firm grip around his waist.

Still standing on the desk close to the back of the class, a female student kept on yelling, "Fight, fight. Somebody getting his ass whop, ha, ha, ha."

"Back off. You're not coming here," shrieked Ms, Bishop as she glared at Mohan. Students circled and pushed each other to get a glimpse of what Mohan was about to do as Orin restrained him.

In the pushing, Ms. Bishop was pushed as well and almost lost her balance. As she stood between Mohan and Francis, she felt a sudden blow in her head. She spun around; her left hand glided up to her head and the spot where she was hit. Her eyes beamed on the floor, where the storybook fell.

"Somebody hit me in my head with that book," Ms. Bishop yelled. "Somebody threw it. Who did it?"

"Ahhhh, ha, ha, ha, ha, ahhhh, ha, ha, ha . . ." Some of the students laughed.

"She got smack." One of the students who prodded on the fight grinned.

"You laughing but it ain't funny. Somebody hit her with a book in her head," rebuked a petite young lady in a black-and-brown sweater. "Somebody threw the book at her."

"Someone hit me with a book," fumed Ms. Bishop, still holding on to the arm of Francis and standing as a shield against Mohan in order to minimize any further aggression.

Mr. Delph and the two students ran into the classroom. His eyes were distended as he glared in the classroom.

"Who's fighting in here?" thundered Mr. Delph, moving toward the teacher. Mr. Delph was a big guy with broad shoulders and a pair of strong arms and bulging, strong biceps. He stood more than six feet.

"These two nuts," the voice of a male student rang out sharp and shrill.

Mr. Delph barreled toward Mohan and Francis and grabbed them, almost sending them off their feet. "You fighting in this class!" Mr. Delph's grip tightened around their arms.

"Yes, both of them were fighting in the class," uttered Ms. Bishop.

"You fighting in here. You're getting suspended," growled Mr. Delph, moving off with the arms of both students in his hands.

"You hurting my arm," said Mohan, somewhat, reluctant in moving.

"And someone hit me in my head, Mr. Delph, while I held on to Francis," Ms. Bishop said. Mr. Delph stopped in his tracks.

Looking over his shoulder, Mr. Delph roared, "Who did it? Who hit the teacher in her head? I have to know."

No one answered. The class suddenly became quiet. Everyone was mute momentarily. Mr. Delph turned about with the two fighters.

"I want to know who hit her. And I want to know now," Mr. Delph's voice boomed and ricocheted off the walls in the room.

"I ain't know who hit her," said one short, stocky male student with bowed legs.

"All I heard she say is that she got hit. I ain't see who do it," a student, small frame, with thick, long hair said.

"I'm waiting to hear who hit her," the dean snarled.

"Don't watch at me. I don't know who hit her," another student said, looking at Mr. Delph.

"The entire class is going to pay for this," the dean uttered.

Students looked at each other, their eyes wide with concern.

One student asked another, "You see who hit her?"

Answered the student, "I ain't see who hit her."

Elonz turned to Mandy and asked, "You know who hit her?"

"No. I don't know who throw the book at her," said Mandy with wide-open eyes.

Most of the students were out of their seats; they stood amongst the disarranged chairs and tables, some of which were tumbled on the floor.

Bellowed Mr. Delph as he turned to fully face the class, "I don't have time to waste. Let me know now who hit Ms. Bishop. And furthermore, sit down, fix the class. Pick up the chairs and desks from the floor and sit down."

Immediately, students began picking up chairs and desks from the floor and straightening and fixing chairs behind desks.

"I want everyone to be seated and let this look like a class," the dean said, still holding the two fighters on opposite sides of him.

Everyone sat and the classroom became very still. A slight whispering went on in the middle and back of the class to find out who hit the teacher.

"You know who hit her?" asked Kendrick, sitting at the back.

"Anton hit her. He threw the book which hit her in the head. I saw him throw it, and he said don't say anything," Monique told Kendrick.

"Tell him to come out and say he did it. Everybody shouldn't suffer because of him. He ain't my buddy, he ain't my homie. He ain't yours either, so why should we suffer if he wanna mess up, hitting the teacher?" Kendrick, a tall, muscular student with a little beard on his chin, said.

Looking over her shoulder, Monique said to Anton, "Tell him you did it. The whole class shouldn't suffer because of you."

"No. I gonna get in trouble," Anton answered with a worried face.

"We gonna get in trouble too. I gonna tell him," whispered Monique, looking straight into the eyes of Anton.

"No, don't," Anton begged, rubbing his chin nervously.

Turning to Kendrick, Monique said, "Anton said he gonna get in trouble if he said he did it. He don't want us tell Mr. Delph."

With a stern face, Kendrick said to Monique, "Tell Delph he did it. I ain't takin' no punishment for da stupid ass. He had no right to pelt Ms. Bishop with da book. She's a teacher. She's a woman. He ain't want nobody hit his mother."

"He gonna say I snitch on him," Monique said, her eyes popping.

"Who cares? He shoulda know that. Tell Delph or I gonna talk. I gonna tell him you know and ain't wanna say nothin'," Kendrick complained.

Mr. Delph noticed the conversation going on at the back and shouted, "What's happening at the back there?"

Getting a little worried, Monique looked across at Kendrick. Kendrick watched her in her full brown eyes and without a blink said, "Tell him now."

Monique jumped up and said in a hushed classroom, "Mr. Delph, Anton hit Ms. Bishop with the book in her head. I saw him and he said not to say anything."

Jaws dropped and eyes popped open wide. "Ohhhh" was the sound that filled the room instantly.

"Come here, Anton, come here, get over here," Mr. Delph bellowed in his deep guttural voice.

"You a snitch, Monique," said Albin, one of Anton's friends who sat next to him.

"You snitch, you make him get in trouble now," said Victor, another friend.

"I didn't mean to do it," Anton said, getting up from his seat and walking to the dean in the front of the class.

"Get over here, boy," Mr. Delph's voice bounced from the walls of the room as Anton approached him, knowing exactly what would be the consequences of his action.

"You hit the teacher with a book in her head as these two crazies fight in the class. Get to my office now," Mr. Delph yelled, anger full in his voice as Anton walked in front of him.

"I didn't mean to do it," said Anton. His voice sounded remorseful since he was a student who normally did not behave in a disruptive manner, and so it was quite a surprise that he was the one who hit the teacher.

Cling, cling, cling-cling, cling, cling. The bell rang ending the period. Students sprang from their seats to dash for the door.

"Stop!" Mr. Delph's voice boomed after the bell. Arlon stopped in his tracks.

Said Ms. Bishop to herself quietly, "I can't believe he did it. He's not normally a troublemaker."

"You're going to line up here. You're not going to leave this room as if you're losing your mind," roared Mr. Delph, still holding on to Mohan and Francis with a firm grip of his sizeable, solid, tough hands.

The young men and women quietly left their seats.

"Push the chairs in. Push them in," the dean's voice sounded again. The students meekly held the back of their chairs and pushed the seats under the desks. Together, they formed two lines. Satisfied that the lines were orderly and the students were quiet, the dean said, "You may go." They hurried out the classroom and then erupted in quarrels and complaints about why Monique snitched and why Anton was so out of place to throw the book at the teacher.

Facing the teacher, Mr. Delph said, "Ms. Bishop, write a report about what happened, and I will deal with these three young men.'

"Yes, I'll get it to you shortly," replied Ms. Bishop, edging to her desk and reaching for a yellow writing pad.

"Let's go," said Mr. Delph, guiding Mohan and Francis out of the room with Anton ahead of them. In his office, he found out what led to the fight and called the parents and told them of the misconduct of their children. The three students were suspended for a number of days after the dean read the report by the teacher.

Chapter 30

The lesson was about to begin. It was after lunch, and many students had started to become disruptive. They talked loudly and walked idly in the classroom. It was a language arts lesson in class 903, and Mr. Naimer, a young, auburn-haired, bespectacled teacher with slight freckles on his flat narrow face, called on the students to take out their reading material.

Standing in front of the class with his brown plaid blazer hanging limply on him, he said firmly, "Class, this is not the time to talk and walk around the room. Kindly return to your assigned seats. Nella, Maria, Latisha, Mortimer, Stephen, Leon, and Trapel, please sit in your assigned seats. How many times do I have to tell you the same thing?"

"Okay, chill, dog. We gonna sit down," said Stephen, edging slowly to his seat.

"I ain't know what's wrong with him. He wouldn't give us a lil break," said Maria with a cross look on her face.

"You already had a break. You had lunch and you were allowed outside for a good twenty minutes," Mr. Naimer reminded Maria and the rest of the class. His face became stern. The feeling of exasperation showed in it.

"What! That's not enough. A lousy twenty minutes," retorted Maria fiercely.

"All he could think about is work. Free up sometimes, man. Free us up. We getting too much work, f—," shouted Trapel, standing beside the window.

"Trapel, are you going to sit down? And mind your language, Trapel, and the rest of you," cautioned the teacher.

Reluctantly, they partly complied, pulling chairs from behind desks and dragging them to the back of the class. They then sat together in a sort of semicircle.

"That's not how and where you sit, students. I want those chairs behind desks and you must sit in your assigned seats. You're not going to sit anywhere that suits you. Kindly get up now," Mr. Naimer ordered, moving off from his position in front of the class and making his way toward Trapel, Maria, Stephen, and the others. "Come on, you have to get up. You just don't disarrange this class."

"Give us a break. We're not bothering you," said Stephen, with a scowl. His eyes now glared and became penetrative as he showed obstinacy at the teacher.

Shouted Marianne, a heavy, young lady with bright starry eyes and broad heavy shoulders, "Mr. Naimer, let's start the lesson. Time is going."

Yes, despite the callousness and stark disregard for authority and an indifference to knowledge by some in the student populace, within the midst were those, even if they did not possess a hunger and yearning for knowledge, who were able to muster a sort of interest in learning.

Realizing that he had already spent some ten or more minutes in attempting to get the class, and in particular the six students, in order, he shook his head perhaps in disgust.

"Kindly move your chairs and take your proper seats behind your desks," Mr. Naimer stressed.

In unison, Stephen and Maria said, "No."

"We're comfortable here, Mr. Naimer," said Trapel, swinging his blue baseball cap around, the peak sticking out at the back of his head.

"Mr. Naimer, don't bother with them," begged Marianne, with her notebook already on the desk in front of her.

With lips tightened and eyes steadfast behind the nickel-framed glasses with tinted lenses, Mr. Naimer walked back to the front of the class. The topic, aim, and objective of the lesson, along with the remainder of the heading, were already written on the board. Picking up the chalk, which was affixed to a blue chalk holder, Mr. Naimer pressed the chalk on the board. A piece broke; the flake fell to the floor, the wood lacquered floor besmirched with scrawls, marks, and lines from the pulling, pushing, and dragging of chairs and desks. Mr. Naimer wrote a "Do Now," on the board: "What would people do if they experience an emergency away from home in a deserted area?" The ninth graders began probing their minds to come up with answers. Not surprisingly, half the class or less got involved.

"Martin, what do you think 'bout this question?" asked Nevol, a tall, thin, blonde student with a ponytail and a ring pierced in his tongue, which he sucked on from time to time.

"I'll use my cell phone to call my paps, man," replied Martin, a thin brown-skinned student. "You can't go those places without a phone, dog."

"You right, that's cool. A phone is important. I got my cell right here," said Nevol.

"I gonna write this down," said Martin.

"Hey, so wha' happen if yuh paps can't get to you in time or if it's a good distance away," questioned Nevol, writing down some points in his notebook.

"I'll call the police." Martin chuckled, twirling his pen.

"Good idea," concurred Nevol. "Naimer, ask us some weird stuff, yo."

Other students were busy coming up with answers. Marianne and her friend Cleo, a petite and affable young lady with a ready smile, brainstormed.

"Marianne, we're coming up with some funny but interesting answers," said Cleo, the white of her even, close teeth gleaming.

"Believe me, we sure do, Cleo," replied Marianne, writing the answers in her green notebook.

"You have just about another minute to conclude what you're doing," said Mr. Naimer, who walked around the class to see what students were doing.

Mr. Naimer then stopped and read what Helena wrote. Said he, "Good points."

Turning to his right as he now stood at the back of the class, he said, "You haven't yet started to work, Trapel, Stephen, Maria, and others. You're just talking and talking."

"We gonna start your work just now. Just relax." Maria grinned, her cheeks spreading wide.

The others totally ignored the teacher and continued with their indulgence. Mr. Naimer moved on and looked at what two or three more students wrote and then headed back to the front of the class.

"Okay, students, our time is up. I'll collect your papers now," he mentioned. He quickly went around the class and collected the written work.

Mr. Naimer then turned the page, with a straight index finger, of the book lying open on the desk. With a slight squint, he adjusted his spectacles in order to give him a better focus on what was written on the board. A flat green paint colored the board, which revealed a film of white residue from the daily dusty chalk marks. Mr. Naimer read the aim and then the objective, emphasizing both. The lesson began. He hung a KWL chart on the board. He asked a few questions about survival, and the responses which students gave he wrote in the K column of the chart. He attempted to access the prior knowledge of a number of students, but only a few responded. Mr. Naimer picked up the storybook that lay on the desk; he flipped the pages and got to page 217.

Said he, "Class, I'll do a model reading to you about this quite interesting story." He read a paragraph from the book as students followed, mainly a few of them. Mr. Naimer stopped and asked, "What is the meaning of the word 'juxtapose'?" He scanned the class for about five seconds. No one answered the question or even volunteered. During the reading and brief discussion, he advised students to use context clues. Since no one seemed inclined to answer he said, "Marianne, could you tell us the meaning of the word?"

Her eyes widened with surprise. The white looked greater; her eyes rolled. She then gazed with concentration on the lines just read.

"Use context clues. There're right there in the paragraph," instructed Mr. Naimer, holding the book in his right hand and glancing at the paragraph.

Marianne read the lines again then thought about what the sentence indicated from the signal words and finally came up with an answer.

Said Marianne, "It means to put things side by side."

"Very good, Marianne. Have you seen how the use of context clues helped you to determine the meaning of the word?" asked Mr. Naimer.

"Yes." Marianne giggled. Her face lit up.

"What signal word did you use?" the teacher questioned, feeling satisfied that he was getting through to a student.

"Compare was the signal word I used," she said confidently.

"Good. Let us move on. I'll continue reading," Mr. Naimer said, bringing the book closer from where he held it. His chest heaved as he took a deep breath.

He read, "The party of campers now traveled into rugged territory after biking through the trail of a wooded area for the last three hours on the first day of the journey. The youngsters were forced to travel by foot. Huge boulders were embedded along their path, large rotted tree trunks lay across the narrow, red, winding track which was full of ditches, with muddy water. The chirp of birds were heard—" Abruptly, Mr. Naimer stopped.

Said he, "What is the landscape of this area, class?"

Richard raised his hand. He was a keen student who could be easily distracted. When that happened, it then became difficult to get him back on track, to focus on the task ahead, but when motivated, he was a very persistent and grudgingly determined student. His brown, piercing eyes mirrored a sense of urgency. He sat still and composed with dark hair flowing and nestling about the shoulders of his slightly athletic body.

"Ah, it's, um, it's changing, it's really a rocky landscape," said Richard, his lower jaw hanging limp.

"Okay, that's good, Richard," said the teacher with a nod. "Let's hear Pamela."

"Well, I'll say it's a jungle and it's rocky. That's the kind of landscape it is. There's a lot of trees and rocks around," explained Pamela candidly.

"Good," assured Mr. Naimer.

"Yeah, yeah, yeah, yeah," filled the air suddenly at the back of the classroom.

Students turned; they looked over their shoulders.

"Pull, pull, get it," was an audible sound from among the yelling students.

"Pull, Nella, pull," Maria's voice rose in a fit of excitement.

"Pull, Maria," Latisha yelled.

"What's going on at the back there?" shouted Mr. Naimer, his neck stiff and straight. "Why all that noise."

"Grab it, Latisha, don't lose," bawled Nella, her lips spread, her teeth bare with wild laughter.

Mr. Naimer rushed forward to get a closer look and to defuse what was happening at the back of the class.

"What's happening with those kids, there," yelled Rebecca, a tall, short-haired student with slight dimples in her cheeks that deepened with a bright smile and a rather hearty laughter.

"I'm trying to learn something, but they don't care. They don't give a sh—t," blurted out Michael. He flipped the pages of his notebook, cupped his face with the palms of his hands, and bit his lower lip. He shook his head in disgust.

"I don't know why they come to school if they don't want to work," stated Francisca flatly, removing the black metal-framed spectacles from her face and placing it on the desk. Her nose twitched as if she picked up a scent traveling in the air.

Said Marianne, "I'm so fed up. The teacher is doing a lesson with us and they're behaving like dim wits."

"What's all this commotion about?" demanded Mr. Naimer curiously.

"Yeah, yeah, yeah . . ." The voices of those distracting the class echoed to the ceiling.

"Don't lose it," a single female voice spouted.

"Hey, what yuh doin', chill mannn," a male voice protested almost hysterically.

"Stop this nonsense right now. Get in your seats," the teacher bawled, with concern and frustration flush on his face, as he made his way among the students.

"Move, Mr. Naimer, move," a voice pitched.

"You students have no discipline," Mr. Naimer called out.

Maria, Nella, Latisha, and Nurleen surrounded Trapel. Their hands were on him. Nella pulled at his blue track pants; Maria tugged at it.

"Hey, get off o' me," Trapel bawled while he sat in a chair. Latisha pulled at the pants and two of the pressed-down buttons running along the sides up to the waist unloosed.

"Ha, ha, ha, ha, ha." Stephen laughed, swaying from left to right in the chair.

"Chill, man. Leave the guy alone," Martin pleaded, leaning back in his chair, his double chin and the fullness of his face quivering as his voice resonated.

"No," Latisha screamed.

"Stop, stop. I said to stop," Mr. Naimer shrieked. "I'll get security in here."

The teacher stepped to the intercom. He yanked the receiver from the base and dialed the security desk. The phone kept ringing. No one answered. It continued to ring. And the commotion in the class heightened. It appeared that no officer was at the security desk at the moment. Perhaps, the officer had just moved away from the desk and did not hear the prolonged ring of the phone. It was a breach of security, but sometimes an officer does it if he or she had to respond to a brief call on the first floor and particularly when the security staff was short owing to the absence of one or more of its members.

With no officer responding from the desk, Mr. Naimer then dialed the dean's office. A voice answered at the other end of the line. He explained what was happening in his room and then hung up.

Trapel managed to get to his feet, but Maria, Latisha, Nella, and Nurleen held on to his pants, tugging and pulling and twitching it.

"Yeh, Latisha, hold, pull," Nurleen squealed, her voice rising to a scream, and she breathed heavy with excitement.

"Yes, yes, yes," Latisha shouted, baring teeth which showed much spacing at the bottom.

Maria pulled and two more buttons unloosed. Latisha tugged with a force, and four buttons flew. Nurleen now grabbed the back of the pants, and three more buttons came apart.

"Hey, no, Maria, don't do that," Trapel begged with eyes bulging and an expression of worry on his flat face. The legs of his track pants were now partly opened. Trapel was unsteady on his feet as if tossed from side to side with the jerks, the pulling, and the tugging. Maria, heavy and full of energy, pushed him, and he stumbled across a desk. And the noise soared. "Yeahhhhh," Nella, Nurleen, Maria, Latisha, and many in the class yelled. Trapel held on to the upper part of his blue track pants. His legs were now visible. The pale skin, devoid of sunlight, was coated with curled black hair. With the scene becoming more unbecoming, Mr. Naimer rushed to the door and pulled it open. He looked to the left and right of the hallway; the tiled brown floor, with its faint glow, created a mirage of narrowness and dimness of the hall. The flat dark-gray walls augmented its bleakness, casting a sense of foreboding. Not unusually, a ruckus. "Yeah," "Wait fuh me," "Where you goin," and the calling of names filled the stretch of the hallway as students dashed back and forth, in and out of classrooms. Mr. Naimer appeared not to have seen them and looked beyond them; he looked for the dean, even an assistant principal or security officer.

He was engrossed in his own problem. Noise soared in his classroom; noise belched in the hallway enough to fray his nerves. "Clear the hallway. Get into your class and be quick about it," would have been Mr. Naimer's reaction. Those words did not echo in the hall, they were not uttered. One thing he was preoccupied or engrossed with, and that was the restoring of order in his class and proceeding with the lesson. No dean or assistant principal was in the hallway. "Gosh," muttered Mr. Naimer. He turned awkwardly, almost lost his balance, and looked back into the classroom. "Be quiet! Sit down! Sit in your given seats!" he bawled.

The students who were previously attentive were immersed in the commotion. They laughed and even banged on desks. Trapel tried to disengage himself from the constraint of the four females. He attempted to raise himself from across the desk. He struggled. He held on to the upper part of the tract pants.

Giggling and tugging, Maria yelled, "Nurleen, don't let go, don't."

"I'm holdin'," Nurleen answered, planting her feet firmly on the floor, and tightening her grip on the split left leg of the pants while Maria and Nella tugged with all their might on the right, several buttons of which were already unloosed. "Leave my f— pants, I say," Trapel barked, his torso still across the desk.

"No, no," Nurleen shot back as she held on.

"You think we can't get it? We gonna show you," Maria blurted, holding her grip.

"Back off o' me. I say back off, yuh hear me?" Trapel grunted, somewhat aggravated, his eyes wide and rolling, but the girls ignored him and pulled at the legs of his pants. His legs above the knees were exposed.

"Ha, ha, ha, ah, ha, ha, ha, ahhh, ha, ha, ha . . ." The rest of the class laughed. It was near hilarious.

Mr. Naimer rushed to the door again and glanced into the hall. He looked back into the room. He was livid. "Stop it! Stop it! Stop the nonsense," he hollered. His head jerked; he pushed it into the hallway. Students leapt in and out of classrooms making a din, as the supervisors were not on the floor. Frustration settled in the heart of Mr. Naimer while he felt helpless that he could not bring order to his classroom as no one listened. The needed assistance was not readily available. He turned sharply and faced the class, the door still ajar behind him. He sighed heavily. The grimace of anger besmirched his narrow, angular face with its straight, tapered nose. Students noted his disgust. One of them pointed a finger at him and burst out, "Ha, ha, ha, ha."

Another said, "Mr. Naimer, stop them."

"Oh gosh, ha, ha, ha, this is crazy." A female student laughed, sitting next to the door in a heavy yellow coat.

"Yeah, yeah, yeah," the class was cracking up with excitement.

Turning to the door, in his leather-soled black shoes, Mr. Naimer peered into the hallway again and saw Mr. Delph walking briskly toward his direction.

"Sir, I need your assistance," Mr. Naimer said loudly. Mr. Delph stepped up his pace. But the foray continued in the classroom. "Pull, Nurleen," Maria called as she held on to the garment of Trapel. With two or three more forceful tugs, the waist buttons snapped, and the track pants were ripped off the waist of Trapel. There was a loud uproar. "Yeah, yeah, yeah, yeah," "Ahhhh, ha, ha, ha, ha, ahhhh, ha, ha, ha, ha," "I can't believe this, ha, ha, ha," "Oh, no, oh, no, oh, my goodness," and "This is crazy, yo" were some of the cries of excitement. Trapel raised himself off the desk. He was pantsless. Maria and Nurleen ran with his blue-and-white track pants to the front of the classroom.

"We got it," Maria shouted in glee.

"He's without pants now," Nella laughed uncontrollably.

"We got your pants, we got it, I tell you," Nurleen taunted, waving the pants like a piece of rag.

Looking down, Trapel couldn't believe his pants had gone. Embarrassment overcame him. "What da f— you did?" Trapel swore, his eyes widening. Mr. Delph barged into the room with fierceness in his eyes.

"Where's your pants? Why you're here with only your drawers on?" Mr. Delph belched.

"They got my f— pants. Da three of them, grinning," Trapel cursed.

"What's going on, Mr. Naimer," the dean questioned. Mr. Naimer explained what happened and who started the disruptive behavior.

The dean started pointing; he pointed to Maria, Nurleen, Nella, and Latisha. His voice boomed, "Get out, get out, get out. Go to my office."

"You a punk, Trapel," snorted Maria, dropping the track pants on the floor.

"Pick it up," the dean roared, looking down at the piece of clothing.

"What!" Maria snarled, bending over, and grabbing and putting the track pants on a front desk. Trapel picked up his pants.

"You, get that pants on and stop allowing the girls to pull your pants off," Mr. Delph warned.

"They jumped me," Trapel said, looking at his legs and his striped blue-and-red boxers.

"Trapel, you a wimp. Make those gals strip yuh," said Roderick.

"Stop! Be quiet," Mr. Delph shouted. The class was hushed.

Maria, Nella, Nurleen, and Latisha left the class and headed to the dean's office.

"I'm totally disgusted by the behavior of your students. This kind of disruption is not going to be tolerated. You came here to work, not to engage in some kind of circus. We're not going to put up with it. There are students among you who want to work, and some of you are preventing them from doing so. The stiffest penalty is going to be handed out to mischief makers," Mr. Delph cautioned in a firm and sharp voice. He sternly warned the class before leaving.

With many minutes still remaining before the end of the period, Mr. Naimer continued reading as students sat in their seats. On the opposite side of the classroom, female students, whites, blacks, Hispanics, Asians, including Chinese and East Indians, sat at their desks and played cards and tic-tac-toe. Mr. Naimer walked up to them and said, "Why aren't you reading?"

"I don't feel like working," said a female student as she drew the face of a person on the desk with her blue-ink ballpen.

"And why are you defacing the desk?" asked Mr. Naimer, looking down at what the student was doing.

"I ain't deface no desk," replied the female student.

"Didn't I see you drawing on the desk?" the teacher inquired, fixing his eyes on the object drawn.

"I was just passing my pen over it. My pen didn't even touch the desk," the student protested.

"Okay. Kindly pay attention to the lesson," Mr. Naimer advised, walking away from her toward another student.

"You're not following the reading, Deonarine," said the teacher.

"I'm bored and my head hurt," uttered Deonarine, resting his head on the desk with his arms circling his red haversack, which lay on the desk.

"But we're reading a story which is part of the lesson," said the teacher.

"I don't care. I don't wanna read no story. I said my head hurt. They making all that crazy noise give me a headache," moaned Deonarine.

"Go to the nurse and get something for your headache," Mr. Naimer said.

"Nah," answered the student without raising his head from the desk.

Turning his body he said to Hung Lai, "Where's your book?"

Tilting his head and eying the teacher Hung Lai said, "In my bag."

"Why aren't you following as I read?" the teacher questioned.

"I got stomach cramps. I didn't eat any breakfast," said Hung Lai.

Still moving around the class to get the students involved in the reading, Mr. Naimer spoke to Himwattie. "I haven't seen you reading."

"I'm not feeling well," replied Hemwattie.

"But I saw you talking with her," Mr. Naimer remarked, looking at her and Aminda.

"I was telling her I wasn't feeling good," answered Hemwattie.

"You weren't reading either, Aminda," accosted the teacher.

"I forgot my book at home," said Aminda. Mr. Naimer continued to read the story and ask the students questions, the responses of whom he wrote on the board.

Turning around, he saw a student get out of his seat and sit on the desk.

Said Mr. Naimer, "Oninga, you cannot sit on the desk. And you are not participating in the discussions."

"I don't have any loose-leaf paper," replied Oninga, blinking his eyes.

"Off the desk, please. And where is your notebook?" questioned Mr. Naimer.

"I forgot it at home," answered Oninga.

"How could you forget your notebook when you're preparing to come to school?" the teacher asked.

"I don't know," Oninga shrugged, getting off the desk and taking a seat in his chair.

Others did not have their notebooks open or any loose-leaf paper. Some claimed their fingers hurt and more. There were also others who sat quietly but did no work although being encouraged by the teacher. When the bell rang, the students pushed and tumbled chairs and tables to make their way out as they jostled each other and stormed into the hallway where a sea of students headed in both directions. It seemed as if their movement was leading to an impending stampede. The situation appeared riotous with cries and yells. It was tumultuous.

Chapter 31

The weather was cooler with light breeze and calm winds. A blue sky arched overhead many days with dazzling, bright golden sunshine. Most students had become extremely excited with the swift dawn of spring and the fast-approaching summer. Many overcasts were seen, with the threat of rain and the turbulence of thunderstorms. Notwithstanding the imminent weather some days of the week, the youngsters of Jones High School took the opportunity to deck themselves in light attire.

With the light breeze chafing his face, Erwin ran with the ball, in his light, long-sleeve green-and-white jersey and blue jeans, bounced it a few times, and shot it at the basket before he was tackled by Peter and Nakon. The ball circled the rim of the metal hoop, rested on it for a second, and dropped into the basket. "Yeah," Erwin shouted and stabbed the air with a firm fist. "I did it." Glee settled on his face. Nakon caught the ball, ran a few yards from the area below the basket, turned around sharply, in his bright royal blue, long-sleeve, open-neck jersey; black tight-fitting jeans and white sneakers; and hurled the ball at the basket and scored three points. The ball landed firmly in the basket. "Wow! Nakon, you done it, dog," shrieked Peter, his eyes bulging with the white of them looking like snowballs.

"Gimme a pound, mannn," hollered Nakon, making a complete turn and pumping his arm in the air. He and Peter bumped fists as they came close together. Peter was lightly dressed in a gray hooded jersey and faded blue jeans which sagged way below his hips, revealing a blue plaid boxer or underpants.

On the opposite side of the court, Nudlun and Wooning ran after the black-and-white basketball. Wooning's long black hair fell in his face. He pushed it back to get a clearer view of the ball. Nudlun, who sported a huge Afro, tackled him for the ball, but Wooning, who ran ahead of him, angled to the right, dribbled the ball, upped it, and shot for the basket. *Bang,* the ball echoed as it struck the metal back and fell into the netted basket. "You playin' mad hard," shouted Nudlun, grabbing the ball from the tarmac after it fell and rolled away since he was yards away from catching a rebound of the ball.

Ortis ran after Nudlun, who bounced the ball several times and turned his back to Ortis. Nudlun held on to the ball as Wooning came from behind while Rozern braced Ortis's shoulder. Nudlun threw the ball to Rupert, who shouted, "To me, Nudlun. Over here." Rupert caught the ball and looked at the basket and then at the other players. "Over here, Rupert," Rozern shouted, raising his arms to catch the ball from Rupert, but Rupert did not respond. He seized the moment to shoot the ball, but Ortis, who ran and got into position, struck it from his hands. The ball fell and Ortis grabbed it.

"Huh," Ortis grunted as he moved away with the ball, his red light coat flapping in the wind as he moved toward the basket. A look of surprise smeared Rupert's face as he lost the ball. "Damn!" he shouted. Ortis moved toward the basket, shot the ball, and scored without being tackled. He smiled. Wooning patted Ortis on the back as he got close to him. "That was a good move, Ortis," shrieked Wooning.

"Yeah," answered Ortis. Jaime, who was near the basket, caught the ball on the rebound and ran in the opposite direction for the other basket, but he was strongly tackled by Rozern, who seized the ball.

The sixth to eighth graders and the ninth to twelfth graders were having a smash time on the basketball courts after school. A few onlookers, student spectators, sat on the benches in light springtime dress and savored the game of basketball played on five of the six courts. "Over here," Rupert bawled for the ball as Rozern dribbled it. Rozern looked over at him. Their eyes met.

"Tackle him, Wooning. Grab the ball," Ortis shouted as he dashed after Rozern, but Rozern was nimble. He got to the three-point line and shot. *Blup.* With a dull thud, the ball entered the basket. "Yeahhhh," Rozern bellowed and ran toward Rupert, whom he high-fived. He turned and gave Nudlun a high five as well.

The youngsters played their game with much gusto even as the afternoon gave way to a slightly chilled evening, but it did not bother the players and their onlookers. They were letting off steam and enjoying the moment. On the courts, the students played ball every afternoon after dismissal. To the southern end of the schoolyard, a group of students relished the spring weather by playing baseball while a small group in the east ran after one of their colleagues who held the ball in a game of football.

The classroom was a venue for hilarity. Students still behaved as if they lost their minds. Some benefited from instruction; they learned while others showed indifference as they headed toward final exams and a long-awaited summer vacation. It was getting warmer though some days were chilly which required students to wear light jackets with good insulation to ward off the chill and sometimes windy conditions.

It was a bright, early spring morning, and the sun rays penetrated the skin even at minutes to eight o'clock.

Almost an hour before, Mrs. Nichols said as she knocked on Erwin's bedroom door, "Erwin."

"Yes, Mom," he answered in a raspy voice.

"I want you to focus at school, hon. You'll soon have your final exams," Mrs. Lorraine Nichols cautioned her son, pushing her head into his room.

"Yeh, I focus," he answered, putting on his gray jersey after dousing himself with a light, fragrant perfume. He combed his hair, hurried to the kitchen, and poured a glass of juice, which he gulped. He yanked his bag from the chair and was out the house. Within an hour, he was bouncing a ball, which he shot at one of the baskets in the schoolyard. Others tackled him as he, again, gained possession of the orange basketball. The schoolyard was crowded with students who basked in the early-morning sunshine. They felt a warmth that they had not felt in months. They had shed the heavy coats and layers of clothes which insulated them from the brisk cold, which had now gone.

Sixth and seventh graders, eighth graders, and students from the senior school seized the opportunity and decked themselves in light free-flowing garment. More than ever, the young men were moving around with their jeans sagging way below their waist, exposing their butt clothed in multicolored boxers, green, red, plaid, brown, gray, blue, and flowered print. A host of colors. Every two steps they made they pulled their pants up before the waists slid to their knees or ankles. Some teachers ordered them to pull their pants up and keep them up, whether they were sixth graders or twelfth graders. Most of them ignored the words of advice that came from faculty and even other staff members.

Quite a number of female students adorned themselves in midriffs and tubes and microminis and denim skirts, which they were prohibited from wearing by school authorities. Many teachers cautioned them about their mode of dress, but they still flaunted in the schoolyard and sneaked into the classrooms with their skimpy attire, covering their upper bodies with slinky, light coats. On a warm day, when the sun shone with brilliance and the weather was hazy, they showed stark disregard for the rules stipulating the mode of dress. They claimed it was hot, and the classrooms did not have air-conditioned units to cool the temperature. Obviously, some rooms did have fans and air-conditioned units, but they chose to dress in a manner that was not appropriate for school. The mood was cavalier with spring looming even as they prepared for final exams.

Maria strode into the yard all decked out in a pink halter-back armless blouse and a mini denim skirt, way above her knees. "Hmm, look at your skirt, child," said Latisha, smiling.

"You try. This weather is hot, and I ain't wearing anything to keep me hot," Maria said, her eyes rolling from one corner to the other.

Cautioned Latisha, "Mr. Linsmun gonna send you home."

"Who? He? He can't send me home. He doesn't buy my clothes. Muh momma would come up here and be right in his face, shu," Maria blurted. "You wearing short skirt too."

"Mine not as short as yours," replied Latisha.

"So?" answered Maria, looking at Latisha with a squint. The two young ladies hung out in the yard as did the rest of the students, many of whom were casually dressed.

The buds appeared on the ashen, brittle-looking limbs of trees that lined the sidewalks of streets. The air was less chill and brisk. Soothing, calm winds and a gentle breeze pawed the faces of all. Spring settled in the air. One felt it from the changing atmosphere. The youngsters thus played more robustly in the yard. Basketball and baseball were more vibrantly played. On good days, the light coats took the place of the heavier, bulky coats in their assorted colors but mainly black. In a jiffy and unnoticeable to many, the full spring season was on the scene with a luster and brilliance. It was springtime and, henceforth, the color spectrum of nature was everywhere. Red roses, yellow sunflowers, and blue dahlias sprang up in their beauty, and the prominence of green was pervasive. The mood among the youngsters of Jones High was hilarious, one of frenzy, as they looked toward summer and a lengthy vacation.

The foolhardiness and the screams and shouts and horseplay did not abate; rather, they intensified. Staff were at their wit's end to bring a semblance of order to their rooms where instructions and learning were to be uninterrupted and unimpinged. Students who were bent on being disruptive spewed all sorts of odious phrases or talked to each other and at their teachers. Some even entertained themselves by listening to some raunchy music on electronic gadgets, which were not allowed in school.

Sitting in Mrs. Baighman's Language Arts 1002 class, decked in a royal-blue T-shirt, blue jersey, and a gray light coat to match the weather, Peter rose from his seat and yelled, "Who pick up my sh—t. I had a red iPod on muh desk. I just turn my back and it's gone."

"Who took your stuff, bro?" asked Ronald, his eyes darting around as if to locate the object.

"I don't know, but whoever pick it up you betta put my sh—t back. I want it now," Peter barked, his blue jeans sagging way below his waist, exposing his gray striped boxers. Eyes looked up at him.

Asked Paulette, "You had stuff on da desk?"

"Yeah, I had muh iPod and I don't see it now. I just turned my back and it's gone. I can't believe this. Somebody betta get muh stuff," Peter remonstrated.

Gliding across to where Peter stood, Mrs. Baighman said, "What's happening over here when we have work to do?"

"Somebody took my stuff," shouted Peter, his jowly face quivering as he spoke.

"What stuff? It doesn't have a name?" Mrs. Baighman demanded.

"My iPod," said Peter furiously.

Rebuked Mrs. Baighman, "You know you're not supposed to have any musical instrument or gadget in here."

"But I wasn't playing it. It was just on da desk," said Peter with anger in his voice.

"Did anyone see Peter's iPod which he's not supposed to have in the classroom?" asked Mrs. Baighman as she stood next to Peter.

"I ain't see his iPod," said Renbert, leaning forward with his arms resting on his backpack, which lay on the desk.

Looking around and casting his eyes on the floor, Clennel said, "Look, his iPod is on the floor."

"Where?" blurted Peter, his eyes widening.

"There." Clennel pointed to where the iPod lay.

Bending over and seeing his gadget on the floor, Peter reached down and picked it up. He breathed a sigh of relief.

"You're going to put that thing away so you could do some work," cautioned the teacher.

"I ain't feel like doin' no work," objected Peter, placing the iPod in his bag and leaning forward and resting his head on the desk.

"You're not going to sit there and do nothing. Take out your book and let's get started," stated Mrs. Baighman firmly.

Reluctantly, Peter sat up in his chair, opened his bag, and took out his books and began to engage in the lesson. Several students were not participating fully in the lesson. They, too, were cautioned by Mrs. Baighman, who threatened to call their parents. Some got the message and started working, half-heartedly. Even though final exams were fast-approaching, many students seemed reluctant or even indifferent in preparing for the tests.

Preparations began in earnest, and the more serious students began to prepare for their final exams. Assignments were submitted, and projects were done and delivered to teachers. The first two weeks in June were reserved for test-taking, and both the junior and senior schools were to be tested in the various subjects. During the last week of May, students, mainly those who were serious with their work, studied in the libraries and did work in the computer and science labs.

The first day of final exams began. Desks and chairs were arranged for the tasks and teachers and aides who were assigned to assist with the administering of tests ensured that everyone was properly seated and had the necessary tools. Yet there were those students who still talked while the testing materials were distributed, much to the chagrin of the teachers.

At nine o'clock, the tests began and continued each day for the rest of the two-week testing period. Most students were the picture of concentration as they worked their way through their exams. Many of the usual disruptive ones tried, made eye contact with each other, whispered, and attempted to pass pieces of paper with information to each other, but they were closely monitored. In each room, they were under the watchful eyes of two teachers and a school aide or teaching assistant. Some students were threatened with disqualification from the test if they continued to talk, as they were distracting others. Nevertheless, the tests were conducted with minimum disturbance.

At the end of each session, which sometimes lasted for two or three hours, some of the serious students looked exhausted. With the conclusion of exams, most students were eager to know their grades. From time to time, they saw teachers marking test papers and inquired about their grades, as many were anxious to know how they performed.

The last week of school approached, and the final day arrived. Students were issued with their report cards. Some were jubilant, particularly the ones who worked and were labeled as nerds; others were indifferent and did not show any emotions, as they knew how they had behaved during the year and had resigned themselves to the fact that they were not going anywhere. And yet there were those who were saddened or distraught. They were the ones who had easily allowed themselves to be distracted even though they did not take part in any disruptive behavior but were distracted to the point that they did not work hard enough even though they were encouraged by their teachers to focus and concentrate on their work. Some wailed; others complained thinking about what their parents would do.

There was an early dismissal at two o'clock, and within half an hour, no student was seen around the school. It was a relief to teachers that for the next thirty minutes they would not have to deal with any discipline issues. At three o'clock, teachers encouraged each other to have a pleasant and restful week since they would be seeing each other shortly. Said Mrs. Baighman, with tiredness engulfing her body, as she stood in the hallway on the first floor, with a bag slung across her shoulder and one held by its handle, "Ms. Cort, I'm tired. I'm going to have a good rest tonight. I'm going to rest for the whole of next week, and I'm going to be back here the following week to voice my opposition about this soaring indiscipline which has plagued this school for years."

"We all are going to let them know how we feel. We're going to share our views and make serious recommendations which they ought to implement," said Ms. Cort.

"We're not going to rest until they do something about this situation. It's a crisis, and we can't work under those conditions next school year. At the conference the following week, I'm going to let the chairman know that they have to do something serious to correct this situation," remarked Mrs. Hutchenson, who appeared very disturbed with the way things went during the school year.

"I can't wait for this conference to begin so I could let those in charge know we can't work in this disruptive and indisciplined environment. These kids were out of control, out of their minds," Mr. Mendez expressed in a vehement way.

"There is so much frustration in this place, and coupled with drab-looking classrooms, there is little wonder that everyone is complaining and is upset," stated Mrs. Baighman as she and the other teachers stood in the hallway.

Ms. Vine approached the small group of teachers and the dean and lost no time in expressing her feelings. "What are you talking about?"

"We're talking about the summer conference the week after next and what the administration should do about the craziness that went on in school," answered Mr. Blair, who listened but did not yet voice his opinion.

"Oh, my goodness, I can't wait to vent my feelings about the chaos that is taking place in this school and that those in authority ought to do something seriously to correct the indiscipline that takes place. I had it up to my throat with disruptions in my class. You prepare and yet you can't teach a thing and you call their parents. They come up here, and it's the same thing. I just want them to know how I feel about teaching here. I hope this conference is not about talk and no action," opined Ms. Vine, feeling very upset.

"They have to do something to bring about changes. I'm waiting to see what the administration and directors are going to say and do at the meeting and how they're going to follow with the decisions made," mentioned Mr. Blair.

"Well, we should all rest and enjoy some peace and quiet next week and return the following week for the summer conference, where we're going to speak our minds," suggested Mrs. Hutchenson with a faint smile.

"I'm sure going to have some rest next week. I need it. But the following week I'm going to be back here like everyone to let those who are in charge know how I feel about the grinding situation at this school. It's wearing me down. It's wearing all of us down. Anyhow, colleagues, enjoy the week," Ms. Vine said and left the building.

"You have a good one, too," hailed Mrs. Baighman as she headed to the office to sign out before leaving the building.

"Enjoy next week. The following week is going to be hectic," said Mr. Blair, shaking hands with Mrs. Baighman before he stepped through the door and left the building.

Mr. Mendez reached out and shook hands with Mrs. Hutchenson and then gave her a hug. "What a year this was. It's unbelievable we survived. Many of us could have become sick with the daily turmoil these kids put us through. Anyway, we made it to the end. Mrs. Hutchenson, enjoy the week."

"You bet, Mr. Mendez, and you enjoy yours too," Mrs. Hutchenson said.

"Sure." Mr. Mendez smiled.

They parted and went their separate ways. Other teachers briefly exchanged pleasantries with each other before leaving to enjoy a week's vacation before returning for the summer conference, prior to beginning their long summer vacation.

The End